The Best of
Montana's
SHORT FICTION

THE BEST OF
MONTANA'S

SHORT FICTION

Edited By
WILLIAM KITTREDGE AND ALLEN MORRIS JONES

THE LYONS PRESS
Guilford, Connecticut
An imprint of The Globe Pequot Press

The Lyons Press is an imprint of The Globe Pequot Press.

10 9 8 7 6 5 4 3 2

Printed in the United States of America

Designed by Cynthia Love Design, Laguna Beach, California

ISBN 1-59228-269-5

Library of Congress Cataloging-in-Publication Data is available on file.

Permissions Acknowledgments

"Days of Heaven," from *In the Loyal Mountains* by Rick Bass, copyright © 1995 by Rick Bass. Reprinted by permission of Houghton Mifflin Company. All rights reserved.

"Big Spenders" by Ralph Beer. Reprinted by permission of the author.

"Custer on Mondays," from *When We Were Wolves: Stories by Jon Billman*, copyright © 1999 by Jon Billman. Used by permission of Random House, Inc.

"Bear and Lions" by Mary Clearman Blew. Reprinted by permission of the author.

"Junk," from *A Stranger in This World* by Kevin Canty, copyright © 1994 by Kevin Canty. Used by permission of Doubleday, a division of Random House, Inc.

"Grounded" by Claire Davis. Reprinted by permission of the author.

"Under the Wheat" by Rick DeMarinis. Reprinted by permission of the author.

"Blue Waltz with Coyotes" by Jeanne Dixon. Reprinted by permission of the author.

"Real Indians" by Debra Magpie Earling. Reprinted by permission of the author.

"Great Falls," from *Rock Springs* by Richard Ford, copyright © 1987 by Richard Ford. Used by permission of Grove/Atlantic, Inc.

"Hoot" by Peter Fromm. Reprinted by permission of the author.

"Jacob Dies" by Allen Morris Jones. Reprinted by permission of the author.

"Do You Hear Your Mother Talking?" by William Kittredge. Reprinted by permission of the author.

"Morphine" by David Long. Reprinted by permission of the author. Originally published in *The New Yorker* magazine.

"Like a Leaf," from *To Skin a Cat* by Thomas McGuane, copyright © 1986 by Thomas McGuane. Used by permission of Dutton, a division of Penguin Group (USA) Inc.

"Heart" by Neil McMahon. Reprinted by permission of the author.

"Ranch Girl." Reprinted with the permission of Scribner, an imprint of Simon & Schuster Adult Publishing Group, from *Half in Love* by Maile Meloy. Copyright © 2002 by Maile Meloy.

"Tough People." Reprinted with permission of Simon & Schuster Adult Publishing Group from *Out of the Woods* by Chris Offutt. Copyright © 1999 by Chris Offutt.

"Father, Lover, Deadman, Dreamer," from *First Body* by Melanie Rae Thon. Copyright © 1997 by Melanie Rae Thon. Reprinted by permission of Houghton Mifflin Company. All rights reserved.

"It's Come to This" by Annick Smith. Reprinted by permission of the author.

"The Mourning of Ignacio Rosa" by Kim Zupan. Reprinted by permission of the author.

CONTENTS

INTRODUCTION
William Kittredge

THIS BOOK OF FAIRLY RECENT STORIES centered on Montana, each by each and taken together, turns on the glories of both place and soul and how they can't ever quite be ours for more than the moment, and on solace and its possibilities. But stories can't be paraphrased in a remotely adequate way, so I'm not going to try.

In the 1980s, while editing *The Last Best Place*, we were swamped with good stories. Nowadays, there are even more fine fiction writers in Montana. This book is clear evidence.

First-rate literary narrative about the American West dates at least back to Willa Cather (*My Antonia*, 1918) and Ole Rölvaag (*Giants in the Earth*, 1926). They were followed by Mari Sandoz (*Old Jules*, 1935), H. L. Davis (the Pulitzer Prize for *Honey in the Horn*, 1935), Walter Van Tilburg Clark (*The Ox-Bow Incident*, 1940), Wallace Stegner (*The Big Rock Candy Mountain*, 1943), and Bud Guthrie (*The Big Sky*, 1947). But, even adding writers like Dorothy Johnson, Thomas Savage, Mildred Walker, and Bernard DeVoto, by the 1960s it was probably still possible to count the significantly insightful literary narratives about the American West on your fingers and toes.

The seeds, however, were planted, and the situation changed. In 1968 Edward Abbey published *Desert Solitaire*, and in 1969 N. Scott Momaday won the Pulitzer Prize for *House Made of Dawn*. A flood of terrific books about the West followed. Some, like Leslie Marmon Silko's *Ceremony* in 1978, Marilyn Robinson's *Housekeeping* in 1981, Cormac McCarthy's *Blood Meridian* in 1985, Molly Gloss's *The Jump-Off Creek* in 1989, and James Galvin's *The Meadow* in 1992, were masterpieces.

In Montana, our longtime tradition of useful narrative thrived. James Welch published *Winter in the Blood* in 1973, and in 1976 we got

Norman Maclean's *A River Runs Through It*. Interest in stories from Montana kept building with the publication of Ivan Doig's *This House of Sky* in 1978. In 1980 Jim Harrison published *Legends of the Fall*. Welch's masterwork, *Fools Crow*, came in 1986, and Richard Ford's brilliant *Rock Springs* in 1987. We began to realize that stories could help us define our lives, and our writers began taking justifiable pride in their stories as American, part of the nation's literature, rather than simply of the West. We began to see stories about Montana in *The Atlantic*, *The New Yorker*, and *Harper's*.

The list of writers in this book is impressive. And there are lots of others who'd be here if there was room for excerpts from novels and for nonfiction narrative—Ivan Doig and Jim Welch, Deidre McNamer and Bryan DiSalvatore, Jon Jackson, Jim Crumley and David James Duncan, Judy Blunt, David Quammen from Bozeman. Doug Peacock, Tim Cahill, and Diane Smith from Livingston. How about an essay from Richard Hugo? But this list could go on and on. Point is, we've witnessed an explosion of profoundly useful writing here in Montana, and it continues.

ASSEMBLING THIS COLLECTION has been a true pleasure. These stories were written by ranch kids and bareback riders, and by semi-émigrés like myself, people from all over the map. But who cares where the writers ran into their stories so long as they move us to redream our lives and yearnings, our losses and recoveries?

People who live in Montana should give thanks for this collection, and those who are thinking about moving in should read it in order to get an idea of what they might be confronting. Profound thanks to the writers who did this work, this making of mirrors in which we see ourselves so vividly reflected. May they keep it going.

Days of Heaven
Rick Bass

THEIR PLANS WERE TO DEVELOP THE VALLEY, and my plans were to stop them. I was caretaking this ranch in Montana that the two of them had bought, or were buying. One of them was an alcoholic and the other was a realtor. The alcoholic—the big one—was from New York and did something on the Stock Exchange.

The realtor had narrow, close-together eyes, little pinpoints in his pasty, puffy face, like raisins set in dough. He wore new jeans and a Western shirt with silver buttons and a big metal belt buckle with a horse on it, and he walked in his new cowboy boots in tiny little steps with his toes pointed in. He always walked that way. The realtor—Zim—was from Billings.

The big guy's name was Quentin. He had a big round stomach and a small mustache, and looked like a polar bear.

The feeling I got from the big guy was that he was recovering from some kind of breakdown, is why he was out here. And Zim—grinning, loose-necked, giggling pointy-toe-walking-all-the-time, always walking around as if he were an infant who'd just shit his diapers—Zim, the predator, had just the piece of Big Sky Quentin needed. I'll go ahead and say it right now, so that nobody gets the wrong idea: I didn't like Zim.

It was going fast, the Big Sky was, said Zim. All sorts of famous people—celebrities—were vacationing there. Moving there. "Brooke Shields," he said. "Tom Brokaw. Jim Nabors. Rich people, I mean *really* rich people. You could sell them things. Say you owned the little store in this valley—the mercantile—and say Michael Jackson—well, no, not *him*—say Kirk Douglas lives ten miles down the road. What's he going to do when he's having a party and realizes he doesn't have enough Dom Perignon? Who's he gonna call?

1

"He'll call your store, if you have such a service. Say the bottle costs seventy-five dollars. You'll sell it to him for a hundred—you'll *deliver* it, you'll drive that ten miles up the road to take it to him—and he'll be glad to pay that extra money.

"Bing! Bang! Bim, bam!" Zim said, snapping his fingers and then rubbing them together, his mindless raisin eyes set so far back, glittering. His mouth was small and round and pale, like an anus. "You've made twenty-five dollars," he said, and the mouth broke into a grin.

What's twenty-five dollars, to a stockbroker guy? But I saw that Quentin was listening.

I'VE LIVED ON THIS RANCH FOR FOUR YEARS NOW. The guy who used to own this place before Quentin—he was a predator, too. A rough guy from Australia, he had put his life savings into building this mansion, this fortress deep in the woods, looking out over the big meadow.

The previous owner's name was Beauregard. He had built the mansion three stories tall, rising up into the trees like one of Tarzan's haunts. Beauregard had constructed, all over the property, various buildings and structures related to the dismemberment of his quarry: smokehouses with wire screening to keep the other predators out, and butchering houses (long wooden tables, with sinks, and high-intensity interrogating lamps over the long tables, for night work). There were even huge windmill-type hoists all over the property, which would be used to lift the hoof-sprawling animals—moose, bear, elk, their heads and necks limp in death—up into the sky, so that their hides could first be stripped, leaving the meat revealed . . .

It had been Beauregard's life dream to be a hunting guide, and he wanted to take rich people into the woods, so they could come out dragging behind them a deer, or a bear—some wild creature they could kill and then take home with them—and Beauregard made a go of it for three years, before the business went down and the bad spirits set in and he got divorced and had to put the place up for sale to make the alimony payments. The divorce settlement would in no way allow either of the parties to live in the mansion—it had to be both or none—and that's where I came in: to caretake the place until it sold. They'd sunk too much money into Beauregard's mansion to just leave it sitting out there in the forest, idle. Beauregard went back to Washington, D.C., where he got a job doing something for the CIA —tracking fugitives was my guess, or maybe even killing them— while his wife went to California with the kids.

Beauregard had been a mercenary for a while. He said the battles were usually fought at dawn and dusk, so sometimes in the middle of the day he'd been able to get away and go hunting. In the mansion, the dark, noble heads of long-ago beasts from all over the world—elephants, and elk, and greater Thomson's gazelles, and giant oryx—lined the walls of all the rooms. There was a giant gleaming sailfish leaping over the headboard of my bed upstairs, and there were woodstoves, and fireplaces, but no electricity. This place is so far into the middle of nowhere. After I took the caretaking position, the ex-wife would send postcards saying how much she enjoyed twenty-four-hour electricity and how she'd get up in the middle of the night—two A.M., four A.M.—and flick on a light switch, just for the hell of it.

I felt like I was taking advantage of Beauregard, moving into his castle while he slaved away in D.C.—but I'm a bit of a killer myself, in some ways, if you get right down to it, and if Beauregard's hard luck was my good luck, well, I tried not to lose any sleep over it.

If anything, I gained sleep over it, especially in the summer. I'd get up kind of late—eight, nine o'clock—and fix a big breakfast, and feed my dogs, and then go out on the porch and sit in the rocking chair, and look out over the valley or read.

Then about noon I'd pack a lunch and go for a walk. I'd take the dogs with me, and a book, and we'd start up the trail behind the house, walking through the centuries-old larch and cedar forest, following the creek up to the big waterfall—heavy, heavy timber. Deer moved quietly through that forest, big deer, and pileated woodpeckers, too, banging away on some of the old dead trees, going at it like cannons. It was shady back in that old forest, and the sun rarely made it down to the ground, stopping instead on all the various levels of leaves. I'd get to the waterfall, and swim—so cold!—with the dogs, and then they'd nap in some ferns while I sat on a rock and read some more.

In midafternoon I'd come home—it would be hot then, in the summer—the fields and meadows all around the ranch smelled of wild strawberries, and I'd stop and pick some when I came out of the forest. By that time of day it would be too hot to do anything but take a nap, so that's what I'd do, upstairs, on the bare mattress with no sheets, with the windows all open, no breeze, and a fly buzzing faintly in one of the other rooms, one of the many empty other rooms.

I would sleep in that sun-filled room upstairs, groggy in the heat—sleeping a pure, happy, dreamless sleep—and then when it cooled down enough—around seven or eight in the evening—I'd wake up and take my fly rod over to the other side of the meadow. It didn't get dark until midnight, in the summer. A spring creek wandered along the edge of that far meadow, and I'd catch a brook trout for supper: I'd keep just one. There were too many fish in the little creek, and they were too easy to catch, so that after an hour or two I'd get tired of catching them, and I'd take the one I'd decided to keep back to the cabin, and fry him for supper.

Then I would have to decide whether to read some more, or go for another walk, or to just sit on the porch with a drink in hand—just one big one—and watch the elk come out into the meadow. Usually I chose that last option—the one about the single big drink—and sometimes, while I was out on the porch, this great gray owl would come flying in from out of the woods. It was always a thrill to see it— that huge, wild, silent creature flying into my front yard.

The great gray owl's a strange creature. It's immense, and so shy that it lives only back in the oldest of the old-growth forests, among giant trees, as if to match its own great size against them. It sits very still for long stretches of time, back in the woods, motionless, watching for prey, until—so say the biologists—*it believes it is invisible,* and a person or a deer can walk right past it—or can even walk right up to it—and so secure is the bird in its invisibility, its psychological cloak of being hidden, that it will not move—even if you're looking straight at it, it's convinced you can't see it, and it won't blink, won't move.

Now *that's* shy.

My job, my only job, was to live in the lodge, and keep intruders out. There had been a "For Sale" sign out front, but I'd taken that down and hidden it in the garage the first day.

AFTER A COUPLE OF YEARS, Beauregard, the real killer, did sell the place, and was out of the picture. Pointy-toed Zim got his ten percent, I suppose—ten percent of $350,000, a third of a million for some place with no electricity!—but Quentin, the breaker of stocks, didn't buy it right away. He *said* he was going to buy it, the first day, the first five minutes he saw it—he took me aside and asked if I could stay on, and, like a true predator, I said, Hell yes. I didn't care who owned it, as long as I got to stay there, and as long as the owner lived far away, and wasn't someone who would keep mucking up my life with a lot of visits.

Quentin didn't want to live there, or even visit—he just wanted to *own* it. He wanted to buy the place, but first he wanted to toy with Beauregard for a while, to try and drive the price down five or ten or twenty thousand; he wanted to *flirt* with him, I think.

Myself, I would've been terrified to jack with Beauregard. The man had bullet holes in his arms and legs; he'd been in foreign prisons, and had killed people. A bear had bitten him in the face on one of his hunts, a bear he'd thought was dead.

Quentin and Zim would sometimes come out on "scouting trips," that summer and fall that they were buying the place—Zim's family back in Billings, and Quentin's back in the Big Apple—and they'd show up unannounced, with a bag of stupid groceries—Cheerios, and Pop Tarts, and hot dogs, and a big carton of Marlboro cigarettes—and they'd want to stay for the weekend, to get a better "feel" for the place. I'd have to move my stuff—sleeping bag, and frying pan, and fishing rod—over to the guest house, which was spacious enough. I didn't mind that; I just didn't like the idea of having them in the house.

Once, while Quentin and Zim were walking in the woods behind the house, I looked in one of their dumb little sacks of groceries to see what stupid things they'd brought this time, and a magazine fell out of one of the sacks—a magazine with a picture of naked men on the cover; I mean, drooping penises and all, and the inside of the magazine was worse, with naked little boys, and naked men on motorcycles.

None of the naked men or boys were *doing* anything—they weren't touching each other—but still, the whole magazine, that part of it that I looked at, was nothing but heinies and penises.

Realtors!

I'D SEE THE TWO OLD BOYS out on the front porch, the cabin all ablaze with light—those sapsuckers running *my* generator, *my* propane, far into the night, playing *my* Jimmy Buffett records, sitting out on the front porch and singing at the tops of their lungs—and then finally, they'd turn the lights off, shut the generator down, and go to bed.

Except Quentin would stay up a little longer. I'd sit on the porch of the guest house, at the other end of the meadow, my pups asleep at my feet, and I'd see Quentin moving through the house, lighting the gas lanterns, walking from room to room, like a ghost, and then the son of a bitch would start having one of his fits.

He'd break things—my things, and Beauregard's things—though I suppose they were now *his* things, since the deal was in the works: plates, saucers, and lanterns, and windows . . . I'd listen to the crashing of glass, and watch his big polar-bear whirling shape passing from room to room—sometimes he'd have a pistol (they both carried 9mm Blackhawks on their hips, like little cowboys)—and sometimes Quentin would shoot holes in the ceiling, holes in the walls.

I'd tense, there in the dark . . . This wasn't good for my peace of mind. My days of heaven—I'd gotten used to them, and I wanted to defend them, and protect them, even if they weren't mine in the first place; even if I'd never owned them.

Then I'd see, in that low lamplight, Zim come into the room. Like some old queen, he'd put his arm around Quentin's big shoulders, and lead him away, lead him to bed.

After they left, the house stank of cigarettes, and I wouldn't sleep in the bed for weeks. I'd sleep in one of the many guest rooms. Once I found some mouthwash spray under the bed, and pictured the two of them lying there in bed, spraying it into each other's mouths in the morning, before kissing . . .

I'm talking like a homophobe here. I don't think it's that at all. I think it was just that realtor. He wasn't in it for the love. He was just turning a trick, was all.

I felt sorry for Quentin. It was strange how shy he was—how he always tried to cover up his destruction—smearing wood putty into the bullet holes in the ceiling and mopping the food off the ceiling—this fractured *stockbroker*, doing domestic work—making lame excuses to me the next day about the broken glass—"I was shooting at a bat," he'd say, "a bat came in the window"—and all the while, Zim, in pursuit of that ten percent, would be sitting out on my porch, looking out at my valley—this *Billings* person, from the hot, dry, dusty eastern part of the state—sitting there with his boots propped up on the railing and smoking the cigarettes that would not kill him quick enough.

Once, as the three of us sat there—Quentin asking me some questions about the valley, about how cold it got, in the winter ("Cold," I said, "very, *very* cold")—we saw a coyote and her three pups go trotting, in the middle of the day, across the meadow.

And Zim jumped up, seized a stick of firewood from the front porch (*my* firewood!), and ran, in his dirty-diaper waddle, out into the field after the mother coyote and pups, running like a madman, waving the club. The mother coyote got two of the pups into the trees, picking them up and carrying them by the scruff of their necks, but Zim, Zim got the third one, and stood over it, pounding, in the hot midday sun.

It's an old story, but it was a new one for me—how narrow the boundary is between invisibility and collusion. If you don't stop it, if you don't single-handedly step up and change things, then aren't you just as guilty?

I didn't say anything—not even when Zim came huffing back up to the porch, walking like a man who had just gone to get the morning paper. There was blood specked around the cuffs of his pants, and even then I said nothing. I did not want to lose my job. My love for this valley had me trapped.

We all three sat there on the porch like everything was the same—Zim breathing a bit more heavily, was all—and I thought I would be able to keep my allegiances secret, through my silence. But they knew whose side I was on. It had been *revealed* to them. It was as if they had infrared vision, as if they could see everywhere—and everything.

"Coyotes eat baby deer and livestock," said the raisin-eyed son of a bitch. "Remember," he said, addressing my silence, "it's not your ranch anymore. All you do is live here and keep the pipes from freezing." Zim glanced over at his big soulmate. I thought how when Quentin had another crack-up and lost this place, Zim would get the ten percent again, and again and again, each time.

Quentin's face was hard to read; I couldn't tell if he was angry with Zim or not. Everything about Quentin seemed hidden at that moment. How did they do it? How could the sons of bitches be so good at camouflaging themselves when they had to?

I wanted to trick them. I wanted to hide and see them reveal *their* hearts—I wanted to watch them when they did not know I was watching, and see how they really were—not just listen to them shooting the shit about their plans for the valley, but deeper. I wanted to see what was at the *bottom* of their black fucking hearts.

Finally Quentin blinked and turned calmly, still revealing no emotion, and gave his pronouncement.

"If the coyotes eat the little deers, they should go," he said. "Hunters should be the only thing out here getting the little deers."

THE WOODS STILL FELT THE SAME, when I went for my walks after the two old boys departed. Yellow tanagers still flitted through the trees, flashing blazes of gold, and the deer were still tame. Ravens *quorked* as they passed through the dark woods, as if to reassure me that they were still on my side, that I was still with nature, rather than without.

I slept late. I read. I hiked. I fished in the evenings. I saw the most spectacular sights. Northern lights kept me up until four in the morning some nights—coiling in red and green spirals across the sky, exploding in iridescent furls and banners . . . The northern lights never displayed themselves while the killers were there, and for that, I was glad.

In the late mornings and early afternoons, I'd sit by the waterfall and eat my peanut butter and jelly sandwich. I'd see the same magic sights: bull moose, their shovel antlers still in velvet, stepping over fallen, rotting logs; calypso orchids sprouting along the trail, glistening and nodding—but it felt, too, like the woods were a vessel, filling up with something of which they could only hold so much—call it wildness—and when they had absorbed all they could, when they could hold no more, then things would change, and that wildness they could not hold would have to spill out, would have to go somewhere . . .

Zim and Quentin came out only two or three times a year, for two or three days at a time. The rest of the time, heaven was mine—all those days of heaven. You wouldn't think they could hurt anything, coming out so infrequently. But how little of a thing does it take to change—spoil—another thing?

I'll tell you what I think: The cleaner and emptier a place is, the less it can take. It's like some crazy kind of paradox.

After a while Zim came up with the idea of bulldozing the meadow across the way, and building a lake, with sailboats and docks. He hooked Quentin up into a deal with a log-home manufacturer in the southern part of the state, and was going to put shiny new "El Supremo" model log homes all around the lake. He was going to build a small hydro dam on the creek, and bring electricity into the valley with it, which would automatically double real estate values, Zim said. He was going to run cattle in the woods, lots of cattle. And set up a little gold mine operation, over on the north face of Roderick Butte. The two boys had folders and folders of ideas, plans.

They just needed a little investment capital, was all.

In the South, where I had come from, tenants held the power of a barnburning if their landlords got out of hand. Even a poor man or woman can light a match. But not here: a fire in this country wouldn't ever stop.

There seemed like there was nothing—absolutely nothing—I could do. Anything I did short of killing Zim and Quentin would be a token act, a symbol. Before I figured that out, I sacrificed a tree, chopped down a big wind-leaning larch so that it fell on top of the cabin, doing great damage while Zim and Quentin were upstairs. I wanted to show them what a money sink the ranch was, and how dangerous it could be, and I told them how beavers, forest beavers, had chewed down that tree that had missed landing in their bedroom by only a few feet.

I know now that those razor-bastards knew everything; they could *sense* that I'd cut that tree. But for some crazy reason they pretended to go along with my story. Quentin had me spend two days sawing the tree up for firewood, and before he could get the carpenters out to repair the damage, a hard rain blew in and soaked some of my books.

I figured there was nothing I could *do.* Anything I did to harm the land or their property would harm me.

MEANWHILE, THE VALLEY FLOWERED. Summer came, stretched and yawned, and then it was early fall. Quentin brought his children out, early that second fall—the fall of ownership. Zim didn't make that trip, nor did I spy any of the nekkid magazines. The kids—two teenage girls, and a teenage boy, a younger Quentin—were okay for a day or two (the girls running the generator and watching movies on the VCR the whole day long), but the boy, little Quentin, was going to be trouble, I could tell—the first words out of his mouth when they arrived were "Is it any kind of . . . is there any season for . . . can you *shoot* anything right now? Rabbits? Marmots?"

And sure enough, they made it two days before discovering there were fish—delicate little brook trout, with polka-dotted, flashy, colorful sides, and intelligent little gold-rimmed eyes, spawning on gravel beds in the shallow little creek that ran through the meadow on the other side of the road—and what Quentin's son did, after discovering this fact, was to borrow his dad's shotgun, and he began shooting the fish.

Little Quentin loaded, blasted away, reloaded—it was a pump-action twelve gauge, like the ones used in big-city detective movies, and the motion was like masturbating—jack, jack, *boom*, jack, jack, *boom*—and little Quentin's sisters came running out and rolled up their pant legs and waded out into the stream and began picking up the dead fish, and pieces of fish, and began eating those fish.

Quentin sat up on the porch with his drink in hand, and watched, smiling.

IN THE FIRST WEEK OF NOVEMBER, while out walking—the skies that sweet, dull, purple lead color, and the air frosty, flirting with snow—I heard ravens, and then scented the newly dead smell of a kill, and moved over in that direction.

I saw the ravens' black shapes taking flight up into the trees as I approached; I could see the huge shape of what they'd been feasting on—a body of such immensity that I paused, frightened, even though the huge shape was obviously dead.

It was two bull moose, their antlers locked up from rut-combat—the rut having been over for a month, I knew—and I guessed they'd been locked up for at least that long. One moose was long-ago dead (two weeks?) but the other moose had died so recently (that morning, perhaps) that he still had all his hide on him, and wasn't even stiff. The ravens and coyotes had already done a pretty good job on the first moose, stripping what they could while his partner, his enemy, was thrashing and flailing, I could tell; small trees and brush were leveled all around them, and I could see the swath, the direction from which they had come—locked-up, floundering, fighting—to this final resting spot.

I went and borrowed a neighbor's draft horse. The moose that had died just that morning wasn't so much heavy as he was just big—he'd lost a lot of weight during the month he'd been tied up with the other moose—and the other one was just a ship of bones, mostly empty air.

Their antlers were locked together as if welded. I tied a big rope around the newly dead moose's rear legs and got the draft horse to drag the cargo out of the woods and down through the forest, to the ranch. It was a couple of miles, and I walked next to the old draft horse, soothing him as he sledded, forty feet behind him, his strange load. Ravens flew behind us, cawing at our theft; some of them filtered down through the trees and landed on top of the newly dead moose's brave, humped back and rode along like that, pecking at the hide, trying to find an opening—but the hide was too thick, they'd have to wait for the coyotes to open it—and so they rode with me like gypsies: myself, and the draft horse, and the ravens, and the dead moose (as if they'd come back to life) moving through the woods like a giant serpent, snaking our way through the trees.

I hid the carcasses at the edge of the woods and then, on the other side of a small clearing, built a blind of branches and leaves where I could hide and watch over the carcasses.

I painted my face camouflage green and brown, and settled into my blind, and waited.

The next day, like buffalo wolves from out of the mist, Quentin and Zim reappeared. I'd hidden my truck a couple of miles away and locked up the cabin so they'd think I was gone.

I wanted to watch without being seen. I wanted to see them in the wild—wanted to see what they were like when humans weren't watching them.

"What the *shit*!" Zim cried as he got out of his big mongo-tire Jeep, the one with the electric winch, electric windows, electric sunroof, electric cattle prod. Ravens were swarming my trap, gorging, and coyotes darted in and out, tearing at that other moose's hide, trying to peel the hide back and reveal the new flesh.

"Shit fire!" Zim cried, running across the yard—hopping the

buck-and-rail fence, his flabby ass getting caught astraddle the high bar for a moment. He ran out into the woods, shooing the ravens and coyotes. The ravens all screamed and rose into the sky as if caught in a huge tornado, as if *summoned*. Some of the bolder ones came back down and made passes at Zim's head, but he waved them away, and shouted, "Shit fire!" again, and then, examining the newly dead moose, said, "This meat's still good!"

Zim and Quentin worked by lanternlight that night: peeling the hide back with butchering and skinning knives, and hacking at the flesh with hatchets. I stayed in the bushes and watched. The hatchets made whacks when they hit the flesh, and cracking sounds when they hit bone. I could hear the two men laughing. Zim reached over and spread a smear of blood, delicately, on Quentin's cheeks, applying it like makeup, or medicine of some sort, and they paused, catching their breath from their mad chopping, and then they went back to work. They ripped and sawed slabs of meat from the carcass and hooted, cheering each time they pulled a leg off the carcass.

They dragged the meat up to the smokehouse—dragging it through the autumn-dead grass—and cut the head and antlers off last, right before daylight.

I hiked over and got my truck, washed my face in a stream, and drove shakily home.

They waved when they saw me come driving up; they were out on the front porch having breakfast, all clean and fresh-scrubbed.

I went up to the porch, where they were talking among themselves as they always had, talking as normal as pie.

Zim was lecturing to Quentin—waving his arm at the meadow and preaching the catechism of development to him.

"You could have a nice hunting camp and send 'em all out into the woods on horses, with a yellow slicker and a gun—boom! They're living the Western Experience. Then in the winter, you could run just a regular guest lodge, like on *Newhart*. Make 'em pay for everything. They want to go cross-country skiing? Rent 'em. They want to race snowmobiles? Rent 'em. Charge 'em for taking a *piss*. Rich people don't mind."

I was just hanging on: shaky. They finished their breakfast and went back inside to plot, or watch VCR movies. I went over to the smokehouse, and peered through the dusty windows. Blood dripped from the gleaming red hindquarters. They'd cut the moose's head off and nailed it, with the antlers, to one of the walls, so that his blue-blind eyes were looking out at his own corpse. There was a baseball cap on his antlers, and a cigar stuck between his big lips.

I went up into the woods.

But I knew I'd come back. I liked living in that cabin, and liked living at the edge of that meadow, and looking out at it.

Later that evening, we were out on the porch again, watching the end of the day come in—the days getting so much shorter—and Quentin and Zim were still pretending to be normal, still pretending that none of the previous night's savagery had happened.

It occurred to me that if they thought I had the power to stop them, they would have put my head in that smokehouse a long time ago. Would have put a baseball cap on my head, stuck a cigar in my mouth.

Quentin, looking especially burned out, had slipped from his chair. He was sitting on the floor with his back to the cabin wall, bottle of rum in hand, looking toward the meadow, where his lake and lots of cabins with lights burning in each of them would someday sit. I was just hanging around to see what was what, to eavesdrop, and to try to slow them down—to talk about those hard winters whenever I got the chance, and to mention how unfriendly the people in the valley were. Which was true, but hard to convince Quentin of, because every time he showed up, they got friendly.

"I'd like that a lot," said Quentin, speaking slowly. Earlier in the day I'd seen a coyote, or possibly a wolf—*sans* pups—trot across the meadow, but I sure hadn't pointed it to anyone. Even as we were sitting on the porch, there was the great gray owl—he'd flown in like a plane, ghostly gray, a four-foot wingspan—perched on the falling-down buck-and-rail fence by the road. I hadn't seen the owl in a couple of weeks, and I felt uneasy. It would be nothing for a man like Zim to walk up to that owl with his cowboy pistol, and put a bullet, point blank, into the big bird's ear—the big bird with his eyes set in his face, looking straight at you, the way all predators do.

"I'd like that so much," Quentin said again—meaning Zim's idea of the lodge as a resort, in winter. He was wearing a gold chain around his neck, with a little gold pistol dangling from it. He'd have to get rid of that necklace if he moved out here. It looked like something he might have gotten from a Cracker Jack box, but was, doubtless, real gold.

"It may sound corny," Quentin said, "but if I owned this valley, I'd let people from New York, from California, from wherever, come out here for Christmas and New Year's. I'd put a big sixty-foot Christmas tree in the middle of the road, up by the mercantile and the saloon, and string it with lights, and we'd all ride up there in a sleigh, Christmas Eve and New Year's Eve, and we'd sing carols, you know? It would be real small-town and homey," Quentin said. "Maybe corny, but that's what I'd do."

Zim nodded. "There's lonely people who would pay through the nose for something like that," he said.

We sat there and just watched the dusk gliding in over the meadow, cooling things off, blanketing the field's dull warmth of the day and making mist and steam rise from the field.

Quentin and Zim were waiting for money, and Quentin, especially, was still waiting for his nerves to calm: almost a year he'd owned the ranch, a full cycle of seasons, and still he wasn't well.

A little something—peace?—would do him good. I could see that Christmas tree all lit up; I could feel that sense of *community*, of new beginnings.

I wouldn't go to such a festivity; I'd stay back in the woods, like the great gray. But I could see the attraction, could see Quentin's need for peace; how he had to have a place to start anew—though soon enough, too, I knew, he would begin taking ten percent from the newness again.

Around midnight, I knew, he'd take to smashing things—and I couldn't blame him. Quentin was wild, and of course he wanted to come to the woods, too.

I didn't know if the woods would have him.

We sat there and watched dusk come sliding in. All I could do was wait. I sat very still, like that owl, and thought about where I could go next, after this place was gone. Maybe, I thought, if I sit very still, they will just go away.

BIG SPENDERS
Ralph Beer

TEENAGERS RODE ROPES FROM CLIFFS above a summer pond. At the final rising instant they kicked free and fell, windmilling their arms through leaf-dappled light. A boy and girl in cutoffs plunged hand in hand toward the glassy surface of water; laughing as they fell, they let go of each other the moment they hit. Their friends on the bank cheered and raised soft drinks to smiling lips.

I shook the ice in my glass and stood. Outside, wind drove snow against the trailer; the windows hummed, and the curtains quivered in cross-drafts. The kids in the commercial cannonballed from over-hanging rocks into the graceful slow motion of endless summer fun.

I turned off the set. The television was new, but reception this far out was seldom clear. A satellite dish would be the ticket, and I smiled to think of my folks' place down in the Big Hole Valley with just a radio.

At the breakfast counter I parted the curtains. Our Christmas tree rolled across the yard, bits of tinsel whipping in the frozen boughs. Snow had drifted to the third cinder block in the tractor shed wall, but it wasn't snow that got you up here, like in the Big Hole. It was wind. And even if this was still Montana, I felt like a stranger so far out in the open.

Cody had started the next day's bread at the sink, and her dark arms were dusted white to her rolled sleeves, her jeans already spot-ted with flour. It seemed unlikely, a woman who looked like that, baking bread in the kitchenette of a mobile home, and as I watched her, I felt again the mild shock of finding myself on leased dry land with her. The difference in our ages alone had been reason enough for doubt, but as time passed, I found that I was willing to believe.

"Twenty below riding a thirty-mile-an-hour wind," I said. "We should have sold the steers in October instead of waiting like the bank wanted." Snow sifted across the yard, rising like smoke through auras of mercury-vapor light above the feed lot.

"The bank is the boss, Pard." Cody folded the dough back on itself and looked at me. "Relax. It could be worse, old man." She blew strands of her jet-black hair away from her face and shook her head. I reached over and brushed her hair back with the flat of my hand, then put two fingers in the flour on the counter and touched her cheek, leaving white dots on her mahogany skin. She ducked away from me with that look of hers and tried to rub the flour off with her shoulder. The smile lingered, though, as she reached up and smudged my nose. "You're a worrier is your problem," she said.

I slipped my arm around her and found her ribs with my fingers. "Worry about this," I whispered and felt her body fill with electric strength. I put my face in her hair and held her just off the floor until she began to relax. The last time we got going we broke a chair in the kitchen set.

After ten months we still played with each other, as proof, perhaps, that we'd be all right, that the distance to town and the fifteen years between us wouldn't matter. But in spite of the teasing, an early winter on a leased place seemed a hard way to start all over.

IT MIGHT NOT HAVE BEEN THE TELEPHONE but wind in the trailer skirts that woke me. The bedroom had gone cold, and it seemed we'd slept most of the night. I could hear Cody's voice down the hall in the spare bedroom we used as an office. The clock radio's luminous digits said 4:37.

I turned up the electric blanket, closed my eyes, and found myself standing in an irrigation ditch, shoveling mud onto a canvas dam and watching the metallic progress of water as it flooded my father's fields. Cottonwoods flanked the river, and under the trees, I could see the Percheron Norman teams we used for haying, lazing in tandem through the shade. The water in the ditch was so cold it cramped my legs.

". . . up," Cody said. "Wake up, Clayton."

I shielded my eyes from the ceiling light with my arm and looked at Cody leaning over me. Her robe fell open, and I slipped my hand inside the terry cloth and let it ride the length of her back. At her thigh, I turned the robe aside to see the rose tattooed on the inside swale of her hip.

"Come have some coffee," she said, taking my hand and pulling me up. "I need to talk to you."

She pulled until I was sitting, then gathered her clothes and went off barefoot down the hallway toward the bathroom, walking hard on her heels. I put my arms on my knees and my head on my arms; I closed my eyes and tried to go back to the ditch. My right knee made a lump under my arm; a knee the size of a grapefruit. It always would be, the doctors said, and it ached if I didn't use the brace.

The smell of black soil soured by water lingered from the dream. It came to me at odd times, that odor of place and youth. The smell of home. My old man had married again at seventy-four. His bride owned the black mud now.

The Mr. Coffee was going when I got to the kitchen. Cody leaned against the counter, standing with one foot on the other as she smoked a Camel Filter. She was wearing a pair of slippers that looked like mallards. Execuducks. I'd ordered them as a joke from an ad in one of Cody's magazines because she did our books. The slippers were for successful people who already had everything.

I pulled back the curtain at the sink. Pellets of snow struck the window like shot. I couldn't even see the diesel tank, twenty yards away. As I stepped back, I saw my reflection on the glass, my sleep-straightened sandy hair standing as if in comic fright.

"Honey," Cody said. "That was TJ's mother on the phone. Are you awake?" She drew on her cigarette as if she needed it to breathe.

"I'm awake." I took two porcelain cafe cups from the drainboard and watched the coffee rise in the Pyrex pot. "TJ's got a mother?" I said.

Cody turned away to snub out the butt, and I looked at the clean lines of her back and legs, the currents of black hair spilling off her shoulders. In profile the blood really showed: Plains Cree and French, although her father, she thought, had been a Harp. I wondered how TJ Rountree, a person we did not often mention, had managed to get me out of bed.

With him it could be anything. I'd known him when he was just starting out on broncs, a skinny kid, who at first took a hell of a beating. But he toughened in his twenties, getting hard and limber as a bullprick whip. Over the years, I'd helped him off some winners, and for a while in the early '80s, it looked like he could be somebody. On his way down, he met Cody, and they ran together for a couple of seasons, until I found her one night passed out in the grass behind the horse trailers at the Last Chance Stampede, lying there where Rountree left her. I got some help and took her to the hospital. After she took the cure, we started seeing each other. When we got married, we acted like Rountree had never been born.

"He's in Missoula," Cody said. She filled our cups and put cream on the table for hers. She lit another cigarette. "In the hospital."

The coffee was strong, although it would have been better the way I used to drink it, with half a shot to the cup. I couldn't do that anymore, living with Cody. I had two drinks a night and put the bottle away. Cody claimed that having whiskey around the house didn't bother her. When she'd been drinking, she went mostly with wine. Still, I kept the bottle out of sight. "He drying out or what?" I asked.

Cody nodded: "Bleeding shits, shakes, scared half crazy. His mom is there with him."

"Now it's Mom," I said. I sat down at the chrome and Formica table. Like the rest of the furniture, it had come with the trailer and had no connection to the past. "So what does Mom want from us?"

Cody stared at her slippers, cigarette smoke boiling from her nose. The one thing you notice right off about reformed drunks is the cigarettes and coffee. "He just waited too long," she said. "He thought he could cowboy up and go cold turkey. He was in some kind of shock by the time they got to him. He's asking for me."

"Well kiss my ass and call me Mildred," I said. "That takes guts." I started to stand, my knee popped, and I almost went down. But in that instant of vertigo before I caught the table, I understood something that had been there all along just under the surface. I saw why we'd never had a real fight, Cody and I. We called it love, but we knew we'd kill each other if we ever got started. As I looked at her I saw that we both understood it now.

"I've got to go," she said. "He's hurting and he's scared."

She walked around the table and put her hand on my arm. I didn't know what to do, and I knew whatever I said would be wrong. I touched her hair. "I'll be needing the truck in the afternoons to feed," I said.

"Maybe the bus then," Cody answered. She slipped her arm under mine and hugged my waist. "If you'd just drive me in."

When it was light enough to see outside I started the truck, fed the horses, and checked the stocktank heaters. The wind tapered off at dawn and morning broke clear, not a cloud from the Missouri to the Rocky Mountain Front. Smoke from the idling truck rose in vertical white contrails against a sea-blue sky. I thought about taking Cody into Great Falls for the bus, and I didn't believe, when it came right down to it, that we'd go. She would change her mind, or I'd say no, or, maybe Rountree would do the right thing for a change and either improve or die before we left.

Cody'd been through a bunch of men when she was running, but I could never understand why she'd ended up with him—a man so obviously out for himself. Winning a few in a row can turn your head, although when I'd been riding saddle broncs I hadn't lasted long enough to discover how I'd act on a roll. A chute post got my knee my second season, and riding pickup was about as close to winners as I got on the summer circuit.

We didn't have much to say during breakfast, and I tried for some restraint. It didn't work. Finally I said, "Okay. Tell me why."

She looked up, butting those black eyes on me. "Just don't," she said with a twist of her mouth. "Just don't you start."

"I need an answer," I told her and heard in the sound of my voice how much I meant it.

"Because," she said and took her dishes to the sink where she started to wash them, then one by one smashed each piece against the divider. She had to hit the cup three times before it broke, but when it did, chips cleared the drainboard and ricocheted off the microwave. When she finished, she took the porcelain handle from her fingers and put it on the table. She looked outside at the glare of sky on empty space. "Because he tried to love me," she said. "It wasn't easy for him, like it is for you, but he tried."

"And you drank yourself stupid, it was so good."

Cody turned her glistening eyes back to me. I'd never seen her cry, and she did not cry then; she stood at the sink, gazing at me through cataracts of ice.

"That's right," she said. "It was good. I just did not know how to face it sober."

I STOOD OUTSIDE IN THE CONCRETE FOREBAY until the driver closed the luggage compartment doors and climbed aboard. Cody looked out the tinted window. Her face was green, her loose black hair clasped behind each ear by a beadwork barrette. A green Indian on her way to town. The driver ground gears and released the brakes, and Cody raised one hand. I shook my head and she looked away.

I went inside and walked around until I could feel my leg. The people waiting on the benches seemed to have been abandoned there in their winter clothes. Three bums sat together by the wall lockers, not going anywhere, just sitting quietly, sharing warmth until someone threw them out. A woman from Rocky Boy or Harlem held a sleeping child—a grandson perhaps. Leaving the reservation or going back; she could have been Cody's mother, the child, mine.

Cody was in motion. As I walked to the truck I knew I had a choice: I could drive home and talk to the cows and wait, or I could move too. Momentum seemed the only answer.

Rising exhaust and river steam yellowed the frozen midday sky. Alone in the lanes of traffic, I felt somehow freed, opened to all the possibilities of so many people moving at such a pace. I drew five hundred dollars in cash at the branch bank on 10th Avenue South and drove on to Holiday Village where I walked the mall looking in all the windows.

At the Westerner's I found a pin-stripe Fenton and a pair of gabardine slacks that matched. The fitting room was tight, but I managed to change without removing my brace. I topped off the shirt and pants with a black scarf and a pearl-gray Resistol Sundance. The clerk put my work clothes in a Westerner's sack. I felt dressed and ready; the sack suggested purchases in reserve.

I was surprised to see kids on every level, crowding the record stores, buying clothes, clowning on the escalators. Some of them wandered in pairs, holding hands. Some embraced in darker passageways near the theater, waiting for the matinee. Most seemed bored by the presence of so much merchandise.

Posters in the windows at Adventure Travel showed mossy castles in the Highlands, high-rise hotels in the Caribbean, an airliner in flight above white-domed clouds, and high-breasted girls in bikinis. I went inside and looked at more posters, at casinos in the desert, at tanned skin fronting white sand beaches, at coconut palms silhouetted against atomic skies. All the places I would never go.

When the travel agent came over, I pointed to an aerial shot of some islands off Santa Cruz. "How much one way?" I asked.

She figured up a flight schedule to Guadalajara by way of Denver and El Paso. "For one?" she asked without looking away from the terminal.

I told her yes and she touched more keys.

"One way, coach, is three hundred and sixty dollars—during our Winter Traveler's Special," she said.

"That's not that much, is it?"

She looked up. "My boyfriend and I went down last year. We stayed on the beach at Teacapan. We fell in love with it." She smiled. Her green eyes were bright as bottle glass in the glow of the screen.

I DROVE OUT TO THE TROPICANA CLUB near the front gate of Malmstrom Air Force Base and went in to plan my future. The place was already in full swing, mostly airmen in civvies, a few wheat farmers in town for the day, a cowboy or two, and some poker machine apes—everyone drinking loud or watching two strobe-lit women who danced in wrought-iron cages swinging from the ceiling on chains. I walked to the end of the bar, as close to the cages as I could get, and put my Carhartt coat on a stool. The bartender gave me a napkin. I noticed a blender on the backbar. "Piña colada," I said, "Make it a pitcher."

The place could have been a warehouse: black cinder block walls with palm trees painted here and there in Day-Glo greens, a tequila sunset mural backing the bandstand. Music throbbed from the darkest corners. Overhead spots threw multicolored cones of light on the dancers. The closest girl took off her top, twirled it, and rotated her small breasts in the opposite direction. The guy next to me squirmed and grinned. He was wearing a mesh cap that read: Ford Tractors and Equipment. "She really puts out," he said and I turned back to love her.

She was Oriental, Korean maybe. She looked into the colored lights and bopped away without seeming to notice the music. The other girl was very white, with dark red hair flounced into lazy curls. She seemed a little stiff, as if, perhaps, she was new to the cage.

The bartender put a fishbowl on my napkin and filled it with froth. "You want the umbrella?" he asked.

"Sure thing," I said and put a fifty on the bar. I rested my weight on my elbows and let the one leg hang.

He left the pitcher beside my glass and put a pink and blue bamboo umbrella, two candied cherries, and a lavender straw in my drink. He raised his eyebrows. "Just right," I told him, and he shook his head and smiled.

I was toying with the umbrella and thinking about Adventure Travel when it came to me: Green Indian. One of the illegals who irrigated for my father used to say that. Anything he didn't like or understand was an Indio Verde. Used to call my old man that behind his back, and son of a bitch, if he hadn't been right. I could see his face, the Mexican, but I had no idea what his name might have been. The old man called them all Manual, as in shovel.

I tried the drink and it was so cold it hurt my heart. It seemed almost perfect. All it needed was more fruit, more booze, and more light. I tried to imagine the perfect piña colada, freshly wrung from the jungle, to visualize the dancers' cages hanging from palm trees that fronted a white crescent beach with breakers coming in and sails like shark fins marking the horizon. One girl would be Polynesian, the other, old-country Irish. I was alone on the beach—the jungle at my back—dressed in a white terry cloth robe and Panama straw the color of cream, drinking the perfect piña colada and watching the waves churn to foam at my feet. In this state of mind, I owned the beach. I owned the dancers.

The music ended, the lights went down, and several airmen struggled to help the women from their cages. They got the job done, handing the dancers down like frozen beef. I closed my eyes. I wanted to stand centered between palms and watch the sea. I wanted it all: salt winds and sea warmth, sand burning the soles of my feet, the glow of endless ocean seared by sky.

I took out my wallet and flipped through my cards. Nothing on American Express or the Discover Card so far this month. The Visa looked good too. The MasterCard could stand another fifteen hundred, and there was my bank card, like an ace in the hole. I took them from their plastic pockets and spread them on the bar like a poker hand. I had some money tucked away at a bank in Butte. I could do it. I could be a wanderer in the world. I could go to the swimming hole every day.

I wondered if Cody was there yet, and how long it would take Rountree to straighten out once she found him. I wondered what she had hoped to accomplish beyond trying to do the right thing. I wondered what she would do if TJ cleaned up his act.

The dancers came along the bar, teasing the drinkers. The girl with red hair stopped to toy with my friend in the Ford cap. He was having fun now, all wiggly on his stool, making signs with his hands. She smiled with her teeth, a thirsty dust-bowl look of accommodation. She nodded at what he was saying, cut her eyes to me, and noticed my drink. I watched as he pulled his wallet to show her something. She looked down the bar at my plastic full house and smiled again.

Her outfit was mostly moccasins and strings of black leather torn into a vampy Mohawk motif. I took my Carhartt from the stool and held it out for her by the collar. She slipped into it like a cape, and the coat made her seem small. "Are those hot?" she asked, looking at the cards.

"Not yet."

She bent over the bar to look closer and pulled the coat tighter from inside, hiding her arms. "I don't get it," she said.

"It has to do with green Indians," I said. "My wife took off this morning. I've got three hundred head of black cattle to feed for the bank and a trailer full of new appliances. If I don't get drunk and kill somebody I might catch a flight to Guadalajara."

"I'm from Omaha," she said. "I know just how you feel."

"A couple weeks on the beach, drinking these beautiful drinks, and watching the water roll in."

"Yeah, right," she said. "Like Jimmy Buffett there."

"Just exactly like Jimmy Buffett, frozen concoctions and all."

She took one arm from inside the coat and fanned the cards with the tips of her fingers. "Are you nice?" she asked.

"Oh, goodness yes, and quite wealthy, too."

"Come on. I mean, are you straight up or what?"

"Maybe if you're not so straight you don't lose so much," I said.

She shook her hair back with a quick movement of her head. "You won't go," she said. "You want it all back. I see guys like you every day, a handful of plastic and a plan. It's talk. It's a country song."

"Maybe you're right," I said, "but I'd lie to you for your love."

"You'll do more than that," she answered.

We laughed. She was on the road where I felt I should be, and the truth was I did feel better. I held out the fishbowl. "Here, kid, try some of this and we'll see if you've got what it takes."

She raised the bowl like a giant shell to her lips and held my eyes as she drank. She closed her eyes then drank again. When she handed it back she said, "My name is Danny . . ." She picked up a card, tipping it to the bar lights, "Mr. Delaney."

"Clay," I said. "Mr. Delaney died." I refilled the bowl, adjusted the umbrella. "One other thing."

"Right," she said and threw back her hair again. "I just knew there would be."

"I am going. I'm just not going alone."

Danny wiped the mustache away with the tip of her third finger and asked for the bowl again with her hands. "Of course you're not," she said.

At Holiday Village, I put the tickets on my American Express and drew a thousand in cash with the bank card. We drove on across town in the blinding late light of afternoon with an accelerating sense of impending joy. From Airport Hill, where the sky cleared, Great Falls was lost beneath a sea of haze the color of sand.

The lady at the American Airlines counter tore our tickets and explained the flight changes at Denver and El Paso. She barely looked at the tickets as she talked, and it worried me that she might make an error. I could just see us boarding the morning flight from El Paso with hangovers, an attendant saying, "Excuse me, sir, but there seems to be a mistake."

". . . luggage?" the airline lady asked.

"Just carry-on," I answered. "We're buying everything new."

Danny had an overnight case with her dancing costume and a tub of cocoa butter for the beach. Between us we didn't have a toothbrush. "I can't believe we're into this," she said on the escalator to the boarding level. She laughed and gave me her palms to slap. I laughed too and slid my hands over hers. We'd been laughing so much the last couple of hours my face had started to stiffen.

"Believe," I said.

We had twenty minutes to kill. At the bank of international clocks in the concourse mezzanine, I told her I had to make a call.

"I'm thinking rum coladas," she said.

"Get some with all the goodies. I'll be right back."

I left her in the flight lounge and found a row of phones. I dumped some bar change on the phone tray and got the operator to ring McDonough's, our closest neighbors, three miles south. The youngest boy, Alfred, worked for me sometimes, when he could escape his old man.

Mrs. McDonough answered, and I asked for her son. When he

came on, I said, "Something's come up, Al. Cody and I are going to be gone a while, and I need you to feed for me."

After a silence so long it seemed we'd been disconnected, he said, "Just a minute." Away from the receiver I heard him call: "Daaad." He sounded like a calf. Alfred, the slow son who would stay home.

"What's going on?" McDonough said in my ear.

"Like I told your boy, something has come up short notice, and I need him to feed for me. Cody and I are going to be away." I heard him breathing on the line. "So would it be all right? Can you spare him?"

"Are you drunk?" he said.

"No. I'm in Great Falls."

"Well, I don't know," he said, "what's going on with you people. That's your business. But I can tell you this: I picked up your wife at Bowman's Corner after she called here this afternoon. I went and got her and took her home drunk as seven hundred dollars. She ain't gone, she's out there with a case of Wild Berry."

"Hang on," I said.

"We get to your place, there's no tracks, no truck. She starts pulling her hair, for Christ's sake. You want my boy to walk into a jackpot like that?"

"You sure she's still there?"

"She's there. It's twelve miles to Augusta."

I felt myself sag. "Sorry about the trouble," I said.

"I've got more to do than ferry . . ."

"Thanks again," I said and hung up.

I went to the wall of east-facing windows and looked out. I could see my one-ton in the lot, and off south, the slope-shouldered rise of the Little Belt Mountains—lit, like a memory of mountains, with alpenglow.

Above the escalators hung a mural of Lewis and Clark making their portage around the Great Falls of the Missouri. The men in the painting looked like Hulk Hogan as they strained to drag their pirogues up onto the prairie. The sky behind them suggested mid-summer and high adventure.

Danny was watching the American Airlines 737 join an accordioned tunnel outside. She'd killed both drinks. I leaned into the bar behind her and looked out through the floor-to-ceiling windows. I touched her hair.

"I've been all over," Danny said. "But every time I see my ship come in I get real goosey."

"Me too," I said. I paid for the drinks, and we walked into the mezzanine toward the boarding gates. Outside, the last direct rays of winter light stoked the Little Belts like bedded coals.

She put her overnight bag on the conveyor at the security check. I emptied my pockets and took off my belt buckle. Danny went through, no problem. The machine went crazy on me. One of the uniformed women behind the counter raised her hand.

"My brace," I said and pulled up my pant leg for her to see.

Danny held the tray with my things, looking at the iron on my leg. The security lady came around the counter with a handheld detector and ran it all over me. It liked the brace. "Okay," she said. "Sorry."

"It's all right," I said. "I'm not boarding anyway."

Danny fingered my buckle. When she looked at me it was with the dryness I'd first noticed at the bar. "Most guys just want to take you to Heaven at the Paradise Inn," she said. "But you, we get to go to the airport first."

I stuffed my pockets with change and put my buckle back on.

"You know something?" she said. "The last time I made it to the airport with a big spender like you we went to Reno."

"How nice for you," I said and took her arm.

"What are you doing, man? I mean, I quit my job! I've got maybe three hundred dollars and no place to stay. It's January, Jack. Just let go, okay? I've had about enough for one shift."

I held her elbow until we got to Gate 4 where a line had formed at the podium for the flight to Denver. An attendant spoke into a red phone. He hung up and began taking tickets.

"Just great," she said. "Now we get to watch the nice people take off before you dump me here. This is getting creepy, you know?" She jerked her arm and I bore down. People leaving the plane glanced at us as they passed.

I took the packet of tickets from the cigar pocket in my coat and let go. I put some one hundred-dollar-bills inside the folder. "I've got to go home," I said. "The beach is no place for a gimp. You can go for both of us."

"Oh, come on!" she said, her palms out, warding off the tickets.

"And get a good Irish burn. And watch the water come in. And drink some real piña coladas."

The line ahead had shortened to three people. "Cash my ticket to get home. Stay as long as you can. Here." I handed her the folder.

"You don't need to rescue me," she said, her eyes beginning to shine. "Do you think I need you to leave town?"

"All you need is a white robe and a Panama straw and some shades. This isn't that complicated, and you'll make me feel better. Go."

"Take a break," she said. "Give me a minute." She stepped into a ladies' room and I walked down to a window to look at the plane. My leg ached. I was beginning to feel the first waves of an afternoon hangover, and I realized that I was hungry. I drew a heart in the condensation on the glass and put a palm tree inside and shot an arrow through it. Cody would be passed out by now.

Danny took my arm. "Listen," she said. "What's going on?" Her hand was deeply freckled, and it was warm in the way of a warmth I needed. In the hard light of the concourse she looked about my age.

"I called home," I told her. "My wife came back. She's a drinker and she's drinking again."

"If you hadn't called, would we have gone?"

"Yes, we would have gone."

"It would be sweet," she said, "the frozen concoctions and all." Then she handed me the tickets and walked her dancer's walk back the way we'd come. At the security station she glanced toward me, shook her head, and kept going.

I waited until the engines gained pitch and the tunnel withdrew from the plane before I walked back to the bar, where I bought a pack of Camel Filters. I asked for a cup of coffee and smoked the first cigarette and watched the plane taxi north, its wing lights bright in the growing dusk. The cigarette made me dizzy.

I sat down and thought about having something to eat before I headed back out to the new place that except for Cody would never be home. I could not go home. But that meadowed valley with its beaver-slide stackers and hayrake teams was always waiting in me. I could close my eyes and smell it; I could turn my head, and it was there.

I smoked another cigarette and drank my coffee and watched as the plane left the earth, leaping south into a winter sky that was turning with slow certainty toward summer.

CUSTER ON MONDAYS
Jon Billman

SUNDAY WAS A BATTLE

Sunday, June 25, was a battle. The last of the smoke cleared in the afternoon, the dust settled in the barley field, and the Sioux, Arapaho, Cheyenne, Crow, and Seventh Cavalry called the horses, picked up the arrows, dusted themselves off, and headed downtown together for cold beers at the Mint. Most of the chiefs and officers had planes to catch in Billings, but the group got on without them. They'd pick up the Indian Wars again at next year's Reenactment of Custer's Last Stand.

On Monday morning, June 26, the day after the big battle, Owen Doggett came home from the Mint to find he was now trespassing on the dirt half acre he used to almost own. Everything the actor now owned formed a crude breastwork ten yards from the chipped cinder-block front step that led to the single-wide he also used to almost own. A buckskin shirt. A few T-shirts. Some socks. A faded union suit. A broken AM radio with a coat-hanger antenna. His Sage fly rod. An empty duffel bag. A brick of pistol rounds, and the title to the '76 Ford Maverick.

Charley Reynolds, the basset hound, was off chasing rabbits in the cheatgrass; he belonged solely to Owen Doggett now. Owen Doggett banged on the window of the locked trailer house with his gloved fists and yelled, "Sweetheart, I'll make you eggs!"

His wife had already begun her day's work, tying flies for an outfitter in Sheridan. Her fly patterns were intricate, exacting, and held the subtle variances of nature usually reserved for spiderwebs, mud-dauber nests, and snowflakes. Through the cloudy window of her workroom, Sue Doggett looked up from her vise and out at her husband in his riding boots and dirty wool tunic. She mouthed, "Read my lips: I am not acting."

THE SIOUX

Mr. and Mrs. Owen Doggett were married three years ago on a moon-lit Monday midnight in Reno, Nevada, after meeting at a Halloween party and dating for exactly sixteen days. The engagement lasted an afternoon and a dinner. They took the red-eye out of Billings and stayed drunk for the entire two-day trip. They were married in the same clothes they met in—his custom Custer buckskin, her star-spangled Wonder Woman bustier. The wedding cost exactly twenty-seven dollars, bourbon and snapshots included.

Sue is a full-blooded Crow. Owen Doggett calls her The Sioux. And sue is what she is doing; she's suing the trooper for all he's worth. No negotiations. Sue gave him an old government Colt revolver as a wedding present. She wanted the valuable relic back. "Indian-giver!" he called her. He cannot afford a lawyer.

THE COLONEL

Owen Doggett is a local, an extra, a private. But Owen will tell you he's a trouter by heart, an actor by trade, and he has faith he will one day soon be the hero, the star, the colonel in the Hardin, Montana, Reenactment of Custer's Last Stand. "Call me Colonel," he'll tell you. He has to stay in character. "I'm an actor from Hollywood. Bred-in-the-bone." Right now he, his trouting buddy, and Charley Reynolds are on their way east so Owen Doggett the actor can audition to be the Black Hills Passion Play's substitute Pontius Pilate. The Colonel will not tell you he is only a private. He will tell you he may soon be cast as Pontius Pilate in a large-scale production of the second-greatest story ever told, the story of Jesus' last seven days in South Dakota. He will not tell you he is from Hollywood, Pennsylvania, and that he has to rent a nineteen-year-old grade horse when he wants to ride.

Hardin's current Custer is a Shakespearean-trained actor from Monroe, Michigan. He looks like Colonel George Armstrong Custer, owns a white stallion like Custer's, pulls a custom four-horse trailer, does beer commercials for a brewery out of Detroit, and calls his wife Libbie. It will not be easy. The Colonel is torn between what he wants to do, what his heart tells him—goddammit, you're an actor!—and what is to be done. "History is the now of yesterday," he says. In his own recent history, the Colonel has caught some nice fish, drunk a few beers, cheated on his wife, and watched some movies. He sees himself on the big screen—not in a factory, not in an office. He hasn't paid many bills, but "hell," he says, "we don't have a satellite dish and we don't get cable. That's a big savings right there."

Libbie Bacon Custer wanted her husband to be President of the United States of America. Sue Doggett wanted the Colonel to get a not-always-have-to-tenderize-a-cheap-cut-of-beef job. Not full-time necessarily, just something where the trooper worked more than one day every two weeks. But that would mean giving up a few Mondays—and Tuesdays, Wednesdays, and the like—of sore-lipping fish.

"Do I not bless you with much fish and bread?" the Colonel asks his wife.

"Whitefish and Wonder Bread every day isn't my idea of heaven," says Sue.

THE PRIVATE

Colonel calls his trouting buddy, Ben Fish, Private. They might be knocking back a few Rainiers at the Mint. They might be boning up on the Black Hills Expedition of '74 over morning coffee at the B-I. They might be casting the Little Bighorn for browns and rainbows on a Monday. They might be, as they are now, rumbling down U.S. 212, on their way only a few hours after dawn, with Charley Reynolds in the middle and the Private riding shotgun. Just the three of them in the old oil-burning baby-blue Maverick, their forage caps cocked back on their heads, spitting the hulls of sunflower seeds out the windows. For the Private this trip is a chance to scout some new country, cast some new water.

The Private is a teacher. He has stitches in the back of the head where the heel of his pregnant ex-wife's cowboy boot caught him from point-blank range. He has lived in a U-Store-It shed for an entire January. The Private has slept in libraries and eaten ketchup soup and melba toast for breakfast. He has talked with lawyers he couldn't afford. He has lived in Wyoming.

The Private is learning not who he is but where he needs to be. It's a process of elimination. Sue gives him flies for simply appreciating them and showing her the little spiral-bound steno pad in which he logs which fly caught which fish under which conditions. The Private is growing older, which means to him that it's harder to have fun.

"One week," he tells the Colonel. "One week and you'll have to find another couch to sleep on."

HARDIN, MONTANA

Every now and then responsibility picks up an ax handle and knocks the Colonel into government service. He delivers mail in Hardin on a substitute basis. "It's a job," he would tell Sue. It's a job.

Hardin is a rough town because it is one thing but also another. Most of it is not part of the reservation. But some of the town, across the Burlington Northern tracks, rests on the Indian land. You can see cattle over there grazing through the front and back yards of the trailer homes. The government prefabs are a little more in need of things—a window that isn't cardboard, siding that doesn't slap in the wind. The roads are mostly gravel and dust. There is the beef-packing plant, where many townspeople, mostly Crow, work. The Crow kids go to school where the Private, Mr. Fish, teaches history: Hardin Intermediate. The Bulldogs.

Every May the Bulldogs take a field trip to the Little Bighorn Battlefield. The Little Bighorn draws people from all over the country, from all over the world. Some of the students live less than ten miles from the national monument, and they've never been to it. Mr. Fish wears his wool Seventh Cavalry uniform, riding boots and all, and acts as if he were there on June 25, 1876, taking fire from all sides.

"Company dismount!" he calls, and the students file off the bus. "Form a skirmish line on the west flank of the bus and hold your ground. Any horseplay and you'll be back in second-period study hall so fast your head will spin."

Mr. Fish and the campaign-hatted guides lead the students around the grounds amid the signs that read WATCH FOR RATTLESNAKES and METAL DETECTORS PROHIBITED. The spring wind whips their hair and makes it difficult to hear, though they understand. There are many questions. Sharp notes fill the afternoon like gun smoke as Mr. Fish bugles the students back on the bus. They talk motives and strategy, treaties and tactics, on the short bus ride back to Hardin.

The Colonel doesn't get called to work much. The Private has summers off and many sick days during the year. On Mondays they go fishing. Sometimes the Tongue River down in Wyoming. Sometimes the Powder River over to Broadus. Sometimes the Bighorn. But most often the Little Bighorn. They take sandwiches and keep a sharp eye out for rattlesnakes, Indians, and landowners. And it's often hot. Very hot. They fish other days, too, but always Mondays.

A Sunday Drive through Custer's Montana

Driving east—going backwards—down U.S. 212, over the Wolf Mountains, through Busby and Lame Deer, the Colonel, Charley Reynolds, and the Private study through the yellow-bug-splattered windshield where Custer and his men camped on their way to the last campaign from Fort Abraham Lincoln, Dakota Territory. It's probably how the outfit would have retreated, if there had been a retreat.

"If you were captured by the Sioux, the idea was to shoot yourself before they had a chance to torture you." The actor steers with his knees, making finger pistols in the air over the steering wheel. "Troopers kept one round, their last round, for just that purpose. Shoot yourself in the head before they could cut your heart out while you watched."

The road is rough here and cuts through the charcoal remains of a forest fire that burned most of the salable Northern Cheyenne Indian Reservation, but it gets better when they get to Ashland, back to everyone's Montana.

"Private," says the Colonel, not shouting over the rattle and thunk of the car so that his words are lost in the noise and it appears that he is just moving his lips, "know what the slowest thing in the world is?" The warm July wind rushes through the open windows and the gaps in the brittle rubber gasket surrounding the windshield. The Private is used to this Maverick lip-reading.

"Besides us right now?" says the Private. The muffler and tailpipe have a few holes in them, like tin whistles, and the sunflower seeds taste like exhaust. "It's either us right now or a reservation funeral procession with only one set of jumper cables," says the Private. The speedometer needle is shaking at around fifty-one miles an hour.

The Private isn't laughing. Charley Reynolds isn't laughing. The Colonel's eyes glass over at the humble recognition that he's just told a joke everyone heard many campaigns ago. But as you get older—he is forty-one, nearly past his Custer prime—you forget. Everything turns to history with daguerreotype eyes and brittle, yellowed edges.

Bugs

Charley Reynolds stands on the Private's lap and sticks his nose into the fifty-one-mile-an-hour prairie wind. The Private lets his palm ride on the stream of air and dreams of becoming a scout. The Colonel talks numbers. Bag limits. Length, girth, weight. Hook size. Tippet strength. Rod action. He talks of the beefiest brown in Montana, the heftiest rainbow in Dakota Territory. "Pleistocene man used shards of bone for hooks," he says. "Indians used rock-hard spirals of rawhide until we traded steel hooks with them. Custer used steel."

What is different about Sue's flies, different from the flies tied by hundreds of nimble-fingered Western women for pennies apiece, is that they are tied for fish, not for fishermen and their aesthetics. Unless, that is, they are true fishermen and know the difference deep inside, like right and wrong.

Her flies have something of the ancient in them, borrowing from her ancestors on the frontier, as well as from evolution: her Darwinian ancestors, the fish. Sue tests her flies in an old aquarium in her workroom. The aquarium is stained, filled with the murky water of the Little Bighorn. With a pair of fencing pliers, she cuts the hook off at the bend and ties it onto a length of leader attached to a two-foot-long willow branch and flings it into the tank from across the small room. Weight. Aerodynamics. Flight. She is looking for balance. In the aquarium are several small rainbow and brown trout.

Sue gets on her back, crawls underneath the aquarium stand, and studies the trout's reactions to the new insects through the tank's glass bottom.

After only a week she throws the burlap water bag over her shoulder and walks to the river to turn the trout back into the Little Bighorn. "Thank you," she tells them, "thank you. Goodbye." She then unfolds the little pack rod from her day pack and ties on one of her new and experimental flies. She casts and catches new fish to help her with her work. Though it rarely happens, if she does not catch new helper-fish, she walks back to the trailer with the empty burlap bag, thinking about how she is going to adjust the new patterns. She enjoys being outsmarted now and then.

What matters is what an imitation looks like on the water, in the water, not warm and dry in a tackle shop that smells like chicken livers and epoxy. Sue's workroom smells like old wool, spruce, and duck feathers. Damp dog, river water, coffee. She rendezvouses with Ben Fish at the river and bails the aquarium out once a week, trout or no trout.

If it is late and he is drunk, the Colonel may tell you Sue ties the most beautiful, most perfect trout flies in the Louisiana Purchase. The Colonel calls them bugs.

THE TREATY

Mr. and Mrs. Owen Doggett celebrated their three-year anniversary by getting a six-pack of Heineken instead of Rainier and toasting the event at home while watching *She Wore a Yellow Ribbon* on video.

A week later, that belly-dancing night at the Mint, Sue said only this: "Three strikes, you're out." The faraway look in the Colonel's eyes was a sure sign he knew she meant it and he didn't shoot back, didn't ask about strike one, strike two.

Sue calls the legal papers the treaty. She'll get the waterbed and the microwave. The banana boxes of Harley Davidson parts. The eight-track player and turntable. The veneer bedroom set. The Toyota Corolla and the single-wide.

The third strike is named Salome.

SALOME ON SATURDAYS

Salome told the Colonel and the Private about the real live camels in the Passion Play on her breaks at the Mint. She is an actress. She works the Passion Play during the week and the Mint most Fridays and Saturdays. She also told the Colonel she could arrange a private audition for him because she happened to know for a fact that Pilate was moving to Florida and the director owed her a few favors that she'd probably never get a chance to cash in on anyway.

Belly dancing is hard work, she also said. So she took lots of breaks. She was not taking a break when Sue walked in after one of the battles to find her Colonel. Sue found him. The Colonel pleaded that it was all part of the act and belly dancing was an art form going back to biblical times and that it should be respected.

Horses, too, they have horses. Doves. Sheep. Donkeys.

THE BLACK HILLS EXPEDITION OF 1995

They stop in tiny Alzada for Cokes, oil, gas, beef jerky for Charley Reynolds, brake fluid, more sunflower seeds. The Colonel says to the Private, "You want to scrub them mustard bugs off the windshield?" It is Sunday afternoon when they cross the twenty or so miles of the townless northeast corner of Wyoming. Yes, the Colonel is trying out for Pontius Pilate, but they will fish, too.

"Nothing between this car and the North Pole but a barbed-wire fence," the Private tells the Colonel.

"Nothing between this car and the South Pole but Mount Rushmore and a fistful of gold mines," the Colonel tells the Private.

They cross the Belle Fourche River and see the Black Hills, the sacred land the Indians were afraid of.

"They heard thunder in there and thought it was the Everywhere Spirit," says the Colonel.

"Maybe they were right," replies the Private. "This wind does blow."

Spearfish, Dakota Territory. The sign at the edge of town has a trout with a spear sticking through it. "Trout are not indigenous to the Black Hills," the Colonel says to the Private and Charley Reynolds.

"They were stocked, all of them. The Indians speared chubs and suckers. That's all there were."

The sun is shining and the summer school coeds are not wearing much. "Welcome to Calvary," says the Colonel.

The Colonel tells Charley Reynolds to stay in the car. The dog jumps onto the gravel parking lot of the Shady Spot Motel (phone, free coffee) and hightails it to a bush, which he immediately sniffs, then waters. The Private tackles him and lugs the hound back to the car.

The Shady Spot rests near the Passion Play amphitheater. Families here enjoy the steady increases in the value of their ranch-styles and don't mind the flash and rumble of the Crucifixion and Ascension three nights a week. There are coffeehouses and bookstores and no bad neighborhoods in Spearfish. No railroad tracks. No reservations. The Passion Play is here because the Mount Rushmore tourists were here first, and the Black Hills seem a fitting place for Christ to appear, should he visit America.

The elderly desk clerk looks them over in their forage caps, Bermuda shorts, T-shirts (the Colonel's Rolling Stones Voodoo Lounge Tour, the Private's Bagelbird), and sandals.

"You fellas with the Passion Play?" asks the desk clerk.

"We're Texas Rangers in town on a pornography bust," says the Colonel. "You rent by the hour, too?" The desk clerk does not think this is funny, is frowning. The Private nods. "Yes, we're here for the Passion Play. There a discount for that?" One dollar.

The Colonel then pays the two-dollar surcharge for Charley Reynolds after the desk clerk says, looking down at the dog no car can contain, "I see you brought a dog."

THE BOY COLONEL

Her flies are small miracles. Tiny damsels, Daisy Millers, opulent caddis flies in all colors and sizes. Shiny Telico nymphs. Little Adams. Noble royal coachmen. Muddler minnows and grasshoppers. Beadheads. Streamers. Hare's ears. Stoneflies, salmon flies. Woolly buggers, black gnats, and renegades. She even invented a fly she calls the Libbie Bacon, tied with the soft hair from Charley Reynolds's belly.

"It's a shame that you'll now have to buy them, pay for them," the Private tells the Colonel. But their fly boxes are still worlds of insects: peacock hurl, elk hair, chicken hackle and deer tail, rabbit fur and mallard feather woven to life around a gold hook.

"And you won't?" asks the Colonel.

Sue gave the Private a full fly box as a Christmas gift the first year he moved to Hardin from Wyoming. Sometimes at night, when he's alone—most every night—and cannot sleep, he opens the box under his reading light and gently touches the flies and his heart speeds up a bit. When he would lose a fly—on a large willow, a snag in the river, maybe a fish—Sue would replace it with one of the same kind but yet different, one thing but also something else. None of her flies are exactly alike. The Private pointed this out to the Colonel, who still calls them bugs.

The Private started keeping the fly journal the first day he fished with the flies Sue tied for him, the morning of the day after Christmas. It was bitter cold and the guides on the rod kept freezing, so that he would have to dip the graphite shaft into the water to de-ice the rod before each cast. Yet he caught more trout than ever before in his life.

While the Colonel ties fresh leader and tippet material onto his line, the Private looks through his fly box. Their plan is to take in tonight's Passion Play (free tickets) and do some fishing tomorrow after the ten o'clock audition. From the motel room window, they can see Calvary, the sturdy cross as big as a pine tree, up the hill to the east of the amphitheater.

They were trying to have children—if not directly trying to prevent them is trying. Sue would often say, "I already have my hands full taking care of one boy. I don't need any more." This concerns the Colonel still. Even more so now. His mustache weighs at his lip when he thinks about it too hard.

Scouting

Spearfish Creek runs strong and clear through the Passion Play neighborhood. Today you can stand on any bridge in town and peer down at fish feeding against the current. Many healthy rainbows and browns. The Colonel's eyes widen as the men count the black silhouettes of trout feeding on the insects that wash their way. Heart-beats quicken. He calls this creek a river.

The detachment of three—a colonel, a private, and a basset hound scout—set out into the afternoon sun from the Shady Spot to scout the holes, the "honey buckets," they will fish tomorrow. There are many of these honey buckets running through the back yards of the people who don't mind living in the New Testament neighborhood.

As they patrol the river, the troopers wave to the grillers and the gardeners and the fertilizers and waterers, crossing now and then through the cool, calf-deep water in their sandals, though only some of the neighbors wave back—some sheepishly from behind their gazing balls and ceramic deer; some annoyed from behind their smoking Webers; some taken aback with beers in their hands as if, Honey, I think Colonel George Armstrong Custer in a Rolling Stones T-shirt and his basset hound just waded through our back yard.

THE COLOR OF SUNDAY

Salome did not tell them about this: the hatchery! How could she have left this out? The creek runs under a stonework bridge, and they wade out from the shadow of the bridge and peer through the chain-link and barbed-wire No Trespasssing fence of what the sign heralds as the D. C. BOOTH FISH HATCHERY, EST. 1896. And for whole moments, minutes, they are old men outside the chain-link of the city swimming pool, Seaworld, Mainland, staring in.

Tall cottonwoods, oaks, and spruce trees, as well as the flowers that have been planted around each of the three stone-and-concrete rearing pools, reflect off the green-gray water. Two lovers and a family with a stroller and children walk along the boardwalk and gaze into the pools. You can, for a quarter, buy a handful of trout meal from the gumball machine bolted to the railing. Many signs: NO FISHING.

A young woman in a khaki uniform sows trout meal from a tin bucket. The water boils with feeding fingerlings. Her auburn hair catches the late-afternoon light and is the color of Sunday. She is singing to the fry as she feeds them. Her hand dips into the bucket and she bows slightly and releases the meal. "I will make you fishers of men, fishers of men, fishers of men." Charley Reynolds chases a butterfly at the edge of the shallow water running over their feet, never catching it, as the men watch, mouths slightly closed, hearts racing. "I will make you fishers of men, if you follow me."

The lovers and the family stop to lean over the railing and look down into another pool, a larger pool. The father buys a handful of trout food and gives it to the young boy, who flings it all at once. The water explodes with trout, trout as big as—or bigger than—the Colonel and Private and Charley Reynolds have ever seen. "Good Lord, will you look at that! Did you see the size of those fins?" asks the Colonel. "Those tails!"

"Yes, she is beautiful," says the Private in a dry-mouthed whisper.

SUNDAY IN JERUSALEM

The Black Hills Passion Play draws people from all over the country, from all over the world. The Colonel and the Private have never been here. Young Christians in purple tunics direct cars, sell tickets, sell programs. An official program costs as much as it costs Charley Reynolds to stay at the Shady Spot. Outside the ticket office/gift shop there is a rather graceless statue, *Christ Stilling the Waters*, by Gutzon Borglum, the artist who blasted four presidents into a mountain just south of here. The Christ of the sculpture looks less like he's stilling waters than waving to friends.

The evening is cool. The tickets Salome gave them are not excellent, not VIP tickets. The troopers are in the center, the fifty-yard line, but back fifty rows, back far enough to wonder how much real weight Salome pulls around here. But they can see downtown Jerusalem. They can see Calvary. They can see the tall cottonwoods that surround the trout hatchery a couple of blocks away. The troopers stand and remove their forage caps and place them over their hearts for "The Star-Spangled Banner." There is a sliver of moon, not yet a quarter. There is an evening star in the west. The fanfare ends. A blond angel appears in the Great Temple and recites the prologue, "O ye children of God . . ."

"It's going to be a long night—look at this program—twenty-two scenes," says the Colonel.

"That which you will experience today, O people, treasure well within your hearts. Let it be the light to lead you—until your last day." With that the angel disappears and the streets of Jerusalem fill with asses, sheep, armored centurions on white stallions, and laughing, running children.

When the play ends, the troopers are not beseiged with passion, which is a little disappointing to both of them. An hour and a half of Sunday left. The actor has an audition in eleven and a half hours. Pontius Pilate is a muscular, tan, deep-voiced man. No long dirty-blond curls to his shoulders. No bushy handlebar mustache. It will not be easy.

FINS THE SIZE OF PRAIRIE SCHOONER SAILS

"Private, you awake?" asks the Colonel at a quarter to midnight.

"Yes," replies the Private. "Thinking about Sue?"

"No."

"The audition tomorrow?"

"No." Those fish. "Private, did you see those dorsal fins?"

CUSTER'S LAST STAND

They are out the door at midnight with an electric beep of the Colonel's Timex Ironman, waders on, vests heavy with tackle, wicker creels, rods in hand, Charley Reynolds in the lead, scouting his way up the creek. They wade through the same back yards, which are now dark except for a few dim yard lights and the electric blue of hanging bug lights and TVs through a couple of windows. Walking, wading slowly, they have enough light to see by. They do not cast, do not hit the honey buckets they mapped in their heads earlier. "Just where are we going?" asks the Private. The troopers are advancing.

They stop under the bridge. Charley Reynolds is up ahead, rustling through some willows along the bank. They take the lines from the reels and thread them through the guides on their graphite rods. The Colonel reaches into a vest pocket and pulls out a tin fly box. He opens it and the insects come to life in the dim glow of a streetlight. Gold bead-heads, hooks, and peacock hurl shine in the low light. The Colonel selects a size ten delta-wing caddis fly, threads his tippet through the eye, cinches down a simple Orvis knot, and slicks the insect up with silvery floatant to keep it on top of the water.

"Fishing dry, huh," says the Private.

"I'm not yet sure what these Dakota fish like for breakfast."

The Private ties on a humble Libbie Bacon in a size fourteen that will sink maybe a foot below the surface in still water, but no more.

Upstream, Charley Reynolds finds a low spot where he ducks under the fence and into the D. C. Booth Fish Hatchery. The troopers watch the basset hound's silhouette as he sniffs around the ponds and lunges at the bugs ticking under the floodlights. "How the hell did he get in?" asks the Private. "Let's advance along the fence line," says the Colonel.

They find the high spot in the rusty cyclone fence. The Colonel goes to his knees and reaches his fragile rod and creel under the sharp steel mesh. "Just how low can you go?" he says and commences to crawl under on his soft neoprene belly, careful not to rip his vest or the three-millimeter-thick waders. He stands erect, brushing the dirt from his waders and vest. "Private, why don't you check that flank over there?" says the Colonel, motioning with his rod toward the tree-lined fencerow at the south end of the hatchery. The rearing ponds are lit from the bottom and they glow in the night.

"Colonel," says the Private, his rod leaning against the fence, both hands grasping the fence like a tree sloth, still outside the hatchery, still looking in. "Colonel, I can't go in there."

"Why in Heaven's name not?" asks the Colonel, nervously adjusting the drag on his reel between glances at the pools after the occasional light smack of a fish on an unfortunate insect.

"Because it's trespassing," says the Private.

The Colonel looks at him, his mustache arched in disbelief.

"Because . . . I'm sorry. I know we've trespassed plenty of times before, but this is different," says the Private. "And right now, I'm sorry, I haven't always, but right now I have just a little more left to lose than you."

"For one?" says the Colonel.

"A job, for starters."

The Colonel reaches into his wicker creel and pulls out the crow-black government Colt. He tucks it back under the fence, handle first, and says, "Here, there's one round in it. You know what to do if we're ambushed."

"You want me to shoot myself?" cries the Private.

"Chrissakes, no. Fire into the air, warn me." The Colonel leaps atop the stone wall and his rod is at once in shadowy motion, the graphite whip whistling in the still summer night. False cast, follow through, false cast, follow through—the fly stays suspended throughout the series of false casts, back and forth, not landing but rehearsing to land. Sploosh! The moment the delicate caddis kisses the surface of the pool, a giant rainbow trout engulfs it, bowing the rod at a severe angle while the Colonel arches his back and sets his arms to play the fish.

The rainbow breaks water and skips a few beats across the surface, tail dancing in the night, its fat belly reflecting white from the floodlights. The Colonel plays out line, careful not to overstress his leader and tippet. The reel drag screams as the furious trout takes more line, across the short pool, around its smooth sides, down, back to the surface, down again.

The Private watches this from underneath a willow tree, sentinel duty. Minutes go by and he watches with his mouth slightly open, jaw set, palms sweating against the cork handle of his fly rod. He can hear the Colonel's heavy adrenalined breathing and the high-pitched din of monofilament leader and tippet, taut as a mandolin string.

Two slaps at the water near the Colonel's feet and the trooper sticks a thumb into her mouth, grasps the lower jaw, and raptures the fish out of the water and into the night air. She is heavy with eggs, heavy with flesh and fins and bone. Upwards of twelve pounds and easily the largest fish the Colonel, or the Private, has ever played, ever captured. Her gills heave as he stuffs her headfirst into his wicker creel, struggling to latch the lid. The Colonel reties another caddis where the tippet is gnawed and stretched. He tosses the old fly on the sidewalk—bent hook, frayed elk hair and hackle.

"Colonel, let's get out of here, I think a car is coming," whispers the Private as loud as he can from a copse of ironwood that runs along the outside of the hatchery's southern length of fence. Fingers of one hand grasp his expensive fly rod, the other fingers curl around the smooth hardwood handle of the government Colt. But the Colonel is in the moment, back on the stone wall, casting in a frantic motion that causes the tippet and leader to jerk and the fly to land a moment after the heavy slap of the line on the water. Maybe the car will cruise on by. Maybe whoever is driving will not see the Colonel playing a big fish under the floodlights of the hatchery. Maybe whoever it is will not hear the gun crack and echo in the peaceful night. "Goddammit, Colonel, a car is coming!" yells the Private, the scout.

Another large trout takes the fly just as the million-candlepower spotlight pans the hatchery like a movie premiere and backs up quickly to light the Colonel on the wall, balancing against the fish, eyes filling with the realization that his stand on the wall is about to come to an abrupt end. He looks at the dark water, then up to the blinding light, back to the water, yells "Ambush!" looks at his expensive rod and reel, up at the spotlight, back at his rod and reel, before dropping them in the water with the trout still attached to the business end. He leaps from the wall and runs for Charley Reynolds's high spot in the fence.

Sploosh!

The government Colt lands in the rearing pond and sinks to the well-lit bottom, next to the expensive reel attached to the expensive fly rod attached to the expensive fish.

The deputy's boot pins the Colonel to the ground between his shoulder blades like a speared suckerfish, the trooper's tail end still in the hatchery, the other half of him a few feet away from the gently running creek he calls a river. His forage cap hides his face until the deputy whips it off and shines a heavy aluminum flashlight in his face. The deputy, a Sioux, looks at his partner, looks at the forage cap in his hand, and says, "Good Lord, we've captured the mighty Seventh Cavalry, red-faced and red-handed."

Charley Reynolds, now on the opposite side of Spearfish Creek, fords the river and licks the Colonel on the face. Insects flit around the yellow glow of the deputy's flashlight. "Have any more scouts in there Colonel . . . Colonel Doggett?" asks the deputy as he reads the

Colonel's Montana driver's license. "By the way, I'll need to see a South Dakota fishing license. The fine for not having one is pretty steep. The fines for illegal fish are pretty steep. The fines for trespassing are pretty steep. Randall, you bring the calculator? Now, about your scouts, Colonel."

The Private waddles out of the willows in his waders with his hands high, forage cap tilted down, rod in the air like a shepherd's staff. "I'm not armed," he says. "I surrender."

"Careful with the Colonel," says the Private, as a deputy cinches the cuffs around his wrists. "He's got a gun."

"Why didn't you shoot in the air to warn me?" asks the Colonel.

"Shoot what?" asks the Private, looking the Colonel in the eyes. "You're the owner of the dripping gun."

The troopers sit, hands cuffed behind them, in the caged back seat of the Lawrence County Sheriff Department Jeep Cherokee.

"She must have gone fourteen pounds," says the Colonel. "A fourteen-pound rainbow on a number ten elk hair caddis. Put that in your fly book."

"That is something that belongs in your history book. It's your story," says Private, "not mine."

"This will probably mean we lose our South Dakota fishing privileges for quite some time," says the Colonel. "Private, it's a good thing we live in Montana."

The engine idles and the radio squawks periodically and the deputies gather little bits of evidence from the scene of the trespassing, the slaughter. The troopers watch the deputies put the trout in a plastic garbage bag, twist it shut, and label it along with the creel. They watch the deputies fish the rod, reel, and pistol from the bottom of the pool, label each, and put them in plastic bags.

The prisoners wait in the Cherokee for what seems like hours. A car pulls alongside the sheriff's vehicle and a woman's silhouette gets out and walks over to the fence and speaks with the deputies. They show her the rainbow in plastic while she crouches, one leg in the dirt along the fence. After a moment the three of them walk toward the Cherokee. It is the Sunday-haired woman.

She looks at the prisoners. The corners of her eyes are sharp and pointed, like arrowheads, the centers glassy and reflective with tears. She is going to say something and the wait for her to begin is agonizing. "They will take anything," she says finally. "They would bite on a pebble, on anything! Those fish will take a bare hook!" The prisoners see she wants to hit them, spit at them, shoot a flaming arrow through their hearts. Though she doesn't.

"Fourteen pounds, Private," whispers the Colonel, then whistles for emphasis after the woman turns for her car. "Fourteen pounds, I tell you. I was going to have that rainbow mounted."

"Owen," says Ben Fish the scout, Ben Fish the teacher, Ben Fish the trouter. "I'd as soon you call me Ben Fish here on out. I've gone civilian."

SPEARFISH ON MONDAY
After nine AM, Lawrence County Jail, Deadwood, South Dakota. The men breathe easily, adrenaline gone, in the tired relaxation of fully realizing that fate has them and there is nothing they can do to undo all they've done. They had their photos taken with Lawrence County license plates around their necks. They have ink on their fingertips. They have called Salome for bail money, who said something to the effect of, "Leave me the hell alone."

"Wild Bill Hickock was shot here in Deadwood," says Ben Fish flatly. "Shot in the back while playing cards."

The Sioux deputy walks into the holding room, what they call the tank, says, "Your basset hound is in the pound and your wife called. She's bailing you out. See you at the courthouse in two weeks," then sets a stack of carboned forms in front of the men to sign and hands the former substitute mail carrier a hastily scrawled note:

Owen Doggett,
Come home. Be quick. Bring Charley Reynolds
and Ben Fish. I'm pregnant.
                    —Sue
P.S. You can't act as if nothing happened here.
But I'm willing to work on it.

Owen Doggett reads the note once, twice, three times. His eyes show that he thinks it over deeply. He takes a long breath, exhales, and, without looking up from the note, says, "I suppose she needs me."

Salt, pepper, and Tabasco fly, and the men eat the scrambled county eggs in their cell instead of auditioning for Pontius Pilate at the amphitheater. "These eggs need mustard," says Owen Doggett. Ben Fish chews his eggs quietly.

"Owen, things are settled between you and me. I don't want to have to worry about the three of you.'

FRIDAY IN OCTOBER

The prairie wind throws dirt and tumbleweeds against the classroom windows. Mr. Fish tells his eighth-graders that on the Black Hills Expedition of 1874 Custer lost a supply wagon full of whiskey and an expensive Gatling gun in a ravine along Boxelder Creek now known as Custer Gap. He also tells them that Custer and four or five of his subordinates shot a bear. The bear was so full of lead and holes that it couldn't be eaten, couldn't be stuffed.

And he tells them this: "There was a troublemaker with the outfit, a private from Indiana. He stole food rations. He stole coffee, blankets, whiskey. He put locust thorns under saddles. He emptied canteens. One bright morning he cross-hobbled the wrong man's horse. The wrong man shot him in the chest. The chaplain said prayers for his soul and a detail buried him in the shadows of sacred Inyan Kara Mountain. Custer knew the dead man was a bad egg and judged the murder justified."

The class watches Mr. Fish and listens intently to these stories, the details once lost in the folds of history, brought to life again by the teacher, though some stories, for the sake of history, Mr. Fish just makes up.

MONDAY ON THE PLAINS

"I have an appointment on Monday," Mr. Fish tells the secretary. "I'll need a sub." He does not tell her the blackflies are hatching on the Little Bighorn. Or that he will be there all day, with his new trouting buddy, Charley Reynolds, fishing, reading, sucking on sunflower seeds, the two of them eating bologna-and-mustard sandwiches. He does not tell her his old trouting buddy, Owen Doggett, has to work on Monday because the packing plant never closes, never shuts down, and days off are best spent tending to legalities in Dakota Territory. The fine for fishing without a license—the teacher's only crime—can be paid by mail and doesn't show up on your permanent record. He does not tell the secretary that Sue Doggett just tied some tiny new blackflies that buzz and dance around a room on their own when a white man isn't looking. He does not tell her she gave him some.

BEARS AND LIONS
Mary Clearman Blew

PLACES OF GREAT SCENIC BEAUTY ALWAYS seem to be hard to make a living on, and certainly that has been true of our ranch. My father tried cattle, sheep, a little logging, but even in my childhood our life here was marginal. My father is dead now, and my mother lives in a subsidized apartment in the town of Fort Maginnis, and my sisters have gone away to cities, but my husband and I keep on ranching. We still raise a few sheep, and of course we have the horses. Most years we try to put up a little hay and harvest some oats, but the growing season is so short, here in the foothills of Montana's Snowies, that crops often don't ripen before first frost. I don't even try to raise a garden. But James and I cut our own logs to build this house on a south slope, above the country road, and from our living room windows we can look down at the old overgrown hay meadows where, at twilight, deer slip in and out of the hawthorn brush and the poplar saplings and vanish into the pines on the steep hill.

"It's so beautiful here," my oldest sister says when she visits, and then she shakes her head. "But how long can you and James hold out?"

And the ranch really is beautiful, only seven miles from Fort Maginnis on a gravel road that winds along Castle Creek through groves of aspens and ravines of haws and chokecherries and wild roses, always within sight and sound of the great pines that heave and murmur in the air currents of summer and will turn mute and ink-dark with the winter snows. But the truth is that we couldn't afford the ranch if it weren't for our jobs. We own eight hundred and fifty acres, which sounds wonderful to the teachers I assist at Sacajawea School down in Fort Maginnis, but too many of those acres are side-hills that were logged off long ago and now hold little but scrub pine growing through the ancient slash. I sometimes worry whether the income from the ranch will stretch to pay the taxes. James and I heat our house with wood we cut ourselves, and I shop at the Goodwill. James delivers mail three days a week on a hundred-mile rural route, and I am a teachers' aide. Our salaries buy groceries and pay the phone and electric bills and stretch to provide Park and Steve with some of their hearts' desires, like baseball gear and Walkmans and Nintendos and their own rifles. Like all kids' lists, theirs are endless.

"Oh but Val, what a great place to raise the boys," say the teachers in the lounge during their free hour, and I know it's true.

FOR INSTANCE, THAT DAY LAST SUMMER when James and I and the boys rode as far as Castle Butte, looking for horses. The draft mares had broken through a fence and gotten lost, and Park and I had split off from James and Steve to search that high flat stretch we call Ballard's Knob, which was a meadow once, on the old Ballard place, but now is grown over with aspens and pine seedlings, stirrup-high and higher. To restore it to pasture would take a bulldozer and defoliant, and it wouldn't be worth it, it wouldn't be economical, not for a short season of wild grass. A consortium of doctors own the Ballard land now, and they've torn out the old fences so they can drive up from Billings every fall and go hunting, but they don't rub shoulders with us locals. The Ballards have been gone for years, and so have most of the old neighbors from my father's time, and our new neighbors down on Castle Creek commute to jobs in Fort Maginnis and build cabins from kits on ten-acre plots and hope to keep their kids away from drugs by living in the country.

My father had known that a time was coming when ordinary people couldn't make a living in the foothills. "Don't want to live to see it," he always said, and he didn't.

I had been thinking about Father as I rode, and how he would have growled at Park for goofing off, riding cross-legged in the saddle and letting old Sandy snatch a bite of bunchgrass anytime she felt like it. And I thought how the high pastures would have seemed just the same to Father in so many ways—the stir of the wind through the scrub, the sandstone boulders rising to meet the ramparts of Castle

Butte, the distant blue outline of the Snowies, the blue, blue sky and rolling clouds. And yet all was so altered, so stark, without traces of human habitation, that I was beginning to feel as though I had ridden into forbidden territory and might, just might, catch a glimpse of some parallel world through gauze or mist or smoke. And then, as though roused by Father's voice inside my head, something rippled through the undergrowth, some fleeing animal.

What? I reined in my mare, stood in my stirrups to see what disturbed the buckbrush. That dark shape, that furry shape that humped like a raccoon as it ran, but bigger and faster than any raccoon, and then I knew. A bear cub, where no bear had been seen for years and years and years, perhaps ever.

I tried to speak, to call to Park to look, and perhaps I did. I spurred my mare into a canter and followed the cub to the edge of the Knob, where the pasture falls off in a slope, and there, in a sunny patch of grass and mountain geraniums, where she had been digging, surprised and rising on her hind legs to get a better look at me, was the sow.

She seemed unafraid. She stood, no farther from me on my horse than the width of a residential street, while the slight breeze disturbed the grass and the pink blooms of the wild geraniums and ruffled her fur. The part of my mind that had separated from me and raced ahead to its own surmise now called back from a distance to ask why, in a good year, did she have only the one cub that had stopped, trembling, to get his own look at me. I had time to think how beautiful she was, with her black fur shading to a sunburned rust, with her serene golden eyes watching me from her own dimension. And then I saw the dark furball clinging to the top of a pine tree at the foot of the slope, the other cub.

"Wow, Mom, bears!" breathed Park, who had kicked old Sandy into a trot and caught up with us. "Cool, Mom!"

I may have blinked, I may have turned to catch the expression on Park's face. In the next moment the breeze stirred empty grass and aspen leaves. The bears had vanished. And I felt awe, and an ache for the deserted grass and the absence of what I had just witnessed.

Never, never, had I dreamed that I would come face to face, as though with a wild neighbor, with a bear sow and her cubs in the Castle Butte pasture.

"WERE YOUR HORSES AFRAID?" asked my oldest sister over the telephone from Seattle when I called to tell her about the bears.

"No. It was the strangest thing. You always read that horses are so terrified of bears, but they just stood there and watched."

"They've probably known all along that the bears are there. They've gotten used to their scent."

"That's what James thinks."

"Ironic, isn't it? The old settlers thought they were clearing out trees and wildlife to make a safe and settled place, and now they're gone and the bears are back. But where are they *coming* from? I mean, I never imagined seeing bears in the foothills when we were growing up, and I never heard of anybody else who did. What's going on? Is it part of some species reintroduction program?"

"James thinks that there have always been a few bears in the Snowies, not many, but a few. In the years that there was a bounty on them, they were hunted hard, but now the bounties are gone, and just the other way around, if you want to hunt a bear, you buy a fifty-dollar tag and draw for a permit. So the bears in the mountains have increased, and their range is overcrowded, and more and more are moving down into the foothills with us."

"So it's political."

"Maybe, but sometimes it seems more personal. I was thrilled to see her and the cubs, but I won't feel so thrilled if she bothers our sheep."

A long silence on the line, and I wondered what Laura was thinking. She often sees so many sides of what seems obvious to James and me, like what will happen when wolves are reintroduced into cattle and sheep country.

But finally she said, "Do you remember the Canadian lynx that Father shot?"

YEARS AGO. THE LAST SUMMER Laura spent on the ranch, so she would have been seventeen and I would have been nine, the same age Park is now. I remember that it was very early in the morning, our reflections in the kitchen window fading to gray light, and Laura was serving breakfast to Father, who was drinking coffee to prime himself for his day's work. He growled something at me, to behave myself, and Laura brought the pot and poured him a second cup of coffee. On her way back to the stove, she stopped at the window, rigid.

"What's that?" she whispered.

Father glanced casually along the line of her gaze, then tensed as though he'd woken fully alive for the first time in years. He shoved his chair back from the table and crossed the kitchen in three strides, lifted down the rifle, the 30.06, from its rack above the refrigerator, and pumped a shell into its chamber as he tiptoed across the creaking floorboards of the old screened porch and eased the door open.

I was right behind him, wanting to see what was happening. The gray predawn light had concentrated in a pink stain behind the log shed, and what at first I thought was a shadow had detached itself from the squat shape of the tractor beside the shed. Then the shadow moved again, taking on a form with a current as powerful as an electric surge, which any country-raised child, even a nine-year-old, recognizes as life, wild life.

Father had braced his left hand on the doorjamb, was taking aim. My heart was pounding on the same frequency as the electric surge. *Get it, Father!*

Then the explosion of the rifle, reverberating inside my head, expanding the porch, echoing from the opposite pine slopes. At first I felt more blinded than deafened, and then my eyes cleared, and the sound of the explosion died away, and the world was still the world.

My mother was running downstairs in her wrapper. "What are you shooting at?"

We all went across the road to look.

Father was a dead shot in those days, and he had hit the lynx in the heart, killing her instantly. The smallest dark stain of blood had oozed from the bullet hole just back of her foreleg, and in the growing daylight we all marveled at the dappled taupe and cream of her fur and the fading gold glare of her eyes. I was hopping around, beside myself with excitement. Father lifted the lynx by her scruff, holding her at shoulder height so her hind pads just brushed the dirt, while my mother ran to get the camera to take pictures as soon as there was enough light, and I felt the tips of the lynx's claws and studied the dirt stuck to her dulled eyes and petted the wild tufts of her ears.

"WHY DO YOU THINK HE SHOT IT, VAL?" my sister asked, over the long-distance line from Seattle.

"Because he was worried that it would bother the sheep."

"But he always said he'd never seen a Canadian lynx down here in Montana, that he supposed this one was passing through the country on its way north. Why did he have to shoot it, if it was just passing through?"

LATER I THOUGHT ABOUT THE UNSPOKEN questions and answers that limned the ones we spoke aloud. Probably there was a bounty on lynxes at that time, fifty or even a hundred dollars, and probably Father sold the pelt for another fifty or a hundred dollars down at Pacific Hide and Fur.

It was always money with Father, she says.

You don't understand, I want to tell my sister. You went off to live in Seattle, where weather is never worse than a nuisance, and wild animals never take bites out of your salary. You can afford to take the long view. James and I have a living to make, and we have a right to protect our livestock.

But this is about more than money, Val.

That's true. Father shot that lynx because she was calling for his bullet. Calling as strong as a power surge. I felt it that morning, and so did you, my sister.

TODAY WHEN I COME ACROSS THE ARTICLE in the newspaper, I call my sister and read it to her over the telephone, about the five-year-old boy in western Montana who was fatally mauled by a mountain lion a hundred yards from his front door. And his body dragged off into the underbrush, where it was found a day later by a sheriff's search party, partially devoured . . .

"God!" says my sister. "But yes, that story was on the news here, too."

Then she tells me about a partner in her law practice who claims that the child's death was the fault of people building subdivisions on old game trails, interfering with centuries-old migratory patterns of wildlife and bringing fatal conflicts upon themselves.

My anger surges up so suddenly that it is a moment before I can trust my voice. "Does he think that if those parents had just moved their house back a few yards, the mountain lion would have stayed on his centuries-old migratory path and not attacked their child?"

"Pretty stupid, I guess."

"Does he know anything about the size of a mountain lion's hunting range?"

My sister sighs. She is trying not to quarrel. "Do you have mountain lions on the ranch now?"

"We haven't seen them. But lions are stalkers, you know. James is sure that he's been watched while he's been working in the timber. He's seen lion tracks, and he's found deer carcasses where some animal has come back more than once to feed, which means it wasn't coyotes. We've been concerned enough to teach Park and Steve what to do if they happen to meet a lion."

"Which is to do what?"

"To stand still. Slide their jackets down over their arms, then raise them over their heads to make themselves look as big as possible. To make a lot of noise. And whatever they do, not to run. Any sudden movement will activate the lion's instinct to pounce, just like any cat."

"When I was growing up on the ranch," says my sister, softly, "I used to slip off in the afternoons with my horse and a book, and I'd dream that I was following a trail through the timber, with a rifle, to protect myself from bears and mountain lions. And it gave me a thrill. But I always knew I was just pretending, that I'd never really see a bear or a lion."

"For Park and Steve, it isn't dream danger."

"I understand that much," she says.

IN THE NATURE ENCYCLOPEDIA we bought for the boys, it says that attacks by mountain lions on humans are rare and usually attributed to animals that are sick or weak and can't catch other game, or animals that are suffering from rabies. It also says that most of the deer killed by mountain lions are diseased or crippled.

Park, who has a science report to write, reads carefully and then looks up. "The lions are nature's way of culling the deer herds, right, Dad?"

James studies the chunk of heart pine he's about to toss into the woodstove as though he expects to read an answer in the splinters. Here we are, it's only September, and already the rain is freezing, and we're stoking the stove at night and firing it up again to take the chill off the house in the mornings. James collects his thoughts, tosses the wood to the flames, and answers Park.

"Now with wolves, they chase down their game, so naturally it's the slow deer they catch first, and so wolves do cull the herds, some. But a critter like a lion stalks his game, and when he's strong and quick enough to bring down a full-grown buck deer with antlers, like the one I found back of the ridge, it's more bad luck than lack of speed for whichever deer happens to pass under his perch."

"Sheep, hogs, and colts have been killed by mountain lions, although usually in areas where deer have been eliminated," Park reads aloud.

"Well . . . ," says James, noncommittal. He pours hot water over his powdered coffee, sets the kettle back on the wood stove, stirs, settles himself in his rocking chair, picks up his own book, and finds his place.

"Dad," insists Park, "a mountain lion couldn't kill a horse. Could it?"

James lays down his book. "Well . . . yes, it could."

"Could it kill *Sandy*?"

"Come on, Park," I tell him. "Let Dad read."

James runs his fingers through his hair, which is beginning to curl around his collar. He lets his hair and beard grow every winter, gets a haircut and shaves again when the weather turns warm in the spring. I worry about the gray in James's hair and the lines in his face.

"A mountain lion *could* kill Sandy, but it won't as long as Sandy's got sense enough to stay out of the trees and graze in open pasture," James explains. "What a mountain lion does is hide and pounce. Just like a cat does. See?"

And he points out to the kitchen, where Steve is teasing the surviving kitten, which crouches and watches from the seat of a chair while Steve drags a knitting needle along the linoleum. Suddenly the kitten reaches down with a lightning paw and bats the knitting needle out of Steve's hand, nearly falling off the chair in the process. Recovering, it regards us with its dreamy gaze.

Me? Lose my balance? It never happened.

I laugh, but I also remember the scene in the barn this morning when Park found the other kitten dead. I had been down in the lower corral, breaking the rime of ice out of the horses' water trough, and I came blowing on my hands and stamping my feet through the broken-hinged door to find the two boys, desolate.

Park had lifted the dead kitten out of the manger. He held it out to me, wordless. It was frozen stiff. Later, when James examined it, he said a weasel had probably killed it, because its blood had been sucked. At the time, I looked at the draggled gray fur on the rigid little corpse, and then at the faces of my two boys, and my breath hung white in the chill air.

Steve was cradling the other kitten in his arms. "Please, Mom! Can't she come inside and live in the house? We don't want her to die, too!"

I was already shaking my head.

"Please, Mom! Please, please, please?"

"We could get a cat box like people in town have for their cats, and put litter in it, and I'd clean it, honestly I would, Mom, please?"

"Please?"

Steve is the one of our boys who looks like the old photograph that was taken of Father when he was five, with eyes so pure and light, and hair so blond that it looks silver in the photograph. Park looks like James, with darker blond hair and transparent skin that holds its tan even deep into winter. They stood in the freezing barn with anxious faces, pleading, and I thought about what Father would have said about cats in the house, and how grouchy he had gotten during his last years, and about good, tired James, and how patient with Father he had been.

"Okay, but you have to promise to feed it and clean up after it and keep it off the bed," I said, and saw their faces break into smiles through the tears.

"We promise, we promise!"

"Oh yay, yay, yay!"

And Steve thrust the surviving kitten at me. It sank its needle claws into the front of my insulated coveralls and clung to me, blank-eyed.

Now, AS I WATCH THE KITTEN PLAY WITH STEVE, lunging at the knitting needle and batting it out of his hands, I realize that I'll soon be lucky to have a straight needle left to knit with. And I look at my little family, James absorbed in his book, Park finishing his homework and turning on the TV, the woodstove radiating warmth in the enclosure of bare floorboards and exposed insulation where we haven't been able to afford Sheetrocking yet, and the black windows mirroring us back through the leaves of coleus and philodendron and spider plants and ficus, and I think that I would like to tell my sister, so what if my only kitchen counter is a home-hewn plank?

Then the thud on the roof.

James looks up with his face so intent that I can't tell myself that I heard nothing. He sits listening with his finger marking the place in his book and the electric light deepening the lines in his face. Park is absorbed in *Rescue 911* and oblivious.

"Turn that down, will you, Park?" says James. Park stares. James lays down his book and gets up out of his chair. He pauses by the gun rack that holds Father's old rifle, the 30.06, and Father's shotguns and James's own .250 Savage, but he leaves the guns on the rack and goes to stand by the window with his face close to the glass.

I can hear nothing, only the snap of a pine knot in the fire. Steve has stopped playing with the cat. The familiar room has taken on a fresh intensity, and I find myself counting the scars and gouges on the chair legs, thinking that I really should sand them down and varnish them. Outdoors the wind has picked up, and the muted roar from the ridges, where the big pines toss and heave in the dark, sounds as familiar to me and yet as alien as the rumble of traffic might be to someone who lives under a freeway. Behind the house the diamond willow shakes its bare twigs, whines and rattles against the logs as it always does in the wind. But I hear no further thud on the roof, no creak of shingles, no stealthy pad of paws over my head.

"Can't see a thing from here," says James in a neutral voice, turning from the window, "what with the overhang of the eaves."

From some strange vantage point I visualize the night. The frozen mud of our driveway, the parked and dark Blazer, and the looming shapes of our clutter: tractor tires and burning barrel, feed buckets and James's overshoes and the motor from the generator and the shovel. The diamond willow, lashing at the solid house, and, like a barn cat magnified by a power of ten, crouched above the eaves and watching the lighted windows and the flickers of movement, the great shadowy beast from the wild world outside ours.

"Don't go outside!"

"I wasn't planning on it," James says. He stops at the sight of the boys' dumb faces. "Well, now, I wonder. Were either of you fellows thinking about playing a hand of cards before bedtime?"

And I understand the part that falls to me. Acting as if this is a normal evening. Finishing the dishes. Setting the boys' thermoses in the refrigerator, making sure that Park has put his homework in his backpack, seeing to all the small tasks that will ease the Monday morning rush. Getting ready for bed. Going to sleep.

Telling myself that, when we open the door in the morning and blink in fresh sunlight, we will face only the usual. The school bus lumbering up the road, a flash of yellow through dark green pines with its horn honking. Park howling that nobody signed his permission slip for P.E. Then the two little boys running down the driveway to catch the bus, James grabbing a last cup of coffee, winding his tattered scarf around his neck, and zipping his coveralls for another day's work in the timber with the screaming chain saw, and me scraping plates into a bowl for the kitten that Park forgot to feed and counting the minutes I need to get myself ready for work. No beast crouching on the roof.

And I imagine what I will say to my sister, days or weeks from now. Do you have any idea how it feels, I will ask her, to lie awake in the dark and know that James, too, is wide awake and listening, although he pretends to be sleeping as quietly as the little boys in their bunks? As the heat of the stoked woodstove fades, do you feel the house gradually cool and creak and settle? Do you hear the child sigh in his sleep in the next room, do you hear the willow twigs scratching to find the chinks between the logs and mortar? Would you be reminding yourself of the measurements of the rafters we sawed, the thickness of the hand-hewn shingles, the wooden skin between ourselves and the wild world?

Can you imagine, I will ask my sister, what it is like to wake suddenly to cold gray light in the window and James's empty side of the bed? To run out in your sweats and bare feet to the *chunk chunk* of wood into the stove and see icicles in James's mustache as he turns from building up the fire and says, "Well, we got an inch of fresh snow last night and a perfect set of cat tracks coming off the roof and headed up toward the north ridge."

Can you imagine, I will ask her, how the mountains might close around Seattle, wrinkling their forests, shrugging the power lines off their shoulders, pouring their muddy floodwater down from the raw sore patches of clear-cut, spilling their scree over the freeways?

Have you seen the lion, my sister will ask, to keep the peace between us.

And then I will tell her about the deer James shot as bait, and the trap he set in the deadfall where the north ridge was logged, long ago, and how, the next morning, the cage of the trap throbbed with a pulse we could feel from the kitchen door.

How the four of us hiked up through the soft snow. How the young female lion looked back at us through the mesh of the cage without apparent fear, with a cat's condescending interest in human doings.

How James handed Park the rifle and asked him if he remembered everything he had been taught.

Ask your law partner, I will say to my sister, if he can imagine being the first in the cold morning to walk out of his Seattle apartment while his wife and little boys sleep. Ask him about walking backward, as James did, into the white light of fresh snowfall, and ask him how the wet flakes felt against his face, upturned for a first glimpse on the overhang of the eaves, of the looming shape, the lightning paw of the beast. Ask him if he would have carried a rifle.

JUNK
Kevin Canty

I WAS OUT ALL MORNING JUNKING with Margaret and her kids, combing the yard sales and estate sales and rummage sales and garage sales, even some of the cheap second-hand stores. Margaret did this every Saturday. She had a business, somewhere between a business and a hobby, where she'd buy up broken small appliances, mixers, blenders, toasters, and fix them up to sell at the swap meet. It didn't seem like much but it was good for the rent on her trailer space and some pocket money besides.

This was the first time I'd spent the night with her, the first time I met her kids. It had taken us a couple of months to work our way up to it, since we met at the Vo-Tech. Margaret was in copier repair, I was in bookkeeping, which still seemed ridiculous whenever I thought about it. Shane and Alicia were dark pretty kids, Indian-looking, which they got from Margaret, who was mostly Crow Indian from up around Hardin, Montana. Shane was five and Alicia was eight and they were shy as deermice. They shook my hand one after the other and then locked their eyes back on the corn flakes. I got the feeling this didn't happen too often, Mom bringing a man home, which was fine with me but scary.

We were both a little gunshy, both of us still married, though I wasn't sure where my wife was that morning. I hadn't seen her in months or maybe years.

Margaret gave me a cup of instant and made me drive while she navigated a route to the sales. It was a good fall morning with the sun just balancing over the plains, already winter in the shadows, the cottonwood trees losing their leaves and the aspens turning yellow. A morning breeze was blowing the refinery haze out of the valley and the sky was almost blue. We were Early Birds, garage-sale pirates and

I felt fine. I woke up with a dream of myself where I would get my job back at the carbon black plant or maybe go out strip-mining up north and then set up housekeeping. I liked the company of women and children, I'd almost forgotten how much.

Margaret had a deadly eye, some places she wouldn't even let me stop, others she'd dart for the pile of junk they hadn't sorted out yet, rooting through the puzzles and picture frames and orphan silverware. She'd go a dollar for a blender, fifty cents for a toaster. The sellers would take it, almost always, no matter how optimistic the price was on the masking-tape tag—they knew she was a professional. Fifteen dollars for a broken mixer, seven-fifty for a popcorn machine that only blew cold air, these prices were the dreams of greed when Margaret came to the yard sale. "Junk," she'd say, holding a blender by the cord and scowling at it. "I'll go a buck."

Part of my mind was on the side of the sellers. I knew what they were thinking: look how much of this thing is perfectly fine, look at how much still works perfect—the mixer bowls, both the original beaters, all this chrome and enameled steel—it *should* be worth more. Only a little part of this is broken. It isn't right, I could hear them thinking. I'm being took. They got it confused, to where it was more about pride than money.

"I don't think so," this one woman told her. "For that kind of money, I guess I'd just as soon keep it." Clutching her little busted mixer, like Margaret had tried to steal it from her.

Margaret just shrugged her shoulders and got in the car. There was another broken mixer someplace. Maybe some optimist would come along and pay the asking price, I thought, though it didn't seem likely. Sell it or get stuck with it.

By two o'clock the garage sales had dried up and Margaret had filled the trunk of her Subaru with broken toasters. It was a big day for toasters. Time to take the kids to McDonald's. They were worn out from the effort of being good all morning and they didn't have anything to show for it, so it was the Happy Meal. They sat in the corner booth and the whole town was passing by them, Saturday afternoon at McDonald's, everybody knew everybody else and they were talking. I lifted one corner of the bun and looked down at the gray circle of meat. "Do you suppose it's true?" I asked.

"What?" Alicia said.

"The thing they say about the meat, where it comes from?"

"Don't be smart-ass around my kids," Margaret said. I thought she was kidding at first but I looked up and she was looking at me cold serious through the heavy black glasses she wore and I thought she looked beautiful, defending her children, like some wild thing. "They get enough of that at school," she said, "all the smart-ass about everything. What's in here is just regular cow meat."

"From Brazil," I said.

"Kids have to believe in something," Margaret said. "They can't just believe in nothing."

Shane paid no attention to his mom and asked me, "What did they say was in the hamburger?"

"You never mind," Margaret said, and gave me a look. I wanted to ask her, just because you have to believe in something does that mean you have to believe in McDonald's? But I didn't. It was good to see her standing up for her kids even if she was wrong. She looked beautiful when she was angry like that. Sitting in Mickey D's in the smell of french-fry grease I thought about how beautiful she was: long dark hair and a long neck, thin, with that Crow wildness in her face. She was good-looking to where her looks could get her in trouble, which is what happened when she was nineteen and afterward for a while. So I heard.

"It was rat, wasn't it?" Shane asked. "They put rat in the hamburgers."

"You shut up and eat," Margaret said. "Parker didn't mean anything like that."

"That's right," I said, although that was exactly what I was going to say. Not that I actually thought there was rat in the hamburgers, but it would impress the kids. Plus you couldn't tell what was in there by looking.

Alicia lifted the corner of her bun and looked in and then looked at her brother. "You are a disgusting human being," she said. "I wash my hands of you."

"All right, enough," Margaret said. "Sit up and eat, sit up!" And when the kids were eating their hamburgers again she turned to me, serious again. "No more kids," she said quietly, for adults to hear. "I've got two kids and my husband was a kid and it just wears me out, okay? Do you know what I mean?"

"Yeah I do."

"I don't mind a little smart-ass, not from you," she said, blinking at me through her glasses. "I mean, you've got to be good for something."

"Well thanks, I guess."

"I don't know if it was a compliment or not," she said. "Eat your hamburger." And she wasn't looking at me then and I don't know what she meant or how she meant it but I felt this warmth all around my body, like I was inside of something, some kind of bubble or cloud with me and Margaret and the kids inside it, and I liked that feeling. Like it wasn't me that was sitting there but some other man who was lucky about these things, lucky about love and about people.

And then we were gone out of there and Margaret was dropping me off at my room at the Sacajawea Apartments and I saw the turquoise Thunderbird from down the block. It was Dorothy's car, my wife. She had that car since high school, a '66, with a white interior and a white vinyl top, a beautiful thing. I noticed that she had Arizona plates on it now, with the little cactus in the middle. I could see the back of her blonde head.

"You want to come out to the swap meet tomorrow?" Margaret asked. "I'll pick you up if you want."

"I'll call you," I said. Suddenly I was nervous to get rid of her, not for her, just so I could think clearly. I was trying to remember how long it had been since I saw Dorothy. Over a year, anyway. Two years? Suddenly I was bookkeeping again.

Margaret said, "Well, I can't get hold of you, so call me if you want to go."

She leaned across the front seat and kissed me, right in front of the kids, and we both said goodbye, goodbye, while I got out of the car and I couldn't even think about them. I watched her little Subaru roll down the street and around the corner but really I was waiting for the door of the Thunderbird to open. Which it did.

One of the things about Dorothy was that whoever made up these Western girl clothes had her in mind exactly. She had on a fringe jacket and spray-on jeans tucked into her boots and she was smoking a cigarette. She was older, though, which was a surprise. There were dark circles under her eyes and wrinkles around her mouth, and you could really tell it by her hands. I saw this with a kind of panic—this was never supposed to happen—as she walked up to me slowly with a grin on her face, not too nice.

"Who's the squaw?" she said.

This was her style, ice water in the face. I stood there blinking for a minute, wondering whether to slap her, and then I remembered: If I slapped her, I lost. Life with Dorothy was one long game of cool.

She said, "I never pictured you as a family man, exactly."

"I just met the woman," I said, although I'd known Margaret for three months then.

"That isn't what it looked like," Dorothy said. "It looked like Mom and Dad on the way to work. Can I come in?"

She didn't wait for an answer but went into the hallway and waited for me to show her which apartment was mine. And then it was like she never left.

"Jesus, Parker," she said, looking around the little room: one bed, one chair, a TV, a desk with my books from the Vo-Tech on it. "Are you sure this is depressing enough? Is that a blood stain?"

She pointed to a blotch on the wall that I'd wondered about myself. But I said, "No, it's just rust or something."

"Well, it looks like blood to me. Have you got a beer?"

She didn't wait but opened up the little dormitory refrigerator and took the last beer and opened it. She drank it like a drowning man, half at once. Then sat down at the table and started chopping out a line of something, crank I guessed, onto my one clean dinner plate. A little silver hunting knife with lumps of turquoise in the handle of the weapon. She chopped it fine and then took a hit in each side of her nose off the sharp point of the blade. Tears welled up in her eyes as she shook her head. "Jesus, that's good," she said. "A little eye-opener. Want some?"

"No, thanks."

"Suit yourself," she said, dipping the point of the blade into the crank again and lining it up her nose. I watched her like a hungry dog watching a person eat, following the point of the knife with my eyes. I'm not that kind of person anymore, I told myself. I'm done with that.

Eyes still shut, making a face from the pain of the hit, she said, "I need some money, Parker. I'm sort of in trouble."

Fuck you, I thought, and then I said it: "Fuck you." Back in town for thirty seconds and already we were playing by her rules and my own life had shrunk to nothing. "You come around here," I said, trying to find the words. "I haven't even seen you for a year and a half . . ."

She just looked at me calm and straight-faced until the words dried up completely. "I wouldn't ask you if I didn't need your help," she said. "You know that."

"So what?"

"I'm just asking for mine," she said.

"What do you mean?" I asked her. "Are you talking about the house?" She looked up, and it was the house, and I started to laugh.

"I'm not kidding you," Dorothy said. "I was your wife for all the time we were making payments on that place. I'm entitled to something."

"You never put a nickel into that house," I said, still laughing. "I mean, don't bullshit me. But it don't matter anyway."

"What do you mean?"

"That money's gone, darling. That money was gone a year ago."

She was all business now, a skinny mean-faced woman, just the way I always liked her. She asked me, "Where exactly did the money go?"

"I don't know, darling," I said, and there was a kind of glory in it. This was not a regular mistake but a big one, a disaster, and I felt a kind of roller-coaster excitement at the memory. Nothing that was good for you. I said, "Most of it I can't remember."

"That was thirty-two thousand dollars," Dorothy said.

"Not after the lawyers got their cut—the lawyers and then the neighborhood association that started the lawsuit got a percentage. And then a big chunk of the rest went into that idiot Ford pickup. You know I wrecked it."

She shook her head.

"Put it around somebody's mailbox out by Ripton. I didn't total it but pretty close."

"You didn't have insurance on it?"

"They canceled me out a couple of days before, I guess I didn't pay the bill. I don't know. I never found the letter. But then when the bank took the pickup back, I had to pay the difference. That and the Visa bill we ran up and after that I don't know. I mean, it went somewhere, I guess. It's gone."

"Thirty-two thousand dollars," she said again, and thought about it for a minute. "Jesus, Parker, you spent that money like it was a dime."

I bobbed my head, like she had just paid me a compliment—and it felt like that, this was the one thing I'd done, the thing they couldn't take away from me. This was the only time I'd ever be bigger than life.

"That was it," I said. "The house, the truck, I quit showing up for work over at the carbon black plant and they canned my ass over there. Did you hear about the guy who played the country record backwards?"

Dorothy shook her head.

"He got his job back, he got his dog back, he got his wife back . . ." I looked down and noticed that Dorothy's hands were trembling. She was holding one of her hands just off the tabletop and watching it shake, like it was somebody else's hand. "What's the matter, baby?" I asked.

"I'm not your baby."

"Whatever you are."

"I'm not kidding about being in trouble," she said. "Your buddy Coy, up here, he's in with a rough crowd."

"How long have you been in town?"

"I've been in and out, the last few months."

I sat on the edge of the bed wondering how I missed her in a town this small, while she went on looking at her hands. I was thinking about Coy, my high school buddy, old junkie friend. I hadn't seen Coy in a while, imagined him fucking Dorothy. I asked her, "What does Coy have to do with it?"

"Oh, fuck you," she said. "I didn't come here to explain myself, I came because I was in trouble and I was hoping you could help me out. I guess I was wrong."

She started to fold the powder back into the little paper envelope and I didn't want her to go. I don't know why, I just have to try to put it together, looking back. I could have let her go, and none of the rest of it would have happened, and my reasons, when I try to put them together, are not all that good. Part of it was that I expected to fuck her, not exactly that I wanted to, although I did. But every time since high school there was always that charge, the one constant. Our bodies fit each other and I knew that if I touched her, if she let me inside we would be the same as we ever were. If she left, the chain was broken, that part of my life was over and I'd be left behind with the others—the good students, church-goers, bookkeepers. I didn't want to be ditched, maybe it was simple as that.

Nobody to blame but myself.

"What do you need?" I asked her.

THAT NEXT DAY, MARGARET TOOK ME ALONG with the kids out to the big swap meet at the Go West drive-in, four hundred cars packed in backwards on the humps, card tables and milk crates, an old turkey-necked buzzard with one cardboard box only, a hole cut in the top: XXX VIDEOS U-PICK $5.00. I was tired and spaced and it was a lie for me to be there. Setting up the folding tables, setting out the popcorn makers and blenders that Margaret brought to sell, I remembered the tangle of Dorothy's legs and mine and the taste of her neck and the burn of the crank as it went down, the old pain and then the rush. But it was a cool clear day with a breeze and after a while my blood started to move. Actually I started to like it.

My job was to hold down the fort, along with Alicia, while Shane and Margaret scoured the back rows for fixable junk. There wasn't any clear line between buyers and sellers at the Go West. Half the business was trades, my junk for your junk, but there was quite a bit of movement here, quite a bit of life. This was hope of a practical kind, people trying to get somewhere. I was a spy in their house, a double agent. I was sitting in my chair watching them and keeping my secrets: Dorothy's laughter and her voice, *book*keeping? *Book*keeping? Jesus Parker that's funny . . . There is no other life, I wanted to tell them, the person that you are is the person you're going to be. Though it was tempting to pretend. Something beautiful in all the movement, all the scurrying around in the clear light, buying and selling, moving forward.

But it was stupid, too, and it wasn't hard to make fun of them: the rusty mag wheels and broken bicycles and cassette tapes in Mexican, the sharp eyes of the bargainers. "This thing work?" they ask, holding up a ten-dollar blender, shaking it, listening for rattles.

"Works fine."

"Mind if I plug it in?"

"I'll get it for you." Then Sherlock Holmes investigates, listening for rattles, trying all twelve speeds: LIQUEFY, PUREE, FRAPPÉ.

"I guess I could go seven and a half," Sherlock says.

"This isn't my booth," I tell him, as instructed. "I can't go lower than nine on my own, but if you want to come back later . . ." He shakes his head, doubtfully. "You could give it a try."

"You guarantee it?"

"If it doesn't work, bring it back next week, we'll give you another." Sherlock still can't make up his mind, so I try to encourage him: "Margaret's here every week."

"This's Margaret's booth?" Sherlock looks around at the stuff and grins. "Course it is, who else would it be—stupid of me, getting stupid. Well, you tell Margaret that Frank Tellers got her blender, and if she wants to make a deal with me she can come see me."

Sherlock leaves with the blender under his arm, which seems to be okay with Alicia—she shrugs at me, elaborately. When Margaret got back with a load of broken toasters, it was okay with her, too, though she immediately went out to track down the deal. She looked happy and purposeful in the hard sunlight. The drive-in was scurrying with things and shoppers, like an ant farm busying itself against the last days before winter, which this might have been. The night before with Dorothy felt like a dream in the hard clear light. It made me happy to be a part of the life, minding the store in my folding lawn chair, making change out of a cigar box, watching the 49ers on a little five-inch black-and-white with Alicia, who was rooting for the Broncos.

"John Elway," she said, serious as ever. "The three amigos. They can't lose."

"It doesn't really matter who wins," I told her, I guess because it sounded like the kind of thing an adult ought to say. "The important thing is the game, not the winner."

Alicia looked at me like I was nuts. "*Somebody's* got to win," she said. "And somebody's got to *lose*."

"Yeah, well," I said, answerless, and tried to interest myself in the game.

Margaret cleared $153 that afternoon, not counting what she had to spend for broken junk. She took us out for hamburgers at the Stockman's Café downtown, then the three of them dropped me off at my room and we all made a lot of plans and promises I couldn't even remember later on.

I couldn't remember because Coy was waiting for me along with Dorothy when I got back to my room and somebody had beaten the shit out of Coy. She was washing his face, which was a mess, bruises rising up around his eyes, lips like burned Vienna sausages, and I looked over at my schoolbooks on the little desk and wondered what the fuck I was doing in the middle of this. *Books for Business* and the *Cash Flow Work Book*.

"What happened to him?" I asked Dorothy.

"His friends happened to him," she said. "The same ones that are going to happen to me if I don't come up with twenty-five hundred dollars."

"Maybe the two of you should leave town," I said. But when I said it I saw Coy and Dorothy fucking again, I saw how tenderly she held the washcloth to Coy's damaged face, and I couldn't stand to let her go. I'm doing this for love, I thought. It seemed like enough of a reason.

"I'm going to Denver," Coy said, though it was hard to understand him because of how swollen up his face was. "I fuck to share."

"What?" I asked him.

"I'm fuckin *scared* of those guys," Coy said. He leaned his head back in the chair until he was looking at Dorothy upside down, behind him. He said, "I'm fuckin scared of you, too. Shit like this didn't used to happen to me," or maybe he said, "doesn't usually happen to me." I couldn't tell. There was a minute of quiet between them in the kitchen where I could feel it slipping away: the swap meet, Margaret, the busy bees getting ready for winter.

The kitchen light was too bright, too clear. I didn't want to see that clearly. When I switched it off, a soft, late-afternoon light came through the dirty window that put us all in twilight. Even Coy's hamburger face looked like it was out of an old painting, the way he looked back at Dorothy, the way she looked down at him. I felt like the light was connecting all of us, holding us in a fold like a soft gray cloth. The place where the world balances, I thought, not knowing exactly what I meant. And a line from an old song: *she loves me better than I love myself.*

"I'm going to Denver," Coy said, and got up out of the chair and got his jacket from the couch and got out the little chrome automatic that was between the sofa cushions. It had been a while since I'd seen a gun and it came as a surprise. "I'm gone," he said, holding the pistol toward Dorothy, grip first. "You want this?"

"Maybe I'd better," she said, and tucked it into her white purse with the long leather fringes, and took her lipstick out while she was in there and freshened up in a little mirror she carried.

And then Coy was gone and it was old times again: she laid the little pistol on the counter and a pint of vodka and a pack of Virginia Slims and the mirror and the knife and the little paper envelope. Like a kit, I thought, a Dorothy kit. "Did I tell you about the radioactive mud?" she asked me.

"I don't remember," I said.

"You'd remember if I told you," she said. "At least I hope you would. It was this resort place down near Phoenix, kind of a shit hole, you know, run-down but it must have been nice once. And anyway they were dumb enough to give me a job . . ."

I eased back in the kitchen chair and it was just like three in the morning, even though it wasn't even five in the afternoon yet. I reached a beer out of the little dorm refrigerator while she told her story. This is what love means, I thought: the thing you can't walk away from. It was just like old times.

AND THEN IT WAS THREE IN THE MORNING for real and I was by myself again in the one-room apartment and I couldn't sleep. Partly it was the crank but mostly it was the old tightrope-walker feeling I got from Dorothy, looking down and seeing the ground so far below . . . Before she left, I gave her a check for the twenty-five hundred, a good check, but it was most of the money I had in the world. She gave me the keys to the turquoise Thunderbird but I knew I couldn't sell it. It was just a loan, a temporary thing, there was no need to transfer the title.

Thinking about this, it was like I had two parts of my brain and one side was always trying to bullshit the other and always succeeding. It was like the old days when every morning I would wake up and say that was the day I was going to quit and every day I was back on the crank by noon. The best part would be when I'd promise myself I was going to quit the next day and the best thing would be to just do up everything in the house, all the crank, drink all the whiskey, smoke all the cigarettes so I wouldn't be tempted . . . The funny part was that one side of my brain really did know what was going on. One side of my brain knew that I'd pissed away the money for rent and food and tuition at the Vo-Tech and it was really gone.

It was all for today. Dorothy was not going to get beat up. It felt crazy, the way that months of my future went down the toilet to pay for good times she already had, good times she had without me. I thought of how I made that money one day at a time: working on the railroad, an extra gang out of St. Regis, Montana. I was swinging a nine-pound spike maul ten hours a day and liking it. After a few weeks the foreman offered to let me switch to machine operator but I told him no, thanks. I liked the feel of the hammer, liked the feeling of getting strong and sleeping well.

The one side of my brain knew what the truth was and the other side had just lies and bullshit: Dorothy would come through, it didn't matter anyway, something would have happened to throw me back into the old life if it wasn't her . . . What made me feel crazy was that I was acting like the truth was nothing and the lies and the bullshit were real. The truth was cold and hard and it was easier to look the other way or to pretend but that didn't keep it from being the truth. That railroad money was going to pay for a new life and now it was gone. I was miles above the ground, looking down, crazy. I thought of the work that I had put into that money. I thought of how long it would take Margaret to make that money with her toasters and blenders and it made me sick, sick in my body. I pulled on my wool coat and my stupid hat with the flaps. I had to get out of this room.

An ice fog and a refinery haze blanketed the street outside and made the air taste like gasoline. The Thunderbird at the curb, the windshield blind with ice. The dings and dents stood out in the yellow light, and you could see the old uneven Bondo job in the back wheel wells. I asked for water, I thought, and she gave me gasoline. Sometimes the blues made perfect sense, three in the morning and drifting down the empty streets, looking for something. Dead leaves rustled in the gutters, like lawyers' papers. Drifting: my feet would take me anywhere but I couldn't tell which way to go. Every direction was as good as any other and the blues came up inside again: I'm just drifting and drifting, baby like a ship out on the sea . . . out in the night and praying for a lighthouse, a signal from shore, anything to tell the rocks from the harbor, crazy . . . My feet took me toward the old neighborhood, where the streetlights ended. Since the company bought the houses up they had gone abandoned and dark. The high school kids shot out the windows and stole the plumbing and painted their names in spray-can splashes and drips, like they pissed red paint onto the wall. TOXIC HAZARD pasted to every door, DANGER PELIGRO.

I turned the corner onto my old block and it was like a mouthful of broken teeth, with the glass still hanging in the window frames and the dark holes where the doors were hammered down. There were winos living in some of these places. I could see Sterno flames flickering on the walls, on the street where I learned to ride a bicycle, fell in love, where my mother and my father celebrated their anniversaries one after the other until the gasoline got into the groundwater. That was where things started turning to shit: when the gasoline started coming through the basement walls. I was still high off Dorothy's crank and I could see everything perfectly clearly, I could see my own life for once. And this street was where my life was, where I had a job and a wife and a twenty-one-thousand-dollar pickup truck with a stereo that would blow the fucking doors off. And then what? The gasoline dissolved the paint so it came off the basement walls in big rubbery sheets and then Dorothy left and since then I didn't know where I was going. Somewhere there was a connection. I was feeling sorry for myself. I tried to stop, I called myself a pussy but there was something missing, just gone, and the emptiness and lonely feeling would not leave me be.

A flickering candlelight was coming from the window of my old living room, and a sound of voices. I edged up toward the house across the battered grass, gone to dirt now, mostly. Trying not to make any noise, I found out how drunk I was. I tripped over a clump of dirt and the voices quit inside. After a minute they started up again and I crept up closer, trying to make out the words but they fell away in scraps on the cold wind. One of the voices belonged to a woman and suddenly I knew it was Dorothy.

I crept up closer, wondering what she was doing there, what she was cooking up, who she was fucking. It came to me like somebody turning on a light: she was going to spend my money and she was going to fuck somebody else and I was going to be out in the cold, always. I pictured her singing in the broken house, sharing a pint of whiskey, the bitch. It wasn't even love, it was just a game I couldn't quit playing, or maybe it was the same thing . . . Everything felt so clear and sharp to me but nothing made sense.

I stuck my head through the window and it wasn't Dorothy at all but a dark-haired woman, maybe an Indian, for a minute I thought of Margaret but then I saw that I didn't know anything at all.

"The fuck out of here," one of the men shouted, and I ran down my own lawn and through the dark, fear mixing with the taste of gasoline in the air. Through the dark and running, and after a minute I liked the feel of running, the punishment I was giving my body. My lungs were suffering, my legs were burning, my face was turning to glass in the cold and it was fine with me. I knew I deserved it, I deserved worse and sooner or later I'd get it. The thoughts came in rhythm with my pumping legs: I don't need this trouble, I don't want this trouble, don't save this trouble for anyone but me . . . Running slowly now, with the crank and alcohol pumping through my blood, I felt like I was about to fall down under a streetlight and that was all right too, whatever happened. I saw myself frozen dead in the weeds and maybe that was what was supposed to happen. The streets were too wide, the people who lived now weren't big enough to fill them up, I wasn't big enough.

I didn't stop until I got to Margaret's trailer. I leaned against a boat-tail Riviera parked across the street and I stared at the dark windows, breathing hard. I didn't know what I wanted from her but I knew that I wanted her, and when I saw the light go on in her bedroom I thought that I'd woken her up with my thoughts.

"Parker, is that you?" she asked. "What are you doing out here?"

I tried to think of what I ought to say, watching her eyes blink, trying to see. A little bit of a moon that night. She was wearing a down jacket and sno-pacs over her nightgown, and her hair was tangled and loose.

"I don't really have an explanation," I finally said.

"Did you want to see me?"

"No," I said, and I could see her face was still confused, full of sleep. "I mean, I want to see you, but I don't think you want to see me."

"That's too much to think about," she said. "It's time to sleep now. Do you want to come in with me?"

"Do you want me to?"

"I'm standing here in my nightgown," she said. "This is stupid."

She took my hand in hers and led my up the little stairs into her trailer. We took our coats off and then our boots and she led me down the narrow hall, to her bed all the way at the back. I wanted to cry and it wasn't just the whiskey: I was full of thanks, so happy to be forgiven. Margaret folded herself back under the covers, watching with her dark eyes as I fumbled with my clothes.

"Don't do this again," she whispered. "I can't do it, not with the kids."

"I won't," I promised, and I meant it. That night, Dorothy was the last mistake of the person I used to be. I was full of plans, the future inside me, bursting to get out.

"You will," she whispered. "Come here."

THERE WERE TWO MORE DAYS AFTER THAT, a Monday and a Tuesday, regular days. Margaret gave me a ride to the Vo-Tech in her little Datsun truck and then I took the bus back to her trailer while she picked the kids up from school and ran the usual errands. I stayed away from the Sacajawea—I didn't want to see Dorothy and I didn't know what the chances were, whether she was already gone or what else she might want from me. I was worn out with her.

The weather turned cold and the wind blew hard out of the north, making Margaret's trailer tremble on its base. We spent the winter nights around her kitchen table, drinking coffee and fixing Mr. Coffees and FryBabys and MixMasters. She did the motors and switches herself, but she let me take things apart and put them back together, while the kids cleaned the cases, using Liquid Secretary to cover spots and stains. She'd shut the TV off when the kids went to bed, then we'd pack all the spare motors back into the milk crates, the tools into her fancy copier-repair tool briefcase, packed it all away and worked on our homework for an hour or so in the quiet, not talking. Watch a little TV, maybe have a beer.

Now these winter nights stand for something, I don't know—
like part of a whole life, like a little patch cut from a big bolt of cloth.
There was a whole everyday life of chores and reasonable plans and
comfort but these were the only two days of it we ever got to live. I
feel like I can remember every minute, but there's nothing to remember: breakfast, dinner, television, work, Shane and Alicia singing
"John Jacob Jingleheimer Smith" until we were both ready to murder them.

The third day was a Wednesday. Margaret had an early class but
I didn't have to be there till noon. I let her go early and hung around
the trailer for a while by myself, drinking coffee and reading the
Nickel Ads: firewood, computers, four-wheel-drives. I tried to figure
out what the Thunderbird was worth but there was nothing in the
paper, and besides, I didn't even have the title. After a minute I had
to stop thinking about it because I felt the craziness again.

Around ten-thirty I walked over to the Sacajawea to check the
mail and get some clothes, taking the long way around to stay out of
the way of the old neighborhood. The Thunderbird was still parked
out front when I got there, which was not quite a surprise. I changed
my clothes and showered and shaved and started to feel pretty good.
My schoolbooks were still there in the room but I wasn't too far
behind. I decided it would be easier to study in the library of the Vo-
Tech instead of my room, and then I decided to take the Thunderbird
to school instead of the bus. Maybe Margaret wouldn't see me, or
maybe I would explain it to her. Maybe I just didn't think about it,
which is how it feels now, trying to figure out why.

The Thunderbird started right up and ran strong. I'd forgotten
what it was like to drive, with the big powerful V8 and the power
steering and power brakes and automatic—a big smooth ride, a mile
of turquoise hood out in front of me and the big chrome dashboard
with the Indian symbols. I punched the buttons on the radio till I
found a rock song, "All Right Now," and turned it up and tapped my
fingers on the steering wheel in time to the music. I felt fast, dangerous, untouchable. Even at the Vo-Tech, the high kept up. I kept
looking back at the Thunderbird on my way into the building, the

best-looking car in the parking lot, nothing but trouble but it was mine, for now, anyway.

The two bikers came into the library about half an hour later. I knew they were looking for me, even before I saw one of the front office staff pointing me out. They both had beards and little black braids. One of them was only big, while the other one was huge, three hundred pounds or more.

The one who was only big said, "Look, we need to get the keys from you."

"What keys?" I said.

"Let's not bullshit this," the biker said. "I mean seriously. Dorothy owes us the money, give us the keys, we'll call it quits, okay?"

And the keys were in my pocket and I could have just given them up, taken them out, handed them over, and that would have been it—no car, no money, no wife, and no future life that was any different. And all of this had already happened, and part of it was that I couldn't admit it to myself. I just felt empty and stupid. It was like looking down from a high place: I felt like I could see it all, my whole life at once. And for some reason at that moment I thought of Shane and Alicia and how I had come from being a child to being here, and the waste of that child's life, and I couldn't do it. With the car I had something, some kind of hope, even if it was a lie. Otherwise there was just nothing.

"That's not your car," I said.

"The fuck it's not," the biker said.

"I have a receipt," I said, sounding puny even to myself. I thought, Here it comes. Part of me wanted it, whatever was going to happen next.

But it was nothing. The biker clapped his hands down on the library table with a loud sound that made the other students stare, and he leaned down to look into my eyes and said, "I wish you'd quit trying to be an asshole about this."

He had a low, raspy voice but he wasn't trying to make it mean. It sounded almost like he cared. I could smell the complicated stink coming off the biker, leather and hair grease and cigarette smoke. I knew a couple of bikers around town and they were good guys to have as friends, good to drink with but sometimes they told stories about this other life, the part that I wasn't allowed into, girls and trains and pool cues. And the other thing was just a dream, there was nothing real about the Thunderbird. But there was nothing real about any of the rest of it, nothing for me.

"Sorry," I said, and left the keys in my pocket.

"It's going to get worse," the biker said, and stood up, and both of them walked out.

I was shaking inside, and the other students were staring at me. I collected my books and went to the window, where I could just see the bumper of the Thunderbird. I expected them just to steal it and I almost wished they would, just get it over with.

Ten minutes passed and the car was still there and I was still there, holding my books in my arms like a high school girl. It was a cold gray day with a wind blowing papers across the parking lot. The snow was melted off everywhere but the shadows of the trees and I was thinking that it was time to quit—time to move on and give it another try somewhere else. Except for trips to here and there, I'd lived in this town for my whole life and I couldn't help thinking I'd made a mess of it. I tried to hate Dorothy for the mess she made but it was my fault as much as hers. I just wish that I had thought of this ten minutes earlier so I could have given the two bikers the keys to the Thunderbird and gotten the whole thing over with.

What happened was I left my schoolbooks on one of the tables in the library and went off to find Margaret. It was noontime so I expected to find her in the cafeteria and there she was, head down over her books, drinking cafeteria coffee along with the brown-bag lunch she brought from home. This was the way I first saw her, and really I can't remember if what I'm telling you is the memory of that particular day or just the way she was. Anyway, she was surprised to see me when I tapped her on the shoulder.

"What are you doing here, Parker?" she asked. "I thought you had a class."

"I did," I said. "I wanted to explain something."

"Like what?" She took her glasses off and rubbed her eyes and looked at me, suspicious. But she must have seen the trouble in me because she changed. "Sit down," she said.

But I couldn't tell her about Dorothy, there in the cafeteria—it was too bright, too normal, too much in the light of day. What I really needed was three in the morning, a couple of drinks, but I had the feeling that I didn't have time for that.

"Come with me for a second," I asked her, and after a minute she said yes. She gathered her books and followed me out into the cold noontime and over to the Thunderbird.

"Whose car is this?" she asked, when she saw me open the door with the key. "Who does this belong to?"

"It's mine for now," I told her, and opened the lock on the other door. She hesitated for a minute before she got in, and I remember that I was angry with her—like she didn't trust me, like I was fooling her all along. "Come on," I said, and started the engine.

She got in, fumbled around for a seat belt before she realized the car was too old to have them. She looked at all the beautiful chrome, the white leatherette. "Where did this come from?" she asked.

"It's a long story," I said. I backed the car out of the space and headed for the exit and Margaret was looking at me from across the seat, a long ways away, like she'd never seen me before.

"Where are you going?" she asked.

"I just want to get away from here for a minute," I said, easing the car out into the traffic on 34th Street, heading west, toward the mountains. I waited a few more blocks, until she was settled back into her seat instead of pressed against the door like she was trying to get away from me, and then I told her: "I'm in all kinds of trouble," I said.

"What do you mean?" she asked.

"I think I might have to go away for a while," I said. I was going to tell her about Dorothy, and about the mess I made, but even at that last minute I didn't want to. It was like saying the words would make them real, and as long as I didn't say them the trouble would go away by itself, like a little balloon flying off.

"There's somebody waving at you," Margaret said.

I looked over two lanes and there were the bikers in a blue Chevy pickup and the one that had done the talking was in the passenger side with the window down, waving his hand for me to stop. I slowed down at first, and the traffic carried them past me and I started looking for a place to turn.

"What's going on, Parker?" Margaret asked, but I was trying to think, and I didn't answer. I looked over and the blue pickup was drifting back toward me through the other cars. I thought that I could get into the parking lot of a gas station but the pickup cut me off, and then I gave the Thunderbird some gas and we shot around them and we were off to the races, Margaret cursing in the seat beside me, cursing at me, "Goddamn you, Parker, stop this fucking car." And after that I can't really sort it out, except that we went back and forth through the traffic and I thought I could make a quick turn and then get away and then Margaret gave this new sound and I looked over and the biker was pointing a sawed-off shotgun at my head. I gunned the engine to get out of the way and went through the red light at Highland and then there was this sound, I don't know, metal and screaming and tires where the Cadillac tried to stop before he plowed into the passenger side. She lived, though the glass made a mess of her face. Her hipbone broke into pieces and still hasn't mended, that's what I hear. I don't know. I don't see her, except in my sleep. I see the last thing, Margaret hanging like a red doll out the hole in the windshield and then the steering wheel breaking apart in my hands and then, most of the time, I wake up.

GROUNDED
Claire Davis

ONLY AN HOUR AGO Wava Haney had grounded her son Kyle forever, but there he was, kicking down the gravel driveway as though he had every right. She knelt on the shop floor, the chair braced against her thigh, one hand supporting the dowel while she cranked on the wood clamp with the other. Her fingers were glossed with glue, and the chair, her best work yet, teetered on the edge of completion. Lifting her fingers from the clamp, she eyed the configuration for balance. She knew what it *should* look like, this Shaker-style, ladder-back chair, bird's-eye maple, with a plank seat chiseled and sanded by her own hands, those hands calloused until she'd lost the tactile details of every day—the embossed flowers on her favorite teacups, the hairs blushing her arms. The chair lingered in a suspension of glue and faith eminently perishable. On her haunches, she looked out the door. Two precious days off from waitressing at the cafe. Two days in which she'd planned to finish this chair. Start another. She'd as soon pretend she hadn't seen Kyle, wipe her hands and wait in the shade of a tree for his sorry return, then give him a piece of her mind. She raised to her feet, studied the chair. This was a critical stage; it could all go so badly.

She slapped her hands across the butt of her jeans, thinking too late, as she always did, that she should have used a towel. He was on the turn in the drive, and if she didn't hurry he would be gone. She hiked her arms and tried running, but her ankles wobbled. Should it feel this way at thirty-six? Her upper arms jiggled and she felt absurd. She slowed to a jog.

The driveway was a piece of work—a half-mile of pitching turns, hills, and dips that in winter meant night shifts burrowing through drifts behind the plow in her four-wheel-drive custom Ford pickup.

You wouldn't think it, to see it now, in the dog days of summer, trees wilted, waiting for the final crisp of autumn. Roadside weeds were varnished with dust. The green grasshoppers of June had turned brown and percolated in the shrubs.

She caught up as he turned onto the highway—two lanes and no shoulders, common to Montana. "Where do you *think* you're going?" she asked.

He slowed. She could see her effect in the set of his chin. She touched his arm and he didn't snatch it from her, and even in her anger, she was grateful for that.

"Did you hear me?"

"Yes, ma'am," he said, as he always did when angry, setting his distance with courtesy.

"You're grounded."

"Yes ma'am."

"Then where are you going?"

"Away from you."

He'd stopped and was watching her with all the astuteness of a fifteen-year-old already gathering his defenses. She stepped to the high side of the shoulder, trying to appear taller. She was no more used to looking up than he was looking down. All that bone didn't fit him yet. He used it like a borrowed body. She supposed he'd gotten his height from his father, though she preferred to think it was some wild-card gene from her own short side of the family. He was dressed in Levi's, T-shirt, and high-top sneakers, a jacket tied around his waist. No water, no food, no spare clothes. "You won't last a day," she said.

"You going to give me the chance to find out?"

"Probably not."

She could see them as others might—a logger, or better yet, a couple on a leisurely drive, startled by the scenery, heads ducked to better see the mountains packed in the frame of car windows. They would welcome the sight of a mother and son on the side of the road. *Isn't that nice*, they would say.

"Get home," she said. "We'll forget it happened."

He walked ahead. She stood a moment in disbelief. "You're too young to run away," she called, though the fact was, he was too old. At five, ten, even thirteen she could have bullied him back up the drive, hauled him by the arm into the house, and sat him on the couch for a dressing-down. But at fifteen he was becoming a man, too strong to tackle.

He lengthened his stride, one to every two of hers.

"Eighteen is old enough. When you're eighteen, I'll lock the door after you." She tried not to breathe heavily. She was past showing weakness to anyone. It had been her first lesson as a single mother in rural Montana where a woman alone didn't so much gather disapproval as disinterest. "This is ridiculous," she said.

He cut into a fallow field, sour with leafy spurge. Knapweed broke flower heads down their jeans and bunched in the cuffs. She chugged behind, convinced he would tire even as she did, that he would grow hot and thirsty and bored with his own dogged rebellion. Wava settled into walking, and jogging in short bursts when she got too far behind. He was having an easy time of it while she struggled: weeds, hummocks, and prairie dog holes. Three-foot conical hills topped the wild oats, the industry of ants shivering on the surface. She believed he could be worn down. There was nothing beyond this valley but the Swan Mountains to the left and the Missions hard on the right. When Kyle hit the bog edging the Clearwater River, his high-tops swilled with water. He looked for a shallow wade, or a felled tree to cross. He must have known he'd be stopped by the river, she thought, and beyond that by the mountains, all that implacable rock. An innocent in the pitting of wills, he must have thought she would give up. She felt disillusioned. He simply did not believe in her.

He appeared disinterested, turning away, his neck craning back to study the side of the mountains where a red-tailed hawk circled on the thermals. "Sharp-shinned hawk," she said, giving him an excuse to talk, an argument to cover his embarrassment. She had a keen sense of what it felt to be fifteen and daring and foolish. She was less certain as to how it felt to be thirty-six and a mother whose son was running away. He started back toward the highway, his sneaker squeezing water with each step. Good: easier to keep up on blacktop.

Given other circumstances, taken at her own accustomed pace, she'd have enjoyed this walk. In the fourteen years she had lived in Montana, much of it had been spent doing just this, striking off across fields, bullying her way through cheat grass, or forests with the pine-pitch smell she'd come to love better than her own baking. It was something perverse in her that preferred this above all others—putting herself in a place where everything most precious could be lost. Time. Direction.

She suspected Kyle had been incubating this idea for some time now. In this he was her son, predicating each move, imperfectly planned perhaps, but planned. It went beyond their fight. It was a product, she thought, of the hours he spent sitting on the back stoop studying the commotion of wind in grass, or the flight of birds. It came of example.

When her husband Joe had first brought them to Montana, enacting the whim and transporting her and one-year-old Kyle out of the Midwest and into the West, she was still young and able to be swayed. Joe was a woodworker, neither adept or inspired, but he tried. "All that lumber," he'd said. "We'll buy a small place with lots of trees." He chucked her under the chin with a finger. "Don't you see it's like free wood then. We're dying here. All the costs—you, the baby, the wood." She wondered how she could have been so witless as to believe that. Five years later he ran off with Katie Hitchet who'd commissioned a set of bookcases. The only redeeming grace was that he'd left his tools. The bookcases Wava burned. She regretted that, in a way—those beautiful birch planks. But it made a hell of a bonfire.

On the highway, Wava kept her pace and temper at twenty feet behind. To the right, a pileated woodpecker knocked its head against a tree, rapping like a determined visitor. They passed the Riding High Ranch, the signpost listing over an assemblage of derelict Studebakers. A flock of peacocks roosted on roofs, shat on windshields and dismembered fenders. They screamed in a frenzied chorus, their fanned tails trembling in the sunlight. Wava and Kyle passed a lumber yard and then a small herd of cattle stupefied with the first heat of the day. When she looked at Kyle again, he'd struck his thumb up for a ride. What next.

"Have you ever heard a thing I've told you?" she asked. "Hitchhiking is *stupid*. You don't know what's out there."

He was jogging backwards, joyfully wagging his thumb in the air. Wava's heart thickened as she looked over her shoulder and in the distance saw a car, a glint off the windshield like the proverbial light at the end of a tunnel, like the oncoming train. Kyle was running to leave her behind, and the car was coming on, nearing, then passing and slowing to a stop fifty yards ahead. The passenger door swung open. Kyle loped up to the car, leaned down to see who was driving, then back at her and got in. The door slammed. Wava ran. She ran, wishing for better shoes. She thought to get the license number but all she could see was sunlight, a frieze on the bumper, two blurs in the front seat. She wanted, more than anything, to see Kyle's face while he was still here, still hers to look at. She was within twenty feet when the gears engaged and the car started pulling away. She could see the driver checking for traffic. "Wait," she yelled. And the taillights flickered. "I'm coming," she called. The exhaust fumed, but the car waited on the side of the road.

THE MISSION MOUNTAINS VEERED OFF as they drove down the highway, she in the back, swathed in dog hair—golden retriever, she thought—Kyle up front, his head rigidly forward, and Jessup Taylor driving. Sup he called himself, with liver-spotted hands and a face of indeterminate age. Sup hummed, his bass voice resonant, out of place in the small car with upholstery tufts seeping out of torn seams and dog hair pooling on the floor. Glancing in the rearview mirror, he smiled. "Where you two going?"

"We're not together," Kyle answered. "As far as you'll take me," he added.

"Seeley Lake," Sup said. "Once a week, need it or not, I go to Seeley Lake for a little excitement. Course, given my age and the nature of the place, it's an exercise in futility, but I try. And you ma'am?"

"Wherever you take my son."

Sup flicked a look into the rearview mirror, then over at Kyle. "Thought you weren't together."

Kyle flinched. His neck looked delicate from behind, white beneath the short-cropped black hair. She'd never seen anything so vulnerable. "He's running away. From me," she said.

"He's not doing a very good job of it," Sup said, downshifting into a turn, five feet from where the bank lolled down into trees— ponderosa, fir, scrub larch, and lanky aspen whose leaves had already gone gold above the red dogwood and bunchgrass.

Sup's head bobbed into each turn, his passengers ignored, as if it were normal to find himself transporting both a runaway and the runned-from in his car, as though there was a world of mothers teth- ered to runaway sons, and perhaps for him this was true because he was old, had seen enough to believe anything possible, and life with all its attendant quirks was no longer a dilemma. Wava envied him.

"Everyone runs away least once in his life, or contemplates the idea," Sup said. "I thought about it, once, maybe two, three times. But it always seemed a coin better saved." They drove in quiet, the road paralleling the forest and link of lakes—Summit, Alva, Inez, bright glimpses in the foliage—unfolding like a drunken stagger, one mile forward, two back on itself in a series of horseshoe curves. They passed a stand of tamarack and a falling magpie. Wava cranked her window open and the dog hair drifted and fell.

"Your dog still got any hair?" Wava asked.

"Sorry," Sup said. "He's lost more than I ever owned." He rolled his window down and the hair wheeled in the air and drafted out. Sup hummed a few notes. "But he's a good dog." He looked over at Kyle. "Stays put where I tell him. Where's it you plan to run to? You got somewhere to go?"

"You can let me out anywhere, sir."

"You trying to get rid of me too? This is not your lucky day, boy." He drove on.

Minnesota, Wava thought. That's where they all go eventually, Minnesota or California.

Kyle leaned forward, his hands fidgeting with the seat belt. "Idaho," he said.

"Idaho?" Sup slapped the steering wheel. "Now *that's* a change for the better." He grinned. "How you going to live?"

"I'll get a job."

"You don't look a day over sixteen—minimum wage and a handful of hours." And from the backseat, Wava could see how Kyle blushed with pleasure to be thought older than he was, even if only a year. "You got money?" Sup asked.

"Yes sir, seventy-three dollars," Kyle said, as if it were all the money in the world—one year's savings, chopping and stacking wood for the elderly Geneva Norwitch who lived alone with her dogs and spavined horses down the valley.

"Well, you're an accommodating boy. Seventy-three dollars, sir, he says. Why don't you just hand it over and get it done with—save yourself a knock on the head?" He shook his finger at Kyle. "You got to consider who you're going to meet on the road. But you're thrifty. I'll say that for you, if not real smart."

"He's an *honors* student," Wava said, feeling defensive, but sounding boastful. And why not? How could she not be proud? Kyle was gazing out the side window.

"No offense, ma'am," Sup said. "We'll be coming into Seeley Lake soon, and all the better that I'm out of it." On the outskirts of town, Sup asked, "Can you tell me why you're leaving?"

"She thinks she owns me." The answer was practiced. Believed.

"She does. Heart and soul, boy," Sup said.

As if that didn't work both ways.

They walked Highway 83 eastbound out of Seeley Lake. As earlier, Wava kept a few steps behind. The road—two lanes of long slow ascents. She thought about the chair in her woodshop, about the glue that might shirk its grip, the laddered rungs slipping, then she looked up and saw her son moving farther from their home with more determination than she could ever account for. He was furious. Embarrassed. His shoulders were slumped under the new backpack he'd bought in the hardware store. He hadn't spoken a word to her since Seeley Lake. As if he had every right to feel angry with her. Wava punched her hands into her jeans. How was she supposed to know what that old man was going to do?

Sup had dropped them off at the True Value Hardware store, an oversized log cabin like all the other Seeley Lake buildings—a tidy collection of logs gummed with oil, antlers and skulls lofted into every available cornice. Wava veered off into the wood finishing aisles. She loved the color cards—pecan, cherrywood, mahogany, teak—the stacked cans of stains and oils, lacquers and waxes. She loved the hiss of a newly opened can, the look of grain revealed with stain, how cheesecloth glided over well-sanded wood. She could use some tung oil. She pulled herself away and followed Kyle. He was looking at hatchets. He eyed the top-of-the-line then pulled a midpriced one from the shelf.

He ran his thumb lightly down the steel while Wava winced. "Good edge," he said.

She took the hatchet from him. The balance was wrong: wrists would pop and ache. It would not cleave cleanly. That's what novices didn't understand. For them the edge was all. She pulled a better one from the rack, placed them both in his hands. "Feel the difference?"

He held them awkwardly. "No," he said.

She moved his hands down the handle. "Yeah," he said. "Oh, yeah." And he handed the new hatchet to her to hold as he moved down the aisle. She swung it as she walked. They could use it at home. A person could always use a good hatchet. It had become an excursion, she thought. There was really nothing desperate about it.

She loved tools—oiling wood handles, cleaning and sizing router bits in the proper felt pockets, alert to the dings, flakes, and splinters that could diminish months of work. Joe'd respected the function of tools but not the tools themselves. The labor and the means always secondary to the product. And wasn't that indicative of something larger in him? "You're too damn critical," he'd say, one foot raised on the table or chair he'd just finished. "I'm just trying to help," she'd offer, and he'd look her over while picking his teeth. *"Yeah,"* he'd say. *"I can tell,"* or *"Who asked for it?"* And so, wasn't it a relief when it all came apart? Yes.

At the counter, Kyle bought the hatchet, a pocket knife, and a backpack. He was down to a twenty, some singles, and odd change. He slipped the items into the pack while she looked at postcards. "We could send this one to ourselves," she teased him. "Having a good time, glad you're here." He broke into a smile. Yes, she thought, this could be turned around.

"Anyone here got a runaway?"

It was a sheriff in the door. Kyle ducked his head and started to move. Wava reached out and snatched at his sleeve, hauling herself back to his side.

"Who's got the runaway?" the sheriff repeated, then spotted them. He was a squat man, a lightweight, bearing down on them with all the authority of Swan County winking from the badge on his front pocket. "You the runaway?"

Wava nodded while Kyle shook his head.

"How old are you?" he asked Kyle.

They spoke at the same time.

"Eighteen."

"Fifteen."

Kyle pulled away and the sheriff's strangely delicate hand circled Kyle's wrist. There were handcuffs prominent in the sheriff's back trouser pocket. She could see Kyle and herself in the back of the sheriff's car, the siren silent, no blue lights, but cruising at sixty with intent down the highway, back to their home and abandoned on the front stoop. Then what? Wait for Kyle to run again. She blamed herself—what, after all, did she know about raising boys? She was an only child, from the Midwest where all the boys she knew in childhood were cornfed at proper tables, wore tight jeans, and carried themselves with the arrogance of their fathers.

"You got some I.D.?"

Kyle shook his head.

"He's got his mother," Wava said. "Is that I.D. enough?"

"It is *if you are.*"

"I am."

"Is she?" He turned to Kyle and the boy kept silent. People were gathering in a cluster, slowing down to see better, leaning in as they walked by.

Wava jabbed Kyle with an elbow and whispered, "This is no time to fool around."

"Maybe we should just go down to the office—"

"She is. She's my mother."

Wava smiled. "Told you so."

The sheriff was breathing through his nose. "This is not a game. I got some old man at the office worrying about a runaway. Now I *got* to investigate."

"I can handle it," Wava said. "I know you're trying to help." She saw herself as he saw her, shirt slipping out of her jeans, sweat stains under her arms and breasts, her hair coarse from the sun. She looked small, foolish, and fierce. The sheriff's eyebrow hitched and she knew he did not believe her. If she could handle it they wouldn't be here. "You're just interfering—"

"Where's your father?" he asked Kyle.

Wava settled on her heels. "I'm divorced," she said, not that it was any of his business.

A woman standing at Wava's elbow nodded and whispered, "It's a hard road."

Wava singled out the woman. "You got something to do?" The woman backed away. And then Wava rounded on the sheriff, because he was the cause of it all—her snapping at the woman who meant only sympathy—because he assumed any father was better than none. She lifted her chin level with the badge on his chest. "Are you done with us? I'm his mother. We're out for a walk." She leaned up into his face. *"This is not your business."*

The sheriff released Kyle's wrist. He was steadying his temper with deep breaths. "Then take your walk somewhere else. Ravalli County maybe." He stepped off and said under his breath, "God damn ungrateful. I'd probably run too."

After that, nothing remained in Seeley but to stand by as Kyle made his purchases at the I.G.A.: a loaf of bread, peanut butter, a six-pack of Coke, and two apples.

They were heading up yet another incline and it stretched onward for a half-mile. They were entering the real heat of the day. Her underwear, damp with sweat, bunched and crept where it had no business. She twisted her hair up and wiped her neck with her shirt collar. She was stewing in her own skin. She considered the sheriff's parting comment. What had she done to merit it? Lose a husband, take on a job while trying to learn a skill to keep the clothes on their backs, the food in their bellies, the sky from falling. *I'd probably run too.* Well God damn it, when was the last time she'd had that luxury?

"Slow down," she yelled. The highway edged a lake sheltered in a hollow of hills; the reflected trees more significant than the real. They passed the island where the millionaire built his log cabin mansion, six kitchens, fifteen fireplaces. A For Sale sign hung roadside. He had one year on the lake before burning his yacht for insurance and firing off his own head. She could not conceive a proper reason for suicide. She could not imagine the necessity of it. The whole prospect of death and dying was deterrent enough. But how much did a person have to lose before the end was worth more than the means? Her mouth went dry. The water looked clean, the hills unmoved. "I'm thirsty," she called.

"You should have bought something to drink," he yelled back.

She jogged to where he waited, pulled her pockets inside out. "No money."

"You should have thought of that before," he said and started walking.

"What? I should have read your mind, grabbed my purse, packed a dinner—"

He stopped.

"I'm thirsty," she repeated. "Pretend I'm a stranger. Pretend I'm some bum on the road who needs a drink and not the mother who gave birth to you, who watched your head crown between her knees."

He opened his pack. "That's gross."

"You don't know the half of it," Wava said as she pulled out two Cokes, handed one to him. "Thanks." She took a long pull. He shrugged the backpack, seated it in the duff of pine needles, then walked down to the lake. Wava folded herself to the ground. Mushrooms whoofed under her and a cloud of brown spoor patinaed her arms. She wiped the sweat under her breasts with the tail of her shirt and leaned back against the tree. Kyle was bending over, picking at the knots in the laces, taking off his shoes. When he was five, she'd bought him a pair with Velcro fasteners. When she showed him how they worked, all he'd said was, *I can tie my shoes.* He put them on, but there was no delight. It was clear he believed she hadn't enough faith in him.

Kyle dove into the water. The afternoon light sliced through the trees. She counted the limbs overhead like a blessing. Pine was good for primitives—plank tables, benches, bookcases. The soft imprint of hammers gave them character, the respect of use and age. After three years of working with the more expensive hardwoods, she retained a fondness for pine. She loved the open-hearted wood with all its knotholes and failings that relentlessly taught forgiveness. If she had a single great attribute, it would be her belief in the character of wood, that each wood had its own best use, each plank its order in design ordained by the symmetry of grain, and that grain preordained by the clemency of weather, by soil or rock face, by the event of seasons.

Belly-up to the sun, Kyle floated in the water. Wava's kidneys felt battered from the long walk and the sudden intake of fluids. She relieved herself in privacy then walked down to the lake. She set her shoes next to her son's and stepped into the lake fully clothed. The cold water wicked up her thigh, her buttocks. She slipped deeper until her breasts floated and the sweat washed away. Dog paddling awhile, she kept her head dry above the water. She had always been a coward about full immersion, each time a battle of will between herself and the unknown. And yet she persisted. She held her breath, squeezed her eyes shut, and ducked under. She floated beneath the surface and when the ringing in her ears faded and her heart calmed, she heard the hum and kick of her son swimming.

HER SHOES SQUEAKED when she walked, the lake water trickling from her jeans into her shoes. But she felt refreshed, ready to do battle. She tried to vary the pitch. "Hey, listen to this," she said, and pumped her foot in her shoe. When she finished he stood there, uncomprehending. "It's 'Stars and Stripes Forever', you know, John Philip Sousa."

He rolled his eyes. "Don't you ever get tired?" he asked.

"You should try an eight-hour shift with the meat loaf special," and she balanced her arms out in front of her. "How about you?" she asked, trying to keep the hope out of her voice.

He turned away and started walking.

"That's my boy," she said. "Never say die." And that was probably her own damn fault too. His stamina—built on long nights at the cafe as a little boy when she couldn't afford a babysitter and he'd play quietly at one of the tables, sneaking sips of cold coffee left by customers. When he faded, she carried him out to the parking lot and lay him in the back of the truck bed—the cap windows cranked open or shut dependent on the weather. She'd check on him in the spare moments, between late-night customers—drunks trying to revive with food, or the truckers hunched over tables talking into the tableside phones, hands cupped around the mouthpiece. Hamburgers hissed, fried chicken crackled and she'd bolt through the back door to lean against the pickup and listen to her son, still safe, still asleep while coyotes choraled in the distance. Hardly an ideal childhood. Not even a reasonable one.

All totaled, including the ride from Sup, they had covered nearly twenty miles. They were still on 83, alongside the Blackfoot-Clearwater Wildlife Management Range, an elk and wildlife preserve. A long flat pasture, with hills bucked up against its western border. They passed signs with binoculars stenciled on—wildlife viewing areas— though in summer when tourists arrived, the elk ranged miles up and away in the high country of the Bob Marshall Wilderness Preserve. A curious idea, given that in season hunting was allowed, the hunters advised to return the radio collars to the department of fish and game. Didn't that make it uncomfortably like shooting a pet? Removing the collar after the dog is hit on the road?

"Could you kill something?" she asked Kyle.

He stopped, shifted the pack on his shoulder. "Why, is there something you want dead?"

"I could carry that pack awhile," she said.

He shook his head. "I can do it. You *never* think I can do it."

"No." She shook her finger at him. "I *know* you can. Why the hell do you think I'm here?"

He stepped back, turning his head so she wouldn't see how pleased he was. Maybe she had done too much. Maybe all the years she worked the extra hours, did the extra chores herself, she hadn't so much given as taken from the boy?

"You never said—could you kill something? Elk? Deer?"

He led off again. "I won't make the county line by dark."

"I could—kill something—but I'd have to be damn hungry first," she said, and thought it couldn't be wearing a collar. He slowed down and she trotted up alongside him. Her son hadn't answered, and that seemed significant. There were things mothers should have of their sons before handing them over—a sense of their experience. "Did you ever see anything die? Something sizable." Her hands spread apart. "Something that counts?"

"Sure." Then he reconsidered. "Do roadkills count?" he asked.

She nodded and thought about her parents, but that was unfair. They had been *in* the car. She had been fifteen hundred miles away with the excuse of raising her own son. She would spare Kyle that, if she could—leaving too soon, too angry and too proud to go back. But she couldn't think about that now—the wages of being someone's child. She had her hands full being a parent. "My father used to slaughter hogs—a sledge to the head." Her arm swung down, and she stopped, fixing the spot at her feet as if there were a pig at the end of her reach. "Jesus, he had *arms* on him." She looked at her own. "Then he'd hoist it up by the hind feet to a crossbar and slit its throat." Kyle was staring at the road, his nose wrinkled. "They were big hogs, hung their length from a crossbar, their heads swinging just about the height of my head. I could look in their eyes if I wanted to." She stepped off. The sun was over the western hills. Meadowlarks sang, perched on the tips of lamb's ear, and the shadows of clouds rolled over the fescue like animals grazing. They stood side by side, watching the shadows, the mountains, the sky around them, everywhere but at each other.

"Did you? Look in their eyes?" he asked.

She nodded her head. "Always."

"Cripes." He walked away. "Why?" he asked over his shoulder.

"Because I was ten years old. Because nothing frightened me then." What kind of child does that? Touches the dead, looks it in the eye? She had been a strange child. So who was she to question Kyle's behavior? Though the only time her father had been upset was when he'd found her, knees crooked over the crossbar and swinging like one of the hogs. She'd wanted to know how they saw the world, inverted, the sky become ground, the grass heaven. Her parents had been horrified. But then what, after all, frightens parents more than their own children's curiosity?

They laid her parents out in oak coffins. Closed caskets. Their neighbor sent her pictures, printed on the back of one, "your father," and on the other, "your mother." A car passed, and another, none slowing down for a better look at the odd pair in the road. Wava slipped a hand into her blouse to ease the stitch in her side.

"I killed a rabbit once," he said.

Wava nodded, as if that were reasonable.

"I lobbed a rock at it, hit it square on the head. It didn't have time to be surprised." His eyebrow lifted, as though he still found that surprising. "Never thought I'd hit it. That it would die."

She studied him from the corner of her eye, the sweat beading on his lip, the chin still hairless—skin like the bottom of a baby's foot. He seemed impossibly young, still bewildered by his own actions, a rock and a rabbit, cause and effect. "Why?" she asked.

He blushed, swiped at the hair over his forehead. "I wanted a lucky rabbit's foot."

The day's sun had wilted the weeds. Wava's arms were lacquered with sweat. In the grasses, beetles drowsed on the underside of the blades, and dragonflies fumbled through the air. She was thirsty, but reluctant to ask him for another drink. The meadow was spent with the day's heat and the first early evening breezes were still moments away, the land pendent with expectation.

"Did you take it?" she asked. "The rabbit's foot?"

"No," he said. "The rabbit was dead. How lucky could it be?"

IT WAS DARK BY THE TIME THEY STOPPED. Their clothes had dried, though the inseams in Wava's jeans remained damp and chafed her thighs. She took off her shoes, rubbed the weals on her feet. Her hair had hardened in snarls. They camped in an abandoned shed, one of many sagging houses and barns along 200 heading south to Missoula. They were in the Garnet Range that had drifted from Idaho almost ninety million years prior along with the Sapphire and Bitterroot Mountains, escaping to Montana. All this traffic, coming and going, Wava thought.

Her skin itched—no-see-ums, whose bite didn't bother until after they'd fled, and what kind of defense could you have against that? Still she slapped at her arms, disinclined to let them get away with it. It was chilly. They had a hatchet and wood but no matches. She sat on the dirt floor, under a star-pierced roof. The wall across from her buckled outward, and through the yawning pitch between wall and foundation, sage and knapweed grew rampant.

Coyotes yapped from the fields outside. "There are big cats around here—mountain lions. Wolves. Rats," Wava said.

"Elk, mule deer, skunk," Kyle said.

"The occasional psychopath," Wava added. "He can use your new hatchet on us."

"You're not going to scare me back home."

Wava stretched her feet in front of her, locked her arms over her chest. "Steaks would taste good."

"We don't have a fire to cook them, anyway."

"I'd eat them raw. Damn I'm tired." She took a bite of the peanut butter sandwich he offered her. "So, remind me. Why are we running away?"

"You grounded me. Forever."

She shrugged. "And you can see how long that lasted. If you'd just done what I told you in the first place—"

"I can't do a *damn* thing without you ordering me around."

"I'm a parent. Your only parent. I'm *supposed* to give you order in your life." She wished she still smoked. She'd have matches then and she could light a fire. Maybe the whole God damn shed. "I take orders every day of my life." Bucking hot plates to customers until her arms were pinked with the heat, and Rod, the owner and cook, shuffled kettles countertop, waiting for the next spurt of customers. He had six daughters, none of whom he thought level-headed enough to work for him. And Wava figured that was his own damn fault.

Kyle had moved off to the far side of the shed, kicking at the sagebrush. She was tempted to list her acts of benevolence like a catalog of his sins. "Checking for snakes?" she asked, and he returned to sit ten feet from her. "You want to be an adult? Then act like it. Adults don't run away." And that was nonsense, of course. They ran with regularity, off to work, to lovers. Put holes in their heads. They had better timing was all, a greater ingenuity for excuses—financial ruin, change of life, you don't understand me. I never meant to fall in love with her, meaning I never meant to fall out of love with you. But there it is. Take care of the boy.

"Well, you're the adult all right," Kyle said. "*You* don't run from nobody."

"You talking about your dad? Christ. Don't bother. He invented his own excuses when he left. No. This is not his doing. This is yours. You take care of your own reasons." She walked over and squatted in front of him. "But you tell me of one time, just one, when I wasn't there."

She stood, dusted her knees, and walked to where her shoes slumped in the dirt.

"Maybe I just want to be alone," Kyle said.

"Funny you should say that. I don't." Wava slipped her shoes on and limped to the door. She leaned on the remnants of the jamb. People were selfish. They learned it as children. They were generous only in blame. The moon hung low and huge in the sky. It would ascend and shrink, but still it would be there, night after night after night. As a child, how many times did it have to rise before she'd believed it would always rise to fall? Such things must have come easier back then.

She could have left. Fifteen years ago. Ten years ago. It was done all the time. She had simply chosen not to. It was all so absurd, her son running from the only one who had stayed, her standing there, tired in the doorway, the moon rising yet another time. She could sleep, and Kyle would run. She could stay awake, and Kyle would run.

"You go on," she said. "You meet other people. Someday, you'll find yourself a woman who knows that you save your peas for the last and assumes it's because you like them least. You'll have to tell her otherwise. Then some morning, you'll slip out of your wife's bed, maybe step on your children's toys and you'll wonder if it's worth it all. You'll think about leaving. I suspect it comes easier with practice."

She shuffled back into the room. She could barely make out his shape against the wall.

"You going somewhere?" he asked.

She shrugged. "Maybe."

"You can hardly walk."

"I'll hitch," she said.

"That's stupid."

She walked out the door. The wind ruffled the grasses and she stepped off into the gratifying silence. She was cut loose and it was terrifying. Wonderful. Wasn't this what she'd been preparing for all along? Marriage and friendship, sons and daughters, were just a respite between you and the knowledge that every choice you make is yours alone. The moon was nearing its zenith and trust seemed a damn thin thing to rely on. She crossed a small hummock, stumbled on the downside, and caught herself short of falling, or turning back to look at the shed a last time. She could not afford to consider what she left behind. The field seemed deeper in the night and the hills kinder—the edges planed clean in silhouette. It was seductive, she thought, this running away. She could just keep going. She watched her feet carefully, stepping clear of the prairie dog holes, through the chewed turf and buckled grasses where elk had rolled out of sleep. Her arms swung at her side and she waded through the knee-high grass. She heard the clatter of Kyle's possessions banging in his back-pack as he raced up from behind.

"You act like it's my fault," he said.

"It is. Surprised?" She struck off toward the road.

He caught up to her, his feet catching in the grass. "How do *you* like it?" he asked.

"I don't know. I haven't been on this end long. Does it scare you? Now that it's me leaving?"

"You going home?"

She stopped. She could see his face in the moonlight, his eyes bright and frightened. She turned away and kept walking. Kyle hesitated and then there was the sound of his feet treading behind her own.

She struck off without direction. They would argue and talk. Perhaps they would walk east, or south to discover what came of the moon's progress. She wondered what they would see, what would become available to them because they'd placed themselves here and now. They'd flush deer whose antlers oriented like a compass against the stars and range behind them to the edges of cities. They'd walk the concrete sidewalks and loiter to hear the street lamps buzzing. Avenues lined in maples, oaks, and weeping birch. There would be homes with dogs yawning on the stoop, doors clamped tight, and hall-ways they didn't know by feel. Where men and women clung to each other, their children spent in fretless sleep under the benediction of gabled roofs. They'd pass like shadows, the city falling behind. Past cemeteries, a march of crosses and stone angels anchored in decline. They'd traverse water and mountains, hillocks of cedar—old-growth groves with hoary skin. And on the downslope where wind shears top-pled trees and lightning forged revelations, they would trace the wood beneath the skin. She would instruct her son—the cambium, the heart wood, the pith, the soul—she would speak as mothers never can and he would understand as sons never have. And in this world, where all things *are* possible, they will turn the corner to find their house, tied to the land, open as they'd left it with the wood shop still redolent of glue and all the clever tools in their ordered place, safe beneath the crown of cottonwoods, beneath the sky, the night suspended.

UNDER THE WHEAT
Rick DeMarinis

DOWN IN D-3 I WATCH THE SKY gunning through the aperture ninety-odd feet above my head. The missiles are ten months away, and I am lying on my back listening to the sump. From the bottom of a hole, where the weather is always the same cool sixty-four degrees, plus or minus two, I like to relax and watch the clouds slide through the circle of blue light. I have plenty of time to kill. The aperture is about fifteen feet wide. About the size of a silver dollar from here. A hawk just drifted by. Eagle. Crow. Small cumulus. Nothing. Nothing. Wrapper.

HOT AGAIN TODAY, and the sky is drifting across the hole, left to right, a slow thick wind that doesn't gust. When it gusts, it's usually from Canada. Fierce, with hail the size of eyeballs. I've seen wheat go down. Acres and acres of useless straw.

But sometimes it comes out of the southeast, from Bismarck, bringing ten-mile-high anvils with it, and you find yourself looking for funnels. This is not tornado country to speak of. The tornado path is to the south and west of here. They walk up from Bismarck and farther south and peter out on the Montana border, rarely touching ground anywhere near this latitude. Still, you keep an eye peeled. I've seen them put down gray fingers to the west, not quite touching but close enough to make you want to find a hole. They say it sounds like freight trains in your yard. I wouldn't know. We are from the coast, where the weather is stable and always predictable because of the ocean. We are trying to adjust.

I MAKE FIVE HUNDRED A WEEK doing this, driving a company pickup from hole to hole, checking out the sump pumps. I've found only one failure in two months. Twenty feet of black water in the hole and rising. It's the company's biggest headache. The high water table of North Dakota. You can dig yourself a shallow hole, come back in a few days and drink. That's why the farmers here have it made. Except for hail. Mostly they are Russians, these farmers.

KAREN WANTS TO GO BACK. I have to remind her it's only for a year. Ten more months. Five hundred a week for a year. But she misses things. The city, her music lessons, movies, the beach, excitement. We live fairly close to a town, but it's one you will never hear of, unless a local goes wild and chainsaws all six members of his family. The movie theater has shown *Bush Pilot*, *Red Skies of Montana*, *Ice Palace*, and *Kon Tiki* so far. These are movies we would not ordinarily pay money to see. She has taken to long walks in the evenings to work out her moods, which are getting harder and harder for me to pretend aren't there. I get time and a half on Saturdays, double time on Sundays and holidays, and thirteen dollars per diem for the inconvenience of relocating all the way from Oxnard, California. That comes to a lot. You don't walk away from a gold mine like that. I try to tell Karen she has to make the effort, adjust. North Dakota isn't all that bad. As a matter of fact I sort of enjoy the area. Maybe I am more adaptable. No, scratch that. I *am* more adaptable. We live close to a large brown lake, an earthfill dam loaded with northern pike. I bought myself a little boat and often go out to troll a bit before the car pool comes by. The freezer is crammed with fish, not one under five pounds.

THERE'S A GHOST TOWN on the other side of the lake. The houses were built for the men who worked on the dam. That was years ago. They are paintless now, weeds up to the rotten sills. No glass in the windows, but here and there a rag of drape. Sometimes I take my boat across the lake to the ghost town. I walk the overgrown streets and look into the windows. Sometimes something moves. Rats. Gophers. Wind. Loose boards. Sometimes nothing.

WHEN THE WEATHER IS OUT OF CANADA you can watch it move south, coming like a giant roll of silver dough on the horizon. It gets bigger fast and then you'd better find cover. If the cloud is curdled underneath, you know it means hail. The wind can gust to one hundred knots. It scares Karen. I tell her there's nothing to worry about. Our trailer is on a good foundation and tied down tight. But she has this dream of being uprooted and flying away in such a wind. She sees her broken body caught in a tree, magpies picking at it. I tell her the trailer will definitely not budge. Still, she gets wild-eyed and can't light a cigarette.

WE'RE SITTING AT THE DINETTE TABLE looking out the window, watching the front arrive. You can feel the trailer bucking like a boat at its moorings. Lightning is stroking the blond fields a mile away. To the southeast, I can see a gray finger reaching down. This is unusual, I admit. But I say nothing to Karen. It looks like the two fronts are going to butt heads straight over the trailer park. It's getting dark fast. Something splits the sky behind the trailer and big hail pours out. The streets of the park are white and jumping under the black sky. Karen has her hands against her ears. There's a stampede on our tin roof. Two TV antennas fold at the same time in a dead faint. A jagged Y of lightning strikes so close you can smell it. Electric steam. Karen is wild, screaming. I can't hear her. Our garbage cans are rising. They float past the windows into a flattened wheat field. This is something. Karen's face is closed. She doesn't enjoy it at all, not at all.

I'M TOOLING AROUND IN THIRD on the usual bad road, enjoying the lurches, rolls, and twists. I would not do this to my own truck. The fields I'm driving through are wasted. Head-on with the sky and the sky never loses. I've passed a few unhappy-looking farmers standing in their fields with their hands in their pockets, spitting, faces frozen in expressions of disgust. Toward D-8, just over a rise and down into a narrow gulch, I find a true glacier. It's made out of hailstones welded together by their own impact. It hasn't begun to melt yet. Four

feet thick and maybe thirty feet long. You could stand on it, blind in
the white glare. You could tell yourself you are inside the Arctic circle. What is this, the return of the Ice Age?

KAREN DID NOT COOK TONIGHT. Another "mood." I poke around
in the fridge. I don't know what to say to her anymore. I know it's
hard. I can understand that. This is not Oxnard. I'll give her that.
I'm the first to admit it. I pop a beer and sit down at the table opposite her. Our eyes don't meet. They haven't for weeks. We are like
two magnetic north poles, repelling each other for invisible reasons.
Last night in bed I touched her. She went stiff. She didn't have to
say a word. I took my hand back. I got the message. There was the
hum of the air conditioner and nothing else. The world could have
been filled with dead bodies. I turned on the lights. She got up and
lit a cigarette after two tries. Nerves. "I'm going for a walk, Lloyd,"
she said, checking the sky. "Maybe we should have a baby?" I said.
"I'm making plenty of money." She looked at me as if I had picked
up an ax.

I WOULD LIKE TO KNOW WHERE she finds to go and what she finds
to do there. She hates the town worse than the trailer park. The trailer
park has a rec hall and a social club for the wives. But she won't take
advantage of that. I know the neighbors are talking. They think she's
a snob. They think I spoil her. After she left I went out on the porch
and drank eleven beers. Let them talk.

THREE FARM KIDS. Just standing outside the locked gate of D-4.
"What do you kids want?" I know what they want. A "look-see."
Security measures are in effect, but what the hell. There is nothing
here yet but a ninety-foot hole with a tarp on it and a sump pump in
the bottom. They are excited when I open the access hatch and invite
them to climb down the narrow steel ladder to the bottom. They want
to know what ICBM stands for. What is a warhead? How fast is it?
How do you know if it's really going to smear the right town? What
if it went straight up and came straight down? Can you hit the moon?

"Look at the sky up there, kids," I tell them. "Lie on your backs, like this, and after a while you sort of get the feeling you're looking *down,* from on top of it." The kids lie down on the concrete. Kids have a way of giving all their attention to something interesting. I swear them to secrecy, not for my protection, because who cares, but because it will make their day. They will run home, busting with secret info. I drive off to D-9, where the sump trouble was.

CAUGHT THREE LUNKERS THIS MORNING. All over twenty-four inches. It's 7:00 A.M. now and I'm on Ruby Street, the ghost town. The streets are all named after stones. Why, I don't know. This is nothing like anything we have on the coast. Karen doesn't like the climate or the people and the flat sky presses down on her from all sides and gives her bad dreams, sleeping and awake. But what can I do?

I'M ON ONYX STREET, NUMBER 49, a two-bedroom bungalow with a few pieces of furniture left in it. There is a chest of drawers in the bed-room, a bed with a rotten gray mattress. There is a closet with a raggedy slip in it. The slip has brown water stains that look like burns. In the bottom of the chest is a magazine, yellow with age. *Secret Confessions.* I can imagine the woman who lived here with her husband. Not much like Karen at all. But what did she do while her husband was off working on the dam? Did she stand at this window in her slip and wish she were back in Oxnard? Did she cry her eyes out on this bed and think crazy thoughts? Where is she now? Does she think, "This is July 15, 1962, and I am glad I am not in North Dakota any-more"? Did she take long walks at night and not cook? I have an impulse to do something odd, and do it.

WHEN A THUNDERHEAD PASSES OVER a cyclone fence that sur-rounds a site, such as the one passing over D-6 now, you can hear the wire hiss with nervous electrons. It scares me because the fence is a perfect lightning rod, a good conductor. But I stay on my toes. Some-times, when a big cumulus is overhead stroking the area and roaring, I'll just stay put in my truck until it's had its fun.

BECAUSE THIS IS SUNDAY, I am making better than twelve dollars an hour. I'm driving through a small farming community called Space-bow. A Russian word, I think, because you're supposed to pronounce the *e*. No one I know does. Shade trees on every street. A Russian church here, a grain elevator there. No wind. Hot for 9:00 A.M. Men dressed in Sunday black. Ladies in their best. Kids looking uncomfortable and controlled. Even the dogs are behaving. There is a woman, manless I think, because I've seen her before, always alone on her porch, eyes on something far away. A "thinker." Before today I've only waved hello. First one finger off the wheel, nod, then around the block once again and the whole hand out the window and a smile. That was last week. After the first turn past her place today she waves back. A weak hand at first, as if she's not sure that's what I meant. But after a few times around the block she knows that's what I meant. And so I'm stopping. I'm going to ask for a cup of cold water. I'm thirsty anyway. Maybe all this sounds hokey to you if you're from some big town like Oxnard, but this is not a big town like Oxnard.

HER NAME IS MYRNA DAN. That last name must be a pruned-down version of Danielovitch or something because the people here are mostly Russians. She is thirty-two, a widow, one brat. A two-year-old named "Piper," crusty with food. She owns a small farm here but there is no one to work it. She has a decent allotment from the U.S. Government and a vegetable garden. If you are from the coast you would not stop what you were doing to look at her. Her hands are square and the fingers stubby, made for rough wooden handles. Hips like gateposts.

NO SUPPER AGAIN. Karen left a note. "Lloyd, I am going for a walk. There are some cold cuts in the fridge." It wasn't even signed. Just like that. One of these days on one of her walks she is going to get caught by the sky which can change on you in a minute.

BILL FINKEL MADE A REMARK on the way to the dispatch center. It was a little personal and coming from anybody else I would have called him on it. But he is the lead engineer, the boss. A few of the other guys grinned behind their hands. How do I know where she goes or why? I am not a swami. If it settles her nerves, why should I push it? I've thought of sending her to Ventura to live with her mother for a while, but her mother is getting senile and has taken to writing mean letters. I tell Karen the old lady is around the bend, don't take those letters too seriously. But what's the use when the letters come in like clockwork, once a week, page after page of nasty accusations in a big, inch-high scrawl, like a kid's, naming things that never happened. Karen takes it hard, no matter what I say, as if what the old lady says is true.

SPACEBOW LOOKS DESERTED. It isn't. The men are off in the fields, the women are inside working toward evening. Too hot outside even for the dogs, who are sleeping under the porches. Ninety-nine. I stop for water at Myrna's. Do you want to see a missile silo? Sure, she says, goddamn right, just like that. I have an extra hard hat in the truck but she doesn't have to wear it if she doesn't want to. Regulations at this stage of the program are a little pointless. Just a hole with a sump in it. Of course you can fall into it and get yourself killed. That's about the only danger. But there are no regulations that can save you from your own stupidity. Last winter when these holes were being dug, a kid walked out on a tarp. The tarp was covered with light snow and he couldn't tell where the ground ended and the hole began. He dropped the whole ninety feet and his hard hat did not save his ass. Myrna is impressed with this story. She is very anxious to see one. D-7 is closest to Spacebow, only a mile out of town. It isn't on my schedule today, but so what. I hand her the orange hard hat. She has trouble with the strap. I help her cinch it. Piper wants to wear it too and grabs at the straps, whining. Myrna has big jaws. Strong. But not in an ugly way.

I tell her the story about Jack Stern, the Jewish quality-control man from St. Louis who took flying lessons because he wanted to be able to get to a decent-sized city in a hurry whenever he felt the need. This flat, empty farmland made his ulcer flare. He didn't know how to drive a car, and yet there he was tearing around the sky in a Bonanza. One day he flew into a giant hammerhead—thinking, I guess, that a cloud like that is nothing but a lot of water vapor, no matter what shape it has or how big—and was never heard from again. That cloud ate him and the Bonanza. At the airport in Minot they picked up two words on the emergency frequency, "Oh no," then static.

I tell her the story about the motor pool secretary who shot her husband once in the neck and twice in the foot with a target pistol while he slept. Both of them pulling down good money, too. I tell her the one about the one that got away. A northern big as a shark. Pulled me and my boat a mile before my twelve-pound-test monofilament snapped. She gives me a sidelong glance and makes a buzzing sound as if to say, *That* one takes the cake, Mister! We are on the bottom of D-7, watching the circle of sky, lying on our backs.

THE TRAILER *STINKS*. I could smell it from the street as soon as I got out of Bill Finkel's car. Fish heads. *Heads!* I guess they've been sitting there like that most of the afternoon. Just the big alligator jaws of my big beautiful pikes, but not the bodies. A platter of them, uncooked, drying out, and getting high. Knife, fork, napkin, glass. I'd like to know what goes on inside her head, what passes for thinking in there. The note: "Lloyd, eat your fill." Not signed. Is this supposed to be humor? I fail to get the point of it. I have to carry the mess to the garbage cans without breathing. A big white fire is blazing in the sky over my shoulder. You can hear the far-off rumble, like a whale grunting. I squint west, checking for funnels.

TROUBLE IN D-7. Busted sump. I pick up Myrna and Piper and head for the hole. It's a nice day for a drive. It could be a bearing seizure, but that's only a percentage guess. I unlock the gate and we drive to the edge of it. Space-age artillery, I explain, as we stand on the lip of D-7, feeling the vertigo. The tarp is off for maintenance and the hole is solid black. If you let your imagination run, you might see it as bottomless. The "Pit" itself. Myrna is holding Piper back. Piper is whining, she wants to see the hole, Myrna has to slap her away, scolding. I drain my beer and let the can drop. I don't hear it hit. Not even a splash. I grab the fussing kid and hold her out over the hole. "Have yourself a *good* look, brat," I say. I hold her by the ankle with one hand. She is paralyzed. Myrna goes so white I have to smile. "Oh, wait," she says. "Please, Lloyd. No." As if I ever would.

MYRNA WANTS TO SEE THE D-FLIGHT CONTROL CENTER. I ask her if she has claustrophobia. She laughs, but it's no joke. That far below the surface inside that capsule behind an eight-ton door can be upsetting if you are susceptible to confinement. The elevator is slow and heavy, designed to haul equipment. The door opens on a dimly lit room. Spooky. There's crated gear scattered around. And there is the door, one yard thick to withstand the shock waves from the Bomb. I wheel it open. Piper whines, her big eyes distrustful of me now. There is a musty smell in the dank air. The lights and blower are on now, but it will take a while for the air to freshen itself up. I wheel the big door shut. It can't latch yet, but Myrna is impressed. I explain to her what goes on in here. We sit down at the console. I show her where the launch-enabling switches will be and why it will take two people together to launch an attack, the chairs fifteen feet apart and both switches turned for a several-second count before the firing sequence can start, in case one guy goes berserk and decides to end the world because his old lady has been holding out on him, or just for the hell of it, given human nature. I show her the escape hole. It's loaded with ordinary sand. You just pull this chain and the sand dumps into the capsule. Then you climb up the tube that held the sand into someone's wheat field. I show her the toilet and the little kitchen. I can see there is something on her mind. Isolated places make you think weird things. It's happened to me more than once. Not here, but in the ghost town on the other side of the lake.

TOPSIDE THE WEATHER HAS CHANGED. The sky is the color of pike-belly, wind rising from the southeast. To the west I can see stubby funnels pushing down from the overcast, but only so far. It looks like the clouds are growing roots. We have to run back to the truck in the rain, Piper screaming on Myrna's hip. A heavy bolt strikes less than a mile away. A blue fireball sizzles where it hits. Smell the ozone. It makes me sneeze.

THIS IS THE SECOND DAY she's been gone. I don't know where or how. All her clothes are here. She doesn't have any money. I don't know what to do. There is no police station. Do I call her mother? Do I notify the FBI? The highway patrol? Bill Finkel?

EVERYBODY IN THE CAR POOL KNOWS but won't say a word, out of respect for my feelings. Bill Finkel has other things on his mind. He is worried about rumored economy measures in the assembly and check-out program next year. It has nothing to do with me. My job ends before that phase begins. I guess she went back to Oxnard, or maybe Ventura. But how?

WE ARE IN THE D-FLIGHT CONTROL CENTER. Myrna, with her hard hat cocked to one side, wants to fool around with the incomplete equipment. Piper is with her grandma. We are seated at the control console and she is pretending to work her switch. She has me pretend to work my switch. She wants to launch the entire flight of missiles, D-1 through D-10, at Cuba or Panama. Why Cuba and Panama? I ask. What about Russia? Why not Cuba or Panama? she says. Besides, I have Russian blood. Everyone around here has Russian blood. No, it's Cuba and Panama. Just think of the looks on their faces. All those people lying in the sun on the decks of those big white holiday boats, the coolies out in the cane fields, the tinhorn generals, the whole shiteree. They'll look up trying to shade their eyes but they won't be able to. What in hell is this all about they'll say, then *zap*, poof, *gone*.

I feel it too, craziness like hers. What if I couldn't get that eight-ton door open, Myrna? I see her hard hat wobble, her lip drop. What if? Just what *if*? She puts her arms around me and our hard hats click. She is one strong woman.

Lloyd, Lloyd, she says.

Yo.

Jesus.

Easy.

Lloyd!

Bingo.

It's good down here—no *rules*—and she goes berserk. But later she is calm and up to mischief again. I recognize the look now. Okay, I tell her. What *next*, Myrna? She wants to do something halfway nasty. This, believe me, does not surprise me at all.

I'm sitting on the steel floor listening to the blower and waiting for Myrna to finish her business. I'm trying hard to picture what the weather is doing topside. It's not easy to do. It could be clear and calm and blue or it could be wild. There could be a high, thin overcast or there could be nothing. You can't know when you're this far under the wheat. I can hear her trying to work the little chrome lever, even though I told her there's no plumbing yet. Some maintenance yokel is going to find Myrna's "surprise." She comes out, pretending to be sheepish, but I can see that the little joke tickles her.

SOMETHING TAKES MY HOOK and strips off ten yards of line then stops dead. Snag. I reel in. The pole is bent double and the line is singing. Then something lets go but it isn't the line because I'm still snagged. It breaks the surface, a lady's shoe. It's brown and white with a short heel. I toss it into the bottom of the boat. The water is shallow here, and clear. There's something dark and wide under me like a shadow on the water. An old farmhouse, submerged when the dam filled. There's a deep current around the structure. I can see fence, tires, an old truck, feed pens. There is a fat farmer in the yard staring up at me, checking the weather. I jump away from him, almost tipping the boat. *I am not the weather!* I want to say. My heart feels tangled in my ribs. But it's only a stump with arms.

The current takes my boat in easy circles. A swimmer would be in serious trouble. I crank up the engine and head back. No fish today. So be it. Sometimes you come home empty-handed. The shoe is new, stylish, and was made in Spain.

I'M STANDING ON THE BUCKLED PORCH of 49 Onyx Street. Myrna is inside reading *Secret Confessions:* "What My Don Must Never Know." The sky is bad. The lake is bad. It will be a while before we can cross back. I knock on the door, as we planned. Myrna is on the bed in the stained, raggedy slip, giggling. "Listen to this dogshit, Lloyd," she says. But I'm not in the mood for weird stories. "I brought you something, honey," I say. She looks at the soggy shoe. "That?" But she agrees to try it on, anyway. I feel like my own ghost, bumping into the familiar but run-down walls of my old house in the middle of nowhere, and I remember my hatred of it. "Hurry up," I say, my voice true as a razor.

A THICK TUBE HAIRY WITH RAIN is snaking out of the sky less than a mile away. Is it going to touch? "They never do, Lloyd. This isn't Kansas. Will you please listen to this dogshit?" Something about a pregnant high school girl, Dee, locked in a toilet with a knitting needle. Something about this Don who believes in purity. Something about bright red blood. Something about ministers and mothers and old-fashioned shame. I'm not listening, even when Dee slides the big needle in. I have to keep watch on the sky, because there is a first time for everything, even if this is not Kansas. The wind is stripping shingles from every roof I see. A long board is spinning like a slow propeller. The funnel is behind a bluff, holding back. But I can hear it, the freight train. Myrna is standing behind me running a knuckle up and down my back. "Hi, darling," she says. "Want to know what I did while you were out working on the dam today?" The dark tube has begun to move out from behind the bluff, but I'm not sure which way. "Tell me," I say. "Tell me."

Blue Waltz with Coyotes
Jeanne Dixon

BEFORE MY BROTHER WAS BORN, Dad promised that if I didn't like the baby we could throw him to the coyotes. I didn't like him. Billy Lee was always wet, he smelled bad, and he got more than his share of attention. By the time he was four he hadn't improved. He still didn't talk. "He don't have to talk," Mom said. "He rolls those big brown eyes of his, and wraps you 'round his finger." Not me, he didn't. I held out for coyotes.

My dad had gone back on his word to the point that when we were ready to move away from the Two Medicine (where we had *plenty* of coyotes, coyotes that left bloody and mutilated sheep carcasses littered across the plains) and moved to a ranch near Columbia Falls, loading all our household belongings into an old '36 Dodge truck with a cattle rack to contain everything, Billy Lee went along.

And I didn't like him any better on the west side than I had on the eastern slope of the mountains. We still had plenty of coyotes. "Nope," Dad said, hunkering down and stroking his chin, the way he did when he had bad news to deliver, "you're growing up. Eight years old is too old to keep fretting about a little brother. Try to get along . . . find something else to occupy your mind."

Most of that summer I didn't have time to think about coyotes; I had to help Mom and neighbor women cook for farm crews. I pumped hundreds of buckets of water to carry to the house, hauled in that many armloads of firewood for the black iron Monarch. I caught fryers, chopped their heads off, scalded them, plucked them, drew them; the women fried them in sizzling fat in black iron skillets. Heat swamped us: meat roasting, baking, stewing; vegetables at the boil; biscuits baking, or white bread, corn bread. And desserts: ice cream to crank in the maker, berries to pick for pies; cakes, gingerbread, cinnamon rolls, strudel rising in the swelter. Tempers flared. Big Anna Anderson, with her baby-fine hair, spattered glasses, and ragged apron always complaining. Bossy Krissi Olmstead, always scolding: "Whad ya go an' do it *that* way for? I told ya, and told ya . . . for gosh sakes!" She'd grab the peeler out of my hand, make potato peels fly like a January blizzard through the hot, unbearable steam of the kitchen. If we opened the door, flies swarmed in. Clouds of flies attacked us, biting our necks, arms, faces. They clamped themselves to our sticky skin like carpet.

While I worked in the kitchen, Billy Lee played in the shade with his dump trucks, or took his nap, or rode into town with Dad to pick up parts for the mower. At the end of haying, Anna Anderson gave him a nickel for being so good. She gave my mother and the other women each a big bottle of Blue Waltz perfume from Woolworth's, a heady concoction of floral scents blended with musk, possibly, or civet. It came in a thick bottle of deepest blue, a gold cap, glass wand, and stopper. Mom said she didn't particularly care for it, that I was welcome to hers; but Anna's leaving me out the way she did stirred up hurt feelings. I thought long and deep about coyotes.

Up in the piney bluffs behind the woods where the aluminum plant would go in one day, coyotes yapped and howled. We had to put the chickens in at night, drive the lambs back into the shed. We found fresh tracks around the farm, but the coyotes seemed content to thrive on what they hunted in the red rock ledges, for they never bothered our stock. The day I got left out of the big perfume giveaway, I decided I'd go and bother them—Billy Lee included.

WHILE MOM AND DAD SLEPT on a blanket under the tree, I told Billy Lee we could play a new game: Party. First we would have to dress up. I doused us both with Blue Waltz, then led him up the ladder to a storage place across from the haymow in the barn. In the musty dark, among spiders, mice, secret packets of dynamite, binder twine, tire chains rusting in a corner, *Rangeland Romance* (with pictures of grown-ups hugging and kissing), we hauled Mom's old rag bag from under a horse collar, opened it up. Long-legged underwear, an Oriental parasol, ostrich plume hat, a Queen Victoria bustled gown, strings of beads, corsets with stays, a whirl-away cape of yellow silk, lace-net petticoats that rustled when we held them up to study them. Billy Lee stuck an enormous brassiere on top of his head. It flopped over his ears like two huge cones. He tied it under his chin.

We laughed.

He skinnied out of his overalls, shirt, shoes, socks. Out of the wealth we had to choose from, he chose a gray shantung dress that looked like Anna Anderson, a multilayered lace-net petticoat over the dress, laddered silk stockings up his arms like long gloves, a string of glass beads that swung to his middle.

I pulled the Queen Victoria velvet over my jeans, pulled a floppy boned corset over the dress, donned the ostrich plume hat, and tied the yellow silk cape around my neck for final effect. We chose high-heeled pumps, mine with jeweled buckles, his with bows. Reeking of mothballs and the floral perfume, we climbed down the ladder, rung by rung. "Careful," I warned him, sweetly, "don't you fall," and we went through the barn, out the back where the cows came in, out into the long summer twilight. Sky and grass had turned the same shade of yellow as the cape on my shoulders. Yellow coulees rose around us, leading us away from the house, out toward the gully, the alkali plain, the long, dark shadow of the mountain. Coyotes. We lifted our skirts over cow pies, dragged them through harsh yellow grass, into the cool yellow wind.

I yapped, three quick barks, a long howl.

A coyote answered.

Billy Lee yapped.

We both yapped.

The breeze grew stronger, cooler, as we moved up the coulee. It caught our veils and billowed our skirts, rattled corset stays and beads, tugged at the yellow cape as we stumbled along in our awkward shoes. Billy Lee tripped and fell; the brassiere flopped one cone over his face. I laughed, loud. He got up, stickers in his foot, looked about to cry, laughed instead. We both shrieked with false laughter, and over the top of a coulee, looking down at us, we saw the silhouette of a coyote. He had drawn his lips back to fangs, he peered down at us through yellow slit eyes, and his sleek body looked rigid as a black paper cutout. My skin, lungs, guts turned to ice. "Come on," I said to Billy Lee, taking his stocking-clad arm, "he won't hurt us."

The coyote disappeared, and the earth cooled in the yellow wind. Billy Lee and I proceeded up the coulee, over the stony ridge, down into a boulder-strewn gully and an ancient streambed. Shadows stirred in the grass, a pheasant flew up, beating the air, squawking. Billy Lee stopped, turned to me. I said, "It's okay, everything's fine." And a coyote sprang out from behind a rock. It flew straight up into the air, jaws open, teeth flashing. It came down in the tussocks of grass, tail between its legs, yipping, yapping. Two more appeared on the ridgeline—the three dashed away. We were close, I thought, to what we had come for.

Down in the gully no air stirred.

Shades of unspeakable vicious things slid across the ground in big, black shapes. Yellow sky turned a yellow-gray; I took Billy Lee's stockinged hand. "Let's dance," I said, shrill with the knowledge of what I was doing. "Like grown-ups," I said.

He bowed deeply, cones flapping at his ears. I curtsied in my velvet, ostrich plume, my stays. Another coyote sprang up, up into the yellow air, all four legs splayed. It yapped, landed in the grass, bounded off, and we chased it. Three others came down from the ridge at the far end of the gully. They raced along in the twilight, a single swath of gray silk, their feet skimming the ground, nose to tail, attached like a single fur neckpiece women wore in those days to the movies, silent.

Billy Lee and I ducked behind a rock. As the line of coyotes rushed past us, we jumped out at them, yipping and barking. They whirled so fast their tails curved around them, and they sprang straight up, barking like our imitation of them. They laughed, chuckled, howled. We chased after them, our skirts held high, my yellow silk flaring out in the falling light. Billy Lee's petticoats lofting about him like sails. He tripped and fell.

One of the coyotes ran back to him.

"No!" I shouted, as if to a dog. "No, go away!"

The coyote pushed the fallen Billy Lee with her nose. Billy Lee got up. The coyote waited, patient, ears twitching forward and back like a mother dog with her pup. She lay down on the grass in front of him, head flat to the ground, ears down, tail swaying gently in the grass. "She likes you," I said. "She does, she really does like you."

Billy Lee put his feet back into the high-heeled pumps with bows, and he did a pirouette in his foolish dress. The coyote danced away, looked back over her shoulder, woofed, trotted ahead, stopped and looked back. She wanted us to go with her, and we went.

Once out of the gully, we danced on an alkali plain in moonlight, the white-poison ground baked hard as a dance floor. Reeking with perfume, we bowed to the coyotes, curtsied. We took hands and whirled around in an allemande-left, a do-si-so, in our too-big shoes, our silks and our plumes. We honored our corners, the watching coyotes, and we danced in the darkening winds as the wild creatures danced with us, coyotes darting in and out, weaving a mystery of wilderness, and easing the hatreds, the violence, all those hard forbidden thoughts that plague us—eased them as wild things always ease heartache.

REAL INDIANS
Debra Magpie Earling

1. BLOOD BROTHERS

We weren't real Indians. We were half of a half breed. We were half of a half of an Indian, but we were enrolled members. We'd carry our cards around in the hidden folds of our wallets, behind the credit card slots, cards that said we were bona fide, genuine, the real deals. In high school we used to carry our cards in our back pockets like loose change. Card-carrying members of the Confederated Salish and Kootenai Tribes. But the Indians didn't buy it. We'd flash those real big Indians our cards when they would threaten us with broken bottles, and they'd look at us, reeling in their drunken stupors, in their alcohol vapors that like near killed us, but most times when asked we'd say naw we weren't. Hell no. And we'd get into fights a lot, the Indians saying we weren't Indians unless they wanted our change, and the whites saying we were Indians until per capita rolled around.

2. SLOW DAYS

One time we were bumming change for cigarettes outside of the Town Pump in Ronan and Kootenai George walks by. My man, my brother says to old George, my man we're looking for a little change brother. Kootenai George tilted his head back squinting, looking at us. No brother of mine, he says, and that's when Jay pulls out his card. Look here, he says. And George, he grabs both of our cards, and looks down at our pictures and then looks back at us, grinning. Jokes, old George says then, and tosses the cards over his shoulder.

3. BAR MEMORIES

My brother and me would sit around the bar at the Ponderay with the white store owners in Polson and we'd run the Indians down. Sons of bitches, we'd say, "wanting to tell us what to do." Damn dumb Indians we'd say to the white bastards. And the old white bastards would timber the house, and we'd drink 'til closing. We'd drink until we were Indians.

4. HITCHHIKING THE BIG SKY

Late at night we'd stumble on past the shining lake with our thumbs held high into the glaring summer traffic and those people would pick us up sometimes. And we'd be what they wanted us to be, we'd be the lost tribe, we'd be the Mexican cherry pickers, we'd be the bored sons home for vacation. And no matter what we'd say those people would believe us. One middle-aged couple in a fading Cadillac, an old El Dorado with rattling doors trying to be something they wasn't too, picked us up at the South Shore around midnight. The wife turns around to look at us closely. You say you're Indians, she said. I don't believe I've ever seen blue-eyed Indians. Oh yeh, Jay told her. Most of us Indians are blue-eyed these days. But my dad, he says, my dad was Jay Silver Heels. Maybe you heard of him, he says. And that woman crooked her neck round to take a good look at us. She snapped on the overhead and took a good long look. You don't say, she says, her hair three times the size of her head, and she had that old lady smell about her, ten years of hair spray and Ambush. That's where I get my name, Jay. He pulled out his card to show her and she nodded impressed. A card always impresses them. Tourists understand laminated cards. They understand credit. She pulls out her half-moon glasses and hums at him. But your last name isn't Silver Heels, she says. Hell no, Jay says to her, you can't just go giving away a name like Silver Heels, he says. No a name like Silver Heels gotta be earned. A load short, the caddie daddy says, I guess that makes you just a heel, he grins thinking he's funny now too. You wouldn't have had to tell me, the woman says, I can see Indian in your cheekbones. Jay turns his head so she can have a better look. You've got the high Indian cheekbones, she says.

5. GUARDING THE SECRETS

The husband cranes his neck to look at us. He snorts. Tell us some of those old Indian stories he says, rubbing his fat head. I can't tell those stories, my brother says. The tribe doesn't like it when I tell our old stories. Anthropologists ripped our stories off years ago, he says. We keep them to ourselves now. Sure you do, the man said. You could tell he thought Jay was lying. Jay grabs the back of the leather seat and pulled himself closer to them. He starts pointing. Over there, he says, we fought the Battle of the Lefthands. Four hundred women raped and slaughtered beneath the waving Calvary flag in 1852. And over there's where we signed the treaty of Indian Buffalo Skull. The moon's full tonight, my brother says, grinning at the woman who now seems a little more interested in him than she should be.

6. INDIAN TRADITION

One story I will tell, my brother says, because you're being so nice to us, and he slips his hand behind the woman's back, and I can see him working her neck just a little with his thumb, and she's leaning into him and humming sweet. They say you can still see the face of those lovers if you look into the full moon on a night like tonight, he tells her. But you have to have a pure heart to see them. It takes a pure heart to be seeing shit like that. Husband turns around quick and gives my brother a can't-you-see-you're-talking-to-a-lady look. Pardon my French, Jay says to the man. We're related to the Dupuis. Wife tilts her head then looking at the moon. I think I can see their faces, the woman starts saying. Yes, yes I can. Just right up there where the shadow curves. It looks like a man's nose, and there are her eyes, she says too eager. My brother continues with his story. The two of them were from two different tribes, he says, Running Bear and Little White Dove. Running Bear loved Little White Dove with a love big as the sky, with a love that wouldn't die. The man pulls his car over then in the spit of gravel but my brother keeps talking. They drowned themselves in the Flathead River because their tribes warred with each other, and their love could never be. I'm cracking up then, and that plaque-haired woman is leaning toward the windshield looking at the moon and thinking of my brother. End of the road fellas, the fat head says. It was just getting interesting, Ma Cadillac says to him. And he shoots back, yeh well, we wasn't born yesterday. Out. It was a good ride up to then even if the old woman did stink.

7. NOWHERE TO GO BUT DOWN

We go into the Conoco after a long night of carousing. We're too old for this shit now but we've been walking since Arlee and even Ravalli looks good. The Buffalo is closed so we decide to stop in for a beer at the all-night gas station. And that's where our trouble starts, not scrapping with a couple Indians calling us white as suyapis, not anything like that. I didn't know how the world could change in one fluorescent bulb flicker with nothing going on at all and I mean nothing. When you walk into trouble like that you don't know it's coming. You don't see it like a movie or anything like that. No music will be thrumming like your heartbeat. You just walk in and the shit hits the fan. I don't know why we didn't notice the old woman tied to the chair first. When we did spot her, her hands were tied behind her back like spoiled meat. Her blouse was ripped off her shoulders and one of her breasts was white and plump and hanging out of her shirt. And I looked at her for a long time, duct tape wrapped round and round her face. I stared at that one big tit and thought I could see back to the time she was pretty.

8. HORN OF PLENTY

My brother was stopped then. He kept saying shit, oh shit because he wasn't looking at the woman; he was looking at the maw of the cash register, wide open with the bills half-hanging out. Big bills too, and coins scattered everywhere, in beef jerky lids, in the peanut box, silver coins littered the splintered wood floor, and he was scooping those coins up with both hands and stuffing his pockets. I was the dimwit gaping, looking at an old woman's tit. I was just standing there jolted by the sight of her when Jay slapped the back of my head. Grab the cash ape shit, he says, grab the cash. I step toward the cash register, one step closer to the woman. Blood's trickling past my boot heel, and every step makes a sound in her sticky blood like ripping tape. That's when her head flings back and we hear the gurgle in her throat and nothing then but the Statler Brothers static on her radio. I lean over the counter pulling thick stacks of bills all the while looking at the woman. I look at her thick ankles bound to the legs of the chair. Think what a piss poor way to die so close to dying anyway while I'm stuffing bills into my pants. My brother's grabbing a six pack of fancy beer and then we're out the door and the night air is so cool and sweet I'm smelling the stink of her blood in my nostrils and I'm running and we're running together. Woowee brother, Jay yells, to the night, we're wild Indians now. We're damn desperadoes.

9. Deer Lodge

We climb the fence at the buffalo range; we're running to Moiese. And we're so damn crazy, the blood is ticking in our ears, the weeds are flying by us, the Indian moon is white and round and resting on our shoulders. We're running warriors carrying the weight of a hundred battle moons, running from the 1852 Lefthand Battle. We could be the white Calvary soldiers too. Because we're Indian and we're not Indian, the hi-bred of Manifest Destiny my brother called us once, and if we don't run fast enough we'll be able to tell all those nonbelieving Indian fuckers we live in the oldest Indian encampment in the West. We live at Deer Lodge we'll say lifting our pen-ink tattooed fists.

10. Night Buffalo

We don't see the herd, well we do, but we don't. We hear them first. We see the hind leg of the bull tossing his head, and the moon lights his breath, and the breath of a hundred buffalo snorts are rising around us, and the winded night has gone still. And the bull paws the ground. I can hear the pop of small stones crunching under hooves the size of my brother's skull. The ground begins to rumble. You never felt rumbling like that, an earth quaking rumble that's shaking the ground so hard your knees are gumby rubber, and running's like a circus ride. You have to hold out your arms just to balance yourself. My brother's clutching that six pack to his chest like a football and his left arm is out and he's running through the herd, switchbacking. The whole herd's forgotten me. The whole fucking bison range is snorting after my crazy brother. They're beating the ground behind him and he's running good. I see the flap of his shirt tail behind him. He's making a go for it and the herd's at his grass-swiping heels with the big one in front right behind him. I see the great head of the buffalo tossed down, clipping Jay's skinny ass, and as the big buffalo head lifts in the wind singing run the world goes slow. The black horn of the bull is suddenly shining in moonlight. And I'm looking at that bull horn and all of a sudden thinking about gunpowder horns in the hands of Indians, and I see my brother's shirt ripping first and I hear the horn as it enters his backbone, it pops and then makes a thick slurping noise like a hunting knife stabbing a red rump roast.

11. Indian Legend

I see my brother lifted high in the night and for a moment he is a silhouette in the moon, but not like the silhouette of those old Indian lovers you're supposed to see in the moon on a moonlit night, no. My brother's lifting his hand to the wide open sky, and I'm already thinking the next time I see a full moon I'll tell the legend of my brother so he'll long be remembered around here as the last, best Indian.

12. The End of the Trail

When the moon rises full, you'll be seeing his face on its surface, emblazoned for all time, even when there are no more Indians, even when the last and only Indian has long since packed his last kinnikinnick pipe forever and has blown his last Indian breath to silver heaven.

GREAT FALLS
Richard Ford

THIS IS NOT A HAPPY STORY. I warn you.

My father was a man named Jack Russell, and when I was a young boy in my early teens, we lived with my mother in a house to the east of Great Falls, Montana, near the small town of Highwood and the Highwood Mountains and the Missouri River. It is a flat, tree-less benchland there, all of it used for wheat farming, though my father was never a farmer, but was brought up near Tacoma, Wash-ington, in a family that worked for Boeing.

He—my father—had been an Air Force sergeant and had taken his discharge in Great Falls. And instead of going home to Tacoma, where my mother wanted to go, he had taken a civilian's job with the Air Force, working on planes, which was what he liked to do. And he had rented the house out of town from a farmer who did not want it left standing empty.

The house itself is gone now—I have been to the spot. But the double row of Russian olive trees and two of the outbuildings are still standing in the milkweeds. It was a plain, two-story house with a porch on the front and no place for the cars. At the time, I rode the school bus to Great Falls every morning, and my father drove in while my mother stayed home.

My mother was a tall pretty woman, thin, with black hair and slightly sharp features that made her seem to smile when she wasn't smiling. She had grown up in Wallace, Idaho, and gone to college a year in Spokane, then moved out to the coast, which is where she met Jack Russell. She was two years older than he was, and married him, she said to me, because he was young and wonderful looking, and because she thought they could leave the sticks and see the world together—which I suppose they did for a while. That was the life she wanted, even before she knew much about wanting anything else or about the future.

When my father wasn't working on airplanes, he was going hunting or fishing, two things he could do as well as anyone. He had learned to fish, he said, in Iceland, and to hunt ducks up on the DEW line—stations he had visited in the Air Force. And during the time of this—it was 1960—he began to take me with him on what he called his "expeditions." I thought even then, with as little as I knew, that these were opportunities other boys would dream of having but probably never would. And I don't think that I was wrong in that.

It is a true thing that my father did not know limits. In the spring, when we would go east to the Judith River Basin and camp up on the banks, he would catch a hundred fish in a weekend, and sometimes more than that. It was all he did from morning until night, and it was never hard for him. He used yellow corn kernels stacked onto a #4 snelled hook, and he would rattle this rig-up along the bottom of a deep pool below a split-shot sinker, and catch fish. And most of the time, because he knew the Judith River and knew how to feel his bait down deep, he could catch fish of good size.

It was the same with ducks, the other thing he liked. When the northern birds were down, usually by mid-October, he would take me and we would build a cattail and wheat-straw blind on one of the tule ponds or sloughs he knew about down the Missouri, where the water was shallow enough to wade. We would set out his decoys to the leeward side of our blind, and he would sprinkle corn on a hunger-line from the decoys to where we were. In the evenings when he came home from the base, we would go and sit out in the blind until the roosting flights came and put down among the decoys— there was never calling involved. And after a while, sometimes it would be an hour and full dark, the ducks would find the corn, and the whole raft of them—sixty, sometimes—would swim in to us. At the moment he judged they were close enough, my father would say to me, "Shine, Jackie," and I would stand and shine a seal-beam car light out onto the pond, and he would stand up beside me and shoot all the ducks that were there, on the water if he could, but flying and getting up as well. He owned a Model 11 Remington with a long-tube magazine that would hold ten shells, and with that many, and shooting straight over the surface rather than down onto it, he could kill or wound thirty ducks in twenty seconds' time. I remember distinctly the report of that gun and the flash of it over the water into the dark air, one shot after another, not even so fast, but measured in a way to hit as many as he could.

What my father did with the ducks he killed, and the fish, too, was sell them. It was against the law then to sell wild game, and it is against the law now. And though he kept some for us, most he would take—his fish laid on ice, or his ducks still wet and bagged in the burlap corn sacks—down to the Great Northern Hotel, which was still open then on Second Street in Great Falls, and sell them to the Negro caterer who bought them for his wealthy customers and for the dining car passengers who came through. We would drive in my father's Plymouth to the back of the hotel—always this was after dark—to a concrete loading ramp and lighted door that were close enough to the yards that I could sometimes see passenger trains waiting at the station, their car lights yellow and warm inside, the passengers dressed in suits, all bound for someplace far away from Montana—Milwaukee or Chicago or New York City, unimaginable places to me, a boy fourteen years old, with my father in the cold dark selling illegal game.

The caterer was a tall, stooped-back man in a white jacket, who my father called "Professor Ducks" or "Professor Fish," and the Professor referred to my father as "Sarge." He paid a quarter per pound for trout, a dime for whitefish, a dollar for a mallard duck, two for a speckle or a blue goose, and four dollars for a Canada. I have been with my father when he took away a hundred dollars for fish he'd caught and, in the fall, more than that for ducks and geese. When he had sold game in that way, we would drive out 10th Avenue and stop at a bar called The Mermaid that was by the air base, and he would drink with some friends he knew there, and they would laugh about hunting and fishing while I played pinball and wasted money in the jukebox.

It was on such a night as this that the unhappy things came about. It was in late October. I remember the time because Halloween had not been yet, and in the windows of the houses that I passed every day on the bus to Great Falls, people had put pumpkin lanterns, and set scarecrows in their yards in chairs.

My father and I had been shooting ducks in a slough on the Smith River, upstream from where it enters on the Missouri. He had killed thirty ducks, and we'd driven them down to the Great Northern and sold them there, though my father had kept two back in his corn sack. And when we had driven away, he suddenly said, "Jackie, let's us go back home tonight. Who cares about those hard-dicks at The Mermaid. I'll cook these ducks on the grill. We'll do something different tonight." He smiled at me in an odd way. This was not a thing he usually said, or the way he usually talked. He liked The Mermaid, and my mother— as far as I knew—didn't mind it if he went there.

"That sounds good," I said.

"We'll surprise your mother," he said. "We'll make her happy."

We drove out past the air base on Highway 87, past where there were planes taking off into the night. The darkness was dotted by the green and red beacons, and the tower light swept the sky and trapped planes as they disappeared over the flat landscape toward Canada or Alaska and the Pacific.

"Boy-oh-boy," my father said—just out of the dark. I looked at him and his eyes were narrow, and he seemed to be thinking about something. "You know, Jackie," he said, "your mother said something to me once I've never forgotten. She said, 'Nobody dies of a broken heart.' This was somewhat before you were born. We were living down in Texas and we'd had some big blow-up, and that was the idea she had. I don't know why." He shook his head.

He ran his hand under the seat, found a half-pint bottle of whiskey, and held it up to the lights of the car behind us to see what there was left of it. He unscrewed the cap and took a drink, then held the bottle out to me. "Have a drink, son," he said. "Something oughta be good in life." And I felt that something was wrong. Not because of the whiskey, which I had drunk before and he had reason to know about, but because of some sound in his voice, something I didn't recognize and did not know the importance of, though I was certain it was important.

I took a drink and gave the bottle back to him, holding the whiskey in my mouth until it stopped burning and I could swallow it a little at a time. When we turned out the road to Highwood, the lights of Great Falls sank below the horizon, and I could see the small white lights of farms, burning at wide distances in the dark.

"What do you worry about, Jackie," my father said. "Do you worry about girls? Do you worry about your future sex life? Is that some of it?" He glanced at me, then back at the road.

"I don't worry about that," I said.

"Well, what then?" my father said. "What else is there?"

"I worry if you're going to die before I do," I said, though I hated saying that, "or if Mother is. That worries me."

"It'd be a miracle if we didn't," my father said, with the half-pint held in the same hand he held the steering wheel. I had seen him drive that way before. "Things pass too fast in your life, Jackie. Don't worry about that. If I were you, I'd worry we might not." He smiled at me, and it was not the worried, nervous smile from before, but a smile that meant he was pleased. And I don't remember him ever smiling at me that way again.

We drove on out behind the town of Highwood and onto the flat field roads toward our house. I could see, out on the prairie, a moving light where the farmer who rented our house to us was disking his field for winter wheat. "He's waited too late with that business," my father said and took a drink, then threw the bottle right out the window. "He'll lose that," he said, "the cold'll kill it." I did not answer him, but what I thought was that my father knew nothing about farming, and if he was right it would be an accident. He knew about planes and hunting game, and that seemed all to me.

"I want to respect your privacy," he said then, for no reason at all that I understood. I am not even certain he said it, only that it is in my memory that way. I don't know what he was thinking of. Just words. But I said to him, I remember well, "It's all right. Thank you."

We did not go straight out the Geraldine Road to our house. Instead my father went down another mile and turned, went a mile and turned back again so that we came home from the other direction. "I want to stop and listen now," he said. "The geese should be in the stubble." We stopped and he cut the lights and engine, and we opened the car windows and listened. It was eight o'clock at night and it was getting colder, though it was dry. But I could hear nothing, just the sound of air moving lightly through the cut field, and not a goose sound. Though I could smell the whiskey on my father's breath and on mine, could hear the motor ticking, could hear him breathe, hear the sound we made sitting side by side on the car seat, our clothes, our feet, almost our hearts beating. And I could see out in the night the yellow lights of our house, shining through the olive trees south of us like a ship on the sea. "I hear them, by God," my father said, his head stuck out the window. "But they're high up. They won't stop here now, Jackie. They're high fliers, those boys. Long gone geese."

THERE WAS A CAR PARKED OFF THE ROAD, down the line of wind-break trees, beside a steel thresher the farmer had left there to rust. You could see moonlight off the taillight chrome. It was a Pontiac, a two-door hard-top. My father said nothing about it and I didn't either, though I think now for different reasons.

The floodlight was on over the side door of our house and lights were on inside, upstairs and down. My mother had a pumpkin on the front porch, and the wind chime she had hung by the door was tinkling. My dog, Major, came out of the Quonset shed and stood in the car lights when we drove up.

"Let's see what's happening here," my father said, opening the door and stepping out quickly. He looked at me inside the car, and his eyes were wide and his mouth drawn tight.

We walked in the side door and up the basement steps into the kitchen, and a man was standing there—a man I had never seen before, a young man with blond hair, who might've been twenty or twenty-five. He was tall and was wearing a short-sleeved shirt and beige slacks with pleats. He was on the other side of the breakfast table, his fingertips just touching the wooden tabletop. His blue eyes were on my father, who was dressed in hunting clothes.

"Hello," my father said.

"Hello," the young man said, and nothing else. And for some reason I looked at his arms, which were long and pale. They looked like a young man's arms, like my arms. His short sleeves had each been neatly rolled up, and I could see the bottom of a small green tattoo edging out from underneath. There was a glass of whiskey on the table, but no bottle.

"What's your name?" my father said, standing in the kitchen under the bright ceiling light. He sounded like he might be going to laugh.

"Woody," the young man said and cleared his throat. He looked at me, then he touched the glass of whiskey, just the rim of the glass. He wasn't nervous, I could tell that. He did not seem to be afraid of anything.

"Woody," my father said and looked at the glass of whiskey. He looked at me, then sighed and shook his head. "Where's Mrs. Russell, Woody? I guess you aren't robbing my house, are you?"

Woody smiled. "No," he said. "Upstairs. I think she went upstairs."

"Good," my father said, "that's a good place." And he walked straight out of the room, but came back and stood in the doorway. "Jackie, you and Woody step outside and wait on me. Just stay there and I'll come out." He looked at Woody then in a way I would not have liked him to look at me, a look that meant he was studying Woody. "I guess that's your car," he said.

"That Pontiac." Woddy nodded.

"Okay. Right," my father said. Then he went out again and up the stairs. At that moment the phone started to ring in the living room, and I heard my mother say, "Who's that?" And my father say, "It's me. It's Jack." And I decided I wouldn't go answer the phone. Woody looked at me, and I understood he wasn't sure what to do. Run, maybe. But he didn't have run in him. Though I thought he would probably do what I said if I would say it.

"Let's just go outside," I said.

And he said, "All right."

Woody and I walked outside and stood in the light of the flood-lamp above the side door. I had on my wool jacket, but Woody was cold and stood with his hands in his pockets, and his arms bare, moving from foot to foot. Inside, the phone was ringing again. Once I looked up and saw my mother come to the window and look down at Woody and me. Woody didn't look up or see her, but I did. I waved at her, and she waved back at me and smiled. She was wearing a powder-blue dress. In another minute the phone stopped ringing.

Woody took a cigarette out of his shirt pocket and lit it. Smoke shot through his nose into the cold air, and he sniffed, looked around the ground, and threw his match on the gravel. His blond hair was combed backwards and neat on the sides, and I could smell his after-shave on him, a sweet, lemon smell. And for the first time I noticed his shoes. They were two-tones, black with white tops and black laces. They stuck out below his baggy pants and were long and polished and shiny, as if he had been planning on a big occasion. They looked like shoes some country singer would wear, or a salesman. He was handsome, but only like someone you would see beside you in a dime store and not notice again.

"I like it out here," Woody said, his head down, looking at his shoes. "Nothing to bother you. I bet you'd see Chicago if the world was flat. The Great Plains commence here."

"I don't know," I said.

Woody looked up at me, cupping his smoke with one hand. "Do you play football?"

"No," I said. I thought about asking him something about my mother. But I had no idea what it would be.

"I *have* been drinking," Woody said, "but I'm not drunk now."

The wind rose then, and from behind the house I could hear Major bark once from far away, and I could smell the irrigation ditch, hear it hiss in the field. It ran down from Highwood Creek to the Missouri, twenty miles away. It was nothing Woody knew about, nothing he could hear or smell. He knew nothing about anything that was here. I heard my father say the words, "That's a real joke," from inside the house, then the sound of a drawer being opened and shut, and a door closing. Then nothing else.

Woody turned and looked into the dark toward where the glow of Great Falls rose on the horizon, and we both could see the flashing lights of a plane lowering to land there. "I once passed my brother in the Los Angeles airport and didn't even recognize him," Woody said, staring into the night. "He recognized *me*, though. He said, 'Hey, bro, are you mad at me, or what?' I wasn't mad at him. We both had to laugh."

Woody turned and looked at the house. His hands were still in his pockets, his cigarette clenched between his teeth, his arms taut. They were, I saw, bigger, stronger arms than I had thought. A vein went down the front of each of them. I wondered what Woody knew that I didn't. Not about my mother—I didn't know anything about that and didn't want to—but about a lot of things, about the life out in the dark, about coming out here, about airports, even about me. He and I were not so far apart in age, I knew that. But Woody was one thing, and I was another. And I wondered how I would ever get to be like him, since it didn't necessarily seem so bad a thing to be.

"Did you know your mother was married before?" Woody said.

"Yes," I said. "I knew that."

"It happens to all of them, now," he said. "They can't wait to get divorced."

"I guess so," I said.

Woody dropped his cigarette into the gravel and toed it out with his black-and-white shoe. He looked up at me and smiled the way he had inside the house, a smile that said he knew something he wouldn't tell, a smile to make you feel bad because you weren't Woody and never could be.

It was then that my father came out of the house. He still had on his plaid hunting coat and his wool cap, but his face was as white as snow, as white as I have ever seen a human being's face to be. It was odd. I had the feeling that he might've fallen inside, because he looked roughed up, as though he had hurt himself somehow.

My mother came out the door behind him and stood in the flood-light at the top of the steps. She was wearing the powder-blue dress I'd seen through the window, a dress I had never seen her wear before, though she was also wearing a car coat and carrying a suitcase. She looked at me and shook her head in a way that only I was supposed to notice, as if it was not a good idea to talk now.

My father had his hands in his pockets, and he walked right up to Woody. He did not even look at me. "What do you do for a living?" he said, and he was very close to Woody. His coat was close enough to touch Woody's shirt.

"I'm in the Air Force," Woody said. He looked at me and then at my father. He could tell my father was excited.

"Is this your day off, then?" my father said. He moved even closer to Woody, his hands still in his pockets. He pushed Woody with his chest, and Woody seemed willing to let my father push him.

"No," he said, shaking his head.

I looked at my mother. She was just standing, watching. It was as if someone had given her an order, and she was obeying it. She did not smile at me, though I thought she was thinking about me, which made me feel strange.

"What's the matter with you?" my father said into Woody's face, right into his face—his voice tight, as if it had gotten hard for him to talk. "Whatever in the world is the matter with you? Don't you understand something?" My father took a revolver pistol out of his coat and put it up under Woody's chin, into the soft pocket behind the bone, so that Woody's whole face rose, but his arms stayed at his sides, his hands open. "I don't know what to do with you," my father said. "I don't have any idea what to do with you. I just don't." Though I thought that what he wanted to do was hold Woody there just like that until something important took place, or until he could simply forget about all this.

My father pulled the hammer back on the pistol and raised it tighter under Woody's chin, breathing into Woody's face—my mother in the light with her suitcase, watching them, and me watching them. A half a minute must've gone by.

And then my mother said, "Jack, let's stop now. Let's just stop."

My father stared into Woody's face as if he wanted Woody to consider doing something—moving or turning around or anything on his own to stop this—that my father would then put a stop to. My father's eyes grew narrowed, and his teeth were gritted together, his lips snarling up to resemble a smile. "You're crazy, aren't you?" he said. "You're a goddamned crazy man. Are you in love with her, too? Are you, crazy man? Are you? Do you say you love her? Say you love her! Say you love her so I can blow your fucking brains in the sky."

"All right," Woody said. "No. It's all right."

"He doesn't love me, Jack. For God's sake," my mother said. She seemed so calm. She shook her head at me again. I do not think she thought my father would shoot Woody. And I don't think Woody thought so. Nobody did, I think, except my father himself. But I think he did, and was trying to find out how to.

My father turned suddenly and glared at my mother, his eyes shiny and moving, but with the gun still on Woody's skin. I think he was afraid, afraid he was doing this wrong and could mess all of it up and make matters worse without accomplishing anything.

"You're leaving," he yelled at her. "That's why you're packed. Get out. Go on."

"Jackie has to be at school in the morning," my mother said in just her normal voice. And without another word to any one of us, she walked out of the floodlamp light carrying her bag, turned the corner at the front porch steps and disappeared toward the olive trees that ran in rows back into the wheat.

My father looked back at me where I was standing in the gravel, as if he expected to see me go with my mother toward Woody's car. But I hadn't thought about that—though later I would. Later I would think I should have gone with her, and that things between them might've been different. But that isn't how it happened.

"You're sure you're going to get away now, aren't you, mister?" my father said into Woody's face. He was crazy himself, then. Anyone would've been. Everything must have seemed out of hand to him.

"I'd like to," Woody said. "I'd like to get away from here."

"And I'd like to think of some way to hurt you," my father said and blinked his eyes. "I feel helpless about it." We all heard the door to Woody's car close in the dark. "Do you think that I'm a fool?" my father said.

"No," Woody said. "I don't think that."

"Do you think you're important?"

"No," Woody said. "I'm not."

My father blinked again. He seemed to be becoming someone else at that moment, someone I didn't know. "Where are you from?"

And Woody closed his eyes. He breathed in, then out, a long sigh. It was as if this was somehow the hardest part, something he hadn't expected to be asked to say.

"Chicago," Woody said. "A suburb of there."

"Are your parents alive?" my father said, all the time with his blue magnum pistol pushed under Woody's chin.

"Yes," Woody said. "Yessir."

"That's too bad," my father said. "Too bad they have to know what you are. I'm sure you stopped meaning anything to them a long time ago. I'm sure they both wish you were dead. You didn't know that. But I know it. I can't help them out, though. Somebody else'll have to kill you. I don't want to have to think about you anymore. I guess that's it."

My father brought the gun down to his side and stood looking at Woody. He did not back away, just stood, waiting for what I don't know to happen. Woody stood a moment, then he cut his eyes at me uncomfortably. And I know that I looked down. That's all I could do. Though I remember wondering if Woody's heart was broken and what any of this meant to him. Not to me, or my mother, or my father. But to him, since he seemed to be the one left out somehow, the one who would be lonely soon, the one who had done something he would someday wish he hadn't and would have no one to tell him that it was all right, that they forgave him, that these things happen in the world.

Woody took a step back, looked at my father and at me again as if he intended to speak, then stepped aside and walked away toward the front of our house, where the wind chime made a noise in the new cold air.

My father looked at me, his big pistol in his hand. "Does this seem stupid to you?" he said. "All this? Yelling and threatening and going nuts? I wouldn't blame you if it did. You shouldn't even see this. I'm sorry. I don't know what to do now."

"It'll be all right," I said. And I walked out to the road. Woody's car started up behind the olive trees. I stood and watched it back out, its red taillights clouded by exhaust. I could see their two heads inside, with the headlights shining behind them. When they got into the road, Woody touched his brakes, and for a moment I could see that they were talking, their heads turned toward each other, nodding. Woody's head and my mother's. They sat that way for a few seconds, then drove slowly off. And I wondered what they had to say to each other, something important enough that they had to stop right at that moment and say it. Did she say, *I love you*? Did she say, *This is not what I expected to happen*? Did she say, *This is what I've wanted all along*? And did he say, *I'm sorry for all this*, or *I'm glad*, or *None of this matters to me*? These are not the kinds of things you can know if you were not there. And I was not there and did not want to be. It did not seem like I should be there. I heard the door slam when my father went inside, and I turned back from the road where I could still see their taillights disappearing, and went back into the house where I was to be alone with my father.

THINGS SELDOM END IN ONE EVENT. In the morning I went to school on the bus as usual, and my father drove in to the air base in his car. We had not said very much about all that had happened. Harsh words, in a sense, are all alike. You can make them up yourself and be right. I think we both believed that we were in a fog we couldn't see through yet, though in a while, maybe not even a long while, we would see lights and know something.

In my third-period class that day a messenger brought a note for me that said I was excused from school at noon, and I should meet my mother at a motel down 10th Avenue South—a place not so far from my school—and we would eat lunch together.

It was a gray day in Great Falls that day. The leaves were off the trees and the mountains to the east of town were obscured by a low sky. The night before had been cold and clear, but today it seemed as if it would rain. It was the beginning of winter in earnest. In a few days there would be snow everywhere.

The motel where my mother was staying was called the Tropicana, and was beside the city golf course. There was a neon parrot on the sign out front, and the cabins made a U shape behind a little white office building. Only a couple of cars were parked in front of cabins, and no car was in front of my mother's cabin. I wondered if Woody would be here, or if he was at the air base. I wondered if my father would see him there, and what they would say.

I walked back to cabin 9. The door was open, though a Do Not Disturb sign was hung on the knob outside. I looked through the screen and saw my mother sitting on the bed alone. The television was on, but she was looking at me. She was wearing the powder-blue dress she had had on the night before. She was smiling at me, and I liked the way she looked at that moment, through the screen, in shadows. Her features did not seem as sharp as they had before. She looked comfortable where she was, and I felt like we were going to get along, no matter what had happened, and that I wasn't mad at her— that I had never been mad at her.

She sat forward and turned the television off. "Come in, Jackie," she said, and I opened the screen door and came inside. "It's the height of grandeur in here, isn't it?" My mother looked around the room. Her suitcase was open on the floor by the bathroom door, which I could see through and out the window onto the golf course, where three men were playing under the milky sky. "Privacy can be a burden, sometimes," she said, and reached down and put on her high-heeled shoes. "I didn't sleep very well last night, did you?"

"No," I said, though I had slept all right. I wanted to ask her where Woody was, but it occurred to me at that moment that he was gone now and wouldn't be back, that she wasn't thinking in terms of him and didn't care where he was or ever would be.

"I'd like a nice compliment from you," she said. "Do you have one of those to spend?"

"Yes," I said. "I'm glad to see you."

"That's a nice one," she said and nodded. She had both her shoes on now. "Would you like to go have lunch? We can walk across the street to the cafeteria. You can get hot food."

"No," I said, "I'm not really hungry now."

"That's okay," she said and smiled at me again. And, as I said before, I liked the way she looked. She looked pretty in a way I didn't remember seeing her, as if something that had had a hold on her had let her go, and she could be different about things. Even about me.

"Sometimes, you know," she said, "I'll think about something I did. Just anything. Years ago in Idaho, or last week, even. And it's as if I'd read it. Like a story. Isn't that strange?"

"Yes," I said. And it did seem strange to me because I was certain then what the difference was between what had happened and what hadn't, and knew I always would be.

"Sometimes," she said, and she folded her hands in her lap and stared out the little side window of her cabin at the parking lot and the curving row of other cabins. "Sometimes I even have a moment when I completely forget what life's like. Just altogether." She smiled. "That's not so bad, finally. Maybe it's a disease I have. Do you think I'm just sick and I'll get well?"

"No. I don't know," I said. "Maybe. I hope so." I looked out the bathroom window and saw the three men walking down the golf course fairway carrying golf clubs.

"I'm not very good at sharing things right now," my mother said. "I'm sorry." She cleared her throat, and then she didn't say anything for almost a minute while I stood there. "I *will* answer anything you'd like me to answer, though. Just ask me anything, and I'll answer it the truth, whether I want to or not. Okay? I will. You don't even have to trust me. That's not a big issue with us. We're both grown-ups now."

And I said, "Were you ever married before?"

My mother looked at me strangely. Her eyes got small, and for a moment she looked the way I was used to seeing her—sharp-faced, her mouth set and taut. "No," she said. "Who told you that? That isn't true. I never was. Did Jack say that to you? Did your father say that? That's an awful thing to say. I haven't been that bad."

"He didn't say that," I said.

"Oh, of course he did," my mother said. "He doesn't know just to let things go when they're bad enough."

"I wanted to know that," I said. "I just thought about it. It doesn't matter."

"No, it doesn't," my mother said. "I could've been married eight times. I'm just sorry he said that to you. He's not generous sometimes."

"He didn't say that," I said. But I'd said it enough, and I didn't care if she believed me or didn't. It was true that trust was not a big issue between us then. And in any event, I know now that the whole truth of anything is an idea that stops existing finally.

"Is that all you want to know, then?" my mother said. She seemed mad, but not at me, I didn't think. Just at things in general. And I sympathized with her. "Your life's your own business, Jackie," she said. "Sometimes it scares you to death it's so much your own business. You just want to run."

"I guess so," I said.

"I'd like a less domestic life, is all." She looked at me, but I didn't say anything. I didn't see what she meant by that, though I knew there was nothing I could say to change the way her life would be from then on. And I kept quiet.

In a while we walked across 10th Avenue and ate lunch in the cafeteria. When she paid for the meal I saw that she had my father's silver-dollar money clip in her purse and that there was money in it. And I understood that he had been to see her already that day, and no one cared if I knew it. We were all of us on our own in this.

When we walked out onto the street, it was colder and the wind was blowing. Car exhausts were visible and some drivers had their lights on, though it was only two o'clock in the afternoon. My mother had called a taxi, and we stood and waited for it. I didn't know where she was going, but I wasn't going with her.

"Your father won't let me come back," she said, standing on the curb. It was just a fact to her, not that she hoped I would talk to him or stand up for her or take her part. But I did wish then that I had never let her go the night before. Things can be fixed by staying; but to go out into the night and not come back hazards life, and everything can get out of hand.

My mother's taxi came. She kissed me and hugged me very hard, then got inside the cab in her powder-blue dress and high heels and her car coat. I smelled her perfume on my cheeks as I stood watching her. "I used to be afraid of more things than I am now," she said, looking up at me, and smiled. "I've got a knot in my stomach, of all things." And she closed the cab door, waved at me, and rode away.

I WALKED BACK TOWARD MY SCHOOL. I thought I could take the bus home if I got there by three. I walked a long way down 10th Avenue to Second Street, beside the Missouri River, then over to town. I walked by the Great Northern Hotel, where my father had sold ducks and geese and fish of all kinds. There were no passenger trains in the yard and the loading dock looked small. Garbage cans were lined along the edge of it, and the door was closed and locked.

As I walked toward school I thought to myself that my life had turned suddenly, and that I might not know exactly how or which way for possibly a long time. Maybe, in fact, I might never know. It was a thing that happened to you—I knew that—and it had happened to me in this way now. And as I walked on up the cold street that afternoon in Great Falls, the questions I asked myself were these: why wouldn't my father let my mother come back? Why would Woody stand in the cold with me outside my house and risk being killed? Why would he say my mother had been married before, if she hadn't been? And my mother herself—why would she do what she did? In five years my father had gone off to Ely, Nevada, to ride out the oil strike there, and been killed by accident. And in the years since then I have seen my mother from time to time—in one place or another, with one man or other—and I can say, at least, that we know each other. But I have never known the answer to these questions, have never asked anyone their answers. Though possibly it—the answer—is simple: it is just low-life, some coldness in us all, some helplessness that causes us to misunderstand life when it is pure and plain, makes our existence seem like a border between two nothings, and makes us no more or less than animals who meet on the road— watchful, unforgiving, without patience or desire.

HOOT

Pete Fromm

I'M ONLY IN TOWN FOR BULLETS—a quick trip to the hardware—no plans to stop and talk to anybody. But waiting at the checkout I get that hinky feeling somebody's watching. I glance down the aisle, but there's nobody there. Making like I'm just checking out the power tools, I take a peek behind me. Only one there is a Hutterite woman, who looks straight at the floor as soon as I see her.

Turning back to the counter, I wipe a little sweat from underneath my jacket collar. Me sweating it over a Hoot, I think, shaking my head. Like she'd be the one staring.

I watch the lady scratching away at my receipt until slowly I realize what I'd seen behind me. At first glance it was just another Hutterite, waiting for the men haggling over steel prices—same long homemade dress, same polka-dot scarf. But somehow she seems different, thinner maybe, or younger. I feel her watching me again.

So I turn around, stare right at her this time. I mean, they must be used to that, right? First thing I see is she doesn't have the standard Hutterite glasses, thick as trough ice. Her eyes are the same watery blue though, and she drops them again as soon as she sees mine. So I take an extra look.

You hardly ever see young ones. Especially girls, unless they're real little. And you never see pretty ones. This one's taller than most, the bright colors of her dress drawn in tighter and stretched out longer than I can ever remember seeing, though, of course, I've never spent much time studying Hoots. But I'm still studying this one when she looks back up, right at me, her eyes never wavering, like she can see thoughts.

For a second I don't turn away but then she smiles and I feel caught. I'm sweating all over and I can't even smile back. I turn to the lady at the register and scoop up my bullets. "Just skip the receipt," I say, and jump the few steps back out to the cold and wind. There are more Hutterites out there, gabbling along in German or whatever, going quiet as I pass.

I fire up my truck, but then wait a minute, watching the Hoots by the door; the old women thick as tree trunks, the men in their black homemades, with their black beards and no mustaches. I wonder how the girl could have come from anything like them—what it must be like having a smile like hers, stuck out in a colony with all of them. With the wind tugging at the tails of their coats they look like ravens and when they glance my way I take off.

By the time I get home the blow off the mountains is moaning through the windbreaks so instead of working on the last stretch of fence I go inside. I wind up walking from room to empty room, turning lights on and then off, listening to the windows rattle in their frames, wishing there was somebody I could tell about the Hutterite girl.

The stairs echo under my boots, reminding me of Carlton thumping up them after Mom whaled on him for one of his outrages. I think maybe I'll write Carlton a letter about the girl, but he's clear down in Texas, working offshore oil. I feel like calling, but Carlton once told me there aren't any phones on the rigs. Not that I could afford a call like that anyway, for nothing but a Hoot girl smiling at me in town.

I find a pad of paper and an old envelope and set them on the kitchen table but by then it's finally dark enough to go out to the hay.

The sky's pretty clear and I walk to the stacked bales without using the light. I crawl up to wait for the elk. They've been at the hay every night lately and my plan is to pop one, hoping it'll scare the rest off. I'm no hunter, but I figure it's what Carlton would do. He was always shooting something.

Mom, of course, always treated the elk like pets and wouldn't let Carlton near them. But, back up on the hill with Dad, I doubt Mom knows a thing about what goes on down here. I kept the graves like a golf green all summer, but now wish I'd let them grow. The elk would probably graze there if I had, and if Mom could know anything now, I bet she'd like that.

The elk are slow tonight and the moon starts wisping in and out of the clouds, the light going from silvery to a kind of foggy black-gray, mostly light enough to see. The wind's still whipping though, and lying freezing in the darkness I get to thinking of later, of crawling between the crackling cold sheets alone. I think of the Hoot girl's eyes, the blue so watered down they were spooky, like glass. When I was a kid we tortured ourselves with the rumor that the Hutterites got so inbred in their colonies they'd pay men to sleep with their wives. Tall, blond, blue-eyed men. Like me. The older guys, like Carlton, said it wasn't much, like they did it all the time. Carlton said there was always a sheet between you, with just a strategic hole, and that the girl just lay there. I'm glad I didn't write him any letter.

Not that I believe any of that about doing it through the sheets. They say all kinds of things about the Hutterites; like they only sell their worn-out roosters at the Farmer's Market, or things are so expensive downtown because they shoplift so much.

I don't know. The only Hutterites I've ever actually talked to are the two we found at the bar at Bowman's Corner, where we used to drink during high school. Senior year we met there to watch the Super Bowl and the first thing we see, even before Joe Montana struggling with the Bengals, is two Hutterite kids, maybe our age. Never seen one in a bar before.

At first we just ignored them, but the owner kept us beered and pretty soon we asked him to bring the Hoots a round, on us. They weren't drinking and we just wanted to see what they'd do with a beer. What they did was bring their beers over and join us, saying "Tank you wery much," and smiling. We could hardly believe it, but somebody managed to ask them what colony they're from, and which team they're for.

We talked about the game for a while and though I was curious about what went on in their colonies—simple stuff, like where they slept and where they ate, who had to do what chores—it seemed too rude just to ask. Pretty soon no one was saying anything and when out of the blue Carlton asked one if he'd trade his thick, home-stitched black coat for Carlton's perfectly good down jacket, it seemed like the funniest thing in the world.

The Hoot had smooth skin, white, and two red spots popped up like bruises on his cheeks. "Na, I coont do dat," he says. After that, every time one of them would say anything one of us would answer, "Na, I coont do dat," and we'd all laugh.

When San Francisco finally pulled it out at the end, the one with the white skin says, "Dat vus wan helluva game," smiling, trying to talk sports. Just like anyone.

Carlton shouts, "Na, I coont do dat," and we all bust up laughing, though really it didn't make any sense and it was getting where it wasn't that funny anymore. But the Hoots keep smiling, like they're having a good time just being with regular people. Like they're one of us or something.

As they get up to go the other Hoot even tips his hat and says, "Tank you wery much," again. For the beer I suppose.

We all got up right after they did. There was maybe five of us. I don't remember exactly how it got going, but we caught them just as they were getting into their truck.

Sitting freezing on the haystacks I hear the elk moving in, their heart-shaped feet crunching over the brittle stubble, but I don't lift myself up. I try to remember how it started in the parking lot out front of Bowman's, but all I can remember is the squeal of the hard-packed snow under our boots, the clouds of our ragged breaths, and the huge ripping sound the black cloth of the Hoot's coat made. They weren't much for fighting and they were outnumbered as hell. We pounded on them until Carlton shouted, "Na, I coont do dat!" as loud as he could, which was all of a sudden so funny we had to stop punching and kicking just to get our breath.

We watched them climb into their truck then, the white-skinned one behind the wheel, wiping at the blood beneath his nose with his torn, snow-covered sleeve. As they drove away, their truck's exhaust densely white in the cold air, we stood quietly in the parking lot, looking at the ground. The Hoots' blood was bright on the snow, and for a long time none of us said anything.

Then somebody, could've been me even, said, "I yust coont do dat," but that wasn't funny at all anymore and without saying another word, or even looking at each other, we got into our trucks and drove home. It was dark by the time we reached our ranch. My knuckles stung like fire and I ground them into the thigh of my jeans. I wondered if back at their colony the Hoots would be able to explain what had happened. I would have liked to have heard.

Picturing the bright red drops of Hoot blood in the snow, so bright and so red it looked fake, I get up on my elbows, my rifle to my eye. I see the shapes of a whole herd spread out below me, dark ghosts against the crust of thin snow in the stubble. I even hear them starting to feed, the crunching grind of their big flat teeth. I watch a while, then hit the spotlight.

A whole field of glaring wall-eyes are caught in the light and the shapes of the closest jump out clear, with perfect hard black shadows etched into the snow behind them. I pick the closest elk. Caught in the sudden glare his eyes never waver. But the others break at the sound of the shot, and still thinking of the terrible brightness of the blood in the parking lot, I empty my rifle into the air, suddenly way madder about hay loss than makes sense.

When my rifle's empty, the barrel hot enough to burn, I look down at the lone dead elk, thrashing around, shot through the head. Carlton, I know, would have wiped out the whole herd, just for the good of the ranch.

I climb down and as I wait for the last kicks to die out, I try to remember if Carlton had really been with us when we thumped the Hoots. For years I was sure he had been, could see him breathing hard and punching right alongside me, but he's older than me and would've been long gone by then.

After gutting the elk I all of a sudden remember I'm freezing and instead of dragging him to the shop I go back to the house instead. The elk can always wait till morning.

I stoke up the woodstove and stand beside it a long time, my hands behind my back, tingling as they warm up. I stare at the yellow-painted kitchen table. I wonder what it would look like to have that

Hoot girl sitting at it, staring at me, her eyes spotlight-bright with knowing what I'd done at Bowman's.

Before long I sit down and pull the pad of paper to me. I draw squiggles for a while. I wrote to Carlton a lot at first, but without him answering I gave it up. This is the first letter I've written since the one last year, letting him know Mom died.

I start out telling him I busted one of Mom's elk and it should make some dandy eating. It's something I think'll make him smile, and I smile myself thinking of the surprise of that gap-tooth grin. But I remember his next to final outrage: Mom and me walking into the shop to find him skinning out a young cow elk. Mom asked real quiet, "Where did that come from?" and just as quiet Carlton says, "The stacks. They're eating us alive." Then Mom was shouting about her pets and how he never acted this way when Dad was alive and Carlton went on working his knife as if she wasn't there. I went and sat on the front porch but I could still hear them, could hear Carlton finally yell, "Go ahead then! Starve!"

He came stomping by me on the porch and then a while later came stomping back out, carrying a big box he threw into the back of his pickup. He said, "See you, kid. You got any sense, you won't be far behind," still so mad he could barely talk.

I didn't realize then he was leaving for good, and nothing he said made sense. Us starve? We were surrounded by cattle. And me follow him? I was twelve years old.

I shake my head and pull my sheet of paper from the tablet and slip it into the stove. I butchered that elk myself. Mom wouldn't touch it. First time I ever butchered anything.

On a fresh sheet I ask Carlton if he was with us at Bowman's when we thumped the Hoots. I tell him I know he couldn't have been. I chew on the end of my pencil a minute, wondering who it could have been if it wasn't Carlton. But I haven't seen any of the high school gang since they blew town and none of their faces come to mind.

Next I ask if he ever really used to do that with the Hoot girls, through the sheets. I tell him I know he couldn't have done that either, but I say it's something I really got to know now. I tell him it's okay if he never did; I know how people talk, how lies like that aren't even lies so much as just a way of talking. So I tell him to just let me know the truth. You're so far away, I say, what difference would it make what I knew about you when we were just kids?

I close talking about the ranch, how I can't really run the whole thing alone, if I get down to admitting it. I don't ask him to come up or anything, but just leave it out there for him to look at. I figure there must be a world of things he looks at while he's out on the rigs with nothing but waves all around him. I lick the envelope and press the flap down with the side of my fist before I have a chance to put in anything about the pretty Hutterite girl, which is why I started the letter in the first place.

I pull some blankets from the closet then and a pillow from the arm of the couch and decide I'll head to town again in the morning, see if there's anything I might need at the hardware. The odds, I figure, of running into the same girl are awful slim, but maybe I'll stay in town all day, checking into the store now and then. I can't believe I bolted like I did when she smiled.

I stretch out on the kitchen bench and pull my blankets up tight to my neck, not wanting to leave the scorching heat of the stove just to drag myself to a cold bedroom. More and more often lately I sleep in the kitchen for just that reason.

I CHECK THE HARDWARE STORE FOUR TIMES, but the Hutterite girl isn't in town the next day. I mail the letter to Carlton and in the next two weeks I start running into town more than ever before, burning up gas I can't afford. Every time I come home I look at the shop and tell myself I have to butcher that elk, but I keep thinking of Carlton's elk hanging in there and I put it off. It's cold enough it won't spoil.

Though I cover every place I've ever seen a Hutterite, I don't find the girl until the middle of December. She's at a craft thing downtown, at a table full of Hutterite women, selling hand-sewn stuff for Christmas presents. By the time I see her she's already seen me and this time I head to the table before I can think, before I realize she's never lowered her eyes, that she's still looking right at me.

"Hi," I say, wondering if she could really remember me.

She smiles, the same way she did at the store, and says, "Vould you like someting." The accent's there, just like any Hoot, and I wonder what I could have been thinking.

"I'd like to know your name," I say anyway.

Not even a blush. The smile stays there and she says, "Amy." Amy, like somebody who sat next to you in kindergarten. I'd been expecting something like Gertrude or Wilhelmina.

An older woman sees me and starts my way and I say, "Where do you live?" and she says fast, "Goodhaven Colony."

Then the older woman is between us, squeezing the girl away from the table, saying, "Vut is it dat you vant?"

I see the girl, Amy, roll her pale eyes toward the ceiling, still smiling. Looking at the big Hoot woman I point at Amy and say, "Her."

Amy's smile actually breaks into a laugh and as the cluster of thick, short women grows she's bustled away and I'm told to, "Shoo, shoo."

I shout my name to Amy, and, "I'm in the book," and I'm laughing myself by the time the men get there, milling around, hoping I'll leave them alone. One of them finally talks, mumbling about the hard times the girl is having now, her confusion. He smiles uncertainly and gives a shrug. "Forget dat girl," he says, "Stay vitch yor own people."

I think of her smile and I say, quiet enough he won't hear, "I yust coont do dat."

I know where Goodhaven Colony is, but, driving out of town, the light fading fast, I know I can't just drive into the colony and ask her to a show or something. Out there, outnumbering me a hundred to one, I wonder how peaceable they'd be.

I park by the back door but night is full on me and I sit in the pickup, listening to the radio, knowing it's cold and empty inside the house. Eventually I dash in and fire up the stove. I listen to the crackling of the kindling and add bigger stuff, then decide to head out and butcher the elk, which I've put off way too long already.

I unlock the shop door and find the elk frozen solid. I slap at him, wondering how I'm going to butcher something as hard as bone. I get into my coveralls and wrestle with the little bull for an hour just to get the skin off. I take a breather then and ask the naked elk if he thinks they have phones at the colonies. "Hello, is Amy there?" I say to the carcass. "Amy who? Amy the pretty one. Amy the confused one." I grin, but begin to admit I don't have a chance.

I cut the elk into front and back halves with a hand saw but it's tough going. Getting impatient, I crank up a chain saw to split him lengthwise along the spine. Curls and chips of meat and bone flick against my coveralls, but as the saw heats up it starts melting things and blood begins to stain the floor.

I'm making a mess and losing every trace of hope I'd had at the craft show. I can't believe how far I've sunk on my own—tearing up an elk with a chain saw just because I've been mooning after some impossible Hoot while the pet elk I poached freezes hard as a statue.

I flip the saw off and when the chain stops rotating I give it a kick. The saw scuttles across the bloody concrete floor and I'm left standing over the pieces of frozen elk. A voice behind me says, "Drew?"

I spin around but before I even see him in the doorway I know it's Carlton. He smiles a little, seeing my surprise, but it doesn't cover the shock on his face. "I got your letter," he says. "I figured you could use a hand."

I jump over to the door, sticking out my hand, but Carlton backs into the darkness, holding up his hands to keep me away. I stop, startled again, but glancing down I see that the chain saw has sprayed me up and down with melted elk stuff. "Let me get this off," I say, starting to strip out of the coveralls. "I was just butchering up . . . ," I start, but Carlton's seen what I was doing. The shop is a wreck.

I unzip the coveralls so fast the zipper sticks and I have to wriggle out. I throw them toward the band saw but instead of catching, the coveralls slip to the floor. I leave them there and leap through the black hole of the door where Carlton had been just a moment before.

"Carlton?" I say.

"Right here," he answers, from over by the truck.

As I crunch over the frozen ground I say, "I'm cleaned up now," and I see him against the light from the house and we shake hands.

We stand there a minute, though the night's cold as can be. "I got up here and couldn't find you anywhere," Carlton says.

I still haven't let go of his hand and Carlton says, "I've called every night since I left Texas."

"Texas," I say, trying to imagine being there so long and then suddenly back here.

"It's darker than the inside of a cow out here," Carlton says, pulling away from me and heading for the house. "What happened to the yard light?"

It burned out months ago. I try laughing. "I leave it off to save money," I say.

"Thin times?" he asks and I catch his accent, southern and slow, and as we head to the house I kid him about it.

We step inside, into the light, and Carlton shrugs and says, "Lived there my whole adult life, Drew." He backs up to the stove and looks over his shoulder. "Can't afford fuel oil?"

"We still got oil," I say. "I just like the wood."

"You'll get over that when the pipes burst," he drawls.

We stand beside the stove with our backs to each other. I hadn't thought of freezing the pipes. "How long you been here?" I ask, looking around the kitchen, at my pillow and pile of blankets on the bench. I wonder what in the world he thinks.

"I've been here for a while," he answers, "waiting for you to show up. I never thought to look in the shop."

He doesn't say anything else so I ask, right out, "What are you doing here, Carlton?"

"I got your letter, like I said."

There's more he's going to say, but he doesn't, so I turn and creak open the stove doors, shoving in a new log and then another. I have to push the second one in and beat on it to get the doors closed again.

"For the record, Drew," Carlton says to my back, "that wasn't me with you at Bowman's."

I stand up and smile at him. "No," I say, "I knew it couldn't've been."

"What did you pound a couple of Hutterite kids for?"

I shrug. Coming from him, it's a pretty dumb question. He was always fighting somebody. "They were Hoots," I say.

Carlton looks as if he still doesn't understand, as if he somehow feels sorry for me, and I ask, "What did you screw them through the sheets for?"

Carlton looks at his feet. "That was just talk," he says. "Punk kids trying to look tough. Nobody ever did anything like that."

I look at him sideways and his grin comes back, sudden and surprising as ever, making me smile. "'Til you said that in your letter I'd forgotten what an asshole I used to be."

My smile dies out. "What are you talking about?"

"We should have a drink," he says, all of a sudden loud and cheerful. "How long's it been since we've seen each other?"

"Not since you blew out of here," I say. "Nine years."

Carlton whistles. "Well, where's the booze? Come on."

I see he's trying hard to sound like his old self and I dip beneath the sink and set a bottle on the table. Carlton wipes at the dust on the bottle and laughs. I interrupt, saying, "It's left over from Mom's funeral. I think the Waldners brought it over."

Carlton isn't laughing anymore and I get glasses. We sit at the yellow table and Carlton pours for each of us. "Nine years, eh? Last time I saw you you were nothing but a pimply-faced kid. Thirteen? Fourteen?"

"Twelve," I say.

"Twelve then," he answers, holding up his glass for me to click mine against. For the first time I realize what a tiny part of his life I must have always been.

"So tell me," Carlton says, "what'd you grow up to be?" Without waiting for an answer he shakes his head. "Pounding Hoots in the bars. Massacring elk with a chain saw. You a tough guy?"

"You were more than tough enough for this family," I say.

He keeps shaking his head and I ask, "What did you grow up to be?" really curious, not just filling up silence like he was. He talks like I was from another planet, instead of just trying to fill his shoes.

"I grew up to be married," he says, sipping and hiding behind his glass at the same time.

I stare at him and he nods.

"Divorced?" I ask, thinking now I know why he's here.

Carlton shakes his head. "Not in a million years. She's a keeper."

I look around the table for my glass.

"She's back in Texas looking after the kids," he tells me.

For a last time I picture Carlton out on the rigs surrounded by waves, only now I see that he probably never once thought about me or Mom or any of the things I pictured him thinking about. He was out there thinking about his own new family the whole time. "Kids?" I say.

"Two. Jen and Olive."

"Olive," I say, like a parrot. Our mom's name.

"Horrible thing to do to a kid, isn't it? Sounds like she's a hundred years old."

I watch Carlton stand up to add more wood to the stove that's still stoked to bursting. He gazes into the open doors, the heat glowing against his face. "How old's Olive?" I ask.

"Two," he says and thumps the stick there's no room for against the floor.

"Mom was alive then. I suppose you could've told her. At least that you were married."

"You could suppose that," he says. The doors squeal as he closes them. "But things like that got to seem harder than maybe they really were."

I can't do anything but stare at him, wondering who he is.

"Anyway," he says, "I came up to see if you'd lost the place yet. Or if you'd driven it so far into the hole it wasn't ever coming back. If it looks all right we're hoping to all come up to stay. What do you think?"

If I'd lost it, I think, if I'd driven it into a hole. I say, "What I think, Carlton, is it probably wasn't much to sit out in the waves and collect oil wages. You want to try to run this place alone, have at it. See how far out of the hole you take it!" I'm shouting, but Carlton worried about frozen pipes right off and I know I'm not making sense.

"I didn't mean it that way," he says, tossing his stick back into the box. I wish he'd just smack me, like he would have when we were kids.

"What I meant was I'm thinking of coming back, with my family. Giving this place another go. With you."

I think of the cattle out there now, hunched up in the draws against the cold and the dark. "You can't just give it a go," I say.

"I'd be in for everything, Drew. This is where I want my kids to grow."

"I can see that," I say. "I mean, after the bang-up job of growing you did here."

Carlton stares at me and I say, "You're a piece of work, Carlton, you know that? Remember your goddamn elk?

"What in the world did you make up down there? What kind of kid did you invent for yourself to be?"

I'm shouting again and I stop suddenly and get up. "Olive!" I snort, and I walk across the house because I don't know what to say next and I don't want him to see how hard I'm shaking.

I snag a coat on my way out and storm straight ahead, going nowhere until I cut the footprints in the snow crust. There's just enough moon for me to see their snaky path heading up the hill. I kneel down to make sure, but I know they're Carlton's. I haven't been up to the hill since the last snow, since I popped Mom's elk.

I fall into Carlton's track. It's a hike and I'm blowing clouds by the time I can see the fence around the stones. Carlton's tracks go straight through, the gate closed neatly over them.

I work the latch and follow Carlton's steps around the whole collection; Mom and Dad, and Mom's parents, and her baby sister's little spot. Carlton's tracks are shuffled around Dad's grave but in front of Mom's there are two long icy grooves, like the spots elk melt into the snow when they bed down, only much smaller.

I kneel down to study them and before I'm even all the way down I realize they're the prints of Carlton's knees, down long enough he melted through. Thinking back to him standing in the bright light of the shop door I can see him perfectly, can see the darkness around his knees, the white, crusty snow sticking to his pants around the edges of the wet.

I feel the cold working into my knees, stiffening them, and I say, "What the hell, Mom?" It's not something to say to someone I don't doubt is in heaven, but I say it again. I picture them fighting over his elk and I hear again the sudden, short chop of Carlton shouting, "Go ahead then. Starve!" and I hear Mom the next morning, even after his final outrage, saying, "We're going to miss him, Drew," and I realize I don't have any idea what there was between them. But, just as suddenly, I know it wasn't Carlton at Bowman's that day. It was me, pretending.

When I get up, I leave the gate open for the elk, though there's precious little left there for them now.

AT THE KITCHEN DOOR I'M STAGGERED by the great heat of the overloaded stove. "Carlton?" I say, before my eyes adjust to the light. There's no answer.

By the time I go through the last room I'm running. The house is empty again. I step back outside and his truck is still beside mine. I lean against it and take a big breath. In the quiet blackness of the night the cold pinches my skin. And then I hear the familiar thin whine of butchering coming from the shop.

I bang the shop door shut behind me so Carlton will know I'm there. He's at the band saw and he peeks over his shoulder, still pushing a piece of the frozen elk through the whirring blade. "That's a good way to lose a finger," I say, which is what he always used to say to me when I tried to help.

He drops a chop into a box on the floor beside him, a box that's already full. He's nearly through the spine and he turns back to the saw to push the last cuts through. The bone smokes a little and the smell is terrible and the whining scream worsens until the teeth are back into meat. I haven't kept the blades sharp.

Carlton drops the last cut into the box and switches the saw off. The blade wobbles as it slows and the scream is gone, which I'm glad for. Just as the blade slows to where I can see each individual shark-like tooth Carlton says, "That's my coat."

I look down and see that I'm wearing his old lineman's jacket, what he used to call his shit-kicking coat. "First thing I grabbed," I say, though I've been wearing it for years, since before the fight at Bowman's.

Carlton's got the blower on high and I hear the first clump of ice drop from the knees of my jeans. "Did you call your wife?" I ask.

Carlton shakes his head. "I was going to," he says. "Even had my hand on the phone, but I thought I better wait, see if we can really talk it over."

"Nothing to talk over," I say. "Everything here's as much yours as it is mine."

Carlton shakes his head again. "Not with the way things've gone."

"Why?" I start, but my voice shakes. "Why didn't you come back when there was still time?"

Carlton wipes some meat and bone from the saw's table. "What did Mom call them?"

"Your outrages," I answer, knowing exactly what he's talking about.

"Outrages," he says, rolling the word around as he nods his head. "Outrages," he says again. "After that last one . . ." He lets the words fade between us as he stands in my coveralls, polishing that old saw table with the sleeve.

When everything is long silent, Carlton looks up again, his grin cracking open. "What say we go back in and finish that drink. We can both call home. Give them the good news."

Home, I think. "Can't," I say. "I got a date."

"A date?" Carlton asks, his smile growing wider, more friendly than I ever remember it.

"Yeah," I answer. I glance at my watch. "I got to meet her at nine. At the Farmer's Market." It's the wrong thing to say, but right then it's the only place I picture seeing a Hutterite.

Carlton watches me. "There's no Farmer's Market in December," he says.

"Just a place she knows," I say.

He glances me up and down. "You're going like that?"

I nod. "She won't mind."

"Must be quite a girl."

I nod again.

"Does she have a name?"

"Amy."

I see him thinking, going over the neighbors' places, trying to picture some little girl from back in his day. "She's not from around here," I tell him.

"A foreigner, huh?"

"She's from Goodhaven," I say, studying the blood on the coveralls, as if I stared at the splotches long enough I'd be able to read our futures.

"Goodhaven?" he repeats, like the name rings some bells.

"Goodhaven Colony. She's not a foreigner. She's a Hutterite."

I can feel Carlton looking at me. "A Hoot?"

"Maybe you know her," I say. "Maybe she's one you did through the sheets."

Carlton looks me in the eye a long time, then takes a big, careful breath. "I told you," he says, "that never happened. To anybody."

"You told me a lot of things," I say.

IT'S BEEN DARK FOR HOURS by the time I cruise through the vacant parking lot where they hold the Farmer's Market in summer. I've got the brights on and I drive to sweep them around, but there's no one there. Carlton's back home, already in his old room. He hasn't called his wife yet, but the yard light was working when I pulled out. He waved from the door and told me to have a good time, and I wonder now what I'm going to tell him.

I make up a story about Amy getting caught, about how at this very moment she's locked in a room somewhere in the colony, the door barricaded by German men all in black. But, though I've made this all up, I start to get the hollow feeling I've been stood up—that Hoots can probably be just as mean as us.

I park and turn off the lights and then the engine. I roll down the window to let the cold in. A few cars make their way past, grinding over the ice in the street, but it's a pretty quiet night.

The cab light flashes on when I open my door and I close it quick to be back in the dark. I walk through the lot, picturing the boxes of baby potatoes and long zucchinis, the giant loaves of bread the Hutterites sell.

I catch a glimpse of someone slipping through the light by the street, a thin blade of a person, walking fast, toward me, and for an instant I think this could actually all come true. But the person hustles on, not swerving an inch my way before disappearing around the corner.

I walk back to the truck and sit down, slicked with sweat from that instant of fear, but with the cold sinking deep inside my clothes, inside my bones. I think again of Carlton at the ranch, of the pipes that'll never freeze, and I turn the engine over, listen to its cranky roar.

After Carlton left us that day, after he'd shouted, "Go ahead then, starve!" Mom and I'd skittered around each other in the big house like it was us that'd had the fight, instead of her and Carlton. I went to bed early just to get away from it. Then I lay in the dark, looking at all the new empty filling my room without Carlton. That's how I heard the shots, a lot of them, hot and fast, and I knew Carlton was still out there somewhere in the dark, killing things.

I don't know if Mom heard or not.

All night I waited for him to come back, and I snuck downstairs before it even got light, still in my pajamas. The kitchen was cold and I shivered, but I decided Carlton really was gone, and that from now on I'd have to give Mom more of a hand. I started the fire in the stove, and got the coffee out. It wasn't till I was getting the water for the pot that I saw what Carlton had done. His final outrage.

The only light on in the house, the one I'd turned on when I reached the kitchen, was just strong enough to cut through the glarey old glass of the sink window. Carlton must've known that. It lit the head of the elk he'd hung from the porch rafters, hung so it'd stare inside the house, stare in at Mom making coffee, which was how every other day had always started here. The elk eyes were already sunken and gray, not shiny black or alive, and its tongue dangled out like something obscene. Its little spike horns looked like the devil's, and I jumped back, my heart oilcanning, quick bile burning my throat.

I went outside without even grabbing a coat, barefooting over the crunching frost to the shop for a ladder so I could get the elk head down before Mom found what Carlton had done. But, once on the ladder, I couldn't get the come-along to let loose, even beating on it with my numb fists.

I ran back inside, breathing hard, like I was barely holding back from crying, and I threw on Carlton's jacket for the first time, his shit-kicking coat, and stepped into a pair of rubber overboots two sizes too big for me. I dashed back out to the shop, judging the coming of day by the strip of gray edging the horizon, and I moved even faster, trip-ping in the big boots, needing to get this done before Mom got up, needing to do that more than I'd ever needed anything.

Grabbing a hammer I made it back up the ladder and I beat on the come-along release until there was the sudden quick shriek of whistling cable and the flat thwap of the head striking the planks of the porch, the wood-on-wood sound of the antlers. It rocked the lad-der, and I hung tight for an instant before starting the careful descent in my clumsy shoes. That was when I saw Mom, tousled from the bed, like she hadn't slept any more than I had. She stood in the center of the kitchen, in her bathrobe, far away from the counters, from any-thing she could grab for support. She was watching me.

I didn't know how much she'd seen, so before going in I rolled the head off the porch, hoping I could get it away before Mom left the house. But as soon as I walked through the door, Mom held her arms open for me and when I stepped into them she held me tight, and I said, "He didn't mean it, Mom."

Mom kept tisking at how cold I was, like I hadn't said a thing, but she stopped dead then, only running her fingers down the seams of the coat she had just noticed was Carlton's. "We're going to miss him, Drew," she said, her voice shivery. "We'll just have to do our best without him."

And that's when, I realized at last, I'd decided that rather than doing that with her, I'd do my best at being both of us instead.

I blow out a big breath that fogs the windshield, then back out of the empty Farmer's Market without looking over my shoulder, knowing there's nothing behind me I could possibly damage. I start down the strip, falling into the cruising line of the few high schoolers waiting for something to happen.

I figure Carlton's calling his wife. Soon his whole family will be living at the ranch and the yard will always be brightly lit and the elk will be pets again. I figure sometime soon, before spring, I'll call and tell Carlton not to mow the graves, so Mom can have the elk up there with her.

In front of me the high schoolers are turning around, starting back the way they came. I rub my face and when it's my turn at the end of the drag, instead of turning around, I keep going. In a minute I'm out of town altogether, the whole world black except for the tiny spot inside my headlights.

I play out the run of road ahead of me. Not too far ahead is the section road cutting off toward Goodhaven, where the pretty Hoot lives with all those grim men in black, those big women in their polka dots. Beyond that is everything else, even, I figure, Texas. With no idea which turn I'll take, I wonder if this is the same way Carlton went.

Jacob Dies
Allen Morris Jones

IF THERE WAS NOTHING BEHIND HIM, it was not an argument for moving on. If there was nothing ahead of him, it was not an argument for staying. He was through with arguments. He stared at his gloved hand around the coil of barbed wire and it was like he could have been holding a pistol, a knife, a can of oil, anything at all: connections were not being made, names were falling away. He wondered if he was going crazy. He wondered if it would snow. He decided that he was in fact crazy, that it would in fact snow.

Half a mile away, he watched as Laura pulled their old Dodge up to the south pasture gate. She stepped out of the truck, opened the gate, then drove through without stopping. The truck chewed its way through the stubble toward him, pushing patterns of ducks out from the steaming, spring-fed ponds.

It had been a cold winter. Of the few things he knew about himself, he was pretty sure he didn't like winter. Even at the age of twenty-eight, his hands cracked in the dry cold and the shoulder that he'd popped out of joint twelve years ago kept him awake at night. His lips sometimes bled after even half a day working in the February wind.

She pulled up beside him and rolled down her window. "Jake," she said.

That was all it took. His name snapped back at him.

He hooked the coil of wire around the post and laid his wire-cutters on top. "You were going to let them bulls on the other side just waltz on through, I guess." He nodded at the half-dozen Angus bulls grazing not a hundred yards from the gate she'd left open.

"It's colder today," she said, smiling lightly. "I thought you might want some coffee."

She was a light-boned woman, and pale; smiling under the kind of cheekbones that made you think of folk singers. Her hair had been long and fine until he'd told her it would get in the way of ranch work and she'd let him cut it. Where was she from? Virginia, maybe. She had a southern accent, though not much of one. Why was her left pinky so crooked? How did she break it?

He stepped forward and took the empty Styrofoam cup from her hand, holding it as she reached through the window and poured from the thermos. He sipped from the cup then immediately tossed it to the ground. "It's cold," he said.

She smiled at him disarmingly, tilting her head. He made sure he remained expressionless, but that head-tilt just melted him.

"I must have let it set for a while," she said.

That stood between them until she took her arms off the truck door and wrapped them around her waist. "God, it's cold."

"Yesterday was colder, I believe," he said.

"I think I'm going to head into town today." She was staring past him up into the Beartooths.

When he didn't say anything, she stepped out of the truck and moved over to kiss him. With the wind blowing, the old snow still skimming along the ground, her lips felt like cold steel, taking his skin with it when she pulled away.

"Get me some cigarettes why don't you. I'm almost out." He touched her hand.

"I may be in there for a day or two. That house gets me a little stir crazy." She pulled away from him.

"Well, hell. I'll go in with you. We'll cut up the town and then just be unstirred crazy together."

"I should go by myself," she said. "Jacob."

He went so still inside.

His cheeks were heavy and hung there. He stared up at the sky, at the highest sheaf of clouds layered not unlike the rough slide of a sand dune, not unlike the deepening wrinkles in his own face. He took a breath. "Your hands," he finally said, reaching forward to touch one again, "have always given you away. First thing. Look at them thin bones. Like the ribs on a housecat. Nobody with hands like that could ever fit in around here."

She took back her hand and stared at him, rubbing her skin as if he had burned her.

Over her shoulder, he saw Mac, his red heeler, come up out of a dry irrigation ditch to run silently toward them. The woman followed his eyes and was just able to jump back into the truck before the dog reached her. Only then did Mac start barking, crouching down and glaring up at her with his thick, muscular head covered with the blood of something small.

"Somebody's going to shoot that dog one of these days," she said, kicking the truck into gear.

HE DROPPED HIS COAT AND GLOVES on the floor, wincing as the gloves peeled away a fresh scab on the back of his hand. He must have scraped through with the barbs. He hadn't felt it.

He stood over the floor vent and held out his hands, glancing around. Her books were gone. A painting she had done, a jumping trout in pastels, was gone. The small black-and-white television with the tin-foil rabbit ears was gone—and that had been his.

So that was it. He walked through the house in his socks, counting up what she had taken. Her books. Her CDs and a few of his—the Hank Williams that she'd liked, the Patsy Cline. But no note on the kitchen table. That was the most conspicuous absence. He brought his hand to his mouth and sucked absently at the blood.

He opened the kitchen cabinets. Her vodka was gone, but she'd left him the Jack. He poured a few fingers into a tin measuring cup, shot in a little water from the tap, and continued stalking around the house, speeding up as he felt the booze.

The guns were still there. His .357, .243, and 7mm. His 12 gauge and sawed-off 10 that his grandfather had given him when he'd said he wanted to go dove hunting.

So this was what it had come down to. Five years of work for that bastard Denton and what did he have? A dog-piss-stained couch. A truck that'd just got stole. A horse. How could anybody have lived like this. It suddenly struck him, with greater strength the faster he walked, that this was no game. No movie. This was his life, and Christ he was fucking it up.

He threw the empty cup across the room, denting the bare wall and sending out a small puff of plaster. He pulled the 10 gauge out of the cabinet: sweet little thing. It'd been years since he'd shot it. The bluing worn away from the barrel. The stock rough and ridiculous looking where he'd tried to checker it with an ice-pick and hammer.

There were fifteen or so shells in the bottom of the cabinet, their box yellow and crumbling. He broke the gun down and slid two of them in, not caring how old they were, not caring that the barrel was wrapped wire and just as likely to explode in his face as not. He wanted noise. He wanted destruction.

The couch got it first. Both barrels from ten feet. Blue smoke and threads of polyester floated down. Then the bookshelf. His tattered copies of Hemingway and Capstick turned to black shreds with one barrel, *The Stockman's Handbook* with the other. After he'd put a round into the wall where her painting had been, he was past hearing the shots and was feeling them only in his chest: a suddenly echoing chamber, an empty network of veins each retaining some measure of the noise, the destruction.

He stopped while he still had a few shells left and stood breathing, the gun loose in his hands. The world was entirely quiet, and his eyes blurred in the smoke. Nothing left but the odor of gunpowder, the odor of slowly smoldering books.

He walked to the window and stared out, the gun like a crossbar in front of him.

BEFORE HE LEFT, he filled a bucket half with grain and went out to feed Caballo, slapping her on the neck and combing through the mane with his fingers.

"You'll be all right," he said. "You'll do good."

He led her through the corral and across the tracks and down into the stubble field: the ponds that stayed open, the fringes of missed grain. A good three months of high winter living in that pasture.

He and Mac slept that first night in an old line shack he knew about from working the Pierson place. He left tracks in the floor dust, and when he sat on the cot, he heard a quick skittering of mice from the floor to the walls. Cold enough to freeze the breath on his mustache and still there were mice. In the night, one of them ran across his face.

He stood and went to lean against the jamb, smoking and slowly waking up, staring out onto the moon-smoothed land, how it rolled and built and gathered into the white shoulders of the mountains.

If he thought about what he was doing for long, if he stopped to consider it, he knew that he would have to go back. Or not go back, not with the ranch house in that shape, but veer off away from her, pursue some other end. So he stood and smoked and thought about nothing at all, bringing his mind, after three cigarettes, down into a peaceful blank.

She had talked about Helena some. He would go there first. About some motel where she'd stayed. What the hell was it called?

And if he caught up to her. What then? Noise and destruction? Tearful apologies? He had no idea.

Behind the glow of his cigarette, he felt like something that had been left behind thirty or forty years before. Most of his life he'd tried for sincerity, for honesty, and when these had failed, had exorcised his frustrations in work: in the patient training of horses and the herding of cattle and the constant smell of shit. He didn't particularly like himself, but then, he liked no one else better. Except, occasionally, for Laura.

Ten years ago, it had still been possible to think of working toward your own place. He'd tied on with Denton with the idea of building a herd and finally, somehow, making a down payment. But then Hollywood had changed everything. Even in eastern Montana, the driest land had gone up to more than a hundred bucks an acre. Hell.

So he had just worked. There was nothing else to do. Bleeding from the lips, bleeding from his hands.

Last year, trying to excise a cheek abscess, one of Denton's steers had kicked him in the ribs. All of a sudden, it had hurt to breathe.

He'd taped himself up and went back out to the pasture, finding the profile of the abscess like a buried fist under the skin of the steer's jaw. He rode up to within twenty yards, rested off his knee, and popped the outer edge of the abscess with his .22 magnum. There was the sudden spray of puss and a bawling, bleeding, shitting steer, and his own feeling of ridiculousness. Later, he'd shot a hawk just to see it fall and bounce off the limbs. And then, feeling so goddamned awful over what he'd done, drove into town to drink and finally get into a fight with the sheriff's son.

Then he'd met Laura. He'd been leaning over the pool table for a shot and she'd put her quarters down. Their eyes met. The jukebox jangled to a stop. The world stopped spinning. All that sort of thing. With her long hair and white sweater over her jeans she'd really been something. And her cheekbones! She'd smiled and tilted her head. And then ran the first two tables she played. She talked like an easterner but he'd never known anybody from the East that could shoot pool like her.

That had been last year.

HE CAME OUT OF THE MOUNTAINS a week later, his dog limping at his heels, his duffel over his shoulder, his shotgun within the duffel: all but the last two shells had been spent on grouse. With a hobo's beard and his jacket tattered at the cuffs and collar, the back of his gloves stained with blood from his lips, he seemed less like a cowboy than some wilderness fugitive, some penniless, lawless drifter: which he was.

But it was a fine afternoon, and it seemed that the mountains—being away from all the light and noise—had wrung something out of him. It had begun to snow again. The road in front of him, whatever road it was, roped through the hills pale as ice. He walked north down the center line, and was soon leaving tracks on the asphalt. Half an hour after dark, when he was just starting to think about building a fire in the borrow ditch, a pair of headlights topped the rise behind him. An old International pickup, and when it pulled up to him its window was already rolled down. He could feel the heat from inside.

"Lookin for a ride?" The driver was Hispanic (although he spoke without an accent), and his black mustache drooped straight and stiff as a gaucho's. He wore a Steelers cap raveling across the brim.

Jacob nodded. "I got me a dog."

"If he don't mind the cold, he can ride in back, I guess."

Jacob went around to drop the tailgate for Mac, then carried his duffel around to throw it on the floorboards next to the gearshift. He pulled himself in after it.

"I'm headin up to Great Falls," the driver said.

Jacob nodded, holding his red and burning hands out to the truck's heater. "Wouldn't have a cigarette on you, would you?"

The driver dug into his shirt pocket and handed him an envelope filled with hand-rolleds. "Take a couple. You look like you been without for a while."

"Appreciate it."

"You much of a talker? We got us a few hours, here."

Jacob lit a cigarette. "What do you want to talk about?"

"Hell, I don't know. Bosnia. Clinton. Tama Janowitz. Anything. My wife left me a week ago and I ain't said five words since."

"So tell me about your wife." He leaned back and crossed his arms. The fresh heat was soaking through his jacket, taking the strength out of him.

"Oh, God, my wife. Jesus Christ." The driver shook his head, and lit one of his cigarettes. "Pretty. Real pretty. But, man! The stuff she was into. I could tell you stories . . ."

Jacob leaned forward and ground out his cigarette in the ashtray and leaned back to tip has hat over his eyes. He woke up only later— it felt like much later—when they pulled into a gas station.

The red and green light was a wash across his face. In the side mirror, he watched the driver (he still hadn't heard, or didn't remember, the man's name) twist the cap on and walk in to pay. Jacob had never stolen a truck before, but it was such a simple thing to move over behind the wheel, twist the ignition key, and drive away.

HELENA HAD CHANGED even in the few years since he'd been there. Congress was in session, and that afternoon, after checking into a motel, he took a stroll up the hill, his thumbs in his jeans.

Even the politicians had changed. Christ. He watched a pair of them climb up the steps: their bodies lean and trim; their briefcases shiny and new. Democrats, probably. The politicians he voted for still walked a little bowlegged, still had honest beer bellies draping down to hide their belt buckles.

He tried to imagine her in Helena.

It was how he hunted deer in the bottoms: a lot of standing and smoking and imagining where a buck should be. In this way, he imagined Laura dancing, head thrown back, laughing above the backward curve of her white neck, one hand held high with a drink. Incongruously, there was a pool table in the corner.

So. A bar with a pool table *and* a dance floor.

He didn't know Helena. It had Government. Did Government drink? Did Government dance?

Not with Laura, he was pretty sure.

He drank his way through three bars, tying Mac up outside each one and easing down into a kind of slow, boiling depression. The fourth bar, mostly empty by one o'clock in the morning, had as its only drinkers a pair of dudes dressed as cowboys. They stood around the pool table, studying the lay of the balls. And when one of them bent to make a shot, a beer sign reflected off the silver on his heel and toe.

"Nice boots," Jacob said. "Pretty."

They both straightened and looked at him. The one closest to the door, with sideburns and a bolo tie, shifted his grip on his pool cue.

"Jack Daniels on the rocks," Jacob said to the bartender, who reached behind him for the bottle without taking his eyes off Jacob.

"So," Jacob said, taking his drink and toasting them, "you pretty boys come here often?"

"Buddy," Bolo-tie said, "you are asking to get your ass kicked." And he stepped forward, hefting the cue.

"Not in this bar," the bartender said, picking up a baseball bat from the corner. "Wayne? Craig? If you want to thump him, you take him outside."

The dudes moved forward together.

Jacob reached into his duffel and pulled out the 10 gauge, dropping the bag and stepping back far enough to cover both the bartender and the dudes.

They all stopped. "Shit," the bartender said. "Put the gun away, mister. You got no reason."

"I got reason."

"What do you want? Money? Booze."

Jacob shook his head and stepped to the side, narrowing the angle between himself and the back of the bar. With no thought, no consideration to the moment, he fired the first of his two barrels along the rows of bottles, sending a wave of broken glass and booze to the floor.

"What do you want?" the bartender asked again, his face expressionless, caught between anger and fear.

"I want people to stop dressing up like goddamned cowboys!" And he blew off his second barrel at the pool table. He scattered the balls, and, from the way they jumped back, managed to put a pellet or two into the dudes. That 10 gauge always did have a wide pattern.

He stood with the gun at his shoulder, amazed at the emotional purge that one pull of the trigger had given him. A clean feeling, all in a rush. Like coming out of the mountains. He was laughing.

Then the bartender was jumping over the bar with the bat. "Two's all you got," he said, coming at him.

Jacob flipped the gun around and ducked under the bartender's first, clumsy swing. It was an easy thing for him to come up out of his crouch, to cold-cock him with the butt of the shotgun.

But then one of the dudes caught the shotgun by the barrel and the other, Bolo-tie, caught his arms. He stepped on the arch of a foot, shoved the stock into a face, and made a break for the door.

Outside, he was fumbling to untie Mac when they blind-sided him against the cold brick of the wall. They held him upright by the neck and chin. He could feel the punches in his ribs, against his cheeks; but there was no real pain. Mac darted in between them, taking pieces out of their calves. They kicked at him uselessly, then finally let Jacob drop in order to turn to the dog.

Jacob slumped to the ground, blind with blood and anger. Through the punch buzz and ring in his ears, he could hear his dog's first, pained yelps. "Mac," he said, struggling back up. "You bastards."

Then the tip of one of the pretty silver boots caught him below the eye; his head snapped back on a loose pivot, and that was all, for a while.

HE WOKE IN STAGES, TASTING BLOOD and the loose change of his broken teeth. It was getting lighter: he could just see out of the alley and onto the street. A bakery truck drove by, its lights still on. He sat up and put his hand down on Mac.

Mac, with old blood pooled around his head and his mouth tensed open against nothing, his legs poised and cold and hard.

Jacob slid down against the wall, already smoothing back the clotted fur. He could feel no line of distinction between the sharp, concentrated pain in his mouth and the dull, formless hurt that was suddenly everywhere else. He tugged at Mac's collar, trying to bring him over onto his lap. There was a dull ripping sound as he came off the pavement, like a sheet being torn apart. Mac lay across his legs.

Bastards, he thought, oh you bastards. And he could think nothing else. Wanted to think nothing else.

IT HAD BECOME NOT SO MUCH A QUESTION of when he would find Laura as to how long they would let him look, how long he could run before they caught him. There was no question of who *They* were. Skinny politicians. Dog shooters. The college professor who had flunked him out of freshman English.

If not Helena, Jacob thought that she would go to Missoula. She had talked about how she missed college, how she would have liked to have gone on to graduate school. She had been mentioning it lately like an accusation.

He drove without consideration, wiping the slow blood away from his nose and lips until the top of the International's steering wheel grew tacky with it.

He drove and imagined her in Missoula, walking around the campus, stopping to stare into dorm windows. He imagined her in the library, among the computers and librarians.

Before Laura, he had never been in love. Was this how it always went? Was this how it was for everyone? In the last few weeks it had almost seemed like they had been trying to steal the comfort from each other. He would find a sopping wet towel left coiled on his side of the bed. She would find her bathwater scalding hot. He thought now that it had all been a way of trying to bring themselves back from the third that had stood between them for a while, that amalgam of love and dependency.

His face was painless. His ribs were painless, although he did find an odd, numbed, restriction there when he tried to breathe. One eye wasn't blinking the way it should. It was like there was nothing left. He had been filled with leaves, with smoke.

Was it worth it? What was he looking for, after all? Was it still Laura? Laura. Who was Laura?

He laughed around broken teeth.

An inversion had dropped a ceiling of frost down onto Missoula, and as he came into town it was like plowing into snow.

He took a turn around the campus, and then another, thinking he might have missed her on the first pass. But no Laura. Hell, this wasn't her, anyway. One thing about Laura, she wasn't a bullshitter.

He worked his way back through town, across one bridge and then another, finally finding himself in front of an old movie theater. On the tattered marquee, barely lit, was *Last Tango in Paris*. And *that* was Laura. Precisely.

He was exultant as he slammed the truck up against the curb, jumping out to feel the first real stabs of pain. As if the rush of blood had finally filled and overloaded fist-weakened vessels. His left eye went black, and he could feel it drooping in its socket.

But what was an eye, after all? He stumbled through into the theater, covering it with his hand. An old man cleaning the popcorn machine backed away and knocked a bottle of Windex off the counter behind him. "Good God," he said, just loud enough for Jacob to hear.

The movie was almost finished, almost empty. He stood waiting for his eye to adjust to the gloom. The few seats with forms in them seemed occupied by groping college students. He stood there until those nearest him turned to tell him to sit down. A girl squeezed up against her boyfriend and the boyfriend almost stood up, but then thought better of it.

He stood in the aisle at a loss, not knowing where he should go from here. Finally, he just yelled out into the rows, sure that she was there somewhere, ducking down. "Laura, you bitch! Get out here!"

A voice behind him yelled, "Put your hands *up*!"

He turned and saw a pair of forms silhouetted in the door, crouched blackly in the light from the lobby. Of course, it was no one he would know. No one he would recognize. No sheriff or sheriff's sons. These were young, ambitious silhouettes. Young sports.

It was not what he had imagined for himself: jail.

He made a motion with his arms, as if he were raising a pistol, then jumped back from the flashes from their barrels. There was screaming, and a sudden rush toward the exits.

He struggled to join the rush, only aware as he was running that he had been shot, that the squelching in his shoes was neither piss nor Coke, and that it was spurting down his leg in an exact rhythm with his steps.

The cops would follow him. They would be smashing him up against a wall.

He made the exit and just managed to duck into a recessed door, standing straight into its shadow. The cops, being too young and sportish, ran right past him, holding their guns awkwardly out in front of them.

It was an easy thing to slip out and run the other way.

But it was only a few steps, a few staggering lurches, before he felt his leg giving out on him. The darkness on the periphery of his one good eye seemed to suddenly grow much darker, and the horizon around him tilted and spun.

The theater exit had been below street level, and he found himself standing under the bridge he'd driven over just a few minutes before.

He leaned against one of the concrete supports and slipped to the ground. Under his hands, his leg was entirely numb. He squeezed it as tightly as he could manage. The bone seemed sound, but the blood . . . his blood was still pulsing out onto the anonymous ground.

He leaned his head back and let his hands fall away. Let them lay flat on a surface of pigeon shit and blood and broken glass. He tried to laugh a little, but found everything that could have given rise to such laughter gone.

There, the cold concrete of the bridge against his back, the heat of his own life spreading out under his legs and growing cold, he imagined Laura someplace warm, someplace with a beach. Dying himself, he couldn't imagine her alive. Couldn't imagine her laughing or dancing or crying.

He closed his eyes against the new blood of the world and found a wave rolling up, cresting above the horizon, and behind it another. And he found Laura within the waves. A light from behind her, or perhaps beneath her, illuminated an electric spread of hair and naked, broken limbs. As he coughed and slid down to rest his cheek on the ground, he saw her poised there, stiff and askew: like some animal come from the ancient depths only to pause at the new edge, finally uncertain.

Do You Hear Your Mother Talking?
William Kittredge

THEY OFFERED ME WORK IN THE MILL when the woods were closed down, but we had enough money and I hate the cold and ringing of the night shift, everything wet and the saws howling. So I stayed home with Ruth.

This is one of those company towns the loggers build on its second-growth hillsides. You can stand at our big window and not see anything but the dripping roofs of green frame houses below us in the brush and piles of split wood covered with plastic tarps and old swing sets and wrecked cars, most of them without glass or tires, which are bright and washed in the rain, and stained with rust, and you can watch the rain dimple the puddles showing black and wet on the black asphalt, and you can wonder.

The place where Ruth parked her DeSoto was empty, and I figured she must have gone down to be at the Mercantile when it opened. My Chevy four-by-four was on blocks in the shed behind the house. I thought about spending the afternoon getting it ready to ship south again.

It surprises me even now. I let the idea go through my mind with the taste of the coffee because I had wondered when I would come to feel that way. It just came to my head. I could feel myself leaving.

It was a dream in which Ruth was staying behind forever. For a long moment I couldn't even get myself to see her face, or understand how I had come to this yellow-painted kitchen in Alaska. The idea of leaving just fell into me like a visitor. I blew my breath on the window, and rubbed my initials in the steamy place.

It was light as it was going to get. The coffee was heavy and sweet, so I poured another cup and lit up another cigarette. Some days nothing moves. You can look out at the evening and see the fog that was there in the morning, feathering off into the canyon where the river cuts toward the ocean. What saved it was Ruth's old DeSoto. She had the headlights glowing. Ruth drives slow and careful.

Outside you could hear the water in the river. I stood on the porch, holding the coffee cup, and watched her park. Ruth got a paper sack in her arms, and stepped around the puddles until she was beside me. Her hair was wet on her forehead and the shoulders of her cloth coat were soaked. She grinned and shoved the sack at me, and I knew I wasn't going anywhere.

During the winter Ruth can look blotched and strange. Some nights she will go alone to a movie and come back after I am sleeping. But she was smiling, and I could read myself, and I had to smile.

"Turn off the headlights," I said, and I took her sack. Ruth ran back through the rain and stuck her head inside the car door and fumbled at the switch. Her skirt was pulled high and it stuck to the backs of her legs, and I could see the dark net of veins behind her knees.

In the summer when we met, Ruth was brown from the sun and her legs looked like something out of pictures. She was working nights as a cocktail waitress in Brownie's, and sleeping away her days on the beach. I caught her there early one morning and I woke her, not so much to start something with her as interested in why these runaway women act like they do. You see them in the mill, dirty and wet and working too hard and determined to be single as possible. And this one was a flirt at Brownie's, which was the other thing.

She told me she could always sleep if she was listening to the ocean, and she smiled and didn't look unhappy with me at all. Her hair was long and yellow and she was hard and tight enough, even after two kids, but she was a little too easy. That was the first thing they told me about her. That she had two kids living with her first husband, but she was eager and not bad. She never talks of her other life and has never hinted at going to see those kids. She slammed the car door and came back. "I got bacon and eggs and juice," she said, taking the sack. "I'm going to cook a regular breakfast."

THE FIELDS SMELLED OF FIRE. You could imagine runs of fire burning behind the combines. My father would shred the heads of the ripe barley between his callused hands, and blow away the chaff and bite down on the kernels, chewing like they were something to eat. I would lie on my back, hidden down in the barley, breathing in the smell while the stalks rattled in the breezes. All I could see was the sky. Ruth might have been with me, listening and quiet. That would have been a fine childhood thing, me and Ruth.

Ruth smiles when she looks away to the window where the rain runs in streaks. You have to wonder who she sees in her reflection, and what kind of family she sees in me and her.

WE LIVE ON A BIG CEDAR-FOREST ISLAND at the edge of the Japanese Current, where it never snows. Everything comes in by boat or floatplane. Ruth and I do not tell each other much of what we came from, letting it go at the fact that we are lucky, and here.

The first morning, after we woke up in her bed, she came along to spend the day with me. It was her funeral. Before noon we were down in the tavern, which is a dark old barn built of cedar planking and shakes, called Brownie's since it was built in the early days of this town. No one knows who it was named for. Big smoky windows look out to the street, if you want to look. All winter while it rains people gather to sit around a barrel stove welded together from sections of culvert, looking at the little isinglass window in the door, where you can see in at the fire. The shadows run up the walls and over our faces.

"We can give them something to talk about," Ruth said that first morning. That's when I said it was her funeral. I should have told her I was proud to walk in with her. That was October, and I was already done falling timber for another winter. The low clouds hung down into the fog coming off the seawater. That afternoon we sat outside Brownie's under the veranda, on the wood bench where everybody has carved their initials. We had our cans of beer and we were out of the rain as we watched the two nuns go along with their tiny steps on the board sidewalk. You could see the trouble they had taken to make themselves precious in the world.

"They think it's something," Ruth said.

I'll give myself some credit. Right then I knew this wasn't just some woman from the night before.

THE DARK RED BEDSHEETS ARE PART OF RUTH, and her saving graces. She changes them every day. She says winter is underwater enough without damp sheets.

The rain was flushing through the galvanized gutter above the window. Ruth would be in close beside the oil stove and reading. I could see her, wrapped in one of the Hudson Bay blankets I bought in Victoria. She keeps a pile of magazines on the floor beside the new platform rocker that was supposed to be mine after we moved in together.

Turned out I like to sit at the kitchen table, under the bare bulb. Ruth wanted to put a shade on the bulb, but I said no. There is a big window in the kitchen. I can see out into the canyon through the mirror of my face on the inside of the window and imagine the runs of salmon, and the old Tlingit fishermen in their round cedar hats.

MY FATHER AND MY MOTHER WERE SLEEPING and I stood in the doorway and watched them sleep in the square of moonlight from the window. I walked away beside the shadows of the long row of poplar trees that ran between the irrigation ditch and the road from the house. Over on the highway at daybreak, while the sprinklers turned their arcs over the alfalfa, I hooked a ride on the back of a stake-bed truck. The last thing I saw was the trees along the high irrigation ditch; I can still see them clear as yesterday. My father was just like me. But Ruth is nothing like my mother. I wonder what a kid would remember from this place we live in Alaska.

THE CARDBOARD PATCHES RUTH NAILED over the knotholes are already turning green. At least we didn't buy the house. I was right about buying the house. This is not the house we want. We want to build a house of cedar logs.

Ruth always keeps a big jug of orange juice in the refrigerator. It burns away the taste of my cigarettes. That first night, in her cabin on the beach, Ruth said she had grown up learning to sleep naked. I can almost taste the feel of her.

All this winter my boots sat over by the wall, ready and oiled for the day when I can go back into the timber. You have to wonder what there is to like about falling those virgin-growth cedar trees, and what kind of man would stay with timber-falling long as I have. The cedars are the most beautiful trees in the world. The red-grained back-wedge comes falling out, and I shut down my long-bladed Stihl, and I sit there letting the quiet settle in. I work alone, which is dangerous, but I want silence when I shut down the saw. The sawdust smells like some proper medicine. Right then I have enough of everything.

The first-growth trees fall true as angels, with the whoosh of their needles through the air, and they are dead. Like the natives I have learned to tell the trees I am sorry, but not so sorry I won't cut another in the afternoon. You kill to fill your belly, and then you tell them it was necessary. You have to smile at such things.

It is my best life, out in the woods, and this winter there have been times I ache for it as I sit through the rainy afternoon in Brownie's and listen to the talk of fish. I wonder if falling trees is a true work. But I forget such worries as Ruth and I walk downhill through the dripping early darkness to the movie house, and we are saying hello to everybody and Ruth is excited like a girl.

———————

"I WALKED IN THE RAIN," Ruth said. "After you went to sleep I walked in the rain."

"You got to tell me what was wrong with you," she said, and she ran her cool fingers down the long scar on my inner arm.

Each step of it seemed right at the time. I can see the pale tender skin along the inner arm separating as the blade traced toward the wrist, my flesh parting along the length of my wound in a perfect clean way, and the tough white sheath and the deeper seeping meat before it is all drowned in blood.

I am telling you about craziness. I lay in those beds and I thought I heard my mother's voice and never slept until I came to believe there was some tiny thing wired into my arm, and electrical circuits flashing along with their messages, right at the core of my arm like a little machine, and all of it a trick. Then I could sleep, because I knew someone could cut it out with a surgeon's blade.

The idea got me in trouble. I found out about doctors, and I went into the office of the best doctor in Klamath Falls. I asked him to cut the wiring out of my arm, and the crazy part was cutting on myself when he refused.

It seemed like a good idea to think my troubles could be solved by the touch of what they call micro-sharpened knives. It was the kind of thing you come to believe like babies believe the things they learn before they are born. It was like knowing which way is up. But the trouble with me is over. I sit in our kitchen and read hunting magazines, and I imagine stalking waterbirds like they were my friends. I am telling you about craziness, but I wouldn't tell Ruth. "We all been born with too much time on our hands." That is what I said.

We have nights to think about our earliest memories. In mine there is a red dog resting in the dust beside a stunted little lawn juniper and the crumbling concrete walkway. There is a thunderstorm breaking. That was out front of the apartment building where we lived when I was a little child in the farmhand town of Malin, on the northern fringes of the potato land that drops toward Tule Lake and California. My mother walked me on the sidewalks, in and out of the stores, and to the barbershop where they smiled when I climbed up to the board across the arms of the chair.

That red dog barked in the night, but usually he was sleeping and wrinkled in the dust. What I see are heavy drops of rain. I can still count them as they puff into the dust. I can close my eyes and call up those raindrops striking each by each. Like my mother would say, "Each thing in its place." I can hear her voice clear as my own.

My father had his two hundred acres of barley-farming property out south of the Klamath Falls airfield; he was hiring winos to herd his few hundred head of turkeys, and he always had my mother. I would ride out with him in the gray pickup truck, gone to check on the well-being of his turkeys, and then home to my mother. Him and my mother, in those good years after the war, they called themselves the free world. But they were playing it like a joke, at parties, with other men and women. Men would come to the kitchen while my father was gone, and my mother would pour whiskey. They would sit at the kitchen table with their whiskey in a tumbler, and my mother would laugh and stand beside them, and those men would hug her around the waist and smile at me while they did it. "You better go outside," my mother would tell me, and she would already be untying her apron.

"We was late with our lives," my father told me. "Me and your mother, so we just stayed with our playground." He told me there was too much room for running with your mind when he was growing up in Tule Lake during the Great Depression. He said he went crazy during those years, and that I should be careful if I got my imagination from him. My father told me this when I was thirteen, maybe as a way to explain his lifetime. That was the first time I left, wishing I could hear my mother say goodbye.

———

"IF YOU WON'T ANSWER ME," Ruth said, " I was only going to tell you what happened." She was at the stove, tending the eggs and bacon.

"You were feeling bad," I said, "and you had a few beers and you walked in the rain and felt better. Like nobody ever did."

"I drove down to the ocean," Ruth said, "and walked the beach. Before daylight." Her back was to me. She was turning the eggs. "It was nothing but that and I felt better."

Ruth colors her hair golden and it was running with seawater when she came walking up from the summer ocean. Ruth shook her head, and I knew her face would taste of salt. Right there was the first time she reminded me of my mother. My mother was young, and her bare arms were red in the summer rain. The drops stood in her dark hair as she was laughing in the yellow light under the thunder.

IT WAS JUST BEFORE THE FOURTH OF JULY and hot and clear and still when I came north. The low fog was banked far out over the ocean.

After some drinking I would see the gray summer tide coming cold over the sand and think about the Lombardy poplar trees you could see for twenty miles over the fields of alfalfa on the right sunny day around Tule Lake. If you imagined them clear enough those trees would come closer until their leaves were real, like they could be touched.

Crazy is really a place you could learn to stay. You could learn to live there forever. It was a reason for drinking. I never imagined myself into somewhere else when I was drinking; it was only afterwards.

Down in Victoria I bought myself a whole set of Alaska clothes as if that would turn me into an Alaska man, got me a barbershop shave, and rode the Alaska ferry north. It wasn't the right way to travel into such a place, but it was easy at hand and it was the season for seeing seabirds and all the fishes from whales on down.

The days were warm and sunlit and you could smell the evergreen trees over the diesel exhaust as we came to dock in midafternoon. I walked out over the sandy flats to the ocean, a wind was coming off the fog on the horizon, and I found a stone fireplace where fish had been cooked. The sand was littered with red berry boxes, and there were torn newspapers in the brush. You had to wonder who had been there.

By nightfall I was sitting on the bench outside Brownie's, listening to some men who talk about the salmon run and lumbering. The inside of Brownie's looked hammered out as a cave. I thought of the mills where I have worked, the howl of saws and wet sawdust, and I wondered if I had come to another wrong place as I sat there being a stranger in the side-angle lights outside Brownie's.

Give it a summer, I thought. There was nobody to notify. I had my clothes folded into a canvas warbag and a half dozen thousand dollar bills. My chain saw pays me a hundred and fifty dollars on a good day. Only a fool does things without money.

"WE OUGHT TO BE MARRIED," Ruth said. She was washing the few dishes and stacking them in the open-faced shelves above the sink.

She went on placing the dishes carefully atop one another, then dried her hands and went to stand before the oil stove. "I could have another baby," she said. "It's not too late. That could be my calling." She smiled like that was going to be funny.

I got up and walked away from her and went into the bedroom. After closing the door, I sat on the bed. That could be my calling. I couldn't hear a thing from the other room, not even Ruth moving around. After a while I pulled my worn old black suitcase from under the bed. With the suitcase open the next move was easy. Ruth could come and stand in the doorway and watch while I packed.

"I'll take a little money to travel on," I would say.

She would look down a moment, and her face would show no sign of anything, and I would think it was going to be easy to get out of here with no trouble. "Watch me," I would say. "I'm gone."

When the suitcase was packed I would head past her into the other room, pull on my slicker and leather cap, and go out to the shed where my Chevy four-by-four was up on blocks. It would be dry inside, with the rainwater splattering from the cedar eaves. The dirt is like dust mixed with pine needles.

There is a pint of whiskey hidden under the seat in the Chevy. Two long swallows and I would think about laughing, and sit in the dirt with my back against the wall and whistle ring-dang-do, now what is that.

My mother beat my ass for that song, and washed my mouth in the irrigation ditch. It's a song I think about when I want to remember my mother and the way she laughed and hugged me as we sat on the grass with water coming from her hair in little streams. Now that is not crazy, thoughts of the water streaming through the little redwood weir in that irrigation ditch and my mother knowing some joke I didn't understand.

Ruth came and sat beside me and my black suitcase on the bed, her elbows on her knees and her head down and her hair hanging forward like she was a wrecked woman with nothing to do but study her hands while some man made up his mind about her life. "My mother told me a joke about times like this," I said.

Ruth didn't answer.

"My mother told me everything you got is like a China cup," I said. "Because it never came from China, and you always got to worry if it's going to break."

"Some joke," Ruth said, and her face was an old woman's face when she looked up at me.

Not that Ruth was crying. Her eyes had just gone old, and the strength in her flesh had lost some of its hold on her bones. Her lower lip fell down, and her teeth were stained by so many cigarettes. I could see the years to come, both of us old in some house where she looked like my mother and the radio was always playing in the other room.

OUT AT THE KLAMATH FALLS HOSPITAL, a nurse unlocked the door and I walked into my mother's care, a man thirty-four years old and unable to even trust his own brain.

My mother's hands were cold. What could I tell her? That I had lived too long watching my father turn hermit in the house he built on the corner of his property out by the airfield where the air force pilots flew jet planes every hour or so like a clock. Could I tell her jet air-planes will make you crazy for answers to everything?

She showed me an old photograph of my father: a young man with just the tip of his tongue between his white teeth, and his hands deep in his pockets and the brim of his city-man hat snapped down over one eye, like the picture-taking was going to stop everything for all time at this moment in his schoolyard. Behind him you can see the painted sign: Turkeys. "He was the best man they ever had," my mother said. "Now he's made you crazy."

You could take the same picture of me, deep in my forest beside some fallen cedar tree, and you might think, Who the hell does he think he is? We've all seen pictures of men who are dead now, with their long saws crossed in front of some great stumpage, and their sleeves rolled up over their elbows.

My mother puckered her soft mouth as she eyed me and didn't talk anymore, as if her tongue had locked and she had lost her speech. Then she shook her head. "I'll tell you the joke," she said. "This is the joke of it." She looked around at the house where she was making her stand; expensive hardwood furniture and a mantel decorated with half a hundred engraved stock-show trophies. Silver spires with imitation silver Angus bulls on the top. She didn't look like anything was a joke.

"Things changed," she said. She was trying to make it sound like a hopeful notion. One afternoon she took off in a Lincoln Continental with a heavy-built man nicknamed Cutty. "Cutty had this house left over from the time he was married," she said. "Your father wouldn't even take me to bed. Cutty knew better, right from the start."

She took off those frameless eyeglasses, and cleaned them. There was a box of Kleenex on every table in that house. I picked up one of those trophies with the little silver Angus bull on top, and I thought like a child, so this is the way to be rich.

The fall-of-the-year sunlight percolated into my mother's house through layers of gauzy curtains, and she never went outside. Twice a week there was a cleaning lady, and every day there was a boy delivering things. My mother just cooked me meals and waited for me to make my peace.

There was nothing to know. Maybe it is true about my mother and Cutty. Maybe they are a great love. Over the years Cutty has worked himself up from auctioneer to purebred-cattle breeder. He's always sending flowers from Bakersfield or some show town. She says it's his busy season.

FOR NINE YEARS I WORKED MY SUMMERS in the woods and batched through the winters with my father in his house. On winter afternoons I would drive over to the Suburban Tavern and shoot some pool, and come home to stir up some tuna and noodles for the microwave oven. Nobody, my father or me, ever really cleaned up the kitchen, and more and more I started to feel tuned to the trembling of those microwaves, all the time closer to discovering I had been wired for other people's ideas.

Just a quarter mile south of my father's house there's a barroom built from a Quonset hut back in World War II, with gas pumps out front. My father is still eager for a walk down to the bar and some drinking and talk first thing in the morning. It's just that you can learn to live in some of those stories. But that is enough about craziness. It's a place you swim like deep in the black ocean with strange fishes. You might never want to come up. It's a country where I could go visit and find a home.

Ruth refolded each thing I owned, her hands trembling as she filled that black suitcase. The unshaded overhead light was on bright in our bedroom, and she moved like an underwater creature. "Fine," Ruth said. "Just goddamned fine."

Her face was flushed with that fallen look you might imagine as secret to animals, her eyes glazed like stones and this way and that quick as lizards. I remember my mother late in the night when she was drunk in our kitchen where the windows were glazed with ice. I would come awake from hearing her laugh, and ease from my bedroom where the people's coats were piled on the other bed, and she wouldn't even see me with those eyes. "Just fucking wonderful," Ruth said. "You pitiful son of a bitch," Ruth said, and I didn't know if she meant me or her.

Ruth unfolded my stiff canvas Carhartt timber-falling pants with the red suspenders, the cuffs jagged off and the knees slick with pitch, and she stepped into them and pulled them up and hooked the suspenders over her shoulders, her dress wadded up inside, and she stood there like a circus girl. "How do you think?" she said. "You think I could work in the woods?"

"You ought to have a baby," she said. "You ought to lie down on your back and come split apart and smell your own blood in the room."

"But you never can," she said. "What can you do?"

THIS IS WHAT I COULD DO. I could lace my boots, and I could get the blocks out from under my Chevy and spend the afternoon cleaning the plugs until she idles like your perfect sewing machine. It would be twilight and the white Alaskan ferry boat would be rolling in the long ocean troughs as I would stand at the rail with a pint of whiskey in my hand and watch the cedar-tree mountains turn to night under the snowy mountains beyond to the east. I could go anywhere in America. But Ruth was smiling, and it wasn't her sweetheart smile. "You better get me," she said, and she dropped those suspenders and stepped out of my canvas Carhartt pants.

"You know what I can do?" she said. "I am going to lie down and come unseamed for a baby."

You wonder what the difference is between men and women, and if women really like to think there is some hidden thing inside them that is growing and will one day be someone else, some hidden thing telling them what to do. There was Ruth at thirty-nine years old, with her babies behind her in another end of the world, too old for what she said she wanted, standing there with her hands open and willing to look at the possibility of dying for some baby.

You think of the old explorers. You have to know there was a time when they smelled their land from out to sea and the clouds blew away, and it came to them that this coastline they had found was a seashore where nobody exactly like them was ever given a chance to walk before.

"I'm going to say, Baby," Ruth said, "do you hear your mother talking? Baby, are you listening?"

Me and Ruth were there in the glare off the glass; I could see us, and I had to wonder what children would see if they were watching and looking for hints about who they should come to be. Ruth looked mottled white like the blood was gone out of her. "Either that," she said, "or you can get the hell out of here."

Those old explorers must have studied their mountains, trying to think this was what they had always wanted, this place they didn't know about. You try to control the shaking of your hands, and you want to say, all right, this will be all right, this is what I'll take, I'll stay here.

"We'll split some shakes," I said. Teetering around that room, picking up my stuff and storing it back into where it belonged, refolding those stiff canvas Carhartt pants along the seams, carefully as they could be folded, I felt like a child on a slippery floor and Ruth eyed my moves like all of a sudden she wasn't sure what she wanted after all. Ruth could see I wasn't going anywhere, and the rest was up to her. There was no one thing to say, and I still cannot name the good fortune I saw except as things to do.

"You coming with me?" I said. In this country they roof their houses with shakes split from pure cedar. We went out that afternoon and bought a straight-grain cedar-tree log, and had it hauled to us. Ruth wouldn't hardly look at me or say anything, but she went along.

That night Ruth slept in her chair with her magazines. By late in the next day we had built a canopy of clear plastic to keep our work dry from the rain, and we started splitting the shakes, side by side. We will build a house where our things to do can be thick with time on our hands.

People will watch us build, and we will be the ones who know the secret. We'll watch strangers on the sand flats. We'll know they envy us our house built of cedar logs. We will live with one garden that grows nothing but red and yellow flowers, and we'll have another garden with cabbages. Our dogs and our cats will sleep on the beds, and me and Ruth will carve faces into the cedar-log walls, and those faces will smile back at us in our dreams and be our friends and warn us of trouble, looking at us like we were the world, and watching what we do like we watch the seabirds picking on the rocks at low tide. There will be cabins with covered walkways to the house. My father could live in one, and my mother could come visit, and Ruth and I and my father and my mother could all go down to the movie house and over to Brownie's after the show.

Your mind is sometimes full of little animals and you have to trick them with things to see. We will live in our house like the old people lived in their houses. Maybe we will come to know what it is like to lie awake in the night while our children listen for our talking and laughing as we listen for theirs.

MORPHINE
David Long

HE'S A HANDSOME MAN, lanky, with black sleepy eyes and soft skill-
ful hands: Gerald Wilcox, a doctor in Sperry, Montana, specializing in
the ear, nose, and throat. He no longer drinks much now—cham-
pagne at a wedding, wine at the table if guests are present. A glass,
maybe two. He's not graced with a huge reservoir of will power. You
do what you can, and what he's been able to do is rein in the drinking. Not give it dominion.

"It makes you morose, don't you see that? Not to mention the
driving around, not to mention people's trust in you. It's too small a
town. Why do I have to say these things?"

This is Charlotte talking, his wife of twenty-two years. Born
Charlotte Timmins—calls to mind "timid," that's the joke of it—she
is a tall, forthright woman, brassy-haired. "Gerald," she tells him, "I
am forty-four years old. I never intended to be a woman who wears a
girdle, a woman with chins." She pinches the excess flesh, creates a
wattle, and exhales with showy contempt. Of their marriage, she has
lately said, "This is not a business arrangement, Gerald. This is something else. Do I make myself clear?"

He pretends bafflement. "Darling," he says, "my feelings have
not changed one iota—in fact they've grown deeper, more complex."

But, yes, he knows what she's talking about. Blessedly, these
complaints are intermittent. Life proceeds, slips from one state to the
next; at odd moments, passions reawaken.

Their only child, Jeanette, is plain-faced, secretive, bookish, as
lanky as Gerald. She has recently asked that he knock off calling her
his Little Bean.

"And what might you prefer," he inquired, "Jeanette, Queen of
the Euphrates?"

"Don't be mean," Charlotte told him.

He said he wasn't. "You don't think I'm being mean, do you, honey?" he asked his daughter.

She cut her eyes at him, made them slits. "No, Daddy."

Last year she was reading *Little Women*, this year—it's 1959—John O'Hara. Wilcox came upon the book among her things while foraging for the stapler. "Well, we don't censor what a person chooses to read in this house," Charlotte said when he showed one passage to her.

Wilcox read aloud: "'He kissed her and put his hand on her breast. Without taking her mouth away from his she unbuttoned the jacket of her suit and he discovered that she was wearing a dickey, not a blouse, and then put his hand down into her brassiere until he was able to cup her breast in the curving palm of his hand.'"

A great arching of Charlotte's brows. She brought her face near his. "Oh *my*," she said. "Would you put your hand down into my brassiere, Gerald? Would you cup my breast?"

He has decided that each of them has a talent for secretiveness. Three secret hearts under one roof.

Nearly every night, he inscribes a few lines in his journal. He notes the ebb and flow of infectious disease. If he and Charlotte have been to a movie, a synopsis appears, a terse critique. He makes reference to the weather, if noteworthy: *Cheated of summer this year. Such gloom.* Or: *Woke last evening to a lightning storm. Jeanette came into our bed, fearing wildfires . . . explained how remote the possibility.* Or: *Walked uptown over the noon hour. Green fuzz on the trees all along First.*

Now and then, something like: *Saw Mrs. D—this forenoon, had the very disagreeable task of telling her that the tumor has begun to encroach on the esophagus. Where some people get their stoicism is more than I can fathom.*

Flipping back a few years—1952, 1949—he finds the occasional entry he can make no sense of: *That business with the Bagnolds continues to nettle me.*

Not a clue.

Strangely, he seldom rereads what he's written. He's not addicted to it. If pressed, he couldn't say why he goes to the trouble, except it pleases him to keep this accounting. Giving up the journal falls outside the realm of what he can do.

In any case, the daily drinking is history, done with two years now and not much missed. But one night perhaps every six weeks, he takes to his office—it occupies the spacious front parlor of the house at 118 Plympton Street, a house of high ceilings spidered with hairline cracks, endowed with several rooms the Wilcoxes barely use—and injects himself with an ampule of morphine. Then he composes longer entries in his journal.

For instance: *I do not feel invincible. Indeed, I feel so near the great powers that it is no trouble to imagine being crushed by them, ground into powder, yet I do feel very much alive, there is no doubt of that. A pity one cannot feel this way more of the God-damned time.* Having written this, he pauses. *No, disastrous,* he writes, lets the fountain pen dawdle in his hand.

The journal books, black and soft-sided, are kept in the top-right drawer of his desk. It's a locking desk, but the key has long ago vanished, so it's conceivable that Charlotte has inspected them at length. Perhaps even his daughter as well. Once, he went to the trouble of plucking a long hair from his head, licking it, and pasting it unobtrusively across the opening of the drawer, a trick he'd acquired from a mystery story. Then he thought better of it, and had a laugh at himself.

And, too, some incidents fail to appear in the journals. The night, for instance, when he drove his car onto the ice of McCafferty's Slough. A luscious, ludicrous evening. This slough had the shape of an oxbow, nearly a full circle segregated from the river's main channel by a narrow, birch-lined dike. A thin crust of snow lay atop the ice, but in places the wind had blown it clear. He drove from one end to the other, spinning gloriously, dodging the occasional squat black icehouse. It was late winter, the air mild and seductive. How had he come to be there, out on the ice? Drinking, yes, he'd been to a roadhouse called Sammy's, but he wasn't very drunk, only softened, estranged from care.

Driving, he had been telling one of his oldest, lamest jokes—*Hey, you in the field there, I been going up this hill close to two hours, don't it ever end? Oh hell, stranger, there ain't no hill here, you just lost your two hind wheels*—when the hind wheels of his own car cracked through the ice. McCafferty's Slough wasn't deep, seven or eight feet at most. It harbored perch and whitefish. Muskrats burrowed in the mud along its bank. Walking the ice, you'd see them squiggle out and follow beneath your boots, elongated, trailing bubbles. But there were—he *did* know this—springs feeding the slough, which left the ice untrustworthy in spots. And so as he finessed a lovely skidding spin, telling his lame joke, the back end of the Buick dropped through, stopping them short. It was quickly apparent that no amount of clever rocking back and forth would help.

"For shit's sake, Gerry," his companion said.

She was Glenny Parker, a slender girl with a ferocious hook nose, and a belly that was literally concave. A shallow white basin. At work, sometimes, he thought of his hand idling there, making quarter-size circles, which seemed to please her. She hadn't believed him at first, that he was a doctor, thought he was teasing her.

They set out across the ice, she gripping his arm, with his topcoat around her shoulders, her shoes red kidskin with straps like fine red wire. The night's hilarity had leached away. They hiked back up the gravel ramp they'd barreled down a half hour before. The air seemed less mild now. Wind poured off the foothills, jangling the snowberries and the brittle remains of the cottonwood leaves. Up the way, not far, was a farmhouse with a light burning. As they drew closer, the light went out.

Wilcox squinted at the mailbox, saw the name "Maki." Old Finn, he thought, starting up the drive. A dog emerged from the blackest patch of shadow and ratcheted off a few congested barks, but made no serious effort to charge him.

A cowled light came on above the door. Glenny Parker didn't know whether to follow or stand back out of sight. She elected to do a little of both.

After a moment, a man in pants and nightshirt came onto the canted slab of concrete that served as a back stoop. Unshaven at this hour, he had a big, fair boy's face gone to thickness.

"Who's there?" he said. "Is someone there?" Then, shielding his eyes, "Dr. Wilcox? Is that you?"

All along, the doctor knew, there'd been the chance he'd be recognized, though, naturally, he'd hoped otherwise. But who was this man? A patient? Husband or son of a patient?

Maki looked beyond him. "Somebody out there with you?"

The doctor hesitated, then, hearing Glenny's feet on the gravel, found himself in the position of saying yes, actually, he did have a friend along.

Maki nodded. "That wouldn'ta been you out on the ice?" he asked.

Wilcox wiped his face, chuckled uneasily. "To be honest with you," he said, "I'm in kind of a jam here."

Maki acknowledged that he was. The girl's hands were plunged up to her elbows in the deep pockets of his coat; she looked tiny, brutally out of place. Maki eyed her without comment.

"Let me get the tractor," he said to the doctor.

Wilcox began to protest. All he really wanted was the use of the telephone, though just who he'd had in mind to call at one in the morning wasn't at all clear.

Maki turned back to the girl. "You better wait inside," he said. Head down, she slipped away from Wilcox, went up the stoop, and passed through the mudroom into the bright-lit kitchen.

Maki secured the door, then the two men made their way back to the slough, Maki a stolid unhurried presence at the wheel of the tractor, and the doctor standing on the back, grasping the back rim of the seat, authentically chilled now. Yet thinking, This could turn out all right.

Maki insisted on doing the work himself, crouching on the ice with his tow chain, grunting out a few words that were lost to the Buick's undercarriage. He hoisted himself back up to the seat of the tractor. A short blast of diesel smoke, a slippage of the tire cleats before they grabbed, and the car bumped from its hole.

Wilcox stood by, rubbing his hands.

Maki got down again to uncouple the chain, dropped it with a clank into the box on the side of the tractor, and climbed back to the seat.

A week later, undressing in their bedroom, Charlotte asked, "You remember Arlette Bledsoe? She said her brother gave you a hand the other day."

Arlette Bledsoe's brother?

"Helped with the car, fixed a flat or some such thing?"

"Oh, that," he said. "Yes."

"You didn't mention it."

"I guess I didn't, no."

"They've had a rotten time of it," Charlotte said. She reminded him that Walter Maki had lost his wife, and that she, Charlotte, had attended the service. At Immanuel Lutheran? In the pouring rain? She was deploying the voice she used for reminding him of things an ordinary person would remember.

He dropped his cufflinks into the wooden tray on his dresser, studying his wife a moment. Nothing accusatory there.

Briefly, he let himself recall the trip back to town with Glenny Parker. Reaching a pint bottle from the glove box, asking if she wanted a little warmup. "Sure, why not?" she said. She took a small mouthful, swished it between her teeth, then bounced the bottle down on the seat between them. She rode with her head against the far window, eyes shut. He drove her into town, back to her apartment on Lancaster Street, but did not go in.

AND SO TONIGHT, THREE WINTERS LATER, Gerald Wilcox is sequestered in his front room, stocking feet on desk, savoring the distant murmur of the furnace, the first swirls of wind brushing the waters of his thoughts. *Morphine, alkaloid derivative of opium . . . from the Greek "morph," the curious shapes seen in dreams.* He can't hear the word in his mind's ear without hearing as well his orotund, long-deceased Grandfather Vail. Each evening, one hand on newel post, the old man would announce he was headed up into the arms of Morpheus, if the seedy bastard would have him. It's an association Wilcox can't shake to this day: morphia and sleep, forgetting. Yet unless he overdoes it, unless the day has drained him, he can bypass the sludgy, soporific effect, and achieve a state he thinks of as *attentiveness.*

Or that's his aim.

His wife is upstairs in bed. She's been soldiering through a life of Michelangelo, so bloated a tome she has to brace it with a pillow. She reads bits aloud, saying, "What that man endured, up on the scaffolding?" She says, "Oh, that Pope, that Julius, what a *monster*."

He hears her neck crack as she turns to see if he's listening, before she chides him. He says he hasn't missed a word. Secretly, it pleases him that Charlotte still gives a good God damn about matters beyond the Sperry Golf Club, the hospital auxiliary, the preparation of sauces, and that she cares that the life they'd set out to lead together is not entirely extinguished. And, beyond that, isn't there a deep, atavistic pleasure in being read to? She has a whiskey voice, as a mystery writer would put it, though in fact the scratchy timbre results from tiny polyps on her vocal cords. Sometimes she lets the book fall, and asks about his patients: the McVicar sisters, Valen and Isabel, six-footers, retired nurses; the Lomasny girl, whose larynx was crushed by a strand of barbed wire; and so on, the human parade, morning and afternoon. He should keep their infirmities to himself, but instead he tells Charlotte these true stories, and none of it goes beyond her. If she knows of his wandering, there's no sign of it. If she knows it's in the past now, there's no sign of that, either.

But tonight he's downstairs, with the latest journal book in his lap. Charlotte will have doused the light and gone to sleep.

The telephone sounds.

The upstairs phone rests on the bedside table. By the third ring, Charlotte will have reached for it; her free hand will be sweeping the empty sheets in search of him. He fetches the thing quickly into his lap, and says, "Yes?"

"Walter Maki," the caller says.

"What's the trouble, Mr. Maki?"

"I was counting on having you," Maki says. Already there's a note of intransigence.

It's Maki's boy, Leonard. Ear problem.

"He's in a certain amount of pain then?"

"I told him to go back to sleep, there wasn't anything we could do till morning, but he was past that."

Infected mastoid, Wilcox imagines. He asks how old the boy is. He wonders, hearing his words go out, if he sounds drugged. No, certainly not.

Maki says the boy is thirteen.

"All right," the doctor says. "Bring him in to the office."

That pushiness in Maki's voice: "I was thinking of you coming out here."

So Wilcox agrees to a house call. Driving out Lower Valley Road, he thinks, isn't it a wonder he's never before been summoned out on a night he's injected himself. He feels robust—*in the pocket*, as the horn players used to say. He lifts his hands from the wheel and the car careers along, hugging the blacktop's soft-edged runnels, bending neither right nor left. Taking hold again, he drives past the old community hall at Aaberg's Landing, past the low spot choked with cattails that floods each spring. A burst of aspen leaves blows through the splay of headlights, the words "gold leaf" appear in his head, and he thinks then about angels. Imagine the ceiling of the world ruptured, spewing forth angels. He's not a believer—not remotely—but this is how his mind works on these nights. Another few miles and he draws alongside the slough. The water is black, still.

Maki admits him, leads his through the mudroom into the kitchen. The boy is on the sofa in the front room. Maki has the stove cranked. There's a smell, a scent added to the water kettle atop it. Mentholatum. The boy's cheeks are fiery, and the skin of his neck clammy. He lacks Maki's square features. His eyes are tipped and melancholy, his face long and weak-chinned.

The swelling is greater than Wilcox had supposed. He palpates the space behind the ear with a light touch. It's too late in the game for medication alone.

"This has been hurting for a few days, hasn't it, Leonard?" he asks.

The boy offers a constricted nod.

"You can lie back down."

To his son, Maki says, fiercely, "Whyn't you say anything before now?"

"You thought it would take care of itself," the doctor says. "Isn't that right?"

Leonard stares at the two men, blinking, his mouth open in a shallow pant.

"Just human nature," Wilcox says. He goes back to the brightness of the kitchen and Maki follows.

"We should get him into town," Wilcox says.

Again Maki balks. He looks intractable, almost menacing.

"We're not going to tussle over this, are we?" Wilcox asks, but immediately he undergoes a change of heart, rises to the challenge. "Never mind," he says. "We can do it here."

Leonard is brought into the kitchen and seated at the enamel-topped table, with his head on a folded towel covered by a sheet. The doctor numbs the skin behind the ear, though this will work only minimally.

"I have a girl," he says to the boy. "She's a little older than you. Jeanette, Queen of the Tigris and Euphrates, I call her."

With one hand he holds the head still, and with the other makes a cut. The boy flinches, but his reaction is remarkably controlled. The incision produces perhaps three tablespoons of pus, viscous green, vile-smelling. "That's it," Wilcox says. "Good." He irrigates the area with antiseptic, bandages it, administers a hefty dose of sulfa, and Leonard is put to bed again in the front room.

"You'll sleep now," Wilcox tells him. The boy stares back, disbelieving, but his eyes already have a glassy, listing look.

"Give you a drink?" Maki says.

"Thanks, no."

"No drink for you?"

"No."

"Can I give you some tea?"

"That's all right," Wilcox says. He has entered the stage where his thoughts wither, when if he were home he might consider a second dose, a touch-up. It's never the right idea. He need only recall the night he lost track and went to his knees, retching in the downstairs lavatory, his heart thready and arrhythmic, his rubbery blue-phantomed skin the skin of a corpse. He was mortified that Charlotte might discover him, horrified that she wouldn't. Nearly three months elapsed before he picked up the needle again. He thought maybe he'd cured himself, but no.

Maki has taken a seat at the table. His palms are turned down upon it, as if to keep it from levitating.

"The boy will be fine," Wilcox says. He's still on his feet, bag in hand.

"Sit down," Maki says.

Wilcox smiles and sits down. "I could stay a minute," he says.

"This evens us out," Maki says.

"Well, now, I wouldn't look at it that way."

"That night on the ice," Maki says. "You were a sorry-looking thing."

Wilcox looks at him, waiting.

"You and that girl."

"Yes, sir."

"So let me ask you," Maki says. "Do you think I ever stepped out on my wife?"

"Mr. Maki, I wouldn't hazard the first thought on that subject," Wilcox says.

So this is a chastising. There are worse things.

"You're sure he's okay," Maki says. "He won't lose his hearing?"

"His hearing will be fine," Wilcox says. "Trust me."

"He plays the trumpet."

"Is that so?"

"His mother was musical," Maki says. "She wanted him to have the lessons."

"This shouldn't hurt a thing."

Maki shakes his head. He says, "You're hopped up on something, aren't you?"

"I'm going to have to be going now," Wilcox says, standing again. "I'll leave you this prescription. Be sure he takes all of it." He pulls out the blank and writes, watching the extravagant looping that is his signature. "Let me see him in a few days," he says.

Maki leaves the paper where it lies. "You and that silly girl," he says.

WILCOX'S HEADLIGHTS JUDDER ON THE WASHBOARD, the Buick's hindquarters drift as he corners at the section lines. Then, abruptly, he's on blacktop again. He pictures Leonard Maki off in a back room with his trumpet, his embouchure, hopes to Christ the boy possesses a little natural aptitude. The idea of him bleating away in his mother's memory is more than Wilcox can take just now.

He lets himself in the rear door of the house on Plympton Street, hangs his coat on the ivory knob in the hall, listens for symptoms of unrest. He pours himself a short inch of bourbon and carries it to his office. Ten past three. No, that's unfair, he thinks. She was not a silly girl, Glenny—just in the wrong company. She had her talents. For a moment, he recalls her lips creeping into the hollow beneath his ear as he drove, keeping to the back roads, her voice tiny but remorseless, *I know what you'd like, Gerry. Stop the car, can't you?* Yet he only saw her one more time after that night on the frozen slough, and it had not gone well.

He sits for a time. Eventually, he takes up the journal, and writes: *Why do you never get used to the stink of pus? If you could smell that exact hue of green, that's how it would be . . . and yet it's just a broth of white cells, the body's defenses. What purpose is served? Why not the rusty smell of blood, the sweetness of breast milk instead? Was I ever taught this?*

Again he finds himself picturing the ceiling of the world, with white cells clustering like a mob of angels.

He writes: *Why this clamoring for purpose?*

There's a footfall outside his door. He slaps the journal shut and braces himself.

But it proves to be his daughter. "What are you writing?" she asks.

"Oh, you know, these notebooks of mine," he says. "You don't mean you've never poked around in them?"

"I wouldn't do *that*," Jeanette says, aggrieved.

Getting to be quite a capable liar, Wilcox thinks, not unhappily.

"What are you doing up?"

Jeanette shrugs, approaches the desk.

"Not sleeping again?" he asks. "Would you like me to give you something?"

"No."

"I could."

"I know," Jeanette says. "Anyway, it's too *late*."

Wilcox checks the filigreed clock hands again and somehow it's gotten to be five past five. "So it is," he says.

Jeanette is barefoot, wearing a long flannel gown with a tiny satin bow at the collar. Her hair is profuse, like Charlotte's, but not nearly so radiant a yellow, and at the moment it looks sea-wracked. She has a long neck and still no bust to speak of, though she's been menstruating for a good two years. Were it not for her gaze—watchful, not in the least dreamy—she might have been painted by Maxfield Parrish.

"Aren't your feet cold?" he says.

"I suppose."

Wilcox asks if she knows a boy named Leonard Maki.

Jeanette shakes her head.

"He plays the trumpet."

"Don't know him," she says.

"I thought you might. From school."

She stands, arms crossed, shifting her weight, her lungs filling and emptying.

After a moment, he asks, "Anything troubling your soul, dear heart?"

"No."

"You can tell me."

But of course she can't.

"Something's always troubling the soul," Wilcox says. "It's an irritable organ."

He offers a smile, which is not returned.

"I'm all right," she says. "I'm not dis*consolate*."

Wilcox smiles inwardly at this word she's plucked from the ether. "Well, it is the way it is," he says. Then it's her turn to nod, and he supposes they understand one another.

"You hungry?" he asks, standing, putting the journal aside. He touches her on the head, works his fingers into the tumbling snarls, which, briefly, she allows.

She follows him down the dim hallway into the kitchen. He opens the refrigerator and stares in at the lighted shelves and closes the door again.

"Do you know how to make that coffee cake?" he asks his daughter. "With the crumbles?"

"In the brown book," Jeanette says, pointing with her chin. "Fannie Farmer."

Wilcox reaches it down, locates the page, which is grease-spattered to transparency in places, with notations in his wife's disheveled, back-slanting hand: "Gerald likes."

"No yeast in this one?" he asks.

"No, Daddy."

He gets out what he needs, also the coffee tin. An easy recipe. In a matter of minutes, he slides the baking pan onto the oven rack.

"Better set the timer," Jeanette says, and so he sets the timer.

He collects the bowl and the utensils and runs water on them in the sink. Over his shoulder, he says, "Why don't you go wake your mother?"

"She won't want to get up this early."

"Oh, I know," he says. "But go anyway. Tell her she won't want to miss this." He shakes his hands, dries them under his armpits, looks his daughter in the eye. "Use those exact words. Say, 'He says you won't want to miss this.'"

No further objection from Jeanette. In fact, he detects a twitch of conspiracy about the lips as she leaves the room. After a moment, he notes her tread along the squeaky boards of the upstairs hall.

He goes and stands at the back door, looking out where a thin silver light is falling through the empty chestnut branches. He doesn't feel too damned awful, considering. Has the makings of a headache, where the neck cords meet the skull, but it will pass. Food will help, and caffeine. Later, in the afternoon, the fatigue will hit, the fuzziness he detests. If there's no one in the office, maybe he can sneak upstairs and lie down and shut his eyes. If not, the tiredness, too, will pass. He pictures himself beginning a new page: *18 November. Made Charlotte a coffee cake.* Maybe he'll record what she has to say about this unusual occurrence. Maybe she'll notice him climbing the stairs, and follow, launching salacious suggestions at him in a stage whisper. Maybe later he'll get to write: *C. and I napped before supper.* He watches a black dog cut through the yard, tail switching. After a while, the timer dings; his whole upper body startles, as if he's been seized from behind. Then he remembers to breathe again.

He slides the baking pan from the oven, sniffs the sugary cinnamon, pokes a toothpick into the center the way Charlotte would. It comes out clean and dry. He sets the pan on a wire rack, runs water into the percolator, taps in coffee, sets the flame. He listens for his wife. He pictures her getting to her feet and pulling on her robe, the slippery blue nylon, yanking the sash, then tousling some life into her night-heavy hair. Waiting, alone here in the kitchen, he suddenly wonders what will become of the journals after his death. He's barely given this a thought before. He's not fifty yet—how many more will have accumulated in the drawer by then, the pebbled-leather volumes swollen with his daily commentary, his nagging queries of himself? And how soon will it be before he relaxes his guard and lets the rest come forth—that chill along his inner arm before the needle slips in. The warming flood of ruminations. He pictures the heap of journals pulled into a lap, flopped open and read, one after another. How can it feel like comfort to him that they will be? And then what? Strange to admit, it's not a thought that troubles him.

Like a Leaf
Thomas McGuane

I'm underneath my small house in Deadrock. The real estate people call it a "starter" home, however late in life you buy one. It's a modest house that gives you the feeling that either you're going places or that this won't do. This starter home is different; this one is it.

From under here, I can hear the neighbors talking. He is a successful man named Deke Patwell. His wife is away and he is having an affair with the lady across the street, a sweet and exciting lady I've not met yet. Frequently he says to her, "I am going to impact on you, baby." Today, they are at one of their many turning points.

"I think I'm coming unglued," she says.

"Now, now."

"I don't follow," she says with a little heat.

"All is not easy."

"I got that part, but when do we go someplace nice?" She has a beautiful voice, and underneath the house I remember she is pretty. What am I doing here? I'm distributing bottle caps of arsenic for the rats that come up from the river and dispute the cats over trifles. I represent civilization in a small but real way.

Deke Patwell laughs with wild relief. Once I saw him at the municipal pool, watching young girls. He was wearing trunks and allergy-warning dog tags. What a guy! To me he was like a crude foreigner or a gaucho.

Anyway, I came down here because of the rats. Read your history: they carry Black Plague. Mrs. Patwell was on a Vegas excursion with the Deadrock Symphony Club.

When I get back inside, the flies are causing a broad dumb movement on the windows. We never had flies like this on the ranch. We had songbirds, apple blossoms, and no flies. My wife was alive then and saw to that. We didn't impact, we loved each other. She had an aneurism let go while carding wool. She just nodded her pretty face and headed out. I sat there like a stupe. They came for her and I just knocked around the place trying to get it. I headed for town and started seeing the doctor. Things came together: I was able to locate a place to live in, catch the Series, and set up housekeeping. Plus, the Gulch, everyone agrees, is Deadrock's nicest neighborhood. A traffic violator is taken right aside and lined out quick. It's a neighborhood where folks teach the dog to bring the paper to the porch, so a guy can sit back in his rocker and find out who's making hamburger of the world. I was one of this area's better cattlemen, and town life doesn't come easy. Where I once had coyotes and bears, I now have rats. Where I once had the old-time marriages of my neighbors, I now have Impact Man poking a real sweet gal who never gets taken someplace nice.

My eating became hit-or-miss. All I cared about was the World Series after a broken season. I was high and dry, and when you're like that you need someone or something to take you away. Death makes you different like the colored are different. I felt I was under the spell of what had happened to me. Then someone threw a bottle onto the field in the third or fourth game of the Series and almost hit the Yankee left fielder, Dave Winfield. I felt completely poisoned. I felt like a rat with a mouthful of bottle caps. All my sense of fairness was settled on Winfield, who is colored, like I felt having been in the company of death. Then Winfield couldn't hit the ball anyway, and just when Reggie Jackson got his hitting back, what happens? He drops an easy pop fly.

What were my wife and I discussing when she died? The Kona Coast. It seems so small. Sometimes when I think how small our topic was, I feel the weight of my hair tearing at my face. I bought a youth bed to reduce the size of the unoccupied area. The doctor says because of the shaking, I get quite a little bit less rest per hour than the normal guy. Rapid eye movement, and so on.

TRUTHFULLY SPEAKING, part of me has always wanted to live in town. You hear the big milling at the switching yard and, on stormy nights, the transcontinental trucks reroute off the interstate, and it's busy and kind of like a last-minute party at somebody's house. The big outfits are parked all over with their engines running, and the heat shivers at the end of the stacks. The old people seem brave trying to get around on the ice: one fall and they're through, but they keep chunking, going on forward with a whole heck of a lot of grit. That fact gives me a boost.

And I love to window-shop. I go from window to window alongside people I don't know. There's never anything I want in there, but I feel good because I am excited when somebody picks out a daffy pair of shoes or a hat you wouldn't put on your dog. My wife couldn't understand this. Nature was a shrine to her. I wanted to see people more than she did. Sit around with just anybody and make smart remarks. Sometimes I'd pack the two of us into the hills. My wife would be in heaven. I'd want to buy a disguise and slip off to town and stare through the windows. That's the thing about heaven. It comes in all sizes and shapes.

ANYONE IN MY POSITION FEELS LEFT BEHIND. It's normal. But you got to keep picking them up and throwing them; you have got to play the combinations or quit. What I'd like is a person, a person I could enjoy until she's blue in the face. This, I believe. When the time comes, stand back from your television set.

I DON'T KNOW WHY DOC KEEPS AN OFFICE in the kind of place he does, which is merely the downstairs of a not-so-good house. I go to him because he is never busy. He claims this saves him the cost of a receptionist.

Doc and I agree on one thing: it's all in your head. The only exception would be aspirin. Because we believe it's all in your head, we believe in immortality. Immortality is important to me because, without it, I don't get to see my wife again. Or, on the lighter side, my dogs and horses. That's all you need to know about the hereafter. The rest is for the professors, the regular egghead types who don't have to make the payroll. We agree about my fling with the person. I hope to use Doc's stethoscope to hear the speeding of the person's heart. All this has a sporting side, like hunting coyotes. When Doc and I grow old and the end is in sight, we're going to become addicted to opium. If we get our timing wrong, we'll cure ourselves with aspirin. We plan to see all the shiny cities, then adios. We speak of cavalry firefights, Indian medicine, baseball, and pussy.

Doc doesn't come out from behind the desk. He squints, knowing I could lie, then listens.

"My house in town is going to work fine. The attic has a swing-down ladder and you look from a round window up there into the backyards. You can hear the radios and see people. Sometimes couples have little shoving matches over odd things, starting the charcoal or the way the dog's been acting. I wrote some of them down in a railroad seniority book to tell you. They seem to dry up quick."

"Still window-shopping?"

"You bet."

"If you don't buy something soon, you're going to have to give that up."

"I'll think about it," I say.

"What have you been doing?"

"Not a whole heck of a lot."

"See a movie, any movie."

"I'll try."

"Take a trip."

"I can't."

"Then pack for one and don't go."

"I can do that."

"Stay out of the wind. It makes people nervous, and this is a windy town. Do what you have to do. You can always find a phone booth, but get out of that wind when it picks up. And anytime you feel like falling silent, do it. Above all, don't brood about women."

"Okay. Anything else?"

"Trust aspirin."

"I've been working on my mingling."

"Work on it some more."

"Doc," I say, "I've got a funny feeling about where I'm headed."

"You know anybody who doesn't?"

"So what do I do?"

"Look at the sunny side. Anyway, I better let you go. There's someone in the lobby with Blue Cross."

So I go.

By hauling an end table out to the porch, despite that the weather is not quite up to it, and putting a chair behind it, I make a fine place for my microwave Alfredo fettucini. I can also watch our world with curiosity and terror. If necessary, I can speak when spoken to, by sipping my ice water to keep the chalk from my mouth.

A car pulls up in front of Patwells'; Mrs. Patwell gets out with a small Samsonite and goes to the house. That saves me from calling a lot of travel agents. The world belongs to me.

I begin to eat the Alfredo fettucini, slow, spacing each mouthful. After eating about four inches of it, I see the lady from across the street, the person, on the irregular sidewalk, gently patting each bursting tree trunk as she comes. Since I am now practically a mute, I watch for visible things I can predict. And all I look for is her quick glance at Deke Patwell's house and then a turn through her chain-link gate. I love that she is pretty and carries nothing, like the Chinese ladies Doc tells me about who achieve great beauty by teetering around on feet that have been bound. I feel I am listening to the sound of a big cornfield in springtime. My heart is an urgent thud.

To my astonishment, she swings up her walk without a look. Her wantonness overpowers me. Impossible! Does she not know the wife is home from Vegas?

I look up and down the street before lobbing the Alfredo fettucini to a mutt. He eats in jerking movements and stares at me like I'm going to take it back. Which I'm quite capable of doing, but won't. I have a taste in my mouth like the one you get in those frantic close-ins hunting coyotes. I feel like a happy crook. Sometimes when I told my wife I felt this way, she was touched. She said I had absolutely no secret life. The sad thing is, I probably don't.

I BEGIN SLEEPING IN THE ATTIC. I am alone and not at full strength, so this way I feel safer. I don't have to answer door or phone. I can see around the neighborhood better, and I have the basic timing of everybody's day down pat. For example, the lady goes to work on time but comes home at a different hour every day. Does this suggest that she is a carefree person to whom time means nothing or who is, perhaps, opposed to time's effects and therefore defiant about regularity? I don't know.

BEFORE I REALIZE IT, I am window-shopping again. Each day there is more in the air, more excitement among the shoppers, who seem to spill off the windows into the doors of the stores. The sun is out and I stand before the things my wife would never buy, not risqué things but things that wouldn't stand up. She seems very far away now. But when people come to my store windows, I sense a warmth that is like friendship. Anytime I feel uncomfortable in front of a particular store, I move to sporting goods, where it is clear that I am okay, and besides, Doc is fixing me. My docile staring comes from the last word in tedium: guns and ammo, compound bows, fishing rods.

WHEN I SAY THAT I AM OKAY, I mean that I am happy in the company of most people. What is wrong with me comes from my wife having unexpectedly died and from my having read the works of Ralph Waldo Emerson when my doctor and I were boning up on immortality. But I am watching the street, and something will turn up. In the concise movements of the person I'm most interested in, and in the irregularity of her returns, which she certainly despises, I sense a glow directed toward me, the kind of light in a desolate place that guides the weary traveler to his rest.

TODAY, SHE WALKS HOME. She is very nearly on time. She walks so fast her pumps clatter on our broken Deadrock sidewalk. She swings her shoulder bag like a cheerful weapon and arcs into the street automatically to avoid carelessly placed sprinklers. She touches a safety match to a long filter brand, as she surveys her little yard, and goes in.

She works, I understand, at the County Assessor's office, and I certainly imagine she does a fine job for those folks. With her bounce, her cigarettes, and her iffy hours, she makes just the kind of woman my wife had no use for. Hey! It takes all kinds. Human life is thus filled with variety, and if I have a regret in my own so far, it is that I have not been close to that variety: that is, right up against it.

I NEED A BREAK and go for a daylight drive. I take the river road through the foothills north of Deadrock—a peerless jaunt—to our prison. It is an elegant old dungeon that has housed many famous Western outlaws in its day. The ground it rests on was never farmed, having gone from buffalo pasture to lockup many years ago. Now it has razor wire surrounding it and a real up-to-date tower like out east.

One man stands in blue light behind its high windows. When you see him from the county road, you think, That certainly must be the loneliest man in the world. But actually, it's not true. His name is Al Costello and he's a good friend of mine. He's the head of a large Catholic household, and the tower is all the peace he gets. The lonely guy is the warden, an out-of-stater, a professional imprisoned by card files: a man no one likes. He looks like Rock Hudson, and he can't get a date.

Sometimes I stop in to see Al. I go up into the tower and we look down into the yard at the goons and make specific comments about the human situation. Sometimes we knock back a beer or two. Sometimes I take a shot at one of his favorite ball clubs, and sometimes he lights into mine. It's just human fellowship in kind of a funny spot.

But, today I keep on cruising, out among the jackrabbits and sagebrush, high above the running irrigation, all the way around the little burg, then back into town. I stop in front of the doughnut shop, waiting for the sun to travel the street and open the shop, and herald its blazing magic up commercially zoned Deadrock. Waiting in front is a sick-looking young man muttering to himself at a high relentless pitch of the kind we associate with Moslem fundamentalism. At eight sharp the door opens, and the Moslem and I shoot in for the counter. He seems to have lost something by coming inside, and I am riveted upon his loss. By absolute happenstance, we both order glazed. Then I add an order of jelly-filled, which I deliver, still hot, to the lady's doorstep.

I'M GOING TO STOP READING THIS NEWSPAPER. In one week, the following has been reported: A Deadrock man shot himself fatally in a bar, demonstrating the safety of his pistol. Another man, listening to the rail, had his head run over by every car of a train that took half an hour to go by. Incidents like these make it hard for me to clearly see the spirit winging its way to heaven. And though I would like to stop reading the paper, I really know I won't. It would set a bad example for the people on the porches who have trained Spot to fetch.

"DID YOU GET THE DOUGHNUTS?" I called out that evening.

Tonight, as I fall asleep, I have a strange thought indeed. It goes like this: Darling (my late wife), I don't know if you are watching all this or not. If you are, I have but one request: Put yourself in my shoes. That's quite an assignment, but give it the old college try for the sake of yours truly.

I KNOW THEY'VE BEEN TALKING when I see Deke Patwell give me the fishy look. I cannot imagine which exact locution she used—probably that I was "bothering" her—but she has very evidently made of me a fly in Deke's soup. There is not a lot he could do, standing next to his warming-up sensible compact, but give me this look and hope that I will invest it with meaning. I decide to blow things out of proportion.

"You two should do something *nice* together!" I call out.

Deke slings his head down and bitterly studies a nail on one hand, then gets in and drives away.

YOU THINK YOU GOT IT BAD? Says here a man over to Arlee was jump-starting his car in the garage; he had left it in gear, and when he touched the terminals of the battery the car shot forward and pinned him to a compressor that was running. This man was inflated to four times his normal size and was still alive after God knows how long when they found him. A hopeful Samaritan backed the car away and the man just blew up on the garage floor and died. As awful as that is, it adds nothing whatsoever to the basic idea. Passing in your sleep or passing as a pain-crazed human balloon on a greasy garage floor produces the same simple result year after year. The major differences lie among those who are left behind. If you're listening, please understand I'm still trying to see why we don't all cross the line on our own, or why nice people don't just help us on over. Who knows if you're even listening?

"So," I CRY OUT TO THE PERSON with exaggerated innocence, illustrating how I am crazy like a fox. "So, how did you enjoy the doughnuts?"

She stops, looks, thinks. "That was you?"

"That was me."

"Why?" She is walking toward me.

"It was a little something from someone who thinks somebody should take you somewhere nice."

My foot is in the door. It feels as big as a steamboat.

"Tomorrow," she says from her beautiful face, "make it cinnamon Danish." Her eyes dance with cruel merriment. I feel she is of German extraction. She has no trace of an accent, and her attire is domestic in origin. I think, What am I saying? I'm scaring myself. This is a Deadrock local with zip for morals.

I decided to leap forward in the development of things to ascertain the point at which it doesn't make sense. We are very much in love, I say to myself. I recoil privately at this thought, knowing I am still okay if not precisely tops. I am neither a detective nor a complete stupe. Like most of the human race, I fall somewhere in between.

"Tell you what," she says with a twinkle. "I come home from work and I freshen up. Then you and me go for a stroll. How far'd you get?"

"Stroll . . ."

"You're a good boy tonight and I let you off lightly."

Mercy. My neck prickles. She laughs in my face and heads out. I see her cross the trees at the end of the street. I see the changing flicker of different-colored cars. I see mountains beyond the city. I see her bouncing black hair even after she has gone. I say quietly, I'm lonely; I had no idea you were not to have a long life. But I'm still in love.

I call Doc. I tell him, You can put your twenty-two fifty an hour where the sun don't shine, you dang quack. John Q. Public says, walk the line, boy, or pay the price. Well, John, the buck stops here. I'm going it alone.

SHE STOOD ME UP AND IT'S MIDNIGHT.

I have never felt like this. This house doesn't belong to me. It belongs to the person, and I'm lying on her bed viewing the furnishings. It's dark here. I can see her coming up the sidewalk. She will come alongside the house and come in through the kitchen. I am in the back room. I guess I'll say hello.

"Hello."

"Hello." She's quite the opposite of my wife, but it's fatal if she thinks this is healthy. She's in the same blue dress and appears to view this as a clever seduction. "It's you. Who'd have guessed? I'm going to bathe, and if you ask nice you can help."

"I want to see."

"I know that." She laughs and goes through the door undressing. "Just come in. You'll never get your speech right. Do I look drunk? I am a little. I suppose your plan was a neighborhood rape." Loud laugh. She hangs the last of her clothes and studies me. Then she leans against the cupboards. "Please turn the water on, kind of hot." When I turn away from the faucets she is sitting on the side of the tub. I think I am going to fall but I go to her and rock her in my arms so that she kind of spreads out against the white porcelain.

She looks at me and says, "The nicest thing about you is you're frightened. You're like a boy. I'm going to frighten you as much as you can stand." I undress and we get into the clear water. I look at the half of myself that is underwater; it looks like something at SeaWorld. Suddenly, I stand up.

"I guess I'm not doing so good. I'm not much of a rapist after all." I get out of the tub, a tremendous stupe.

"You're making me feel great."

"That Deke has caused you to suffer."

"Oh, crap."

"It's time he took you someplace nice." I'm on the muscle now.

I am drying off about a hundred miles an hour. I go into the next room and pull on my trousers. I don't even see her coming. She pushes me over on the daybed and drags my pants back off. I am so paralyzed all I can do is say, Please no, Please no, as she clambers roughly atop me and takes me, almost hurting me with her fury, ending with a sudden dead flop. Every moment or so, she looks at me with her raging victorious eyes.

"Just don't turn me in," she says. "It would be awful for your family." She bounces up and returns to the bathroom while I dress again. There is a razor running and periodic splashes of water. Whether it is because my wife has to sit through the whole thing or that I can't bring her back, I don't know, but the whole thing makes me a different guy. In short, I've been raped.

SHE TOWS ME OUTSIDE, clattering on the steps in wooden clogs, sending forth a bright woman's cologne to savage my nerves. I see there is only one way my confused hands can regain their grasp: I burst into tears. She pops open a small flowered umbrella and uses it to conceal me from the outside world. It seems very cozy in there. She coos appropriately.

"Are you going to be okay now?" she asks. "Are you?" I see Deke's car coming up the street. The Impact Man, the one who never does anything nice for her. I dry my tears posthaste. We head down the street. We are walking together in the bright evening sky under our umbrella. This foolishness implies an intimacy that must have gone hard with Impact Man, because he arcs into his driveway and has to brake hard to keep from going through his own garage with its barbecue, hammocks, and gap-seamed neglected canoe, things whose hopes of a future seem presently to ride on the tall shapely legs of my companion.

I can't think of something really right for us. The only decent restaurant would seem as though we were on a date, put us face to face. We need to keep moving. I feel pretty certain we could pop up and see Al Costello, my Catholic friend in the tower. He always has the coffeepot going. So we get into my flivver and head for the prison. It makes a nice drive in a Tahiti-type sunset, and by the time I graze Staff Parking to the vast space of Visitors, the wonderful blue-white of the glass tower has ignited like the pilot light on a gas stove.

"I want you to meet a friend of mine," I tell the lady. "Works here. Big Catholic family. He's a grandfather in his late thirties. It looks like a lonely job and it's not."

The tower has an elevator. The gate guards know me and we sail in. The door opens in the tower.

"Hey," I say.

"What's cooking?" Al grins vacantly.

"Thought we'd pop up. Say, this is a friend of mine."

"Mighty pleased," Al says. He has the lovely manners of some-one battered beyond recognition. She now glues herself to the window and stares at the cons. I think she has made some friendly movements to the guys down in the yard. I glance at Al and evidently he thinks so too. We avert our glances and Al says, "Can I make a spot of coffee?" I feel like a fool.

"I'm fine," she says. "Fine." She is darn well glued to the glass. "Can a person get down there?"

"Oh, a person could," says Al. I notice he is always in slow move-ment around the tower, always looking, in case some geek goes haywire. "Important thing I guess is that no one can come here unless I let them in. They screen this job. The bad apples are soon gone. It takes a family man."

"Are those desperate characters?" she asks, gazing around. I move into the window and look down at the minnowlike movement of the prisoners. This would have held zero interest for my wife.

"A few, I guess. This is your regular backyard prison. No celebri-ties. We've got the screwballs is about all we've got."

"How's the family, Al." I dart in.

"Fine, just fine."

"Everybody healthy?"

"Oh, yeah. Andrea Elizabeth had strep but it didn't pass to nobody in the house. Antibiotics knocked it for a loop."

"And the missus?"

"Same as ever."

"For Christ's sake," says my companion. We turn. He and I think it's us. But it's something in the yard. "Two fairies," she says through her teeth. "Can you beat that?"

After which she just stares out the window while Al and I drink some pretty bouncy coffee with a nondairy creamer that makes shapes in it without ever really mixing. It is more or less to be polite that I drink it at all. I look over, and she has her wide-spread hands up against the glass like a tree frog. She is grinning very hard and I know she has made eye contact with someone down in the exercise yard. Suddenly, she turns.

"I want to get out of here."

"Okay," I say brightly.

"You go downstairs," she says. "I need to talk to Al."

"Okay, okay."

My heart is coated with ice. Plus, I'm mortified. But I go downstairs and wait in a green-carpeted room at the bottom of the stairs. There is a door out and a door to the yard. I think I'll wait here. I don't want to sit in the car trying to look like I'm not abetting a jail break. I'm going downhill fast.

I must be there twenty minutes when I hear the electronics of the elevator coming at me. The stainless doors open and a very disheveled Al appears with my friend. There is nothing funny or bawdy in her demeanor. Al swings by me without catching a glance and begins to open the door to the yard with a key. He has a service revolver in one hand as he does so. "Be cool now, Al," says my friend intimately. "Or I talk."

The steel door winks and she is gone into the prison yard. "We better go back," says Al in a doomed voice. "I'm on duty. God almighty."

"Did I do this?" I say in the elevator.

"You better stay with me. I can't have you leaving alone." He unplugs the coffee mechanically. When I get to the bulletproof glass,

I can see the prisoners migrating. There is a little of everything: old guys, stumblebums, Indians, Italians, Irishmen, all heading into the shadow of the tower. "We're just going to have to go with this one. There's no other way." He looks crummy and depleted but he is going to draw the line. We have to go with it. She will signal the tower, he tells me. So we wait by the glass like a pair of sea captains' wives in their widow's walks. It goes on so long, we forget why we're waiting. We are just doing our job.

Then there is a small reverse migration of prisoners and she, bobby pins in her teeth, checking her hair for bounce, waves up to us in the tower. We wave back in this syncopated motion that is almost the main thing I remember, me and Al flapping away like a couple of widows.

As we ride down in the elevator again, Al says, "You take over from here." And we commence to laugh. We laugh so hard I think one of us will upchuck. Then we have to stop to get out of the elevator. We cover our mouths and laugh through our noses, tears streaming down our cheeks, while Al tries to get the door open. Our lady friend comes in real sternlike, though, and we stop. It is as if we'd been caught at something and she is awful sore. She heads out the door and Al gives me the gun.

In the car, she says with real contempt, "I guess it's your turn." Buddy, was that the wrong thing to say.

"I guess it is." I am the quiet one now.

There is a great pool on the river about a mile below the railroad bridge. It's moving but not enough to erase the stars from its surface, or the trout sailing like birds over its deep pebbly bottom. The little homewrecker kneels at the end of the sandbar and washes herself over and over. When I am certain she feels absolutely clean, I let her have it. I roll her into the pool, where she becomes a ghost of the river trailing beautiful smoky cotton from a hole in her silly head.

It's such a relief. We never did need the social whirl. Tomorrow we'll shop for something nice, something you can count on to stand up. There for a while it looked like the end.

HEART
Neil McMahon

AFTER THE FIGHT I COUGHED for a long time, hunched over on a chair beside the ring while Charlie cut my hand wraps off. When he finished he stared at me with his fists on his hips. "For Christ's sake," he said. "You sound like you got tuberculosis." He tossed the soggy wads of gauze on the floor and came back with a plastic cup of water. It helped some.

A black fighter carrying an athletic bag stenciled ANACONDA JOB CORPS nodded to me as he walked by. Earlier, I had watched him knock out one of the toughest of the prison middleweights and make it seem easy. "You look real good out there," he said. He was wearing a wide-brim hat with a plume, patent leather boots that laced to the knee, and a crimson satin shirt. Underneath the shirt, I knew, were hand-sized patches of pink skin. They made me think of a drowned man I had seen once in Chicago. The drowned man had been in the water three days, and his outer layer of skin had peeled like chocolate latex paint, leaving spots the color of old milk. When the black fighter bent close I could smell his sweat.

"You move real good," he said. His long thin hands hung loose at his waist. "You *slim*. You stay away from them big fat boys you be all right." He flipped up his palms and offered them. I slid my own across them. He grinned again, a flash of white on his unmarked face.

"You do all right tomorrow," he said. "You jus keep movin." He turned and sauntered back across the stage, jerking slightly with each step.

"A plume," Charlie said. "Now that's what I call fancy. Get dressed, let's get the hell out of this place." He walked to the ring, spread his hands on the ropes, tested them for tautness: remembering.

My fight had been the last of the day. The stage in the prison auditorium was almost empty now. The convicts were mingling with the audience, mainly friends and relatives who had come to see the tournament. All were men; women were not allowed past the visiting room. The boxers who had come from outside were gathering near the doors. I was bracing myself to rise when a hand clamped on my shoulder. It was the man I had just beaten, a three-time loser named Grosniak.

Before the fight, he had taken me aside and recited his record meaningfully: "Armed robbery, grand larceny, and assault with a deadly weapon." He had only been out a week on his second parole when he and a friend got drunk and took a Mini-Mart in Butte. The police were waiting when he drove up to his house. "Eight years this time," he said, with what seemed like satisfaction. "There was bullets in the gun."

Grosniak's hair was bristly and unevenly cut, and he had a wandering eye that I had kept trying to circle around. The roll of flesh above his trunks was still red from punches. He was standing so close his hip almost touched me.

"I got to admit, you beat me fair and square," he said. "I dint think you could, but you did."

"Thanks," I said. Sweat was still running down the pale loose skin of his chest and belly, collecting in little drops on the sparse hair around his navel.

"You got a hell of a left hand," he said. "Your arms are too long for me. I couten figure out how to get inside you. But I'm gonna work on it. Maybe I'll get another shot at you sometime."

"Maybe so," I said.

"I knew you couten knock me out, though. I told you that before. You can pound on me all day, but you can't knock me out. Nobody's ever knocked me out." Dried blood and snot were still streaked across his chin, and dark red bubbles sucked in and out of his nose as he breathed. He was clenching and unclenching his fists.

"You couten take me on the street, neither," he said.

Earlier in the day, it had seemed I could not take a step without a guard eyeing me. Now there was none to be seen. But Charlie was walking back from the ring, thumbs hooked in his pockets, head lowered.

"Let's go," he said to me.

Grosniak's hand stayed on my shoulder. "That's gonna be a real show tomorrow," he said. "Heavy Runner hasn't lost a fight in five years."

Charlie ignored him as if he was invisible. "Build a fire under it," he said.

"Two hundred fights," Grosniak said. "He's won them all by knockouts."

I stood, shaking off his hand, and started toward the locker room. From the corner of my eye I saw him take a step after me, but before I could turn back, Charlie had shouldered him out of the way and was facing him, hands quiet at his sides. Grosniak's feet shifted in an impatient little dance, his walleye squeezing open and shut so it looked like he was winking.

"Too bad you're not in the tournament," he finally said.

"Real too bad," said Charlie. "I love to watch fat boys go down, they make such a nice splat when they hit."

Grosniak stepped back, and Charlie wheeled and walked after me.

"Maybe I'll get a shot at you sometime," Grosniak called.

I fell into step beside Charlie.

"I'll get you both on the street!"

We passed through the door into the locker room, and Charlie turned so fast I ran into him. "Why *ever*," he said, "didn't you take him down?"

"No need," I said. "I knew I had him."

"I god damn well guess you had him. One shot with your right would have done it. You remember what your right is?" He slapped my forearm hard.

"I didn't want to hurt him," I said, already hearing the words sound wrong.

"*Hurt* him? He's been convicted of armed robbery and aggra-vated assault."

I turned away, but he gripped my bicep and jerked me around, veins standing out on the back of a hand hard from years of working red iron. "Boy," he said, "you think that Indian's going to give you a break when he gets you on the ropes tomorrow?"

His face was tilted back and cocked to one side above his stocky body: tight-clamped jaw, bristly Fu Manchu worn in honor of Hurri-cane Carter, and a nose that had been redone in rings and bars all over the West. You could tell from his eyes that he wanted to be kind, but he understood when kindness would not do. I had not knocked Gros-niak out because I could not stand the smack of my glove against his rubbery flesh, and the sudden fear in his eyes when my left came for his nose again, too quick for him to stop. In the last round, when he lumbered out with his fists drooping, trying to get enough air into his heavy body, I had hit him only to keep him away.

Charlie let go of my arm, looking suddenly tired. "I'll be in the lobby."

"I'll hurry," I said. "I just need a quick shower."

He stooped in the doorway, face gone wry. "You looking to get gang-raped?"

I shook my head.

"Just get dressed," he said. "I can put up with the smell of you for the drive home."

I stripped off trunks and cup and took my clothes from my bag. But I hated the evil-smelling sweat of fighting, and there was no one else around. I went quickly to the sink. The porcelain was covered with greenish scum, and the hot water tap would not turn. I rinsed handfuls of cold under my arms and down my chest and groin. There was no sting when the water touched my face; if one of Grosniak's wild flurries in the first round had scored, I could not yet feel it. When I finished I was shivering. I turned to see a shape, blurred from the water in my eyes, leaning against the doorjamb. I thought Charlie had come back, and said, "Toss me my towel, hey?"

The shape did not move. I blinked my eyes clear, and with a jolt, recognized the man: Louis Heavy Runner, the prison heavyweight champion.

He was not much over six feet tall, two or three inches shorter than me, but his tremendous chest and shoulders filled the doorway. Gleaming black hair hung in a ponytail to his waist. His forehead was high and broad, his jaw narrow, making him look Oriental. He seemed to be staring slightly to the side of me, and I could not tell if he missed my nod or ignored it. Because of a quirk in the seeding, he had fought twice that afternoon. Both times he had ended the bouts in the first round, leaping in with left hooks so fast I had not quite seen them, so savage they knocked two-hundred-pound men clear off their feet. The first got up to take the eight-count. Heavy Runner clubbed him back to the mat in seconds. The other man went down a half-minute into the fight and stayed there.

I started looking in my bag for a towel and realized I had forgotten to bring one, but I rummaged until Heavy Runner pushed off the doorjamb with his shoulder and went back outside. Then I dried off quickly with my jeans. The auditorium was empty when I came out except for a bored-looking guard near the entrance. I went to the ring and lined up even with the ropes. It took me just over four full strides to reach the other side.

I had thought so.

The lobby was crowded with visitors and boxers, standing around sipping Cokes from the concession stand the convicts had set up. Everybody's eyes looked watchful over the brims of their cups. Charlie was leaning against a wall with his arms folded. He pointed with his chin at the coach of the Great Falls club, a three-hundred-pounder named Fletcher, who was joking with a group of the inmates. We saw him at most of the tournaments, and he sometimes seconded for me in the corner.

"Looks like the big man's renewing old acquaintance," Charlie said.

It had never occurred to me to wonder what Fletcher did for a living. "Is he a cop?"

"He did three years here. I thought you knew that."

I shook my head.

"Blew his old lady away," Charlie said. "I remember it, I was in high school. That was back when they used to say, 'If you can't divorce your wife in Nevada, bring her to Montana and kill her.'"

Fletcher saw us, waved, and started toward us. The convicts and boxers stepped quickly out of his way.

"Shot her *down* in the kitchen," Charlie said softly.

Fletcher slapped me on the back. I started coughing again. "You looked terrific out there," he said. "That Joe Grosniak's a pretty tough old boy."

"He's a meat," Charlie said.

"Well, he's no Louis Heavy Runner," Fletcher admitted. His thumb and forefinger squeezed the muscle above my shoulder as if he was testing me for the oven. "I'll be straight with you, I don't think you have a chance tomorrow." He sounded cheerful. "He's the toughest fighter in the joint, probably in the whole state. But he hasn't had a fight go past the first round in so long, you might be able to wear him out if you can stay away from him. Whatever you do, don't let him tag you with that hook. He killed a guy with it, you know, in a bar fight. That's why he's in here." He looked directly at me, and for the first time, I realized his inky hair and dark skin were those of a half-breed. He slapped me on the back again and said, "I'll be in your corner tomorrow. Sleep tight."

After a long time, two guards separated from the crowd and stood in front of the doors. "Everybody here?" one called. He had small shoulders and wide fleshy hips, and his nightstick and radio seemed too big for him. The other guard yelled into the auditorium that this was the last call for visitors to leave. "Anybody still here's gonna spend the night," the first guard said. The inmates laughed and whistled.

The guards separated the convicts back into the auditorium and counted us twice, then led us across the exercise yard through the raw windy March twilight. Dead grass sprouted through cracks in the concrete where the snow had blown off. Scraps of rusty chain nets hung from basketball hoops, clinking in the wind. The fence around the yard was chain-link topped with barbed wire, eighteen or twenty feet tall, and I could see the guard towers at all four corners of the old stone building, a silhouette in the window of each.

The corridors were wide and brightly lit, with lines painted down the centers of the floor. Metal doors with grilles were set into the walls at intervals that looked too close. Some were open, showing empty cells with bunks and seatless toilets; at others, a man's face would appear, silently watching us pass. At the end of every corridor, a grate of iron bars spanned wall to wall, floor to ceiling, with an armed guard sitting in a barred alcove. He would look us over, exchange words with the guards who led us, then throw the switch that slid the grate aside. Nobody pushed to get through, but nobody lagged behind.

At the last checkpoint, a booth in the main lobby, each of us had to push our hand through another grille and be examined for the invisible fluorescent stamp we had gotten when we entered. I did not think such a stamp would wash off with soap and water, but I was glad I had not showered.

IT WAS ALMOST DARK BY THE TIME we reached the outskirts of Deer Lodge and passed the last of the signs that read: WARNING: STATE PENITENTIARY AND MENTAL HEALTH FACILITY ARE LOCATED IN THIS AREA. DO NOT PICK UP HITCHHIKERS. From there it was a dozen flat miles through soggy hayfields to the Highway 12 turnoff at Garrison. Charlie lit a Camel, but the smoke tickled my cough. Irritably, he stubbed it out.

"Maybe I should just drop you off at the state hospital," he said. The truck veered as he leaned down to rummage beneath the seat. He came up with a pint of Jim Beam that always looked the same, about half full.

"Shelley's got some codeine," I said.

He swiveled to stare at me, the pint in his fist. "*Shelley.* The night before a fight?"

"I told her I'd come by."

He grunted and sank lower in the seat, chin almost to his chest.

Abruptly there was a dark shape on the roadside ahead to the right, too close to the speeding truck. I jerked up straight, my hands gripping the dash. Charlie swerved, and the shape turned as we roared by: an old Indian woman, coat blown open by our passing, thin hands clutching a bundle. Her black eyes looked like the hollows of a skull.

"You can take that son of a bitch if you just stay away from him," Charlie said. "Don't listen to Fletcher's bullshit. He's trying to set you up."

I craned around. The old lady had already faded into the dark of the Warm Springs Valley.

"You hearing me?" Charlie said.

I turned back. "That ring's three feet short of regulation," I said. "I paced it off."

He shrugged. "I've told you a thousand times, you're an outside fighter. You go in and mix it up with a guy like Heavy Runner, sure you're going to get hurt. But you've got a good three inches reach and you're in top shape."

"And he's got thirty pounds on me and he's twice as fast. Did you see him with those other guys? It was like they were in a cage with a gorilla."

Charlie drank from the pint, then offered it to me. "Just a sip. Clear your throat."

I shook my head.

We topped a rise to see the lights of Garrison, and a minute later we drove through. It consisted of a truck stop, a mill of some kind, and a string of run-down houses along a railroad siding. Only the big diesel rigs idling in front of Welch's Cafe kept the place from looking deserted. Then we accelerated again onto the highway east.

"You want to go in there already whipped, it's okay with me," Charlie said. "It's your ass either way."

I closed my eyes and willed sleep.

IN THOSE DAYS SHELLEY LIVED in the part of town called Moccasin Flats. The streets were mostly dirt, and what was left of her fence was always plastered with windblown paper. A cat's eyes glowed in the headlights as we pulled up, then disappeared into the abandoned chicken house across the street.

"About ten tomorrow," Charlie said.

I gripped my bag and stepped out. He leaned suddenly across the seat, his eyes hard in the argon light. "You let that woman suck all the juice out of you, you ain't gonna be worth a rat's ass." Then the truck's tires crunched on frozen snow, and I was alone.

The faint smell of marijuana smoke hit me when I pushed open the door, old, like it had soaked into the curtains and furniture. "Don't move," she said. I turned slowly to where she was sitting cross-legged in a corner, with a sketch pad across her knees. She was wearing a long peasant skirt and a blouse I had bought her, Central American, with wide bands of deep red and blue. Her pupils were dilated, and her face had a look of almost childish concentration. "The conquering hero returns," she said, and the pencil began to move across the pad.

I tossed my bag on the couch and pulled off my jacket.

"Hey," she said. "Hold still."

"Later."

"But I've got to catch you in your moment of glory." Her voice had an edge that was not quite teasing.

"I'm not in the mood for screwing around, Shelley," I said, and walked into the kitchen.

She came in and stood with her hands clasped in front of her. "Sorry," she said. "Your face isn't beat up, so I thought maybe you won."

"I did," I said. I was tired but did not want to stop moving. "You got any beer?"

She put her hands on my cheeks and turned my face both ways, examining it. "Okay, the sketch can wait." she said, then kissed me. I tasted smoke on her breath. "Tough fight?"

"No," I said. We kissed again, longer this time, then she pulled away and went to the refrigerator. She set a six-pack of San Miguel and two fat New York steaks on the counter.

"Celebrate," she said. "Victory in your last fight. If you lost, you would have gotten Hamm's and tuna fish."

"Shelley, what are you doing spending money on stuff like this?" I said, trying to sound angry. She worked part-time in an art supplies store and could hardly pay the rent.

Her eyes widened mockingly. "I keep telling you, I found a sugar daddy."

I snorted, but I thought of all my out-of-town construction jobs.

She opened two bottles of beer, and when we raised them, touched hers to mine. "To heroes," she said, with the edge back in her voice. She had never once come to watch me fight. I took a long drink. It was so cold it made my teeth hurt, sharp at first but then soothing to my raw throat.

"It wasn't the last fight," I said.

"Oh, don't tell me," she said, setting her bottle down hard. "You let Charlie talk you into that stupid Golden Gloves thing."

"Tomorrow," I said.

"To*morrow*?"

"This was just eliminations. I've got to go back for the finals."

"I thought you were going to take me to Boulder Hot Springs."

"That was if I didn't win."

"You sort of forgot to tell me that," she said. She walked to the small window above the sink and stood there, gazing out. When I met her eyes, reflected in the glass, she was looking at me from a long way away. "So how do you want your steak?"

I circled her with my arms, her body tight and resisting. "I'm sorry," I said. "I didn't know what my chances were. I'd a lot rather go to the hot springs with you."

"Then why don't you?"

"I have to go back. I won."

She shook her head impatiently. Her hair smelled of lemon and tickled my nose. "Who's going to care if you don't? A bunch of jerks who can't get off on anything but pounding each other's brains out. I could even see it if you got paid."

"That's not the point."

"What *is* the point?" After a moment she leaned back against me and covered my hands with hers. "You hate it, don't you," she said quietly.

I watched the old school clock on the wall, twelve minutes after seven on a Saturday night.

"If you're trying to prove something, lover, I can think of better ways," Shelley said. She twisted around and ran the tip of her tongue along my neck. "Now how about that steak?"

"Rare," I said.

AFTER DINNER I TOOK A LONG SHOWER and stretched out on the bed. It was too short for me, so I always ended up sticking my feet through the iron posts at the end. The walls were hung with her sketches and paintings. Many were nudes, and some of couples, mating. The figures were exaggerated, the females with voluptuous breasts and thighs, the men large-boned and heavily muscled, and they grappled and strained like giants. But beneath the sexual quality there was an honesty, a need to get to the heart of whatever it was that made men and women behave in such an outwardly absurd way. Her work had just begun to sell, a few landscapes and wildlife sketches at a gallery in Helena. The nudes remained private. Several were new, and I tried to be interested, but the phlegm rose in my throat and I started coughing again. The stereo was playing quietly in the next room, the dark rhythmic chords and lonesome harmonica of *Blonde On Blonde*. I knew that when she finished the dishes, she would sit for a few minutes with her water pipe.

After a while she came in and lit a candle on the dresser. I watched her take her earrings off, burnished copper teardrops that glowed dully in the flame light. Another night, I might have asked her to leave them on. She undressed, her small breasts stretching flat as she reached into the closet for her robe. I could not stop the coughing, and when she turned back she said, "You sound just awful."

"Have you got any more of that codeine?"

"I think so." She went down the hall and came back with a small brown bottle and a spoon, then said, "I have to brush my teeth," and left again. I drank the cough syrup straight from the bottle. It was cherry flavored, but you could tell there was something under the sweetness. Across the room, a small dark shape of a moth moved patiently, in silhouette, down the wall, fluttering toward the candle.

An instant cold ache would still touch the base of my nose whenever I thought of the Samoan at the Golden Gloves the year before. He was the Northwestern United States light-heavyweight champion; I had not yet had a dozen fights in a ring. Early in the first round, he had stepped in under one of my jabs and hooked me to the ribs. I remembered the blows like jolts of painless electricity, sparking inside my skull, and then blackness caving in the edges of my vision. When I opened my eyes, the referee was on three.

I remembered the glare of the overhead lights, the crouched referee's finger stabbing the air in front of my face with every number he shouted; remembered seeing for the first time the rust-colored stains on the canvas as my head rolled to the side; remembered thinking that the roar of the crowd was just as it is always described. I got up, and then got up again, trying to follow that grinning kinky blueblack head, trying to lash out and destroy it. But as in the dream I had when I was younger, I could not make my arms obey me. There comes a moment when you realize you are not what you have thought. I went home that night with three broken ribs and a nearly dislocated jaw.

You can drive in cars all your life and never think a thing about it, until one night a drunk doing sixty comes across the center line and you wake up wrapped in plaster, sucking liquid through glass tubes. After that, getting in a car is not the same. Being knocked out was a little like that, only it was not the pain. It was just something I never wanted to happen to me again.

When Shelley came back she was fragrant with soap, toothpaste, and a trace of perfume. She slipped off her robe and shook free her hair, a dark mane that came halfway down her back. Then she turned to me, slender and ivory, and commanded, "Lie on your stomach." She straddled me, her hands cool, then warm, on my back, surprisingly strong, kneading out the hours of tension. After a while she told me to turn over. Her face was dreamy, absorbed in the movement of her own hands. As she swayed, her hair would brush my skin. Then her lips began to follow her fingers, moving down my chest and belly. I pressed my palms to her face and pulled her up beside me.

"What's the matter?" she whispered.

I stroked her head, rounding the curve of her skull with my fingers. Finally I said, "That Indian's going to beat the piss out of me tomorrow."

She reared up and put her hands on my shoulders. "My God, are you crazy? You *know* you're going to get hammered, but you're going to go anyway?"

"He's knocked out everybody in the state," I said.

She pressed me back into the bed, leaning forward until her face was only inches from mine. The scent of her perfume pulsed from the soft place where her jaw met her neck. "Stay here with me. You're sick. We'll lie in bed all day. I'll do anything you want."

"It's already set," I said. "Charlie's coming by at ten."

"The hell with Charlie! You think he's your friend, but he's just using you, pushing you to do it because he can't anymore. Call him and tell him you can hardly breathe." Her eyes were fiercer than I had ever seen them. "Call him."

"I can't do that."

"Well, *I* can." She slid off me, her feet thumping on the wooden floor. I hooked my arm around her waist to pull her back. "Let me *go*, god damn you," she panted, and twisted my fingers until she broke free.

When she got to the door I said, "Wait. If I'm still coughing in the morning, I won't go."

"Promise?"

I hesitated. She jerked open the door.

"I promise," I said.

Back in bed, she stretched herself over me like a blanket, spreading arms and legs to cover mine. "Sweetie, when are you gonna understand, you're not like Charlie and those others. It's okay. You don't have to be." Her fingers moved to my groin, but I caught her hand. She rose up on an elbow and looked into my face. Then she said, "Okay. See you in the morning." She turned so her back was against me and pulled my arm across her breasts. After a while, her breathing evened.

For a long time I lay there, listening to the ticking of the bedside clock, like a tiny mechanical heart: thinking about what Charlie had said on the drive to the prison. "Most of those poor bastards in for their second or third time, it's because things are too complicated out in the world. So they pull shit until they get caught, and once they're in, somebody tells them what to do every minute and feeds them breakfast."

Grosniak, yes. He wore it like a uniform and so did most of the others I had seen. But a man like Louis Heavy Runner—he was there because there was no place else to put him. A hundred years ago, he would have been riding with Sitting Bull or Joseph, a hero instead of a criminal. That he had broken the law seriously, that he was dangerous, there was no doubt. But what were you supposed to do with a man like that: Give him a job in a tire shop? Hope he stayed on the reservation and drank himself to an early death?

Climb into a tiny arena with him, and for a few desperate minutes, give him a chance to somehow get even?

I did my best to explain to Heavy Runner and all the other convicts who slept alone in cell bunks year after year why I could not make love to the woman beside me tonight. Then I turned onto my other side and stepped into the ring in my imagination, waiting for the bell.

THE WEIGH-IN ROOM WAS SMALL and crowded, although not so many boxers had come back for the finals. Several of the inmates were standing in a group at the door, forming a sort of gauntlet. They stopped talking when we walked in. Grosniak stared at me as if he had never seen me before and Louis Heavy Runner, wearing jeans and a navy watch cap like a logger, again seemed to be looking off to the side. I found a space at the room's far end and undressed, then wrapped a towel around my waist.

The inmate operating the scale was a puffy man with pale skin and watery eyes, dressed entirely in white. Ahead of me a black welterweight stepped up. I had noticed him the day before, long, lean, muscled like a greyhound. The attendant's hand lingered on his back as he slid the balance weights around.

"One forty-eight," he said, and shook his head. "You got a pound to go."

The black fighter stepped down, forehead wrinkled. "I guess I go run," he said to no one. He pulled on a jock and went out to the gym.

The scale attendant's hand went to the small of my back as if to help me up the four-inch step. He gave the towel a playful tug. "You're not going to weigh with that, are you?" I tightened my grip. For heavies the weighing was a formality. "What do you think it'll be?"

"One eighty-six," I said.

"Eighty-five with the towel. You must not of slept too good." The group of convicts at the door laughed in a sudden burst at something I could not hear. I stepped down, got the gym bag from Charlie, and took out my jeans.

"You might's well not bother," the scale man said, watching. "They're about to start." Charlie nodded. Today, with only one fight in each division, it was going to go fast. I put away the jeans and found the trunks and cup. The black welter trotted in, gleaming with sweat, and stepped back up. The attendant took a long time with the balance weights.

"Forty-seven and a half," he said finally. The fighter groaned and looked around the room as if for help.

"Try and take a shit," one of the convicts said. "That ought to be worth a half pound."

I put on my robe and laced my shoes carefully. The room was still filled with jostling men and Charlie said, "Come on, I'll wrap you out in the gym." When we reached the door one of the inmates was blocking it, his back to us. Charlie said, "Excuse me, pardner," and when the man did not turn, laid a hand on his shoulder.

He turned then and so did all the others, and for the first time Louis Heavy Runner met me with his eyes. They were hard and black and calm, his mouth a line, leathery skin taut over his thrusting cheekbones and fierce hooked nose, and for all of my years in the city I had never before understood as I did in that instant what it was to be white. Charlie pushed past and walked out to the gym and I followed, not looking to the sides.

We unfolded chairs and sat across from each other, me facing the wall. Around the gym the other boxers hung alone or in groups, pacing, shadow boxing, bouncing. Some of the Job Corps blacks were crouched on a gym mat shooting craps. Their laughter had a nervous sound. Charlie taped my shoelaces down, then took two rolls of gauze and another of white athletic tape from the bag. "Left hand," he said. I rested my elbow on my thigh and extended the hand. Charlie automatically touched his pocket for his knife, but the guards had taken it away in the lobby yesterday and today he had remembered to leave it in the truck. He tore a two-inch slit in the gauze with his teeth, hooked it around my thumb, and began to wrap the wrist.

After each turn he would snug it and say, "Okay?" He worked slowly and carefully, taking several turns around the wrist, then down between each finger, then looping around the thumb to keep it from hooking and tearing back. His hands were strong, rough as sandpaper, the knuckles misshapen. Beads of moisture formed on his forehead and the smell of coffee was strong on his breath. I looked over his head at the wall. It was flat green and peeling like all the others. Charlie finished, taped the wrist and ran strips down between the fingers, then said, "Now the right." Far away, a bell rang.

"Let's get the bantams and lightweights out here," a voice called. I recognized it as the scale attendant's, loud, important, aggressive. Most of the others left, the Job Corps fighters in a group, and it was quiet.

"Keep your left in his face," Charlie said. His voice was low and he kept his gaze on the hand as if he was talking to it. "Use that looping hook, get him moving into your right. And god damn it, when he comes in, throw it." He knotted the gauze with a hard tug.

I was remembering the soundless painless explosions in my head, the shouting face too close to mine, the awakening sense that I had been somewhere unknown through that vague roar and blur of hot lights and hand on my arm leading me away. I tried to swallow. The taste was sour and would not go all the way down. I thought about Shelley, how there was still time to get out of here, and I said, "Charlie."

He raised his eyes, the deep scar under the left one sunken and red, and I looked in and understood what it was about them, that they held immeasurable trouble but not a trace of fear, and I looked away. "Nothing."

"Take a lap," he said, standing. "Easy, just to get the blood going. Then we'll warm your hands." I slipped off the robe and trotted the circuit of the gym, shaking my arms loosely. They were heavy and when I spat it came out in a spray like tiny balls of cotton floating to the floor. The bell in the auditorium rang several times in quick staccato, the signal for a knockout.

When I came back Charlie was waiting, holding a pair of ten-ounce gloves, the size of ski mitts. "Put some snap in them," he said after we started and I tried, but I saw in Charlie's face what I already knew, that the strength that came so easily working the bag and sparring was gone.

THE AUDITORIUM WAS FILLED and the crowd on its feet as I walked to the ring. Over the pounding in my head I recognized the black fighter with the pink spots on his chest, holding a trophy. When he saw me he grinned and raised a clenched fist. Louis Heavy Runner was surrounded by other inmates like a king. He was wearing white trunks and no robe and muscles slid shadowed under his dark torso as he stretched and bounced. Someone slapped me on the back too hard and I turned to see Fletcher's face, looking the size of a pumpkin. His leering eyes were yellowish and set too close together, his breath foul, his fatman sweat oozing through his oily pores. "Stay in there as long as you can kid," he said. "We'll have the towel ready."

Charlie climbed the three steps to the ring ahead of me and held apart the ropes. I climbed the first, the second, the third. A man in the audience wearing a cowboy hat was raising a handful of popcorn to his mouth. I stepped through the ropes.

The referee was a short neat man with sandy hair and a bow tie. He cleared his throat into the microphone. "Ladies and gentlemen," he said, even though there were no women. "The feature event of today's exhibition: the heavyweight championship of this tournament." There came a pause and a rustle of paper. "In this corner, from Helena, wearing green trunks, weighing one hundred and eighty-five pounds—" A few cheers floated in from the audience and from near the ring someone yelled, "*Git* his ass, Slim!"

". . . two hundred and fourteen pounds, the defending champion for the fifth consecutive year—" The crowd howled and stamped as Heavy Runner strode to the ring and up the stairs.

"Come on out here, fellows," the ref said, and in the center of the ring we stood a foot apart. Heavy Runner was a few inches shorter and a few wider and his eyes were shiny, black, calm.

". . . punches below the belt," the ref was saying. "Break clean . . . return to a neutral corner for the eight-count . . ." The bell rang three quick times. "Good clean bout. Shake hands and come out fighting." We touched our four gloved fists together and turned back to our corners.

"Water," I said, and Charlie got the squeeze bottle in my mouth fast. I swished it around and spat into the bucket Fletcher held. The taste was still there.

"Seconds out," the timekeeper called. Charlie shoved my mouthpiece in and he and Fletcher stepped back. I held the ropes and bounced, trying to force air all the way into my lungs.

The bell rang.

Heavy Runner came out fast, loping to my left, hands held loosely in front of his chest, face exposed. I circled with him, knowing I was stiff, too straight, that I had to reverse our direction. Heavy Runner was closer, and I threw a jab that flopped out, a thing with no strength or bone. He made no attempt to slip or block and a trickle of blood started from his nose. Glints of white teeth showed at the corners of his mouth but in his eyes no anger or hatred showed: only that fierce calm that spoke of something I had never felt. Around and around we circled, and I thought that at any second my legs would give out from under me.

Heavy Runner shifted his weight and I leaped back, feeling the rope brush my hip. Heavy Runner closed the distance impossibly fast, looming like a truck. I slipped a hard right, hearing its hiss, feeling the sting of leather on my ear. In the center again we danced, the crowd's roar an ocean of sound that battered against us. I had forgotten about direction, about everything except that Heavy Runner was moving closer again. I backpedaled, almost running, until I hit the ropes, then threw another desperate left. This time Heavy Runner was around it and in the air before it could land.

When I came back I was still on my feet. Everything was almost the same, but I knew I had been gone. It was like being touched with something very hot. I bounced off the ropes with my forearms tight around my head, elbows in my gut, and bulled my way past the jarring blows, trying to get clear enough to see. When I did Heavy Runner was there and a punch to the temple buckled my knees. I closed up again and stayed crouched in the corner, taking blow after blow with machine gun speed, feeling shaken apart into a sack of flesh. I knew I had to look, but I could not make my eyes stay up.

Then for just an instant Heavy Runner paused, and I pulled my gaze up from the blue of brown gloves and brown body swirling in front of me. His face came into focus, looking thoughtful, and I understood that the next one I took was going to be the last. I dropped my knee and drove my right at the center of those black eyes.

The jar to my shoulder made me bite deep into my mouthpiece. I covered tight and waited but the face was gone and after a few seconds I realized that no one was hitting me anymore. Then, as if someone had plugged in a radio with the volume turned up high, I was aware of the noise. I dropped my gloves enough to take a look. Around the ring fists were waving in the air and eyes and mouths were stretched in contortions. The referee was dancing around with his hands out palms down. Louis Heavy Runner was on the other side of the ring, facing away. One of his arms hung over the ropes, the other at his side. He was walking slowly along as if taking a stroll. When he rolled around he lurched, his mouth slack and his eyes unseeing.

"Seven, eight!" The ref jumped forward, tugged on Heavy Runner's gloves, spoke sharply to him. Heavy Runner nodded vaguely. The ref glanced at his corner and whatever he saw there made him shrug. He stepped back, signaling to me that the fight was on.

"Finish him, god damn it!" a voice was shouting. I recognized it as Charlie's. I started forward. Heavy Runner was blinking and shaking his head, his gloves risen but still purposeless. I stopped.

"For Christ's sake, *go get him!*"

I dropped my fists and bounced through the next seconds, aware of the crowd's different sound, until Heavy Runner looked at me again. This time I could tell he saw me. Slowly, he began his lope, and I joined him in our dance for the remaining few seconds before the bell.

In the strange deep clarity of the next minute, I swirled water in my mouth and listened to Fletcher growl excitedly about glass jaws and right crosses, while Charlie, tight-lipped, said nothing. This time when the ten-second whistle blew and Fletcher held up the bucket, I missed and a glob of blood-streaked spit landed on the pointed toe of his cowboy boot. His eyes turned flat as glass. The roar was starting again. When the bell rang I could feel Charlie watching me.

The next round lasted longer than I had expected, almost two minutes. Heavy Runner came out with the glitter back in his eyes but I was moving now, loose and cool, and stung him with a couple of jabs that got the blood flowing from his nose again. I even managed to get us circling my way. But then I dropped my right three inches, planting my feet to throw it, and in the time it took me to do that Heavy Runner was leaping forward. The hook dropped me to a knee. The ref had to push Heavy Runner back to his corner while he shouted the eight-count, and on the last number Heavy Runner shoved past him and lunged in again. I tried the looping hook to move him left but he was in with that same speed. This time I went down to a hand and a knee and while I was getting my feet under me something clubbed me on the back of the head.

When I opened my eyes it took me a moment to remember where I was and what I was supposed to do. I rolled onto my side, then sat up to see the referee holding Heavy Runner's gloved fist high in the air. The crowd was yelling for him and Charlie was yelling at the ref and I got up and walked unsteadily back to my corner.

As I gripped the ropes I heard my name called. A gloved hand touched my shoulder. I turned and looked once more into those black eyes, almost shy now.

"We need you two over here," an inmate with a camera called. He handed us trophies, posed us with our arms around each other's waists, and took a picture.

THE MIDAFTERNOON WIND WAS COLD and wet and fluttered the lapels of my jacket. We walked in silence to the truck. Charlie paused, gazing down the street toward the distant mountains. "You got a right hand, no doubt about that," he said. "His feet just flat came off the canvas. All you had to do was throw it once more."

"Whatever that takes, Charlie, I just don't have it."

"They still should have given you the fight. Clubbing a guy on the head when he's down doesn't fly."

"It wouldn't have changed anything."

"What the hell's that supposed to mean?" he said, but then got into the truck without waiting for an answer. A station wagon drove by full of passengers, and the black fighter with the pink spots leaned out and called, "We catch you next time, Slim." I raised my hand.

Charlie took the pint from the glove box and handed it to me. The whiskey tasted wonderful, sweet and raw. My throat still hurt but the cough was gone. I passed it back. Except for the bars, Main Street in Deer Lodge was empty and closed, cold and lonesome on a Sunday afternoon in the early Montana spring. Flashes of sunlight gave the prison's old stone and brick a warmer color than yesterday, but it was no place I ever wanted to spend any time.

"Must be eight, ten years ago I went to Calgary to fight a spade from Tacoma," he said. "About ten seconds into the first round the little bastard sucker-punched me and knocked me right on my ass. After driving six hundred miles. I lay there and listened to the ref count and I could of got up again, but I was too disgusted. Thought that was it. My last fight." He pulled into the Circle K at the town's edge and set the brake, leaving the engine idling.

"You'll be back," he said. "It gets in your blood." He got out and came back with a twelve-pack of Pabst and a sack of ice. We cracked beers and drove on. After a while he started to whistle, a tune I had never heard.

To the east the high craggy peaks of the Flint Range stood out white against clouds of blue and gray, changing shade by the instant, glowing as they thinned before the sun then darkening again into threat. Shelley had not spoken to me all morning, but then ran out barefoot as I was getting into Charlie's truck and handed me what was left of the codeine. I imagined her now sitting by her front window, maybe sketching. Her hair would be tied back loosely with a silver clasp, that would come undone at my touch.

Ranch Girl
Maile Meloy

IF YOU'RE WHITE, AND YOU'RE NOT RICH or poor but somewhere in the middle, it's hard to have worse luck than to be born a girl on a ranch. It doesn't matter if your dad's the foreman or the rancher— you're still a ranch girl, and you've been dealt a bad hand.

If you're the foreman's daughter on Ted Haskell's Running H cattle ranch, you live in the foreman's house, on the dirt road between Haskell's place and the barn. There are two bedrooms with walls made of particleboard, one bathroom (no tub), muddy boots and jackets in the living room, and a kitchen that's never used. No one from school ever visits the ranch, so you can keep your room the way you decorated it at ten: a pink comforter, horse posters on the walls, plastic horse models on the shelves. Outside there's an old cow-dog with a ruined hip, a barn cat who sleeps in the rafters, and, until he dies, a runt calf named Minute, who cries at night by the front door.

You help your dad when the other hands are busy: wading after him into an irrigation ditch, or rounding up a stray cow–calf pair when you get home from school. Your mom used to help, too—she sits a horse better than any of the hands—but then she took an office job in town, and bought herself a house to be close to work. That was the story, anyway; she hasn't shown up at the ranch since junior high. Your dad works late now, comes home tired and opens a beer. You bring him cheese and crackers, and watch him fall asleep in his chair.

Down the road, at the ranch house, Ted Haskell grills steaks from his cows every night. He's been divorced for years, but he's never learned how to cook anything except steak. Whenever you're there with Haskell's daughter Carla, who's in your class at school, Haskell tries to get you to stay for dinner. He says you're too thin and a good beefsteak will make you strong. But you don't like

Haskell's teasing, and you don't like leaving your dad alone, so you walk home hungry.

WHEN YOU'RE SIXTEEN, HASKELL'S RANCH HOUSE is the best place to get ready to go out at night. Carla has her own bathroom, with a big mirror, where you curl your hair into ringlets and put on blue eye shadow. You and Carla wear matching Wranglers, and when it gets cold you wear knitted gloves with rainbow-striped fingers that the boys love to look at when they get drunk out on the Hill.

The Hill is the park where everyone stands and talks after they get bored driving their cars in circles on the drag. The cowboys are always out on the hill, and there's a fight every night; on a good night, there are five or six. On a good night, someone gets slid across the asphalt on his back, T-shirt riding up over his bare skin. It doesn't matter what the fights are about—no one ever knows—it just matters that Andy Tyler always wins. He's the one who slides the other guy into the road. Afterward, he gets casual, walks over with his cowboy-boot gait, takes a button from the school blood drive off his shirt and reads it aloud: "I Gave Blood Today," he says. "Looks like you did, too." Then he pins the button to the other guy's shirt. He puts his jean jacket back on and hides a beer inside it, his hand tucked in like Napoleon's, and smiles his invincible smile.

"Hey," he says. "Do that rainbow thing again."

You wave your gloved hands in fast arcs, fingers together so the stripes line up.

Andy laughs, and grabs your hands, and says, "Come home and fuck me."

But you don't. You walk away. And Andy leaves the Hill without saying good-bye, and rolls his truck in a ditch for the hundredth time, but a buddy of his dad's always tows him, and no one ever calls the cops.

Virginity is as important to rodeo boys as to Catholics, and you don't go home and fuck Andy Tyler because when you finally get him, you want to keep him. But you like his asking. Some nights, he doesn't ask. Some nights, Lacey Estrada climbs into Andy's truck, dark hair bouncing in soft curls on her shoulders, and moves close to Andy on the front seat as they drive away. Lacey's dad is a doctor, and she lives in a big white house where she can sneak Andy into her bedroom without waking anyone up. But cowboys are romantics; when they settle down they want the girl they haven't fucked.

WHEN HASKELL MARRIES AN EX-HIPPIE, everyone on the ranch expects trouble. Suzy was a beauty once; now she's on her third husband and doesn't take any shit. Suzy reads tarot cards, and when she lays them out to answer the question of Andy Tyler, the cards say to hold out for him.

On the spring cattle drive, you show Suzy how to ride behind the mob and stay out of the dust. Suzy talks about her life before Haskell: she has a Ph.D. in anthropology, a police record for narcotics possession, a sorority pin, and a ski-bum son in Jackson Hole. She spent her twenties throwing dinner parties for her first husband's business clients—that, she says, was her biggest mistake—and then the husband ran off with one of her sorority sisters. She married a Buddhist next. "Be interesting in your twenties," Suzy says. "Otherwise you'll want to do it in your thirties or forties, when it wreaks all kinds of havoc, and you've got a husband and kids."

You listen to Suzy and say nothing. What's wrong with a husband and children? A sweet guy, a couple of brown-armed kids running around outside—it wouldn't be so bad.

There a fall cattle drive, too, but no one ever wants to come on it. It's cold in November, and the cows have scattered in the national forest. They're half wild from being out there for months, especially the calves, who are stupid as only calves can be. The cowboys have disappeared, gone back to college or off on binges or other jobs. So you go out with your dad and Haskell, sweating in heavy coats as you chase down the calves, fighting the herd back to winter pasture before it starts to snow. But it always snows before you finish, and your dad yells at you when your horse slips on the wet asphalt and scrapes itself up.

IN GRADE SCHOOL, IT'S OKAY TO DO WELL. But by high school, being smart gives people ideas. Science teachers start bugging you in the halls. They say eastern schools have Montana quotas, places for ranch girls who are good at math. You could get scholarships, they say. But you know, as soon as they suggest it, that if you went to one of those schools you'd still be a ranch girl—not the Texas kind, who are debutantes and just happen to have a ranch in the family, and not the horse-farm kind, who ride English. Horse people are different, because horses are elegant and clean. Cows are mucusy, muddy, shitty, slobbery things, and it takes another kind of person to live with them. Even your long curled hair won't help at a fancy college, because prep-school girls don't curl their hair. The rodeo boys like it, but there aren't any rodeo boys out east. So you come up with a plan: you have two and a half years of straight A's, and you have to flunk quietly, not to draw attention. Western Montana College, where Andy Tyler wants to go, will take anyone who applies. You can live cheap in Dillon, and if things don't work out with Andy you already know half the football team.

When rodeo season begins, the boys start skipping school. You'd skip, too, but the goal is to load up on D's, not to get kicked out or sent into counseling. You paint your nails in class and follow the rodeo circuit on weekends. Andy rides saddle bronc, but his real event is bull riding. The bull riders have to be a little crazy, and Andy Tyler is. He's crazy in other ways, too: two years of asking you to come home and fuck him have made him urgent about it. You dance with him at the all-night graduation party, and he catches you around the waist and says he doesn't know a more beautiful girl. At dawn, he leaves for spring rodeo finals in Reno, driving down with his best friend, Rick Marcille, and you go to Country Kitchen for breakfast in a happy fog, order a chocolate shake, and think about dancing with Andy. Then you fall asleep on Carla's bedroom floor, watching cartoons, too tired to make it down the road to bed.

Andy calls once from Reno, at 2 A.M., and you answer the phone before it wakes your dad. Andy's taken second place in the bull riding and won a silver belt buckle and three thousand dollars. He says he'll take you to dinner at the Grub Stake when he gets home. Rick Marcille shouts "Ro-*day*-o" in the background.

There's a call the next night, too, but it's from Rick Marcille's dad. Rick and Andy rolled the truck somewhere in Idaho, and the doctors don't think Rick will make it, though Andy might. Mr. Marcille sounds angry that Andy's the one who's going to live, but he offers to drive you down there. You don't wake your dad; you just go.

THE DOCTORS ARE WRONG; it's Andy who doesn't make it. When you get to Idaho, he's already dead. Rick Marcille is paralyzed from the neck down. The cops say the boys weren't drinking, that a wheel came loose and the truck just rolled, but you guess the cops are just being nice. It's your turn to be angry, at Mr. Marcille, because his son will live and Andy is dead. But when you leave the hospital, Mr. Marcille falls down on his knees, squeezing your hand until it hurts.

At Andy's funeral, his uncle's band plays, and his family sets white doves free. One won't go, and it hops around the grass at your feet. The morning is already hot and blue, and there will be a whole summer of days like this to get through.

Andy's obituary says he was engaged to Lacey Estrada, which only Lacey or her doctor father could have put in. If you had the guts, you'd buy every paper in town and burn them outside the big white house where Lacey took him home and fucked him. Then Lacey shows up on the Hill with an engagement ring and gives you a sad smile as if you've shared something. If you were one of the girls who gets in fights on the Hill, you'd fight Lacey. But you don't; you just look away. You'll all be too old for the Hill when school starts, anyway.

AT WESTERN, IN THE FALL, in a required composition class, your professor accuses you of plagiarism because your first paper is readable. You drop the class. Carla gets an A on her biology midterm at the university in Bozeman. She's going to be a big-animal vet. Her dad tells everyone, beaming.

But the next summer, Carla quits college to marry a boy named Dale Banning. The Bannings own most of central Montana, and Dale got famous at the family's fall livestock sale. He'd been putting black bulls on Herefords, when everyone wanted purebreds. They said he was crazy, but at the sale Dale's crossbred black-baldies brought twice what the purebreds did. Dale stood around grinning, embarrassed, like a guy who'd beaten his friends at poker.

Carla announces the engagement in Haskells' kitchen, and says she'll still be working with animals, without slogging through all those classes. "Dale's never been to vet school," Carla says. "But he can feel an embryo the size of a pea inside a cow's uterus."

You've heard Dale use that line on girls before, but never knew it to work so well. Carla's voice has a dreamy edge.

"If I don't marry him now," Carla says, "he'll find someone else."

In his head, Haskell has already added the Banning acreage to his own, and the numbers make him giddy. He forgets about having a vet for a daughter, and talks about the wedding all the time. If Carla backed out, he'd marry Dale himself. For the party, they clear the big barn and kill a cow. Carla wears a high-collared white gown that hides the scar on her neck—half a Running H—from the time she got in the way at branding, holding a struggling calf. Dale wears a string tie and a black ten-gallon hat, and everyone dances to Andy's uncle's band.

Your mother drives out to the ranch for the wedding; it's the first time you've seen your parents together in years. Your dad keeps ordering whiskeys and your mother gets drunk and giggly. But they sober up enough not to go home together.

That winter, your dad quits his job, saying he's tired of Haskell's crap. He leaves the foreman's house and moves in with his new girlfriend, who then announces he can't stay there without a job. He hasn't done anything but ranch work for twenty-five years, so he starts day-riding for Haskell again, then working full-time hourly, until he might as well be the foreman.

WHEN YOU FINISH WESTERN, you move into your mother's house in town. Stacks of paperwork for the local horse-racing board cover every chair and table, and an old leather racing saddle straddles an arm of the couch. Your mother still thinks of herself as a horsewoman, and buys unbroken Thoroughbreds she doesn't have time or money to train. She doesn't have a truck or a trailer, or land for pasture, so she boards the horses and they end up as big, useless pets she never sees.

Summer evenings, you sit with your mom on the front step and eat ice cream with chocolate-peanut-butter chunks for dinner. You think about moving out, but then she might move in with you—and that would be worse.

You aren't a virgin anymore, thanks to a boy you found who wouldn't cause you trouble. He drops by from time to time, to see if things might start up again. They don't. He's nothing like Andy. He isn't the one in your head.

When Carla leaves Dale and moves home to Running H, you drive out to see her baby. It feels strange to be at the ranch now, with the foreman's house empty and Carla's little boy in the yard, and everything else the same.

"You're so lucky to have a degree and no kid," Carla says. "You can still leave."

And Carla is right: You could leave. Apply to grad school in Santa Cruz and live by the beach. Take the research job in Chicago that your chemistry professor keeps calling about. Go to Zihuatanejo with Haskell's friends, who need a nanny. They have tons of room, because in Mexico you don't have to pay property tax if you're still adding on to the house.

But none of these things seem real; what's real is the payments on your car and your mom's crazy horses, the feel of the ranch road you can drive blindfolded and the smell of the hay. Your dad will need you in November to bring in the cows.

Suzy lays out the tarot cards on the kitchen table. The cards say, Go on, go away. But out there in the world you get old. You don't get old here. Here you can always be a ranch girl. Suzy knows. When Haskell comes in wearing muddy boots, saying, "Hi, baby. Hi, hon," his wife stacks up the tarot cards and kisses him hello. She pours him fresh coffee and puts away the cards that say go.

TOUGH PEOPLE
Chris Offutt

THE BELL RANG FOR THE FIRST ROUND and I stepped across the canvas holding the red gloves high to guard my face. The crowd was rooting for my opponent, a big Indian with plenty of reach. All I could do was duck, go inside, and go to work. I'd never fought before and I was scared.

We circled each other and I blocked two jabs, then dodged a roundhouse right. The only rules were no kicking, biting, or elbows. Blurred tattoos covered his chest and arms. He came at me again. I ducked and popped him in the face, and the jolt went up my arm and into my body. I stung him twice more the same way. My mouth was dry. It seemed like we'd been fighting for hours. He led with his jab and I ducked again, but this time he was waiting for me. His haymaker got me on the temple and I felt two days pass.

When I woke up, the cornerman was removing the gloves. He led me out of the ring to a folding chair. I sat there breathing hard, mad at myself. A little piece of my mind wondered if Lynn had run off with the guy who'd beat me, but I knew that was bad luck talking in my head. Bad luck was how I got here, and now my luck had dipped again.

Lynn dropped into the chair beside me. She doesn't sit in a regular way. She gets near a chair and lets gravity pull her onto the seat. It's her only bad habit.

"Are you hurt?" she said.

"I'll have a shiner."

"I wish I took some pictures."

"Where you been?"

"I signed up for tomorrow."

"I'm out of it. You only get one chance."

"Not you," she said. "I signed up for the Tough Woman contest."

"No way."

"Way," she said. "There's only three women so I'm automatically in the finals. I get five hundred bucks for stepping in the ring. We can go back to Billings."

She and I had been traveling together before we went broke here in Great Falls. Entering the Montana Tough Man Contest had seemed like a good way to raise bus fare out of town. Now it just seemed stupid.

Lynn held my arm as we walked to the motel, and after a quick shower, we put that mattress through its paces. I guess the main reason we were together was sex. I know that has a bad sound to it, like we're just wild, but that's not exactly true. I'd left Kentucky a while back and was a cook at the same diner where she worked as a waitress. She was a photographer, but had pawned her camera to cover our motel bill. We'd been hanging out for two weeks. We got along okay. We talked. It's just that our bodies could sing.

In the morning my eye was puffed and black as a burnt biscuit. I'm not even an athlete, let alone a fighter, and my body was pretty sore. Lynn went out for coffee while I took a long bath. The notion of her fighting for money went against my raisings. It made me feel responsible for her and I didn't want that. Neither of us did. We just wanted to be free.

She came back to the room and held her hands in front of her face, thumbs touching, fingers pointing up. She tilted her head and squinted. It was how she practiced taking pictures.

"That would make a good photograph," she said. "The boxer in the tub."

"I don't want you to fight," I said.

"It's not up to you."

"I ain't trying to tell you what to do, Lynn. Going broke was my fault and I hate you had to hock your camera."

"Get off it," she said. "I bought it used. I'll get a better one next."

"We could sell our blood," I said. "Maybe volunteer for medical tests."

"It'll take too long. I can make half a grand in three minutes."

"It just ain't right. A woman ain't supposed to fight for a man."

"What's fair for you is fair for me. Besides, I might win. We'll get two thousand cash and have a great life. This is just a rough patch. Even rich people have it rough sometimes."

"I reckon."

"Let's pretend we are rich," she said. "Let's just think that way and act accordingly."

"First thing is to get a fancy camera."

"I'll take a thousand pictures of you a day. That's like twenty-five rolls."

I got out of the tub and dried myself while she practiced taking pictures, squatting to change angles, and making a whirring sound as she advanced the film. Even though she was faking, I felt embarrassed by a nude shot.

"Let's go to Seattle," she said. "Everybody I know is moving there."

"It's your money."

"No, it's ours. There's better jobs there."

We laughed and talked and made plans to open a photo gallery and diner in Seattle. It would be old style, with good food cheap. Lynn's pictures would hang on the walls, and the menu would be shaped like a negative with holes along the side. We'd have specials called F-Stop Burger, and Zoom Lens Soup. Photographers and Kentuckians could eat there free.

Lynn needed rest and I took a walk. The sky was haired over solid gray. There was no sun, just a dull light, and I figured snow was coming. Great Falls reminded me of towns in Kentucky that hadn't changed since the fifties. The buildings were low and made of stone, and people strolled from store to store. I thought about home and wished I'd never left. Kentucky's idea of a tough man contest is to get through the season at hand.

In a pawnshop window was a camera that came with a bunch of lenses. I wanted to buy it all and go back to the room and throw the whole rig on the bed. That would make Lynn and me square. I hated the idea of owing somebody. I stood there for a long time thinking that having money gave you freedom, but getting the money took freedom away. What I needed was luck.

I started worrying that Lynn might get hurt in the fight, break her nose or lose a tooth—and blame me. The more I thought about it, the madder I got. Inside I felt like I was about to bust, but there was nowhere for me to go with it.

I went back to the motel and stopped at the bar. It was called the Sip & Dip, and had a tropical decor with plastic parrots, bamboo walls, and fake torches. Any minute you expected a cannibal to jump out at you. An older couple was arguing at a table shaped like a kidney bean. A tall man about forty came in, ordered a whiskey ditch, and began talking to me. He was from Mississippi. His southern accent made me feel good, as if I were talking to a countryman.

"Luck always turns," he said. "There's nothing you can do when you're running bad but develop yourself a leather ass. How did you happen to be here for the Tough Man Contest?"

"I borrowed a car from a guy at work. Me and Lynn wanted to get out of Billings and run around."

He told the bartender to bring a couple of drinks.

"On me," he said. "You're a guy who needs a lot of outs right now."

"You know I can't buy the next round."

"There was a time when all I owned was on my back. So you and Lynn were on the loose."

"Yeah," I said. "We had a couple hundred bucks and four days off from work. We're thinking maybe we'll hit the Chico Hot Springs when bang, we're pulled over by the Highway Patrol. I'm sober and we're not carrying dope, so I'm not worried. I'm good with cops, I say yes sir and no sir, and all that. They have a tough job. I respect that because my job ain't the best. When you're a cook, everything will cut you or burn you."

He said he understood. The older couple who'd been arguing were kissing now, pecking at each other's faces like a pair of chickens.

"Do you live here?" I said.

"No. I have a cabin up in Big Sandy. I'll do some bird hunting this week."

"There's a river in Kentucky with the same name."

"I suppose that's possible," he said. He looked at me like he was gauging worth. "Is Lynn beautiful?"

"Definitely."

"Beautiful women make me fear death."

I sat and studied on that for a while. Dying never scared me, but life does every day. I couldn't tell him that, though. I wondered if he was sick with some disease, or maybe he was older than I thought.

"What's your name," I said.

"Jack," he said. "Jack King. I'm in the deck."

"I don't get you."

"A deck of cards."

"Is that your real name?"

He gave the bartender the sign for more drinks. The older couple had quit smooching and seemed to be resting. Keno machines blinked in the corner.

"I'm a gambler," Jack said. "I've been down to those riverboats in Louisiana for quite some time. I like to come up here and hunt and play a little poker."

"Whereabouts do you play?"

"The Butte game goes all night."

"Is that what you like?"

"The minute you sit down, you have to be willing to play for days. You could learn from that."

"What do you mean?" I said.

"You need to cowboy up."

"I'm doing the best I can. It just don't feel right to have your girl-friend out fighting for money."

"I once had a girlfriend who worked as a dancer in a topless joint. It was the worst two weeks of my life, but she made a bankroll to choke a horse. We had a nice run."

He twisted a heavy gold ring, and I noticed that he wore them on the last two fingers of each hand. He spoke without looking at me. "You never finished telling about that cop pulling you over."

"Well, that's when everything just went to hell in a handcart. The guy I borrowed the car from had stolen it. The cops held me in jail for three days until they found him. Lynn had to stay in a motel. When I got out, we pretty much blew the rest of our money at karaoke night downtown."

Behind the bar was a glass window that looked into the deep end of the motel pool. You couldn't see past the surface of the water, which made the swimmers seem headless. A pair of pale legs floated past the window and I recognized them as belonging to Lynn. She wore a black one-piece. I liked watching her, knowing she didn't know I was there.

The older couple was working on another drink. He was singing to her, one of those old songs you don't hear anymore, and I imagined Lynn and me still together at their age. Jack was right. Things were about to change.

"In your line," I said, "you must learn a lot about luck."

"I knew a gambler who ran into a losing streak for three months down in Reno. By the end of it, he'd sold his watch, ring, and belt buckle. He owed money to everyone he knew. He sublet his place and slept in his car. Then he sold his car and kept playing. Out of the blue he got so lucky he could piss in a swinging jug. Won a hundred grand in two days."

"Wow," I said.

I wondered if Jack's story was about himself. He told it in a personal way, as if recounting the good old days.

"Tell me," he said, "do people bet on these fights?"

"I don't know."

"Seeing as how you're on the ankle express, I'll give you a ride over there. Meet me in the lobby at six."

He left and I wished I could go somewhere and start all over, which is how I've felt all my life. As soon as I get somewhere, I'm ready to leave. I finished my drink and went back to the room, where Lynn was sitting in bed. There was an intent look on her face that I'd seen only during the height of breakfast rush at the diner.

"Hey," I said, "I got us a ride."

"Borrow another car?"

"I met this guy who said he'd give us a lift. You'll like him."

"I'm not in a frame of mind to like anyone."

"You don't have to fight."

"I don't see any choice."

"We can get restaurant jobs here. In a month we'll be in Seattle."

"I don't care about Seattle," she said. "I just want out of this hotel, this town, and everything else. I don't care how."

She looked at me like I was her enemy. I could see she wanted privacy so I stayed in the bathroom until time to meet Jack. I don't know if she was getting mad because she had to fight, or so she could fight. Either way, it gave me a bad feeling.

We met Jack in the lobby at six, and when I introduced them, she wouldn't talk. We went outside to his car. I'd never been in a Cadillac before and it was not something I minded. I've heard they can go anywhere a pickup can go. We followed the Missouri River to a filling station with a store attached. I asked if he wanted me to gas it up, and he shook his head and went inside. Lynn stared through the windshield at a neon sign that glowed orange. I tried to think of something to say. Jack came back with two quarts of water, an energy bar, a box of Band-Aids, and a ballpoint pen. He made Lynn eat and drink.

We parked at the fairgrounds and walked across the lot to the arena. Jack was talking to her in a low voice, his arm across her shoulders like a coach. It was a nice night, the clear sky covered by stars like dew. At times I missed Kentucky, but never at night. When I couldn't see the land out there, I forgot I wasn't at home. Sometimes I wished it was always night.

We checked Lynn in, then went to the fighters' area, which was just some metal chairs in the corner. The center of the arena held a boxing ring on a platform, surrounded by rows of people who'd paid extra to sit close. Along two sides were rising sets of bleachers. The lights gleamed above the ring. Jack used three Band-Aids to build a strip across Lynn's nose, holding it open to get more air. He told her not to drink the water yet, and walked away. I sat beside her.

"You scared?" I said.

"Yes," she said. "Jack said it was okay to be scared. He said if I wasn't, there was something wrong with me."

"There's nothing wrong with you."

"I don't want to get hurt."

"The gloves are thick and the headgear covers you. Plus women wear that belly pad."

"They're still hitting you."

"The time goes fast, Lynn."

I looked away when I said that because it was a big fat lie. That round I fought was the slowest minute of my life. It felt like a month of Sundays.

"Whatever happens," I said, "you just remember I'm right here and I always will be."

She looked at me with an odd expression on her face, then stood and began to stretch. I walked to the concession stand. The arena was jammed with Indians and I looked them over carefully. They dressed like people in the hills at home—flannel shirts, jeans, boots, and work jackets—men and women alike. Quite a few wore glasses. I thought maybe Indians just had bad eyes, until I remembered that a lot of people at home wore glasses because they couldn't afford contact lenses. I wondered if it was the same here.

The first bout had just ended. The fighters left the ring to sit with their families. Smoking was not allowed, but you could drink beer, and a few people were already staggering. A couple of young men gave me dirty looks for being white, until they saw my black eye. Then they said hello.

The guy who knocked me out stopped and shook my hand. He was a little bit drunk. His name was Alex. He wore a rodeo buckle and fancy cowboy boots. His long braids were tied together behind his neck.

"I lost the last fight last night," he said.

"I didn't see it."

"Came all the way from Browning to find a man who hits as hard as my horse kicks."

"Well," I said, "ours was a good fight."

"You got your licks in."

"You won it."

"Yes," he said, "even a blind squirrel finds a nut sometimes."

The P.A. announced the women's finals. When I got to Lynn, Jack was already there, rubbing her shoulders and whispering in her ear. He'd used the pen he'd bought to write on her fists. Her left hand carried the word "kiss," and her right hand said "kill." He was telling her to jab with the left, kissing her opponent on the mouth, then kill her with the right.

We walked Lynn to the ring. She wasn't blinking.

"Go for the face," Jack said. "Keep your chin down and your eyes open. Circle but don't back up. Say this over and over—kiss, kiss, kill."

She nodded and climbed the stepladder to the ring. The other fighter was a short Indian woman with a powerful body. I knew Lynn would lose and I felt awful for having put her there. If I hadn't left Kentucky, she'd be with a guy who had more to offer.

The bell rang. The crowd was yelling, and the announcer chanted into his microphone, "Here kitty, kitty, kitty." The Indian woman moved slowly, waiting to see what Lynn would do. Lynn's little white legs looked pathetic below the torso pad. She wore her swimsuit, and I wished that she was still in the pool, that they were fighting in the water where Lynn would have a chance. They circled each other three times. Jack stood beside me muttering, "Kiss, kiss, kill."

The people in the crowd were yelling for blood. Lynn's fists were up and her chin was down, and suddenly she jumped through the air, swinging both fists wildly at the woman's head. Lynn connected two or three times before the woman shoved her away and hit her in the face, opening a cut above her eye. When I saw the red smear, my guts just folded up on themselves.

The doctor called time and the referee took the fighters to neutral corners. The doctor examined the cut, put ointment on it, and left the ring. Lynn had a look I'd seen when a customer stiffed her at the diner. She was mad. The other woman just looked serious, like she could face a sideways ice storm and walk all night. She moved forward a step at a time. Everybody in the place understood that Lynn was no fighter, but she was in there, and she wasn't afraid.

The Indian woman walked to Lynn as if to shake hands and hit her very hard on the cut eye. Lynn's head jerked to the side, spattering blood on the canvas floor of the ring. I started to cry. When I looked up, the fight was over. The doctor had stopped it and the crowd was booing.

The doctor worked on the cut while a man from the judge's table handed Lynn an envelope. Jack helped her to a chair. He held her chin with one hand and lifted the water to her mouth like a baby's bottle. He was very gentle. I sat beside Lynn. She was gasping for breath, her chest rising and falling, barely able to drink. There was a butterfly bandage across her left eyebrow. A sheen of sweat covered her skin.

"The doctor said it won't scar," Jack said.

"I want it to," she said.

The woman who won the fight leaned over the chair to hug Lynn. Her arms were strong, with raised scars on them. The two women reeked of sweat in a way that I had only smelled on men in a work crew. They whispered in each other's ears. After Lynn got control of her breathing, Jack helped her to the rest room where she could change clothes.

I sat there thinking that Lynn was tougher than me. She hadn't gone down, she'd just got cut. I watched the winner walk the aisle. Someone gave her a cup of beer and someone else gave her a cigarette and I suddenly wanted her for a girlfriend. I wanted to treat her as tenderly as Jack had treated Lynn. The woman was beautiful in the garish lights of the ring that spilled shadows on the bleachers. Whatever she'd gone through to get so tough soaked me with sorrow.

Lynn and Jack joined me. The flush had faded from her skin. She'd wet her face and hair, and she looked fine. We went outside, past teenage boys smoking cigarettes and faking punches at each other. The dry cold air snapped against my face. Snow drifted down, one of those early autumn snows before the hard cold sets in. The flakes were the size of silver dollars falling from the sky, turning the black night white.

"If they hadn't stopped it," I said, "you'd have won. It was your fight."

"No, it wasn't," Lynn said. "It was never my fight."

Jack unlocked the Cadillac and sat behind the wheel. Lynn gave me the envelope that contained her prize money.

"I'm going with Jack," she said. "I'm sorry."

I nodded.

"The motel is paid through tomorrow," she said. "We can drop you there, if you want."

I shook my head no.

"This isn't about you," she said. "This is about me."

She hugged me then, squeezing me tighter than she ever had. My face pushed against her neck and I smelled the cheap soap from the rest room. I put my arms around her, but I couldn't hug back. My knees felt wobbly. She stepped away. She was sad but trying to smile. A strand of hair fell over her face. I lifted my hands and pretended to take a picture.

She got in the car and I watched the red taillights move around a corner.

I headed for the motel and stopped at the bridge that crossed the Missouri River. I stood there a long time. Snow was thick in the air. My family had been in the hills for two hundred years and I was the first to leave. Now I was pretty much ruined for going back. The black water ran fast and cold below.

I started walking.

FATHER, LOVER, DEADMAN, DREAMER
Melanie Rae Thon

I WAS A NATURAL LIAR, like my mother. One night she told my daddy she was going to the movies with her girlfriend Marlene. Drive-in, double feature, up in Kalispell. Daddy said, *How late will you be?* And my mother said she didn't know.

Hours later, we tried to find her. I remember my father hobbling from car to car while I sat in the truck. The faces on the screen were as big as God's. Their voices crackled in every box. I was certain my mother was here, stunned and obedient. Huge bodies floated over the hill. They shimmered, lit from inside. This was how the dead returned, I thought, full of grace and hope.

It was midnight. I was nine years old. By morning I understood my mother was five hundred miles gone.

I remember the clumsy child I was. Bruises on my arms, scabbed knees. Boys chased me down the gully after school. I remember falling in the mud. They stole things I couldn't get back, small things whose absences I couldn't explain to my father now that we lived alone: a plastic barrette shaped like a butterfly, one shoelace, a pair of white underpants embroidered with the word *Wednesday*. I was Wednesday's child. I wore my Tuesday pants twice each week, the second day turned inside out.

Careless girl, the nuns said, immature, a dreamer. They told my father they had to smack my hands with a ruler just to wake me up.

I was afraid of the lake, the dark water, the way rocks blurred and wavered, the way they grew long necks and fins and swam below me.

I was afraid of the woods where a hunter had killed his only son. An accident, he said: the boy moved so softly in his deer-colored coat. When the man saw what he'd shot, he propped the gun between his feet and fired once more. He bled and bled. Poured into the dry ground. Unlucky man, he lived to tell.

I was afraid of my father's body, the way he was both fat and thin at the same time, like the old cows that came down to the water at dusk. Bony haunches, sagging bellies—they were pitiful things. Daddy yelled at them, waving his stick, snapping the air behind their scrawny butts. They looked at him with their terrible cow eyes. Night after night they drank all they wanted, shat where they stood. Night after night the stick became a cane, and my father climbed the path, breathing hard. He'd been a crippled child, a boy with a metal brace whose mother had had to teach him to walk a second time when he was six, a boy whose big sister lived to be ten. She drowned in air, chest paralyzed, no iron lung to save her. I thought it was this nightly failure, the cows' blank eyes, that made my mother go.

My daddy worked for a man twelve years younger than he was, a doctor with an orchard on the lake. We lived in the caretaker's cottage, a four-room cabin behind the big house. Lying in my little bed, the one Daddy'd built just for me, I heard leaves fluttering, hundreds of cherry trees; I heard water lapping stones on the shore. Kneeling at my window, I saw the moon's reflection, a silvery path rippling across the water. I smelled the pine of the boards beneath me, and the pines swaying along the road. Then, that foot-dragging sound in the hall.

I remember the creak of the hinge, my father's shape and the light behind him as he stood at my door. This was another night, years before the movie, another time my mother lied and was gone. He said, *Get dressed, Ada, we have to go.* He meant he couldn't leave me here alone. I wore my mother's sweater over my nightgown, the long sleeves rolled up.

This time we drove south, down through the reservation, stopping at every bar. We drove past the Church of the Good Shepherd, which stayed lit all night, past huddled trailers and tarpaper shacks, past the squat house where two dogs stood at the edge of the flat tin roof and howled, past the herd of white plaster deer that seemed to flee toward the woods.

We found my mother just across the border, beyond the reservation, in a town called Paradise, the Little Big Man Bar. Out back, the owner had seven junked cars. He called it his Indian hotel. For a buck, you could spend the night, sleep it off.

My mother was inside that bar, dancing with a dark-skinned man. Pretty Noelle, so pale she seemed to glow. She spun, head thrown back, eyes closed. She was dizzy, I was sure. The man pulled her close, whispered to make her laugh. I swear I heard that sound float, my mother's laughter weaving through the throb of guitar and drum, whirling around my head like smoke. I swear I felt that man, his hand on my own back, the shape of each finger, the sweat underneath my nightgown, underneath his palm.

Then it was my father's hand, clamping down.

I am a woman now. I have lovers. I am my mother's daughter. I dance all night. Strangers with black hair hold me close.

I remember driving home, the three of us squeezed together in the truck. I was the silence between them. I felt my father's pain in my own body, as if my left leg were withered, my bones old. Maybe I was dreaming. I saw my mother in a yellow dress. She looked very small. A door opened, far away, and she stumbled through it to a field of junked cars.

The windows in the truck were down. I was half in the dream, half out. I couldn't open my eyes, but I knew where we were by smell and sound: wood fires burning, the barking of those dogs.

I remember my prayers the morning after, boys lighting candles at the altar, my mother's white gloves.

Green curtain, priest, black box—days later I was afraid of the voice behind the screen, soft at first and then impatient, what the voice seemed to know already, what it urged me to tell. I was afraid of stained glass windows, saints and martyrs, the way sunlight fractured them, the rocks they made me want to throw.

Sometimes my father held me on his lap until I fell asleep. He stroked my hair and whispered, *So soft*. He touched my scraped shin. *What happened, Ada, did you fall down?* I nodded and closed my eyes. I thought about the boys, the gully, the things they stole. I learned that the first lie is silence. And I never told.

Then I was a girl, twelve years old, too big for my father's lap. I dove from the cliffs into the lake. I told myself the shapes waffling near the bottom were only stones.

I played a game in the woods with my friend Jean. We shot each other with sticks and fell down in the snow. We lay side by side, not breathing. My chest felt brittle as glass. If I touched my ribs, I thought I'd splinter in the cold. The first one to move was the guilty father. The first one to speak had to beg forgiveness of the dead son.

I worked for the doctor's wife now. My mother's words hissed against those walls. I knew the shame she felt, how she hated that house, seeing it so close, getting down on her knees to wax its floors, how she thought it was wrong for an old man like my father to shovel a young man's snow.

But Daddy was glad the snow belonged to someone else. That doctor had nothing my father wanted to own. He said, *The cherry trees, they break your heart.* He meant something always went wrong: thunderstorms in July; cold wind from Canada; drought. I remember hail falling like a rain of stones, ripe fruit torn from trees. I remember brilliant sunlight after the storm, flowing ice and purple cherries splattered on the ground. My father knelt in the orchard, trying to gather the fruit that was still whole

Then I was sixteen, almost a woman. I went to public school. I knew everything now. I refused to go to mass with my father. I said I believed in Jesus but not in God. I said if the father had seen what he'd done to his child, he would have turned the gun on himself. I thought of the nuns, my small hands, the sting of wood across my palms. I remembered their habits, rustling cloth, those sounds, murmurs above me, that false pity, *poor child*, how they judged me for what my mother had done.

I knew now why my mother had to go. How she must have despised the clump and drag of my father's steps in the hall, the weight of him at the table, the slope of his shoulders, the sorrow of his smell too close. He couldn't dance. Never drank. Old man, she said, and he was. Smoking was his only vice, Lucky Strikes, two packs a day, minus the ones I stole.

He tried not to look at me too hard. I was like her. He saw Noelle when I crossed my legs or lit my cigarette from a flame on the stove.

He gave me what I wanted—the keys to his truck, money for gas and movies, money for mascara, a down vest, a cotton blouse so light it felt like gauze. He thought if I had these things I wouldn't be tempted to steal. He thought I wouldn't envy the doctor's wife for her ruby earrings or her tiny cups rimmed with gold. Still, I took things from her, small things she didn't need: a letter opener with a silver blade and a handle carved of bone; a silk camisole; oily beads of soap that dissolved in my bathwater and smelled of lilac. I lay in the tub, dizzy with myself. The dangerous knife lay hidden, wrapped in underwear at the bottom of my drawer. Next to my skin, the ivory silk of the camisole was soft and forbidden, everything in me my father couldn't control.

The same boys who'd chased me down the gully took me and Jean to the drive-in movies in their Mustangs and Darts. Those altar boys and thieves who'd stolen my butterfly barrette pleaded with me now: *Just once, Ada—I promise I won't tell.*

I heard Jean in the back seat, going too far.

Afterward, I held her tight and rocked. Her skin smelled of sweet wine. I said, *You'll be okay. I promise, you will.*

I am a woman now, remembering. I live in a trailer, smaller than my father's cottage. I am his daughter after all: there's nothing I want to own. I drive an old Ford. I keep a pint of whiskey in the glovebox, two nips of tequila in my purse. I don't think I know as much as I used to know. I sit in the car with my lights off and watch my father, the slow shape of him swimming through the murky light of his little house. He's no longer fat and thin. It scares me, the way he is thin alone. He's had two heart attacks. His gallbladder and one testicle are gone. In January, the doctors in Spokane opened his chest to take pieces of his lungs. Still he smokes. He's seventy-six. He says, *Why stop now?*

I smoke too, watching him. I drink. I tell myself I'm too drunk to knock at the door, too drunk to drive home.

In the grass behind my father's cottage, a green truck sits without tires, sinking into the ground. If I close my eyes and touch its fender, I can feel everything: each shard, the headlight shattering, the stained glass windows bursting at last, the white feet of all the saints splintering, slicing through a man's clothes.

Twenty-one years since that night, but if I lie down beside that truck, I can feel every stone of a black road.

Fourth of July, 1971. This is how the night began, with my small lies, with tepid bathwater and the smell of lilac—with ivory silk under ivory gauze—with the letter opener slipped in my purse. I was thinking of the gully long before, believing I was big enough to protect myself.

Jean and I knew other boys now. Boys who crashed parties in the borderlands at the edge of every town.

I asked my father for the truck. I promised: *Jean's house, then up the lake to Bigfork to see the fireworks and nowhere else.* I said, *Yes, straight home.* I twisted my hair around my finger, remembering my mother in a yellow dress, lying to my father and me, standing just like this, all her weight on one foot, leaning against the frame of this door.

We drove south instead of north. A week before, two boys in a parking lot had offered rum and let us sit in the back seat of their car. They said, *Come to the reservation if you want to see real fireworks.*

We scrambled down a gulch to a pond. Dusk already and there were maybe forty kids at the shore.

We were white girls, the only ones.

Jean had three six-packs, two to drink and one to share. I had a pint of vodka and a quart of orange juice, a jar to shake them up. But the Indian kids were drinking pink gasoline—Hawaiian Punch and ethanol—chasing it down with bottles of Thunderbird. They had boxes full of firecrackers, homemade rockets and shooting stars. They had crazyhorses that streaked across the sky. Crazy, they said, because they fooled you every time: you never knew where they were going to go.

The sky sparked. Stars fell into the pond and sizzled out. We looked for the boys, the ones who'd invited us, but there were too many dressed the same, in blue jeans and plaid shirts, too many cowboy hats pulled down.

One boy hung on to a torch until his whole body glowed. I saw white teeth, slash of red shirt, denim jacket open down the front. I thought, *He wants to burn.* But he whooped, tossed the flare in time. It spiraled toward the pond, shooting flames back into the boxes up the shore. Firecrackers popped like guns; red comets soared; crazyhorses zigzagged along the beach, across the water, into the crowd.

The boy was gone.

In the blasts of light, I saw fragments of bodies, scorched earth, people running up the hill, people falling, arms and legs in the flickering grass, one head raised, three heads rolling, and then the strangest noise; giggles rippling, a chorus of girls.

They called to the boy, their voices like their laughter, a thin, fluttery sound. *Niles.* They sang his name across the water.

Then I was lying in the grass with that boy. Cold stars swirled in the hole of the sky. In the weird silence, bodies mended; bodies became shape and shadow; pieces were found. Flame became pink gasoline guzzled down. Gunfire turned to curse and moan.

This boy was the only one I wanted, the brave one, the crazy one, the one who blazed out. He rose up from the water, red shirt soaked, jacket torn off. I said, *You were something,* and he sat down. Now I was wet too, my clothes and hair dripping, as if he'd taken me into the sky, as if we'd both fallen into the pond.

I whispered his name, *Niles,* hummed it like the girls, but soft. He said, *Call me Yellow Dog.*

My purse was gone, the letter opener and my keys lost. The boy kept drinking that pink gasoline and I wondered how he'd die, if he'd go blind on ethanol or catch fire and drown. I'd heard stories my whole life. The Indians were always killing themselves: leaping off bridges, inhaling ammonia, stepping in front of trucks. Barefoot girls with bruised faces wandered into the snow and lay down till the snow melted around them, till it froze hard.

But tonight this boy was strong.

Tonight this boy could not be killed by gas or flame or gun.

He had a stone in his pocket, small and smooth, like a bird's egg and almost blue. He let me touch it. He said it got heavy sometimes. He said, *That's when I watch my back—that's how I know.* I kissed him. I put my tongue deep in his mouth. I said, *How much does it weigh now?* And he said, *Baby, it's dragging me down.*

My clothes dried stiff with mud. I remember grabbing his coarse braid, how it seemed alive, how I wanted it for myself. I thought I'd snip it off when he passed out. His hands were down my cut-off jeans. He knew my thoughts exactly. He whispered, *I'll slit your throat.* I let his long hair go. His body on me was heavy now. I thought he must be afraid. I thought it must be the stone. He held me down in the dirt, pressed hard: he wanted to stop my breath; he wanted to squeeze the blood from my heart. I clutched his wrists. I said, *Enough.*

I imagined my father pacing the house, that sound in the hall. I heard my own lies spit back at me, felt them twist around bare skin, a burning rope.

I remember ramming my knee into the boy's crotch, his yelp and curse, me rolling free. I called to Jean, heard her blurred answers rise out of some distant ground.

I remember crawling, scraping my knees, feeling for my purse in the grass. Then he was on me, tugging at my unzipped jeans, wrenching my arm. He said, *I could break every bone.* But he didn't. He stood up, this Niles, this Yellow Dog. He said, *Go home.*

He was the one to find my purse. He took the letter opener, licked the silver blade, slid it under his belt. He dropped my keys beside me. He said, *I could have thrown these in the water.* He said, *I didn't. You know why? Because I want your white ass gone.*

When I looked up, the stars above him spun.

I yelled Jean's name again. I said, *Are you okay?* And she said, *Fuck you—go.*

I staggered up the hill. I saw my father at the kitchen table, his head in his hands. I heard every word of his prayers as if I were some terrible god. I felt that tightness in my chest, his body. I felt my left leg giving out.

I saw what he saw, my mother's yellow dress, me standing in the door. I smelled his cigarettes. He said, *The cherry trees, they break your heart.*

I drove up that road through the reservation, my mother's laughter floating through the open windows of the truck. She made me dizzy, all that dancing—I felt myself pulled forward, twirled, pushed back, hard.

The lights of the steeple still burned. I was Noelle, the same kind of woman, a girl who couldn't stand up by herself. I wanted to weep for my father. I wanted not to be drunk when I got home, not to smell of boy's sweat, sulfur and crushed lilacs, mud. I wanted to stop feeling hair between my fingers, to stop feeling hands lipping under my clothes.

The dogs on the roof growled. All the white plaster deer surged toward the road. Wind on my face blew cold.

Past the Church of the Good Shepherd, a hundred pairs of eyes watched from the woods, all the living deer hidden between trees along this road. I practiced lies to tell when I got home. I thought, My mother and I, we're blood and bone. I saw how every lie would be undone. I watched a dark man wrap his arm around my pale mother and spin her into a funnel of smoke.

Then he was there, that very man, rising up in a swirl of dust at the side of the road—a vision, a ghost, weaving in front of me. Then he was real, a body in dark clothes.

There was no time for a drunken girl to stop.

No time to lift my heavy foot from the gas.

I saw his body fly, then fall.

I saw the thickness of it, as if for a moment the whole night gathered in one place to become that man, my mother's lover. A door opened at the back of a bar in Paradise. His body filled that space, so black even the stars went out.

I am a woman now, remembering, I am a woman drinking whiskey in a cold car, watching the lights in my father's house. I am a woman who wants to open his door in time, to find her father there and tell.

Twenty-one years since I met Vincent Blew on that road, twenty-one years, and I swear, even now, when I touch my bare skin, when I smell lilacs, I can feel him, how warm he was, how his skin became my shadow, how I wear it still.

He was just another drunken Indian trying to find his way home. After he met me, he hid his body in the tall grass all night and the next day. Almost dusk before he was found. There was time for a smashed headlight to be reassembled. Time for a dented fender to be pounded out and dabbed with fresh green paint. Time for a girl to sober up. Time for lies to be retold. Here, behind my father's cottage, I can feel the body of the truck, that fender, the edges of the paint, how it chipped and peeled, how the cracks filled with rust.

I waited for two men in boots and mirrored glasses to come for me, to take me to a room, close the door, to ask me questions in voices too low for my father to hear, to urge and probe, to promise no one would hurt me if I simply told the truth.

Imagine: *No hurt.*

But no one asked.

And no one told.

I wanted them to come. I thought their questions would feel like love, that relentless desire to know.

I waited for them.

I'm waiting now.

I know the man on the road that night was not my mother's lover. He was Vincent Blew. He was mine alone.

He lies down beside me in my narrow bed. I think it is the bed my father built. The smell of pine breaks my heart. He touches me in my sleep, traces the cage of my ribs. He says, *You remind me of somebody.* He wets one finger and carves a line down the center of my body, throat to crotch. He says, *This is the line only I can cross.* He lays his head in the hollow of my pelvis. He says, *Yes, I remember you, every bone.*

He was behind me now, already lost.

I didn't decide anything. I just drove. My hands were wet. Blood poured from my nose. I'd struck the steering wheel. I was hurt, but too numb to know. Then I was sobbing in my father's arms. He was saying, *Ada, stop.*

Finally I choked it out.

I said, *I hit something on the road.*

And he said, *A deer?*

This lie came so easily.

All I had to do was nod.

He wrapped me in a wool blanket. Still I shivered, quick spasms, a coldness I'd never know, like falling through the ice of a pond and lying on the bottom, watching the water close above you, freeze hard. He washed the blood from my face with a warm cloth. His tenderness killed me, the way he was so careful, the way he looked at the bruises and the blood but not at me. Every gesture promised I'd never have to tell. He said, *You'll have black eyes, but I don't think your nose is broken.* These words—he meant to comfort me—precious nose—as if my own face, the way it looked, could matter now.

He said he had to check the truck. He took his flashlight, hobbled out. I couldn't stand it, the waiting—even those minutes. I thought, My whole future, the rest of my life, like this, impossibly long.

I moved to the window to watch. I tried to light a cigarette, but the match kept hissing out. I saw the beam moving over the fender and grille, my father's hand touching the truck. I imagined what he felt—a man's hair and bones. I believed he'd come back inside and sit beside me, both of us so still. If he touched me, I'd break and tell.

But when he came inside, he didn't sit, didn't ask what, only where. I could have lied again, named a place between these orchards and Bigfork, that safe road, but I believed my father was offering me a chance, this last one. I thought the truth might save us even now. I described the place exactly, the curve, the line of trees, the funnel of dust. But I did not say one thing, did not tell him, *Look for a man in the grass.*

He said, *You sleep now.* He said, *Don't answer the phone.*

I had this crazy hope. I'd heard stories of men who slammed into trees, men so drunk their bodies went limp as their cars were crushed.

Some walked away. Some sailed off bridges but bobbed to the surface faceup. I remembered the man's grace when we collided, the strange elegance of his limbs as he flew.

I believed in my father, those hands holding blossoms in spring, those fingers touching the fender, my face—those hands wringing the rag, my blood, into the sink. I believed in small miracles, Niles flying into the pond hours ago, Yellow Dog wading out.

I imagined my crippled father helping the dazed man stumble to the truck, driving him to the hospital for x-rays or just taking him home. I thought my father had gone back alone so that he could lift the burden of my crime from me and carry it himself, to teach me suffering and sacrifice, the mercy of his God.

Even if the police came, they'd blame the Indian himself. He'd reel, still drunk, while my father, my good father, stood sober as a nun.

For almost an hour I told myself these lies. Confession would be a private thing, to my father, no one else. He would decide my penance. I would lie down on any floor. I would ask the Holy Mother to show me how I might atone. I would forgive the priest his ignorance when wine turned to blood in my mouth.

I thought of the cherries my father found after the hail, the bowl of them he brought back to the cottage—I thought of this small miracle, that any had been left whole. We ate them without speaking, as if they were the only food. I saw my father on his knees again, the highway. He gathered all the pieces. Glass and stone became the body of a man. My father's fingers pressed the neck and found the pulse. I knew I couldn't live through fifteen minutes if what I believed was not so.

Two hours gone. I saw the bowl slipping from my hands, my faith shattered, cherries rolling across the floor. I saw the man more clearly than I had on the road, the impossible angles of his body, how he must have broken when he fell.

I heard my father say, *Thou shalt not kill.*

But this was not my crime. The Indian himself told me he accepted accidents, my drunkenness as well as his own. Then he whispered, *But I don't understand why you left me here alone.*

I knew I should have gone with my father, to show him the way. I imagined him limping up and down that stretch of highway, waving his flashlight, calling out. On this road, wind had shape and leaves spoke. A bobcat's eyes flashed. A coyote crossed the road. I felt how tired my father must be, that old pain throbbing deep in the bone.

I tried not to count all the minutes till dawn. I tried to live in this minute alone. I wanted to speak to the man, to tell him he had to live like me, like this, one minute to the next. I knew the night was too long to imagine while his blood was spilling out. I promised, *He'll come.* I said, *Just stay with your body that long. There's a hospital down the road where they have bags of blood to hand above your bed, blood to flow through tubes and needles into your veins—enough blood to fill your body again and again.*

I went to the bathroom, turned on the heater. I needed this, the smallest room, the closed door. I crushed the beads of lilac soap till I was sick of the smell. I heard the last crickets and the first birds, and I thought, *No, not yet.* I heard the man say, *I'm still breathing but not for long.* He told me, *Once I sold three pints of blood in two days.* He said, *I could use some of that back now.*

Then there were edges of light at the window and the phone was ringing. Jean's mother, I thought. I saw my friend naked, passed out in the dirt or drowned in the pond. This too my fault.

The phone again. The police at last.

I must have closed my eyes, relieved, imagining questions and handcuffs, a fast car, a safe cell. Soon, so soon, I wouldn't be alone.

I must have dreamed.

The phone kept ringing.

This time I picked it up.

It was the Indian boy. He said, *I'll slit your throat.*

Past noon before my father got home. I understood exactly what he'd done as soon as I saw the truck: the fender was undented, the headlight magically whole. I knew he must have gone all the way to Missoula, to a garage where men with greasy fingers asked no questions, where a man's cash could buy a girl's freedom.

I couldn't believe this was his choice. Couldn't believe that this small thing, the mockery of metal and glass, my crime erased, was the only miracle he could trust.

He said, *Did you sleep?* I shook my head. He said, *Well, you should.*

I thought, How can he speak to me this way if he knows what I've done? Then I thought, We, not I—it's both of us now.

The phone once more. I picked it up before he could say *Stop*. The police, I hoped. They'll save me since my father won't. But it was Jean. *Thanks a lot*, she said. *I'm grounded for a month.*

Then she hung up.

Vincent Blew was long dead when he was found. The headline said, UNIDENTIFIED MAN VICTIM OF HIT AND RUN. One paragraph. Enough words to reveal how insignificant his life was. Enough words to lay the proper blame: "elevated blood alcohol level indicates native man was highly intoxicated."

I thought, Yes, we will each answer for our own deaths.

Then there were these words, meant to comfort the killer, I suppose: "Injuries suggest he died on impact."

I knew what people would think, reading this. Just one Indian killing another on a reservation road. Let the tribal police figure it out.

Still, the newspaper gave me a kind of hope. I found it folded on the kitchen table, beside my father's empty mug. I thought, He believed my lie about the deer until today. He is that good. He fixed the truck so the doctor wouldn't see. He was ashamed of my drunkenness, that's all.

I was calm.

When he comes home, we'll sit at this table. He'll ask nothing. Father of infinite patience. He'll wait for me to tell it all. When I stop speaking, we'll drive to town. He'll stay beside me. But he won't hang on.

I was so grateful I had to lean against the wall to keep from falling down.

I thought, He loves me this much, to listen, to go with me, to give me up.

All these years I'd been wrong about the hunter. Now I saw the father's grief, how he suffered with his wounds, how his passion surpassed the dead son's. I saw the boy's deception, that deer-colored coat. I understood it was the child's silent stupidity that made the father turn the gun on himself.

I meant to say this as well.

But my father stayed in the orchard all day. At four, I put on dark glasses and went to the doctor's house. I polished gold faucets and the copper bottoms of pots; I got down on my hands and knees to scrub each tile of the bathroom floor. The doctor's wife stood in the doorway watching me from behind.

She said, *That's nice, Ada.*

She said, *Don't forget the tub.*

When I came back to the cottage, I saw the paper stuffed in the trash, the mug washed. My father asked what I wanted for dinner, and I told him I was going to town. He said I could use the truck, and I said, *I know.*

I meant I knew there was nothing he'd refuse.

He saw me held tight in the dead Indian's arms. He was afraid of me, the truth I could tell.

Sometimes when I dream, the night I met Vincent Blew is just a movie I'm watching. Every body is huge. Yellow Dog's brilliant face fills the screen. He grins. He hangs on to that torch too long. I try to close my eyes, but the lids won't come down. His body bursts, shards of light; his body tears the sky apart. Then everything's on fire: pond, grass, hair—boy's breath, red shirt.

But later he's alive. He's an angel rising above me. He's Vincent Blew hovering over the road. The truck passes through him, no resistance, no jolt—no girl with black eyes, no body in the grass, no bloody nose. There's a whisper instead, a ragged voice full of static coming up from the ground. It's Vincent murmuring just to me: *You're drunk, little girl. Close your eyes. I'll steer. I'll get us home.*

And these nights, when he takes the wheel, when he saves us, these nights are the worst of all.

Three days before the man was known. His cousin claimed him. She said she danced with him the night he died. In Ronan, at the Wild Horse Bar. Then he was Vincent Blew, and she was Simone Falling Bear. It amazed me to think of it, the dead man dancing, the dead man in another woman's arms.

She said he died just a mile from her house. I knew then that her cousin Vincent was her lover too, that her house was a tarpaper shack at the end of a dirt road, that her refrigerator was a box of ice, her heater a woodstove. She'd have a bag of potatoes in a pail under the sink, a stack of cans with no labels on the shelf.

I saw that even in his stupor Vincent Blew knew the way home.

She said he'd been an altar boy, that he knew the words of the Latin mass by heart. She said he'd saved two men at Ia Drang and maybe more. She had his Medal of Honor as proof.

She said he wanted to open a school on the reservation where the children would learn to speak in their own tongue.

But that was before the war, before he started to drink so much.

He had these dreams. He had a Purple Heart. *Look at his chest. They had to staple his bones shut.*

I don't know what lies the reporter told to make Simone Falling Bear talk. Perhaps he said, *We want people to understand your loss.*

That reporter found Vincent's wife in Yakima, living with another man. He asked her about Vietnam, and she said she never saw any medals. She said Vincent's school was just some crazy talk, and that boy was drinking beer from his mama's bottle when he was three years old. When the reporter asked if Vincent Blew was ever a Catholic, she laughed. She said, *Everybody was.*

In a dream I climb a hill to find Vincent's mother. She lives in a cave, behind rocks. I have to move a stone to get her out. She points to three sticks stuck in the dirt. She says, *This is my daughter, these are my sons.*

September, and Vincent Blew was two months dead. I was supposed to go to school, ride the bus, drink milk. But I couldn't be with those children. Couldn't raise my hand or sit in the cafeteria and eat my lunch. I went to the lake instead, swam in the cold water till my chest hurt and my arms went numb. Fallen trees lay just below the surface; rocks lay deeper still. I knew what they were. I wasn't afraid. Only my own shadow moved.

I came home at the usual time to make dinner for my father. Fried chicken, green beans. I remember snapping each one. He didn't ask, *How was school?* I thought he knew, again, and didn't want to know, didn't want to risk the question, any question—my weeping, the truth sputtered out at last, those words so close: *Daddy, I can't.*

The next day I lay on the beach for hours. I burned. My clothes hurt my skin. I thought, He'll see this.

But again we ate our dinner in silence, only the clink of silverware, the strain of swallowing, his muttered *Thank you* when I cleared his plate. He sat on the porch while I washed the dishes, didn't come back inside till he heard the safe click, my bedroom door closed.

I saw how it was between us now. He hated each sound: the match striking, my breath sucked back, the weight of me on the floor. He knew exactly where I was—every moment—by the creak of loose boards. I learned how words stung, even the most harmless ones: *Rice tonight, or potatoes?* He had to look away to answer. *Rice, please.*

His childhood wounds, his sister's death—those sorrows couldn't touch his faith. My mother, with all her lies, couldn't break him. Only his daughter could do that. I was the occasion of sin. I was the road and the truck he was driving. He couldn't turn back.

The third day, he said, *They called from school.*

I nodded. *I'll go*, I said.

He nodded too, and that was the end of it.

But I didn't go. I hitched to Kalispell, went to six restaurants, finally found a job at a truck stop west of town.

That night I told my father I needed the truck to get to work, eleven to seven, graveyard.

I knew he wouldn't speak enough words to argue.

I married the first trucker who asked. I was eighteen. It didn't last. He had a wife in Ellensburg already, five kids. After that I rented a room in Kalispell, a safe place with high, tiny windows. Even the most careless girl couldn't fall.

Then it was March, the year I was twenty, and my father had his first heart attack. I quit my job and tried to go home. I thought he'd let me take care of him, that I could bear the silence between us.

Three weeks I slept in my father's house, my old room, the little bed.

One morning I slept too long. Light filled the window, flooded across the floor. It terrified me, how bright it was.

I felt my father gone.

In his room, I saw the bed neatly made, covers pulled tight, corners tucked.

I found him outside the doctor's house. He had his gun in one hand, the hose in the other. He'd flushed three rats from under the porch and shot them all.

He meant he could take care of himself.

He meant he wanted me to go.

I got a day job, south of Ronan this time, the Morning After Café. Seventeen years I've stayed. I live in a trailer not so many miles from the dirt road that leads to Simone Falling Bear's shack.

Sometimes I see her in the bars—Buffalo Bill's, Wild Horse, Lucy's Chance. She recognizes me, a regular, like herself. She tips her beer, masking her face in a flash of green glass.

When she stares, I think, She sees me for who I really am. But then I realize she's staring at the air, a place between us, and I think, Yes, if we both stare at the same place at the same time, we'll see him there. But she looks at the bottle again, her loose change on the bar, her own two hands.

Tonight I didn't see Simone. Tonight I danced. Once I was a pretty girl. Like Noelle, shining in her pale skin. It's not vain to say I was like that. I'm thirty-seven now, already old. Some women go to loose flesh, some to hard bone. I'm all edges from years living on whiskey and smoke.

But I can still fool men in these dim bars. I can fix myself up, curl my hair, paint my mouth. I have a beautiful blue dress, a bra with wires in the cups. I dance all night. I spin like Noelle; I shine, all sweat and blush and will.

Hours later, in my trailer, it doesn't matter, it's too late. The stranger I'm with doesn't care how I look: he only wants me to keep moving in the dark.

Drifters, liars—men who don't ask questions, men with tattoos and scars, men just busted out, men on parole; men with guns in their pockets, secrets of their own; men who can't love me, who don't pretend, who never want to stay too long: these men leave spaces, nights between that Vincent fills. He opens me. I'm the ground. Dirt and stone. He digs at me with both hands. He wants to lie down.

Or it's the other way around. It's winter. It's cold. I'm alone in the woods with my father's gun. I'll freeze. I'll starve. I look for rabbits, pray for deer. I try to cut a hole in the frozen earth, but it's too hard.

It's a bear I have to kill, a body I have to open if I want to stay warm. I have to live in him forever, hidden in his fur, down deep in the smell of bear stomach and bear heart. We lumber through the woods like this. I've lost my human voice. Nobody but the bear understands me now.

Last week my lover was a white man with black stripes tattooed across his back. His left arm was withered. *Useless,* he told me. *Shrapnel, Dak To.*

He was a small man, thin, but heavier than you'd expect.

He had a smooth stone in his pocket, three dollars in his hatband, the queen of spades in his boot. He said, *She brings me luck.*

He showed me the jagged purple scar above one kidney, told the story of a knife that couldn't kill.

The week before, my lover was bald and pale, his fingers thick. He spoke Latin in his sleep; he touched my mouth.

It's always like this. It's always Vincent coming to me through them.

The bald one said he loaded wounded men into helicopters, medevacs in Song Be and Dalat. Sometimes he rode with them. One time all of them were dead.

He was inside me when he told me that.

He robbed a convenience store in Seattle, a liquor store in Spokane. He did time in Walla Walla. I heard his switchblade spring and click. Felt it at my throat before I saw it flash.

He said, *They say I killed a man.*

He said, *But I saved more than that.*

He had two daughters, a wife somewhere. They didn't want him back.

The cool knife still pressed my neck. He said, *I'm innocent.*

I have nothing to lose. Nothing precious for a lover to steal—no ruby earrings, no silver candlesticks.

In my refrigerator he'll find Tabasco sauce and mayonnaise, six eggs, a dozen beers.

In my freezer, vodka, a bottle so cold it burns your hands.

In my cupboard, salted peanuts, crackers shaped like little fish, a jar of sugar, an empty tin.

In my closet, the blue dress that fooled him.

If my lover is lucky, maybe I'll still have yesterday's tips.

When he kisses me on the steps, I'll know that's my thirty-four dollars bulging in his pocket. I'll know I won't see him again.

He never takes the keys to my car. It's old, too easily trapped.

But tonight I have no lover. Tonight I danced in Paradise with a black-haired man. I clutched his coarse braid. All these years and I still wanted it. He pulled me close so I could feel the knife in his pocket. He said, *Remember, I have this.*

I don't know if he said the words out loud or if they were in my head.

When I closed my eyes I thought he could be that boy, the one who blew himself into the sky, whose body fell down in pieces thin and white as ash and bread, the one who rose up whole and dripping, who slipped his tongue in my mouth, his hands down my pants.

He could have been that boy grown to a man.

But when I opened my eyes I thought, No, that boy is dead.

Later we were laughing, licking salt, shooting tequila. We kissed, our mouths sour with lime. He said we could go out back. He said if I had a dollar he'd pay the man. I gave him five, and he said we could stay the week for that. I kissed him one more time, light and quick. I said I had to use the ladies' room.

Lady? he said, and he laughed.

I decided then. He was that boy, just like him. I said, *Sit tight, baby, I'll be right back.* He put his hand on my hip. *Don't make me wait,* he said.

I stepped outside, took my car, drove fast.

Don't get me wrong.

I'm not too good for Niles Yellow Dog or any man. I'm not too clean to spend the night at that hotel. It wouldn't be the first time I passed out on a back seat somewhere, hot and drunk under someone's shadow, wrapped tight in a man's brown skin.

But tonight I couldn't do it. Tonight I came here, to my father's house, instead. Tonight I watch him.

He's stopped moving now. He's in the chair. There's one light on, above his head. I can't help myself: I drink the whiskey I keep stashed. It stings my lips and throat, burns inside my chest. But even this can't last.

I don't believe in forgiveness for some crimes. I don't believe confessions to God can save the soul or raise the dead. Some bodies are never whole again.

I cannot open the veins of my father's heart.

I cannot heal his lungs or mend his bones.

Tonight I believe only this: we should have gone back. We should have crawled through the grass until we found that man.

If Vincent Blew had one more breath, I should have lain down beside him—so he wouldn't be cold, so he wouldn't be scared.

If Vincent Blew was dead, we should have dug the hard ground with our bare hands. I should have become the dirt if he asked. Then my father could have walked away, free of my burden, carrying only his own heart and the memory of our bones, a small bag of sticks light enough to lift with one hand.

IT'S COME TO THIS
Annick Smith

NO HORSES. THAT'S HOW IT ALWAYS STARTS. I am coming down
the meadow, the first snow of September whipping around my boots,
and there are no horses to greet me. The first thing I did after Caleb
died was get rid of the horses.

"I don't care how much," I told the auctioneer at the Missoula
Livestock Company. He looked at me slant-eyed from under his Stet-
son. "Just don't let the canneries take them." Then I walked away.

What I did not tell him was I couldn't stand the sight of those
horses on our meadow, so heedless, grown fat and untended. They
reminded me of days when Montana seemed open as the sky.

Now that the horses are gone I am more desolate than ever. If
you add one loss to another, what you have is double zip. I am wet to
the waist, water sloshing ankle-deep inside my irrigating boots. My
toes are numb, my chapped hands are burning from the cold, and
down by the gate my dogs are barking at a strange man in a red log
truck.

That's how I meet Frank. He is hauling logs down from the
Champion timberlands above my place, across the right-of-way I sold
to the company after my husband's death. The taxes were piling up. I
sold the right-of-way because I would not sell my land. Kids will
grow up and leave you, but land is something a woman can hold onto.

I don't like those log trucks rumbling by my house, scattering
chickens, tempting my dogs to chase behind their wheels, kicking
clouds of dust so thick the grass looks brown and dead. There's nothing I like about logging. It breaks my heart to walk among newly cut
limbs, to be enveloped in the sharp odor of sap running like blood.
After twenty years on this place, I still cringe at the snap and crash of
five-hundred-year-old pines and the far-off screaming of saws.

Anyway, Frank pulls his gyppo logging rig to a stop just past my house in order to open the blue metal gate that separates our outbuildings from the pasture, and while he is at it, he adjusts the chains holding his load. My three mutts take after him as if they are real watchdogs and he stands at the door of the battered red cab holding his hands to his face and pretending to be scared.

"I would surely appreciate it if you'd call off them dogs," says Frank, as if those puppies weren't wagging their tails and jumping up to be patted.

He can see I am shivering and soaked. And I am mad. If I had a gun, I might shoot him.

"You ought to be ashamed . . . a man like you."

"Frank Bowman," he says, grinning and holding out his large thick hand. "From Bowman's Corners." Bowman's Corners is just down the road.

"What happened to you?" he grins. "Take a shower in your boots?"

How can you stay mad at that man? A man who looks at you and makes you look at yourself. I should have known better. I should have waited for my boys to come home from football practice and help me lift the heavy wet boards in our diversion dam. But my old wooden flume was running full and I was determined to do what had to be done before dark, to be a true country woman like the pioneers I read about as a daydreaming child in Chicago, so long ago it seems another person's life.

"I had to shut off the water," I say. "Before it freezes." Frank nods, as if this explanation explains everything.

Months later I would tell him about Caleb. How he took care of the wooden flume, which was built almost one hundred years ago by his Swedish ancestors. The snaking plank trough crawls up and around a steep slope of igneous rock. It has been patched and rebuilt by generations of hard-handed, blue-eyed Petersons until it reached its present state of tenuous mortality. We open the floodgate in June when Bear Creek is high with snowmelt, and the flume runs full all summer, irrigating our hay meadow of timothy and wild mountain grasses.

Each fall, before the first hard freeze, we close the diversion gates and the creek flows in its natural bed down to the Big Blackfoot River.

That's why I'd been standing in the icy creek, hefting six-foot two-by-twelves into the slotted brace that forms the dam. The bottom board was waterlogged and coated with green slime. It slipped in my bare hands and I sat down with a splash, the plank in my lap and the creek surging around me.

"Goddamn it to fucking hell!" I yelled. I was astonished to find tears streaming down my face, for I have always prided myself on my ability to bear hardship. Here is a lesson I've learned. There is no glory in pure backbreaking labor.

Frank would agree. He is wide like his log truck and thick-skinned as a yellow pine, and believes neighbors should be friendly. At five o'clock sharp each workday, on his last run, he would stop at my blue gate and yell, "Call off your beasts," and I would stop whatever I was doing and go down for our friendly chat.

"How can you stand it?" I'd say, referring to the cutting of trees.

"It's a pinprick on the skin of the earth," replies Frank. "God doesn't know the difference."

"Well, I'm not God," I say. "Not on my place. Never."

So Frank would switch to safer topics such as new people moving in like knapweed, or where to find morels, or how the junior high basketball team was doing. One day in October, when redtails screamed and hoarfrost tipped the meadow grass, the world gone crystal and glowing, he asked could I use some firewood.

"A person can always use firewood," I snapped.

The next day, when I came home from teaching, there was a pickup load by the woodshed—larch and fir, cut to stove size and split.

"Taking care of the widow." Frank grinned when I tried to thank him. I laughed, but that is exactly what he was up to. In this part of the country, a man still takes pains.

WHEN I FIRST CAME TO MONTANA I was slim as a fashion model and my hair was black and curly. I had met my husband, Caleb, at the University of Chicago, where a city girl and a raw ranch boy could be equally enthralled by Gothic halls, the great libraries, and gray old Nobel laureates who gathered in the Faculty Club, where no student dared enter.

But after our first two sons were born, after the disillusionments of Vietnam and the cloistered grind of academic life, we decided to break away from Chicago and a life of mind preeminent, and we came to live on the quarter section of land Caleb had inherited from his Swedish grandmother. We would make a new start by raising pure-bred quarter horses.

For Caleb it was coming home. He had grown up in Sunset, forty miles northeast of Missoula, on his family's homestead ranch. For me it was romance. Caleb had carried the romance of the West for me in the way he walked on high-heeled cowboy boots, and the world he told stories about. It was a world I had imagined from books and movies, a paradise of the shining mountains, clean rivers, and running horses.

I loved the idea of horses. In grade school, I sketched black stallions, white mares, rainbow-spotted Appaloosas. My bedroom was hung with horses running, horses jumping, horses rolling in clover. At thirteen I hung around the stables in Lincoln Park and flirted with the stable boys, hoping to charm them into riding lessons my mother could not afford. Sometimes it worked, and I would bounce down the bridle path, free as a princess, never thinking of the payoff that would come at dusk. Pimply-faced boys. Groping and French kisses behind the dark barn that reeked of manure.

For Caleb horses meant honorable outdoor work and a way to make money, work being the prime factor. Horses were history to be reclaimed, identity. It was my turn to bring in the monthly check, so I began teaching at the Sunset school as a stopgap measure to keep our family solvent until the horse-business dream paid off. I am still filling that gap.

We rebuilt the log barn and the corrals, and cross-fenced our one hundred acres of cleared meadowland. I loved my upland meadow from the first day. As I walked through tall grasses heavy with seed, they moved to the wind, and the undulations were not like water.

Now, when I look down from our cliffs, I see the meadow as a hand-made thing—a rolling swatch of green hemmed with a stitchery of rocks and trees. The old Swedes who were Caleb's ancestors cleared that meadow with axes and crosscut saws, and I still trip over sawed-off stumps of virgin larch, sawed level to the ground, too large to pull out with a team of horses—decaying, but not yet dirt.

We knew land was a way to save your life. Leave the city and city ambitions, and get back to basics. Roots and dirt and horse pucky (Caleb's word for horseshit). Bob Dylan and the rest were all singing about the land, and every stoned, long-haired mother's child was heading for country.

My poor mother, with her Hungarian dreams and Hebrew upbringing, would turn in her grave to know I'm still teaching in a three-room school with no library or gymnasium, Caleb ten years dead, our youngest boy packed off to the state university, the ranch not even paying its taxes, and me, her only child, keeping company with a two-hundred-and-thirty-pound logger who lives in a trailer.

"Marry a doctor," she used to say, "or better, a concert pianist," and she was not joking. She invented middle-class stories for me from our walk-up flat on the South Side of Chicago: I would live in a white house in the suburbs like she had always wanted; my neighbors would be rich and cultured; the air itself, fragrant with lilacs in May and heady with burning oak leaves in October, could lift us out of the city's grime right into her American dream. My mother would smile with secret intentions. "You will send your children to Harvard."

FRANK'S BEEN MARRIED TWICE. "Twice-burned" is how he names it, and there are Bowman kids scattered up and down the Blackfoot Valley. Some of them are his. I met his first wife, Fay Dell, before I ever met Frank. That was eighteen years ago. It was Easter vacation, and I had taken two hundred dollars out of our meager savings to buy a horse for our brand-new herd. I remember the day clear as any picture. I remember mud and Blackfoot clay.

Fay Dell is standing in a pasture above Monture Creek. She wears faded brown Carhartt coveralls, as they do up here in the winters, and her irrigating boots are crusted with yellow mud. March runoff has every patch of bare ground spitting streams, trickles, and puddles of brackish water. Two dozen horses circle around her. Their ears are laid back and they eye me, ready for flight. She calls them by name, her voice low, sugary as the carrots she holds in her rough hands.

"Take your pick," she says.

I stroke the velvet muzzle of a two-year-old sorrel, a purebred quarter horse with a white blaze on her forehead.

"Sweet Baby," she says. "You got an eye for the good ones."

"How much?"

"Sorry. That baby is promised."

I walk over to a long-legged bay. There's a smile on Fay Dell's lips, but her eyes give another message.

"Marigold," she says, rubbing the mare's swollen belly. "She's in foal. Can't sell my brood mare."

So I try my luck on a pint-sized roan with a high-flying tail. A good kids' horse. A dandy.

"You can't have Lollipop neither. I'm breaking her for my own little gal."

I can see we're not getting anywhere when she heads me in the direction of a pair of wild-eyed geldings.

"Twins," says Fay Dell proudly. "Ruckus and Buckus."

You can tell by the name of a thing if it's any good. These two were out of the question, coming four and never halter broke.

"Come on back in May." We walk toward the ranch house and a hot cup of coffee. "I'll have 'em tamed good as any sheepdog. Two for the price of one. Can't say that ain't a bargain!"

Her two-story frame house sat high above the creek, some Iowa farmer's dream of the West. The ground, brown with stubble of last year's grass, was littered with old tennis shoes, broken windshields, rusting cars, shards of aluminum siding. Cast-iron tractor parts emerged like mushrooms from soot-crusted heaps of melting snow. I wondered why Fay Dell had posted that ad on the Sunset school bulletin board: "Good horses for sale. Real cheap." Why did she bother with such make-believe?

Eighteen years later I am sleeping with her ex-husband, and the question is answered.

"All my wages gone for hay," says Frank. "The kids in hand-me-downs . . . the house a goddamn mess. I'll tell you I had a bellyful!"

Frank had issued an ultimatum on Easter Sunday, determined never to be ashamed again of his bedraggled wife and children among the slicked-up families in the Blackfoot Community Church.

"Get rid of them two-year-olds," he warned, "or . . ."

No wonder it took Fay Dell so long to tell me no. What she was doing that runoff afternoon, seesawing back and forth, was making a choice between her horses and her husband. If Fay Dell had confessed to me that day, I would not have believed such choices are possible. Horses, no matter how well you loved them, seemed mere animal possessions to be bought and sold. I was so young then, a city girl with no roots at all, and I had grown up Jewish, where family seemed the only choice.

"Horse poor," Frank says. "That woman wouldn't get rid of her horses. Not for God, Himself."

March in Montana is a desperate season. You have to know what you want, and hang on.

FRANK'S SECOND WIFE WAS TALL, BLOND, AND YOUNG. He won't talk about her much, just shakes his head when her name comes up and says, "Guess she couldn't stand the winters." I heard she ran away to San Luis Obispo with a long-haired carpenter named Ralph.

"Cleaned me out," Frank says, referring to his brand-new stereo and the golden retriever. She left the double-wide empty, and the only evidence she had been there at all was the white picket fence Frank built to make her feel safe. And a heap of green tomatoes in the weed thicket he calls a garden.

"I told her," he says with a wistful look, "I told that woman you can't grow red tomatoes in this climate."

As for me, I love winter. Maybe that's why Frank and I can stand each other. Maybe that's how come we've been keeping company for five years and marriage is a subject that has never crossed our lips except once. He's got his place near the highway, and I've got mine at the end of the dirt road, where the sign reads, COUNTY MAINTENANCE ENDS HERE. To all eyes but our own, we have always been a queer, mismatched pair.

After we began neighboring, I would ask Frank in for a cup of coffee. Before long, it was a beer or two. Soon, my boys were taking the old McCulloch chain saw to Frank's to be sharpened, or he was teaching them how to tune up Caleb's ancient Case tractor. We kept our distance until one thirty-below evening in January when my Blazer wouldn't start, even though its oil-pan heater was plugged in. Frank came up to jump it.

The index finger on my right hand was frostbit from trying to turn the metal ignition key bare-handed. Frostbite is like getting burned, extreme cold acting like fire, and my finger was swollen along the third joint, just below its tip, growing the biggest blister I had ever seen.

"Dumb," Frank says, holding my hand between his large mitts and blowing on the blister. "Don't you have gloves?"

"Couldn't feel the key to turn it with gloves on."

He lifts my egg-sized finger to his face and bows down, like a chevalier, to kiss it. I learn the meaning of dumbfounded. I feel the warmth of his lips tracing from my hand down through my privates. I like it. A widow begins to forget how good a man's warmth can be.

"I would like to take you dancing," says Frank.

"It's too damn cold."

"Tomorrow," he says, "the Big Sky Boys are playing at the Awful Burger Bar."

I suck at my finger.

"You're a fine dancer."

"How in God's name would you know?"

"Easy," Frank smiles. "I been watching your moves."

I admit I was scared. I felt like the little girl I had been, so long ago. A thumb-sucker. If I said yes, I knew there would be no saying no.

THE AWFUL BURGER BAR IS LIKE THE RED CROSS, you can go there for first aid. It is as great an institution as the Sunset school. The white bungalow sits alone just off the two-lane on a jack-pine flat facing south across irrigated hay meadows to where what's left of the town of Sunset clusters around the school. Friday evenings after Caleb passed away, when I felt too weary to cook and too jumpy to stand the silence of another Blackfoot night, I'd haul the boys up those five miles of asphalt and we'd eat Molly Fry's awful burgers, stacked high with Bermuda onions, lettuce and tomato, hot jo-jos on the side, Miller for me, root beer for them. That's how those kids came to be experts at shooting pool.

The ranching and logging families in this valley had no difficulty understanding why their schoolteacher hung out in a bar and passed the time with hired hands and old-timers. We were all alike in this one thing. Each was drawn from starvation farms in the rock and clay foothills or grassland ranches on the floodplain, down some winding dirt road to the red neon and yellow lights glowing at the dark edge of chance. You could call it home, as they do in the country-and-western songs on the jukebox.

I came to know those songs like a second language. Most, it seemed, written just for me. I longed to sing them out loud, but God or genes or whatever determines what you can be never gave me a singing voice. In my second life I will be a white Billie Holiday with a gardenia stuck behind my ear, belting out songs to make you dance and cry at the same time.

My husband, Caleb, could sing like the choirboy he had been before he went off to Chicago on a scholarship and lost his religion. He taught himself to play harmonica and wrote songs about lost lives. There's one I can't forget:

Scattered pieces, scattered pieces,
Come apart for all the world to see.

Scattered pieces, lonely pieces,
That's how yours truly came to be.

When he sang that song, my eyes filled with tears.
"How can you feel that way, and never tell me except in a song?"

"There's lots I don't tell you," he said.

We didn't go to bars much, Caleb and me. First of all we were poor. Then too busy building our log house, taking care of the boys, tending horses. And finally, when the angina pains struck, and the shortness of breath, and we knew that at the age of thirty-seven Caleb had come down with an inherited disease that would choke his arteries and starve his heart, it was too sad, you know, having to sit out the jitterbugs and dance only to slow music. But even then, in those worst of bad times, when the Big Sky Boys came through, we'd hire a sitter and put on our good boots and head for the Awful Burger.

There was one Fourth of July. All the regulars were there, and families from the valley. Frank says he was there, but I didn't know him. Kids were running in and out like they do in Montana, where a country bar is your local community center. Firecrackers exploded in the gravel parking lot. Show-off college students from town were dancing cowboy boogie as if they knew what they were doing, and sunburned tourists exuding auras of camp fires and native cutthroat trout kept coming in from motor homes. This was a far way from Connecticut.

We were sitting up close to the band. Caleb was showing our boys how he could juggle peanuts in time to the music. The boys tried to copy him, and peanuts fell like confetti to be crunched under the boots of sweating dancers. The sun streamed in through open doors and windows, even though it was nine at night, and we were flushed from too many beers, too much sun and music.

"Stand up, Caleb. Stand up so's the rest of us can see."

That was our neighbor Melvin Godfrey calling from the next table. Then his wife, Stella, takes up the chant.

"Come on, Caleb. Give us the old one-two-three."

The next thing, Molly Fry is passing lemons from the kitchen where she cooks the awful burgers, and Caleb is standing in front of the Big Sky Boys, the dancers all stopped and watching. Caleb is juggling those lemons to the tune of "Mommas, Don't Let Your Babies Grow Up to Be Cowboys," and he does not miss a beat.

It is a picture in my mind—framed in gold leaf—Caleb on that bandstand, legs straddled, deep-set eyes looking out at no one or nothing, the tip of his tongue between clenched teeth in some kind of frozen smile, his faded blue shirt stained in half-moons under the arms, and three bright yellow lemons rising and falling in perfect synchronicity. I see the picture in stop-action, like the end of a movie. Two shiny lemons in midair, the third in his palm. Caleb juggling.

IT'S BEEN A LONG TIME COMING, THE CRYING. You think there's no pity left, but the sadness is waiting, like a barrel gathering rain, until one sunny day, out of the blue, it just boils over and you've got a flood on your hands. That's what happened one Saturday last January, when Frank took me to celebrate the fifth anniversary of our first night together. The Big Sky Boys were back, and we were at the Awful Burger Bar.

"Look," I say, first thing. "The lead guitar has lost his hair. Those boys are boys no longer."

Frank laughs and points to the bass man. Damned if he isn't wearing a corset to hold his beer belly inside those slick red-satin cowboy shirts the boys have worn all these years.

And Indian Willie is gone. He played steel guitar so blue it broke your heart. Gone back to Oklahoma.

"Heard Willie found Jesus in Tulsa," says Melvin Godfrey, who has joined us at the bar.

"They've replaced him with a child," I say, referring to the pimply, long-legged kid who must be someone's son. "He hits all the right keys, but he'll never break your heart."

We're sitting on high stools, and I'm all dressed up in the long burgundy skirt Frank gave me for Christmas. My frizzy gray hair is swept back in a chignon, and Mother's amethyst earrings catch the light from the revolving Budweiser clock. It is a new me, matronly and going to fat, a stranger I turn away from in the mirror above the bar.

When the band played "Waltz Across Texas" early in the night, Frank led me to the dance floor and we waltzed through to the end, swaying and dipping, laughing in each other's ears. But now he is downing his third Beam ditch and pays no attention to my tapping feet.

I watch the young people boogie. A plain fat girl with long red hair is dressed in worn denim overalls, but she moves like a queen among frogs. In the dim, multicolored light, she is delicate, delicious.

"Who is that girl?" I ask Frank.

"What girl?"

"The redhead."

"How should I know?" he says. "Besides, she's fat."

"Want to dance?"

Frank looks at me as if I were crazy. "You know I can't dance to this fast stuff. I'm too old to jump around and make a fool of myself. You want to dance, you got to find yourself another cowboy."

The attractive men have girls of their own or are looking to nab some hot young dish. Melvin is dancing with Stella, "showing off" as Frank would say, but to me they are a fine-tuned duo who know each move before they take it, like a team of matched circus ponies, or those fancy ice skaters in the Olympics. They dance only with each other, and they dance all night long.

I'm getting bored, tired of whiskey and talk about cows and spotted owls and who's gone broke this week. I can hear all that on the five o'clock news. I'm beginning to feel like a wallflower at a high school sock hop (feelings I don't relish reliving). I'm making plans about going home when a tall, narrow-hipped old geezer in a flowered rayon cowboy shirt taps me on the shoulder.

"May I have this dance, ma'am?"

I look over to Frank, who is deep in conversation with Ed Snow, a logger from Seeley Lake.

"If your husband objects . . ."

"He's not my husband."

The old man is clearly drunk, but he has the courtly manner of an old-time cowboy, and he is a live and willing body.

"Sure," I say. As we head for the dance floor, I see Frank turn his head. He is watching me with a bemused and superior smile. "I'll show that bastard," I say to myself.

The loudspeaker crackles as the lead guitarist announces a medley—"A tribute to our old buddy, Ernest Tubb." The Big Sky Boys launch into "I'm Walking the Floor Over You," and the old man grabs me around the waist.

Our hands meet for the first time. I could die on the spot. If I hadn't been so mad, I would have run back to Frank because that old man's left hand was not a hand, but a claw—all shriveled up from a stoke or some birth defect, the bones dry and brittle, frozen half-shut, the skin white, flaky, and surprisingly soft, like a baby's.

His good right arm is around my waist, guiding me light but firm, and I respond as if it doesn't matter who's in the saddle. But my mind is on that hand. It twirls me and pulls me. We glide. We swing. He draws me close, and I come willingly. His whiskey breath tickles at my ear in a gasping wheeze. We spin one last time, and dip. I wonder if he will die on the spot, like Caleb. Die in midmotion, alive one minute, dead the next.

I see Caleb in the kitchen that sunstruck evening in May, come in from irrigating the east meadow and washing his hands at the kitchen sink. Stew simmers on the stove, the littlest boys play with English toy soldiers, Mozart on the stereo, a soft breeze blowing through open windows, Caleb turns to me. I will always see him turning. A shadow crosses his face. "Oh dear," he says. And Caleb falls to the maple floor, in one motion a tree cut down. He does not put out his hands to break his fall. Gone. Blood dribbles from his broken nose.

THERE IS NO GOING BACK NOW. We dance two numbers, the old cowboy and me, each step smoother and more carefree. We are breathing hard, beginning to sweat. The claw-hand holds me in fear and love. This high-stepping old boy is surely alive. He asks my name.

"Mady."

"Bob," he says. "Bob Beamer. They call me Old Beam." He laughs like this is a good joke. "Never knowed a Mady before. That's a new one on me."

"Hungarian," I say, wishing the subject had not come up, not mentioning the Jewish part for fear of complications. And I talk to Mother, as I do when feelings get too deep.

"Are you watching me now?" I say to the ghost of her. "It's come to this, Momushka. Are you watching me now?"

It's odd how you can talk to the ghost of someone more casually and honestly than you ever communicated when they were alive. When I talk to Caleb's ghost it is usually about work or the boys or a glimpse of beauty in nature or books. I'll spot a bluebird hovering, or young elk playing tag where our meadow joins the woods, or horses running (I always talk to Caleb about any experience I have with horses), and the words leap from my mouth, simple as pie. But when I think of my deep ecology, as the environmentalists describe it, I speak only to Mother.

I never converse with my father. He is a faded memory of heavy eyebrows, Chesterfield straights, whiskery kisses. He was a sculptor and died when I was six. Mother was five feet one, compact and full of energy as a firecracker. Every morning, in our Chicago apartment lined with books, she wove my tangled bush of black hair into French braids that pulled so tight my eyes seemed slanted. Every morning she tried to yank me into shape, and every morning I screamed so loud Mother was embarrassed to look our downstairs neighbors in the eyes.

"Be quiet," she commanded. "They will think I am a Nazi."

And there was Grandma, who lived with us and wouldn't learn English because it was a barbaric language. She would polish our upright Steinway until the piano shone like ebony. I remember endless piano lessons, Bach and Liszt. "A woman of culture," Mother said, sure of this one thing. "You will have everything."

"You sure dance American," the old cowboy says, and we are waltzing to the last dance, a song even older than my memories.

"I was in that war," he says. "Old Tubb must of been on the same troopship. We was steaming into New York and it was raining in front of us and full moon behind and I saw a rainbow at midnight like the song says, 'Out on the ocean blue!'"

Frank has moved to the edge of the floor. I see him out the corner of my eye. We should be dancing this last one, I think, me and Frank and Old Beam. I close my eyes and all of us are dancing, like in the end of a Fellini movie—Stella and Marvin, the slick young men and blue-eyed girls, the fat redhead in her overalls, Mother, Caleb. Like Indians in a circle. Like Swede farmers, Hungarian gypsies.

Tears gather behind my closed lids. I open my eyes and rain is falling. The song goes on, sentimental and pointless. But the tears don't stop.

"It's not your fault," I say, trying to smile, choking and sputtering, laughing at the confounded way both these men are looking at me. "Thank you for a very nice dance."

I CRIED FOR MONTHS, OFF AND ON. The school board made me take sick leave and see a psychiatrist in Missoula. He gave me drugs. The pills put me to sleep and I could not think straight, just walked around like a zombie. I told the shrink I'd rather cry. "It's good for you," I said. "Cleans out the system."

I would think the spell was done and over, and then I'd see the first red-winged blackbird in February or snow melting off the meadow, or a silly tulip coming up before its time, and the water level in my head would rise, and I'd be at it again.

"Runoff fever" is what Frank calls it. The junk of your life is laid bare, locked in ice and muck, just where you left it before the first blizzard buried the whole damn mess under three feet of pure white. I can't tell you why the crying ended, but I can tell you precisely when. Perhaps one grief replaces another and the second grief is something you can fix. Or maybe it's just a change of internal weather.

Frank and I are walking along Bear Creek on a fine breezy day in April, grass coming green and thousands of the yellow glacier lilies we call dogtooth violets lighting the woods. I am picking a bouquet and bend to smell the flowers. Their scent is elusive, not sweet as roses or rank as marigolds, but a fine freshness you might want to drink. I breathe in the pleasure and suddenly I am weeping. A flash flood of tears.

Frank looks at me bewildered. He reaches for my hand. I pull away blindly, walking as fast as I can. He grabs my elbow.

"What the hell?" he says. I don't look at him.

"Would you like to get married?" He is almost shouting. "Is that what you want? Would that cure this goddamn crying?"

What can I say? I am amazed. Unaccountably frightened. "No," I blurt, shaking free of his grasp and preparing to run. "It's not you." I am sobbing now, gasping for breath.

Then he has hold of both my arms and is shaking me—a good-sized woman—as if I were a child. And that is how I feel, like a naughty girl. The yellow lilies fly from my hands.

"Stop it!" he yells. "Stop that damn bawling!"

Frank's eyes are wild. This is no proposal. I see my fear in his eyes and I am ashamed. Shame always makes me angry. I try to slap his face. He catches my hand and pulls me to his belly. It is warm. Big enough for the both of us. The anger has stopped my tears. The warmth has stopped my anger. When I raise my head to kiss Frank's mouth, I see his eyes brimming with salt.

I don't know why, but I am beginning to laugh through my tears. Laughing at last at myself.

"Will you marry me?" I stutter. "Will that cure you?"

Frank lets go of my arms. He is breathing hard and his face is flushed a deep red. He sits down on a log and wipes his eyes with the back of his sleeve. I rub at my arms.

"They're going to be black and blue."

"Sorry," he says.

I go over to Frank's log and sit at his feet, my head against his knees. He strokes my undone hair. "What about you?" he replies, question for question. "Do you want to do it?"

We are back to a form of discourse we both understand.

"I'm not sure."

"Me neither."

MAY HAS COME TO MONTANA with a high-intensity green so rich you can't believe it is natural. I've burned the trash pile and I am done with crying. I'm back with my fifth-graders and struggling through aerobics classes three nights a week. I stand in the locker room naked and exhausted, my hips splayed wide and belly sagging as if to proclaim, Yes, I've borne four children.

A pubescent girl, thin as a knife, studies me as if I were a creature from another planet, but I don't care because one of these winters Frank and I are going to Hawaii. When I step out on those white beaches I want to look good in my bathing suit.

Fay Dell still lives up on Monture Creek. I see her out in her horse pasture winter and summer as I drive over the pass to Great Falls for a teachers' meeting or ride the school bus to basketball games in the one-room school in Ovando. Her ranch house is gone to hell, unpainted, weathered gray, patched with tarpaper. Her second husband left her, and the daughter she broke horses for is a beauty operator in Spokane. Still, there are over a dozen horses in the meadow and Fay Dell gone thin and unkempt in coveralls, tossing hay in February or fixing fence in May or just standing in the herd.

I imagine her low, sugary voice as if I were standing right by her. She is calling those horses by name. Names a child might invent.

"Sweet Baby."

"Marigold."

"Lollipop."

I want my meadow to be running with horses, as it was in the beginning—horses rolling in new grass, tails swatting at summer flies, huddled into a blizzard. I don't have to ride them. I just want their pea-brained beauty around me. I'm in the market for a quarter horse stallion and a couple of mares. I'll need to repair my fences and build a new corral with poles cut from the woods.

My stallion will be named Rainbow at Midnight. Frank laughs and says I should name him Beam, after my cowboy. For a minute I don't know what he's talking about, and then I remember the old man in the Awful Burger Bar. I think of Fay Dell and say, "Maybe I'll name him Frank."

Frank thinks Fay Dell is crazy as a loon. But Fay Dell knows our lives are delicate. Grief will come. Fay Dell knows you don't have to give in. Life is motion. Choose love. A person can fall in love with horses.

The Mourning of Ignacio Rosa
Kim Zupan

Delbert Handcamp swung a dull ax at the catch pond ice, chopping to open water for the hundred head of Angus heifer cows milling around him in a black circle. The anxious cattle steamed the air with their breath and Handcamp sweated in it. He hacked a rough outline, and then breaking it through, nearly put the ax blade into the bloodless face of his hired man Ignacio Rosa, looming from under five hard inches of January ice.

Half an hour later, as he drove the county road to town, Handcamp's heifers gaped after him from the fence line. In the back of the pickup, the stiff body of Ignacio Rosa skidded and bumped between the fender-wells. Ignacio Rosa: handler of horses, feeder of stock, midwife to cattle. Through the water hole he'd looked asleep and dreaming, but on the snowy catch pond bank he'd gone white and hard as oak. Now, in Handcamp's truck, he was just a brittle dead load for town.

The ragged line of men filed out of the Rodeo Club Bar and stood around in a half-hearted snowfall watching Christian Finney bag the hard body of Ignacio Rosa and transfer it to the trunk of the county sheriff cruiser. They stood in the snow in shirtsleeves, the whole red-faced line numb from the inside out, just drunk enough not to feel the wind. Deputy Yvonne Nevala stood on the sidewalk talking to the one hard woman who'd ambled from the bar-dark with all the rest to watch the show. Finney hugged the bag to his chest and held his breath. Across the river the town dump smoldered up black plumes, and the smell of trash and tire rubber came on the wind up the street. But for Finney it was the smell of the dead and he held his breath against it.

IN THE WARMTH OF HIS OFFICE, Christian Finney watched the snow disappear from Delbert Handcamp's shoulders. From his chair he could see out a fractured window Yvonne Nevala angling across the street. She came in with a swirl of snow, her red hair undone and unruly down her back. She stood to the side of Finney and leaned against a file cabinet. Handcamp hadn't looked up when she came in and did not look at her then, but had stopped talking.

"So anyway," Finney said, "you were saying."

Handcamp shifted in his chair. "All I know," he said, "is he had a boyfriend from Great Falls who came out once a week, twice sometimes, seemed like. They'd meet down at the old Sullivan place and get tight."

Though he did not look at her—he stared straight ahead across the desk and through Finney—the movement of Yvonne Nevala tying her mane of hair made Handcamp stop again. Finney held in his stomach self-consciously under the far-looking gaze and waited. He did not look to Nevala but watched Handcamp work his jaw back and forth, grinding his teeth. The snow on his shoulders went up in steam so he seemed to smolder under his jacket.

"Go on ahead," Finney said. "The Sullivan place."

"Afterwards when he come back," Handcamp went on, "he'd go to the barn and talk to the work team. My two mares. Coming up across the yard I'd hear him in there. I go in and he's got his ear laid down on their back, talking to them."

"What's that about?"

"Liked to listen to their heart work," Handcamp said. "Anyways, that's what he told me."

"Well," Finney said, smiling, "he was a horse-lover. I heard that of him."

"That's right."

"And the guy from town, now. You ever meet him or see the man?"

"Christ, no. Rosa sure as hell wasn't going to bring him around the ranch. I told him that. 'Don't bring him around or I'll kick his ass' is what I told him. None of that."

Yvonne Nevala turned to the window. Beyond the glass, snow covered over the bare oblong in Handcamp's pickup box where the icy body of Ignacio Rosa had lain like cordwood. She'd watched Finney lug the corpse to the car trunk, but now pictured Rosa in a different embrace, roughly loved against the boards of a decaying sheep shed. She stood beside Finney, in front of the window, her red hair reddening from the window light and a vision of Rosa's last moments working in her head.

"So they'd meet up there at the old Sullivan place, get high, and then make love, is that what you're saying?" she asked.

Handcamp turned his eyes finally to her. "I don't know what they did, goddamn it. He said he was in love. Little fag Mexican bastard, in love with a queer from town and my two work mares." His gaze moved to the stove then, in front of him, and he stared back at the red eyes of the vent holes. Yvonne Nevala shifted slowly behind the protection of the bank of cabinets, away from the cold creeping around the window edge. The stove was doing nothing for her.

Behind his desk, Christian Finney held in the excesses of his belly and studied Handcamp. The broad chest and shoulders bulging like burls in a cottonwood, black hair curling from under a worn Scotch cap, and a beard thick and dark as mink fur. He's really a beautiful sonofabitch, Finney thought. A goddamn specimen. He suits that country out there, mean right back at it. Doesn't get him down like some of these folks, either, only makes him better at fitting it. He's a goddamn piece of work all right.

Handcamp glowered at the fire holes and the red-haired deputy slid a file drawer in and out to break up the quiet.

"Well, Del," Finney said finally, "you might as well go home and feed. I'll be out and poke around, let you know anything at all we might get on this, soon's we get anything at all."

He extended his hand to Handcamp, wanting to shake hands more to feel the kind of grip than out of courtesy. But Handcamp went to the door without looking at Finney or Nevala, without a word or nod. He opened it and turned, silhouetted there in the white rectangle of the door frame with the snow-covered street beyond. He waited, and the cold flooded around him into the room. Finney still stood behind his desk, embarrassed by his own white hand that Handcamp had refused. It felt alien to him and he stuck it in his pant pocket. He could see his breath now in the office.

"The county will burn him," he said, "so don't worry about any of that."

Delbert Handcamp turned up his jacket collar and adjusted his cap to the side. "I'll tell you this," he said. "You're right, he was good with animals. That's what he knew."

Finney said, "I heard that," to the closing of the door, and he and Yvonne Nevala watched out the window as Handcamp went to his truck and drove away, across the clattering plank bridge and out of town, the same trip alone he'd made an hour earlier with his hired man as dunnage, folded in a grain tarp.

Yvonne stood close to the window, pulling at her hair, undone again, and breathed the pane to a blur.

"Some elegy," she said.

"Coming from him it is," said Finney. "That's what he knows."

"Well, I don't care. He reminds me of a goddamn caveman. He's one of these kind that belong on the ranch and nowhere else. Get him away and he doesn't know how to act. And did you notice," she said, turning from the fogged glass, "I wasn't even here."

"No, I didn't." Finney, his chair swiveled back to his desk and his hands over his eyes, wasn't really there either, but moving around in the darkness behind his fingers, his mind lurching among hard notions and gut feelings. He held out all distraction: the room, Nevala, the vacant street outside the window, everything but the deathsmell of slow-burning rubbish that had come in on the draft.

Finney's deputy crossed the small office and stood in front of him. "Well," she said, "so." She rolled her knuckles along the desktop and stared hard at the backs of Finney's pale hands. "Why'nt I take a ride out and talk to those Meekses or what's their name, that Bohunk family up there above Sullivan place?"

The office was cold now, and the stove gasped out the vent holes from the wind sucking at the chimney pipe.

"No," said Finney, taking his hands down, "no, you take the body on in to Great Falls and we'll wait on the coroner's report. I'll call you in so they expect you."

"But I could get up to Sullivan, see folks, and be back in three hours. Then at least we might know something."

"And I said take Rosa to town and we'll wait and that's what I goddamn well meant," Finney said. "He's rode around this country enough that way, like a dead calf you haul to the dump."

He swung around to the window. Even through the muffling snow, the rattle of planks from a car on the bridge came up the empty street and through the ineffective pane to Finney. He looked there, toward the comfort of the river, where beyond, smoke still billowed from the burning trash. Most of the midmorning drunks had ambled back to their own comfort of the Rodeo Club, but a die-hard red-faced pack now stood around the trunk of the cruiser, passing among them a bottle in a bag and huddling close, as if there was a fire there and they were warming from the memory of frozen Rosa.

And these few scattered back to the bar with hurried nonchalance as Yvonne Nevala slammed the office door and strode to the car. She glared at the retreating men who shuffled slow-motion through the snow, lugging their shabby defiance and their own recollections of Rosa, fuel enough to drive them dully through another long afternoon of booze.

Christian Finney took it all in from his window, watched as the cadaverous drunks moved off and his deputy jerked the car angrily into gear and set off on the last lap of Rosa's passage. Finney took consolation from having wedged the awkward package of Rosa in the car trunk so the body would not slide or bounce, that the lover of horses and men should ride with dignity; maybe not a man any longer but the shape of a man yet, before they ruined him for the sake of investigation.

Finney looked beyond to the river for solace. Beyond it, the smoke had flattened out on the faint wind and lain down on the water like a black reflection.

THEIRS HAD BEEN A LIFE IN THE COMPANY of animals, Delbert Handcamp and the little Mexican Ignacio Rosa who had one day walked down from the county road lugging packsack and wide-pommeled saddle, looking for board and room and winter haven. And Rosa stayed on, five years from that January day, tending with Handcamp the three hundred head of black bald-faced cattle and hundred black heifers through every season of growing. Everywhere in the far sphere of vision above the ranch house, antelope roamed the high plateau ground, rolling like mercury in the distance across plowed fields and among Handcamp's secure Angus. Deer bedded in every thorny pile of buckbrush in every side coulee that drained runoff from the tableland to the canyon below the house. And in the farthest part of the canyon, two miles along the creek from the ranchyard, where a boundary fence cut off retreat or escape or avoidance, Handcamp's horses loitered. At the sight of the two men they circled and sulked, ran the fence line hunting for exit before at last being cornered, pawing, blowing, and still pretending at being wild. But when Ignacio Rosa emerged from the shape of the pickup, the two Percheron work mares would move away from the herd, and without even the promise of the oat pan would go to Rosa and nuzzle him between them like a lover in a triangle.

Not calendar winter but actual winter came to Handcamp's treeless country on the short dark days of early November, and the whole circle of beasts came closer around the two men and scant lee of the canyon. The antelope haunted put-up feed and the deer kept to the creek bottom below the house where the snow would not drift. Saddle horses were moved up, penned in, and fed. From November on till April, every movement in the ranchyard and among the outbuildings was followed by eyes, from the hilltop, from the bottomland and horse pasture. Even the slamming of a truck door became significant: deer jerked up their heads in alarm and hungry cattle bellowed in despair.

The barn strained against ground-anchored cables, toppling by inches after eighty years of wind. Here Ignacio Rosa pampered the Percheron team. He prepared them for work almost with regret, rigging them up with the deliberate care of an undertaker about his business, smoothing each leather line as if he were knotting a tie under the chin of a corpse. Rosa stood atop an orange crate to reach his work, teetering over the backs of the blue and dapple mares. He lay across them, ran his arms down each huge neck to check the collar fit, moved his hands along the belly bands, throat latches, and hold backs, talking a half singing, murmuring talk as he slipped among thick legs and brushed under the heavy bellies of the mares.

At the end of the day's cold work, inside the barn, Rosa fed his team only the brightest, cleanest feed. He ran his hands over the sweat-white muscles of the mares, loving the lines of flanks and necks and withers unfettered by gear, checking for burrs in the tails that reached nearly to the floor, tottering on his box to check the manes, combing his girl-like fingers even through the showy feathers of each fetlock above the toe-resting hooves. And last, in the muggy dark of the Percherons' stalls, the Mexican rubbed, curried, and combed, listening between ribs to the soothing rumble of massive hearts.

DELBERT HANDCAMP LEFT THE SHERIFF'S OFFICE, the town and its river, and, climbing, left off the paved road, slewing the pickup between frozen ruts winding toward home. He fretted cattle now, worried over the moon coming full in the northeast behind a malignant tower of clouds—an awful eye of light, leering from behind the black gouts of cumulus, that would tug at the fluid in the bellies of his cows and coax calves out into a January storm.

Three days Ignacio Rosa had been gone before he rose up in the ice hole, and Handcamp would face a third night alone. For five winters he'd awoken each night to the ignition grind of the old Chevy flatbed, and listened as the Mexican eased the doddering rig out of the yard to make the two A.M. check on cattle. And he had gone to sleep again to the comfortable, fading grinding of gears as Rosa went away up the road to the heifer pasture. Here Rosa would climb the fence and prowl the calving ground, flashing his light, recognizing animals like people on the street, talking with familiarity to drowsy cattle working cuds, rubbing the backs of tamer cows and calling them his Spanish pet names, and examining hundreds of flanks for the kinked nervous twitch of tail, for the gleaming bulb of water bag or the near-transparent hoof pointing from the womb.

And each cold morning for five winters, Handcamp heard the jangle of the rigging as the mares shook in their gear, and from his kitchen would see the tiny man holding the two eighteen-hundred-pound pawing Percherons in check. Now, driving the empty country from town toward the storm, Delbert Handcamp pictured Ignacio Rosa smiling down from his seat on the hay sled, offering his hand for a lift up, waiting to go about the long morning of feeding stock together as the sun came up white, just clearing the coulee edge.

This afternoon the winter sun was far away and white but going down, and the huge moon rose up. Handcamp fretted over unfed cattle and fresh calves, the tide of clouds, and Rosa's blue mares caged in the barn.

BEHIND FINGERS PRESSED INTO HIS EYES to blot out the small distraction of light, Christian Finney juggled the new complications of his life, trying to urge his mind into another higher working gear after years of small-town routine. Handcamp had come with dead Rosa less than twenty-four hours ago. Now, in his hot office, Finney considered the cycle that was his balm: the steady passing of nature's one phase to another in the expected, comfortable way of things. For the last quiet week he'd parked beside the river, and through his field glasses counted and identified each south-moving species of duck that swirled out of the Montana January sky and set down in the slow current. His radio never crackled and the days slipped on. The river passed steady in its channel, the sun rolled down its winter slope, and as he tallied and scrawled in his battered notebook, mallards and gadwalls, teal, bufflehead, and widgeon set down in numbers much the same as the year before and many pages of other years, marking for Finney a notch in the soothing easing of one season into another. This year, the birds' late coming and the slow pile-up of snow gave Finney comfort: to witness fall grow peacefully old and slough by inches into long winter.

In his small town, Christian Finney's work was a regular cadence of neighborly investigations into matters of poached deer and stolen hay, drunken wife-beatings and gutter duels, drunks dead in cars in borrow ditches. At his littered desk, Finney hid in the darkness behind his hands and felt the pang of a kind of homesickness for the tranquil commotion of his routine. But outside, the snow on the front edge of a genuine storm was coming in hard, and in the city on the pathologist's steel tray, the body of Ignacio Rosa lay naked, twisted, and split, his heart beside him in a bag.

Finney blinked at the morning white light that came from his street window, a candescence not from a bright sun, as it was weak and far off, but from the all-whiteness of everything beyond the glass. Finney leaned his fast-hammering heart to the desk edge and began to reread the pathologist's report that had been delivered an hour earlier by an impatient, insolent deputy from Great Falls. Finney was determined this time to see beyond the sterile jargon, to conjure a picture of the fragile man he himself had zipped into a bag the day before and sent to town in the trunk of a car. The report was not his language, and he drew no image of dead Rosa from it.

"The body is positioned on the dorsal aspect," he read, "with spine contour curved, the concave aspect to the left side." And Finney thought, Good Christ, I don't even know what that means. Makes me think of a fish, a dorsal fin. He paused, read on, "The right upper arm is extended perpendicular to the right side and the right forearm is flexed, the hand located near the head." Finney remembered suddenly that, as he threw back the tarp from the pickup bed, he thought for an instant that it was all a disgusting joke, that Rosa was an imposter corpse, feigning sleep with his wide-eyed smooth face laid on his hand the way a baby sleeps. Finney remembered expecting a smile to spread across the corpse face.

"The body appears to be that of a well-developed, well-nourished Latin male of approximately 30 years of age. The body measures 166 cm. (65 inches) in height and weighs 62 kg. (136 pounds)." Yes,

Finney thought, he was nothing to carry, like a calf. Or do you go light when you freeze? No, a deer hanging is the same. You don't change. What's you is you. He read on in the bleak window light. The last pitchy knot burned and snapped in the stove and the cold radiated in through the stone walls. "Brown-black hair present over the skull and a small amount of similar colored hair is present over the pubic area. Irises are blue and pupils are round, each measuring 3 mm. in diameter. Natural teeth appear in good repair, though some stain present on front teeth. Rigidity is marked in muscles of the neck and extremities. Livor mortis present in back and buttocks."

And Christian Finney imagined then the man behind these pages, the bored coroner bending to his chore, drawing a tape along the stiff carcass, measuring even the pupils in their drying sockets, checking teeth like a man dickering on a horse. He pictured those muscles bulging in Rosa's neck, his angled arms straining against the scalpel, and the black stain all the length of him where lifeblood had finally seeped and pooled after the stubborn muscle of the heart stopped working. On the following page was the section that began "evidence of recent physical injury," and Finney was drawn up and in, reeling along with the bloodied doctor now, felt himself tracing flesh with the surgeon's tools and blades, sectioning the butchered body into "extremities," "head," and "trunk," coolly sawing and cutting, reading the body like a map and following a course of traverse lacerations, compressive abraded contusions, sliding type abrasions, lacerated hemorrhaged organs stacked in bags, and eviscerated loops of bowels glistening under a light.

His own pounding heart muscle beat against the desk edge, the pulse throbbed at his ears, and his empty belly constricted and creaked as he read along, or, seeing it now, traced along with probing fingers the semicircular bruising pattern over the body, measuring each deep geometric arc and near-circle. This whole picture had been hidden under the bulk of frozen clothes, and he recalled only the red scarf around the slim neck and the sleepy look of the corpse. The dozen crushing bruises he couldn't have seen. He considered weapons: tire, irons, bottles, posts, pieces of machinery: sections of Cat track, brake rods, clutch handles, drill ends, a cultivator steel duck foot.

Finney tracked the topography of Rosa's ruined body at last to the head, and read without comprehension, "lacerations of the scalp involving the left posterior parietal area," "fractured calvarium," "subarachnoid hemorrhage chiefly parieto-occipital," and "hemorrhage over the basilar aspect of the brain and the vessels forming the Circle of Willis." The Circle of Willis, thought Finney. He rested his elbows on the desktop and covered his eyes. The vessels forming the circle of Rosa. They had found it and stood watching, clutching it under the light, this circle of Rosa, the insidemost place going round and round like a flywheel in the middle of the center of your head, keeping you going, the spinning circle of Rosa or Finney or whoever, that deepest part where another man could not ever touch. But they had, they'd cut it out of him and sliced it on a tray—the one and only thing it seemed that might have kept him whole.

Christian Finney felt his pulse throb along his neck as he sat still with his white hands over his eyes. He was remembering some old country proverb about knowing a man only by seeing the blood beneath the skin. And here they've gone beyond any of that, he thought. They've plowed up his soul. But it was me as much as them. It was me sent him to it. I put him in the trunk and sent him to town. And in the darkness behind his soft hands, Finney was envisioning, too, the day five years ago when he had dropped off the smiling Rosa at the in-road to the Handcamp place, delivered him to the last five years of his life. At the in-road cattle-guard, Rosa offered his little-girl hand, and the slight pressure was less farewell than a touching, really, as if he were testing that sense in himself, in Finney. And for that second, Finney was touching him, too. Then Rosa was gone, packing his meager circumstances down the road and into that coulee of Handcamp's that took him in and was his life: Handcamp, animals, and the great windless ditch in the center of that blowing country.

Christian Finney fought for air in the office like the sputtering coals in the stove. That was the rest of his life, he thought, and I was at both ends of it, bringing him into the country and taking him out, leaving him there at the in-road gate in the cold and shipping him finally away from it frozen hard in a car trunk. And the only warmth in between—the one secret and windless place—he found in a tumbledown sheep shed, hiding out from everything cold this country had to offer.

YVONNE NEVALA HELD HER FACE CLOSE over a cup of tea. She'd come in, stoked the dying fire in the stove, and put a chunk of cottonwood log on it. Finney was in his chair. He'd put on his coat against the cold. The pathologist's report was in his desk. He'd been sitting there for a long while before Nevala came in, and had dropped the report into a drawer when he heard her boots at the door.

Finney swiveled to the window. A few cars were moving up and down the street. A red neon in the Rodeo Club Bar window flashed COORS COORS COORS through the curtain of heavy snowfall.

Nevala set down her cup and leaned across a file cabinet. "Think it's fixing to snow?" she said. Once, she recalled, the old gag would've warmed Finney to her, but now he did not laugh or turn or lift even a shoulder in acknowledgment. Nevala watched him. She put her head down and eyed along the cabinet edge as though aiming a rifle, sighting across the desk and chair and through Finney's head and eyes, to the unhealthy smolder of the neon that transfixed him. She galloped her fingertips along the metal beside her cheek.

"So what's on your mind, then?" Finney said. Nevala squinted down the edge. She picked up her cup.

"So?" said Finney.

"Just that I heard a couple things last night," Nevala said. "I heard they all liked him."

"Who all liked who?" Finney said, spinning the chair around.

"All of them, all those drunks and Social Security stiffs from right over there." Nevala motioned with her cup toward the window and the red light from the bar across the street.

"What do you mean 'liked him.' Hell, everybody liked him."

"I don't know, just that a lot of attention was paid to him in there and scuffles he was in the middle of. Or about him, I mean. And Jewel was saying some things. I mean she liked him too, but it was like he was competition."

"Your friend Jewel," Finney said. "I saw you two talking outside the bar the other day when Rosa came in. Not much you can believe from a one o'clock drunk."

Nevala bent down and adjusted the stove vents. "I saw it, too," she said.

"In the bar you mean? What the hell, you're supposed to be a goddamn deputy around here. There's a thing called discretion in this business, you might recall."

"Just a couple of times with Jewel is all."

"So then you probably knew your friend Jewel has been known to make some money in there? Your friend Jewel takes a lot of that Social Security money home by doing private showings down by the river in cars, brush-humping anybody with a buck or two to gamble against the clap." Finney was talking loud, the emotion that had ebbed in him after studying the coroner's sterile notes now welling up in him like a rush of bile. "What could that old whore possibly know about Rosa that would mean anything? What could she know at all?"

"She may be that, I don't know. It was always just her and me having a drink and that was it. She's the only company I have in this goddamn place. I like her. She's the one and only company I have."

"There are other women around here," Finney said, "some fairly respectable ones, if it's company you want."

"Oh, but I know all of them. I talk to them a half an hour in town when they're getting groceries. The rest of the time they're penned up on the ranch, cooking for animals like your friend Handcamp and making kids. Or they're feeding cattle with the old man. Feeding is all they know, one way or another, either at the supper table or off of a tit or kicking hay off the back of a truck." With her long hair hanging along her pale face, Yvonne Nevala seemed to peer from a dim interior, as if speaking from the crack of a door. "I don't have a friend here. So I talk to Jewel. She's one who escaped all that in her own way, even if it's not a beautiful way."

"It's not beautiful, all right," Finney said. "It's not even anywhere close to that."

"It's no ways worse than your friend Handcamp and his type. All your old boys, slapping backs and going fishing. Or them across the street. That type."

"He's really eating on you, isn't he? There's nothing wrong with Handcamp outside of being quiet. Or is it that he didn't pay you attention when he was in here?"

"That's the last thing. But there's more than quiet to Handcamp, something else Jewel told me last night. About a couple of months ago the two of them were drinking in his truck out front of the club one night, passing a bottle after close-up, and Jewel—she was pretty laid-out she told me, pretty tight—she gets to rattling his chain about Rosa, about how he was so popular with the regulars in there. She's laying this on pretty thick, and then Handcamp has her hair rolled up in the window and he's knocking her around, I mean really hammering. Jewel's no delicate flower so she gave him some back, but that's your Handcamp, who's only so nice and quiet."

"Well why didn't she come to me then?" Finney asked, "if any such thing ever happened."

"It's not that. It doesn't matter to her. Her husband had gone after her quite a bit. She doesn't care so much. She only wanted me to see about Handcamp and Rosa, about how it was."

The blue-white outside light flooding through the frosting panes made Yvonne Nevala's face more white, the veins coming out along her temples more blue, as she stared at Christian Finney behind his desk. He swiveled away, once more toward the window, and covered his eyes with his fingers. He only breathed.

"Of course the other type of man in this town," Nevala said, "is the one who'd rather spend time counting mallards at the river. There's that type here. For company."

Finney did not move, but sat listening to his pulse beat faster and feeling it on his eyeballs with the light touch of his fingers. He heard coals in the stove-box. All of that with them was long, long dead but would not heal, the ulcer of it still festering up a purulence without warning or cause. He waited there like that, listening to his own pulse and the cottonwood burning in the stove, until Nevala went across to the door and out.

Finney took down his hands and opened his eyes to the window light. And in the brief blindness of constricting pupil, Finney dreamed the violent movement of Handcamp's limbs, shoulders, long arms and thick hands, muscles, sinews and tendons in perfect interaction, pounding away in the whiskeyed inside of a pickup, the whole fast storm of it lit just by the red-flashing glow of the neon bar sign.

The radiance of the neon was comforting, and Christian Finney was surprised to be watching it. His eyes adjusted to the light and he stared as the club's beer sign burned through the snow. Beyond it, silhouetted against a blue jukebox light, he could make out the dark heads of patrons, nodding and turning in the gloom of the bar. It was two o'clock in the afternoon. The neon gleamed like an ember, and Finney envied the men who were warm and drinking beyond it. He looked down the street to the bridge. In this kind of weather, he thought, every duck in the country will be down on the river. Or coming in hard, he thought, coming in and setting down anywhere in the storm.

DELBERT HANDCAMP WALKED ACROSS the whitening ranchyard, his eyes on the ground, not looking to the hills going blue behind the storm, not to the corrals and drifting pens or parked equipment, or to the slanted barn looming through the snow. He went straight from the main house to the weathered bunkhouse, where he eased open the cracked door from its jamb, stood inside, and studied the leavings of Ignacio Rosa's life. The light filtering through the decayed gauzy curtains was faint and the outside cold froze every scent and last action: a Bull Durham smoke twisted out in a cup, overboots staining a newspaper, a small pair of graying long underwear draped across the back of the one overstuffed chair like a skin; the smell of tobacco, Vitalis hair cream, and sweat. Hung on sixteen-penny nails driven into the wall were bale chaps, a battered summer straw hat, a wool jacket covered with feed hay. On another wall, a picture of a Percheron work team cut from the Great Falls Sunday newspaper, and a painted crucifix, obscene with its pink weeping Jesus.

The winter sun was weak behind the full storm and was just sliding under the drifting coulee edge. The last rays shimmered on dozens of capsized flies that lay dead on the windowsill where they'd beaten themselves against the murky glass months before for the freedom of light.

Beneath the window, framed in a rectangle of gray light, was the Mexican's narrow bunk. Delbert Handcamp went across the room and sat down on the edge of the bed in the fading light. He pulled back the wool blanket, took up the pillow, and buried his face in the dingy linen. He pressed it tight, pressed out the half-light, and breathed the smell of Vitalis and sweat—the smell of his hired man, Ignacio Rosa.

I ACCEPT THE SNOW, FINNEY THOUGHT. I accept that it's got to snow, but there is no comfort in the wind. Instead of a nice, soft postcard picture it comes like this, piles ten feet deep behind anything that won't blow down and all this dead country as hard as iron, not a clean and white pretty landscape picture like you see, no, but the dead ground bared off and the snow snaking and shifting and piling up wherever it cares like it's alive. Finney tried to occupy his mind with ranting against the storm after he'd clutched and braked and gunned the black-and-white Cascade County Bronco across the river's floodplain and up humped-back ridge upon ridge, up and toward the heart of the boiling dark sky until finally gaining the top of the great benchland, where in the windy center, like a vein, stretched the protected coulee of the Handcamp place. In the town on the flat among the cottonwoods, the snow was still coming hard, but here on top, moving toward the blackest part of it, the storm was bearing wind.

Finney drove for two miles, fighting the ratcheting dozer tracks and deep ruts of the county road and checking his watch against the lowering sun. Then ahead he could see it, at first just an angular, unnatural shape amid all the round and bare country. His heart beat faster and seemed to swell. He picked up speed and then was beside it—the long low-sagging sheep shed on a rise above the road, the last standing thing on the old Sullivan place—and was past it. Through his rearview mirror, Finney saw into the dark rectangle of the fallen door, a black open mouth in the storm, made out in the line of pole uprights receding in the gloom. He sped past the gate and where he knew the drifted entry road breached the borrow ditch. Whoever Sullivan was, Finney thought, he made a good shed. Even now it would be warm there, even in this wind. To be out of it, that was the thing. This is the only place for miles. Far in the back, past where even the door light reaches, it would be warm. A blanket, straw, a corner still intact in all this old decay. It is the one place in all this country, far as you can see.

As the shed went out of sight in his mirror beyond a hill, Christian Finney began to weary with each jolt of the truck spring. He felt as though he was collapsing upon himself, and that, like Rosa, his organs had been pulled out, but then misplaced back among the loops and creases of his bowels, and the one thing still painfully in place was the circle of himself, the Circle of Finney swinging around his head: his own imagined soul still untrammeled but grinding at the raw mews of remembering.

In a shallow coulee just beneath the brunt of the wind, Finney stopped the truck in the road to piss, leaning heavily against the open door and spraying the ground. Bulldozer tracks, tread marks of snow lugs and the huge prints of workhorse teams were frozen in the mud like fossils. Finney zipped his pants, held out his dead-white hands and eyed them as if they were the unattached meat of some other animal, and stared beyond them to the frozen roadbed. His eyes followed the spoor of machine and animal up the opposite rise to where they disappeared over the crest. Standing misshapen, his head cocked into the wind that even here now began to drag at his clothes, he watched snow gather in the perfect crooks of the diminishing prints of horses. And suddenly the wind was on his spine, gripping it like the hand of a corpse. He stood frozen by cold and horror, staring up the hard roadbed at the realized picture of death there before him. Rosa. Rosa, smooth face looming in the ice hole, placid corpse slumbering in the pickup box, as if not destroyed at all. But under his sodden winter clothes he was crushed like a trampled calf. Finney had read the coroner's gibberish, had pictured since then a hundred times the black near-circles preserved in Rosa's flesh. And now the death was as real as this, real as geometry, perfect arcs locked in mud until April thaw and runoff and going out of sight toward the dimming top of the hill.

Finney drove too fast on the last miles of rutted road, tracking it between the overflowing borrow ditches. Beside the ditches were the half-buried right-of-way fences and beyond that was all white. Finally, ahead, he could make out the vague shapes of Handcamp's cattle, pressed into a fence corner at the head of the ranch in-road, the intersection where he had left Ignacio Rosa five years before and then U-turned back to town. Above the engine noise and the howl of the wind, Finney could hear the bellowing of cattle. They were gaunt and wild-eyed and bawled at the sight of Finney's truck as if he were a hay sled and team.

Apart from the main herd, a rough-haired heifer licked at a fresh calf and prodded it around on the ground with her nose. The calf had been licked dry of newborn mucus, but now its lush tongued hair stood up in frozen black curls. And despite the mother's dim urgency, her tight bag ripe to suck, the calf could not get up. Its big head lolled, eyes bulging in fear and wonder at its own roaring mother and the sudden white universe, nothing like a womb.

By the time Finney turned in and came abreast of the heifer on the in-road, the calf was dead. Most of the cows jogged the fence line beside his truck, swinging their heads and bawling. They had given up any notion of forage and were spending their last energy following the vision of salvation of a man in a truck. They swung along the fence line after Finney. Long strands of saliva hung from their mouths as they bawled for feed.

When he stepped from the Bronco in the ranchyard, Finney could still hear them, above the coulee rim, their bellowing coming on the wind. He saw them lined up at the fence, looking down and moaning.

He knocked at the back door of the house and got no answer. He went around to the front. Inside somewhere a radio hissed static cattle futures and stockmen's advisories. The lights were off and nothing moved. Finney stood under the porch awning but it was no shelter at all. The snow slanted in under it. The coulee seemed to provide no relief from the storm, but only funneled the wind. Everything in the ranchyard was buried and drifting, and except where the cattle stood in ranks above, there was no skyline or ridgeline, but only white from the yard upward.

Across the road, set back into the cutaway hill, the barn leaned with the storm. Finney shouldered the wind and made for it. He found the door latch, slid it back, cracked the heavy door, and stood panting in the barn's dark fug. His eyes adjusted slowly to the dwindling light filtering through two dusty windows. The barn groaned and Finney heard the panicked flapping of wings and the wind tuning the anchor cables outside. Then all around him he could make out wreckage: loose hay, fragments of planks, spilled oats and piles of manure, orange pools of urine shimmering in the weak light. Farther back the sharp ends of broken holding pen boards hung down from posts by nails. Trace lines dangling from a peg lay uncoiled across the floor like tentacles. Pigeons wheeled among the rafter joists. Everywhere was disarray and Finney's heart hammered against his breastbone. From the corner of his eye he glimpsed movement low against a wall, and he turned quickly to a pair of cat's eyes glaring from the back of a horse stall. A growl swelled up from the animal's throat.

The air was warm and rank like a breath in his face, and Finney barely breathed of it as he walked across the litter to the center of the barn. The eyes that reflected window light from the darkest corner were huge, and they gleamed and rolled in fear. Finney froze at the sound of alarmed snorting and the clattering of hooves. His pounding heart surged from his viscera to his throat as he distinguished in the darkness the two work mares standing together, their flanks pressed to the stone foundation in defense. They jerked back their heads, and their rolling eyes showed white. The birds weaved above them through the barn's teetering ribs and the two horses pounded their shod feet on the ground, pressing together against the rough wall, blowing and fearfully pawing, their great mournful eyes fixing on another enemy.

Before he found the power to move, to finally backstep across the dank wreckage to the distant barn door, Christian Finney stood for long minutes before the horses. They shuffled and goggled at him from the shadows and he waited with hopes of decision. He listened to his heart and to the howl of the storm beyond the walls. But it was not for him to decide, was it, the Finney indicted by Yvonne Nevala, Finney at the river's cold edge content to sit and witness the predictable current and the erosion of seasons? He was here, wasn't he, and wasn't that enough of a decision for her? Decisions were made for you, and now he stood resigned before Rosa's mares, the Mexican's minions, his enormous and affectionate killers. Miles away across the raw flat, Finney had stood in judgment like this in the ruined sheep shed, had studied those blue wrong Mexican eyes shining out of the darkness, the smile, the small hands palm up and shoulders shrugging in lame apology, while other eyes out of sight in the familiar humid corner of the shed peered out and another heart raced from arousal and the fevered anticipation of decision.

The mares clashed their hooves and blew sorrowfully in the dark. Finney turned his back to them, went to the door and out in the snow, latching the door behind him. From this angle he could see a drifting trench of footprints leading to the door of the bunkhouse, and he plowed across the yard toward it, circling around to the single south-facing window. Beyond a skeletal row of Russian olive, a swath of tracks went off down the coulee from the opened gate of the horse corral. Finney huddled breathing hard in the slipstream of Rosa's house. Two roostertail wakes of snow curled around the weathered corners. Finney strained to see through the curtains in the dim window. As his eyes adjusted to the interior light, he was suddenly watching Delbert Handcamp sob into a pillow. His black head was buried in the down and his body spasmed like a poleaxed slaughter cow.

Snow piled quietly around the corners of the building. Finney, hypnotized by the jerking muscular shoulders, stared at Handcamp on the illuminated bed. Then beyond him, on the edge of the window light, Finney saw the suit of underwear, draped across the chair like Christ's image on the shroud. He could make out vaguely the photo of horses on the wall, bale chaps dangling from a hook like withered legs, Rosa's twisted hats hung on nails.

The white sun slid below the hills somewhere in the storm and the light seemed to come from the snow itself. Finney huddled in the lee watching Handcamp weep among his hired man's leavings, until at last the great shoulders stopped twitching. Handcamp turned and set the pillow at the head of the bed under the window, not seeing Finney there beyond the curtain or not showing it: turned like a man in pain and slowly stretched on the mattress. His big hands lay at his sides and he stared up at the water-stained ceiling. Finally, and without any turning or shifting of weight, he rolled his eyes slowly back in his head and the two men regarded each other through the glass.

DELBERT HANDCAMP LAY ON Rosa's bed talking. "Five years ago Monday he came on the place, come down the road with his gear out of nowhere." Handcamp glared at the ceiling and Sheriff Finney stood beside the bed. "Now it was rough on him at first. Before long he was wanting to leave, but I wouldn't take him. As I say, it was this time of year and all, lot of snow all drifting in. It was for his own good. He had to stay on until he come to like it here." Handcamp lifted his rough hand from the mattress and motioned vaguely around the room. "He had this, and then I give him over the team to work too. He had it good."

Among the cracks and water marks of the ceiling Handcamp seemed to be deciphering a script of action that had gone on without him. He spoke without inflection or emotion.

"It was five years ago that day, and it was like I said, he had the guy from Great Falls or somewheres. Maybe you found him by now, I don't know. But he'd just come back from down there at the Sullivan place with this bastard. Five years from that very day, and it was a special kind of day, you understand. But he went anyway to that son of a bitch from town. He comes into the kitchen then afterwards and just sits there, fooling at a scarf he was wearing, waiting for me to say something. But I never said a thing. He messes with it and finally says it was a present, a gift from a friend, and I told him, 'Get the hell out.'

I watch him from the window and he walks across the yard and stops under the light over there." Handcamp pointed toward the door, still ajar, and through the crack Finney could see the yard light flickering on, cued by the dark. "He stops under the light there and fools with the knot of that scarf. Because he knows I'm watching, you understand. Then he goes on into the barn."

Handcamp closed his eyes tight and pointed again, across the yard toward the barn, looming askew just beyond the arc light, horses caged inside.

"I wait a while before I go across and I know he hears me come in, but he has his ear laid on that mare's side, listening to her heart like I told you about. But he don't look around. I picked up a spud bar that I'd been chipping ice with. It was there by the door."

And as the wind pounded the bunkhouse, Christian Finney imagined the little Mexican's last moment, attending the rumble of that huge heart echoing in the chest of his mare.

"He heard me all right," Handcamp said, "but he kept looking away, making out like I wasn't there and hugging the horse in his way. I took that bar and kind of got him behind the ear with it. He went down noisy, saying like, 'Oh, no, oh, no' and hollering Mexican gibberish, and those horses are getting excited. You know, I believe he must have pissed his pants or something because they were used to him crawling around under them and such. But something set them off, the smell maybe, and they start pounding him into the floor. He yelled out for a little bit while he could, but they kept on. And it's peculiar, you understand, those goddamn horses would do anything for him, pull any goddamn thing on the wagon or sled, and they end up stomping him in their own stall."

Handcamp stopped to consider the strangeness of it. He opened his eyes to the decaying ceiling and then quickly closed them.

"I just couldn't look at him then," he said. "I left him in there for two days. And they made a hell of a mess of the place, spooked like they were. Trying to get away from him, I imagine. Saturday I took him to the catch pond, buttoned some rocks up in his coat, chopped a hole, and lowered him in. But then he came back up and, I don't know, I felt bad about him. And he looked better then too, just asleep. He just rose up, bobbed up through the ice hole like I told you. I was feeling bad. I didn't know what to do with him, so I brought him to you. I figured he'd anyway keep coming every time I chopped a hole.

"It was all like I said. He had a guy from Great Falls who came out, maybe some others, I don't know." For the first time, Handcamp opened his eyes and looked hard at Finney, turning his black eyes on him like a weapon and sizing him. Finney looked beyond him, out the window, and there in the gloaming again imagined the sheep shed, remembered the warmth of it amid all that cold, like it was the belly of the storm.

Handcamp did not move on the bed. His chest rose and fell like a giant bellows. He studied Finney up and down, only his eyes moving in their sockets. "This is a hell of a life here sometimes," he said. "You need something else outside of these cows for company. Like now, you get out there in the yard and all there is for company is all these eyes looking at you. And now that's too cold. But it's all there is now since Rosa's gone, is all these eyes from over the coulee top, all of them looking to you and you can't just go up and get rid of them."

Handcamp reached out his thick hands and grasped the bed railings on each side of the mattress. "And now it's you, coming around looking at everything, eyeing over the edge at me moving around, looking through the window, looking at everything a man does on his own place in his own way and not bothering nobody. This is my place here. This is my own place."

Finney turned his back on Handcamp. He squinted through the opened bunkhouse door and was lulled by the snow swirling into the violet gush of the yard light. Yes, Finney thought, it surely is his place, just as I thought when he sat in the office back-staring the stove vents, looking like some kind of beautiful wolf. And they did have a life here, the dead horseman Rosa and this Handcamp with his own way of lasting against so much hardness.

He swung around slowly to look at Handcamp, who stared at him from the thin bed. So you make a choice, he thought, the way Rosa once did, or the way he was forced to make one, you go or you stay, you hold to your own steady line or you take warmth where you find it. Or maybe it takes you.

Beyond the radiance of the light, snow gathered around the outbuildings and abandoned equipment, and farther out, atop the ridge where the one light would seem like the weakest of stars through the storm, the drifts sifted over fence lines. Fallen cattle and the town road.

Handcamp sat up on the bed.

"It's time we went, Del," Finney said.

"No," Handcamp said, "in this kind of storm you don't go anywhere until the county plows you out." He swung his jaw toward the barn. "Outside of you go with the team."

"Chain up all four wheels and I make it."

"No you don't," Handcamp said. He glanced from Finney to the door, gauging the distance. "I don't think so." He stood up.

"No," Finney said. He backstepped slowly to the door as Handcamp stepped toward him. "No." Finney turned and ran across the drifted ranchyard. Overtaken halfway to the barn, his legs buckled under Handcamp's great weight and he fell. A strong hand held his face down in the snow and with Delbert Handcamp on him, he could not move. He could not breathe. After a few seconds of struggle, he gave in to it. But it was not how he'd imagined it, this embrace beneath the bloodstone areola of the arc lamp: not here in the light, not going, like Rosa, into darkness.

AFTERWORD
Allen Morris Jones

FEELS LIKE IT SHOULD BE HARDER THAN THIS, editing an anthology. Late nights with coffee and cigarettes, fists on tables, furious sulks. Good friends gone bad and art as the final common denominator. Turns out, though, these things come together like shuffling cards. The only real trick is in deciding what to exclude. When William Kittredge and I first started talking about this project, we both came to the table with a handful of ideas, a few restrictions to keep the thing from overflowing into flotsam. We wanted themes, we wanted coherency. Keep it down to writers who are still alive, we said. Restrict the work to actual stories (versus, say, novel excerpts). And keep it in Montana, at least thematically. Otherwise, let the stories pick themselves.

Given this admittedly haphazard approach, it's surprising now how the collection manages to hold itself together, how certain themes have risen *ex nihilo* from the soup. Through no real talent or planning of our own, we have here an anthology that hits on all cylinders. Each of these writers, so unique in style and voice, nevertheless complements the next, taking up where the others leave off. Twenty-one separate styles and voices, yes, but each with some attachment to the place, some new insight or spin, some original (often skewed) look at who we are, where we come from. If you read this anthology with the right kind of eyes, it's possible to see a reflection of Montana, a rare portrait of who we are, where we've come from.

Consider how many of the stories explore the ideas of alienation and disenfranchisement, of reconciliation and peace, the search for some damn thing. If you live in Montana, you most likely came here from somewhere else, running away or running toward, searching or hiding. We have been the malcontents and immigrants, second sons and disgraced daughters. There's the cuckolded father in Richard Ford's classic story "Great Falls," for instance. Blue collar and desperate, standing finally with a pistol, torn between decisions. Or Ralph Beer's protagonist in "Big Spenders," sitting with his umbrella drink, dreaming about palm trees and white crescent beaches. And Thomas McGuane's narrator in "Like a Leaf," eavesdropping on the neighbors, watching other people's lives, always from a distance. And Chris Offutt's protagonist in "Tough People," trying to earn enough money in amateur boxing to get out of town, to find bus fare and maybe a little peace. Damaged souls, all of them, looking only for a few answers, for a brief moment of respite.

Of course, it's the *looking* that's essential, the ubiquitous key to most all of these narratives. Pete Fromm's narrator in "Hoot" has spent most of his adulthood envying his brother's escape and perhaps planning his own. Mary Clearman Blew's narrator in "Bears and Lions" describes how her home is moving away from her, how the changing West is leaving her behind. A theme that emerges again in Rick Bass's remarkable and much-lauded "Days of Heaven." Then there's Maile Meloy's "Ranch Girl," with its wonderful first line, "If you're white, and you're not rich or poor but somewhere in the middle, it's hard to have worse luck than to be born a girl on a ranch." In Melanie Rae Thon's contribution, "Father, Lover, Deadman, Dreamer," she dwells on (among other things) ideas of escape and avoidance: how it's impossible to avoid our own identities, our inherited notions of who we are. A theme approached from yet another angle by Claire Davis in her story "Grounded," wherein a mother follows her runaway son, trying to convince him that he can't leave her behind.

These are stories that have all found their way to light via the most varied and circuitous routes imaginable. David Long's excellent study in family and community, in privacy and exposure, "Morphine," was first published in *The New Yorker*. Kim Zupan's "The Mourning of Ignacio Rosa" (having circulated hand to hand for years, a secret jewel of the Montana community) is seeing print here for the first time. Neil McMahon's boxing tale, "Heart," was published in the *Atlantic Monthly* in the late seventies, and Debra Earling's "Real Indians" was being printed in the literary magazine *Prairie Schooner* even while this anthology was going through its final edits.

In a way, it's the community itself that is responsible for this collection. All these friends and familiar faces, pressed elbow to elbow under one cover. For such a big state, it's sure a small neighborhood. A phone call to the magazine *Northern Lights* gave us Jeanne Dixon's wonderful story "Blue Waltz with Coyotes." Rick DeMarinis's tale "Under the Wheat" has been taught and read and (safe to say) imitated by Missoula's creative writing students since it was published almost twenty years ago. I found Jon Billman's hilarious and touching story "Custer on Mondays" in a copy of *Zoetrope* that I pulled off the newsstand. I immediately contacted him for possible contributions to my own magazine, touching off a friendship that's only grown over the years. Kevin Canty teaches at the university in Missoula, and while we hadn't yet met, after a similar phone call and brief conversation he was kind enough to e-mail me his superb story "Junk." I remember reading William Kittredge's "Do You Hear Your Mother Talking?" more than ten years ago, standing by the magazine rack in the University of Montana bookstore, buying the magazine so I could read it again. A naive kid hungry for anything literary, studying Montana letters from a distance, Bill's story knocked everything off its tracks for a while. It feels like something has come full circle, being able to reprint the same story now. And finally, Annick Smith (who is certainly one of the essential hearts of this literary world) was generous enough to contribute her award-winning tale "It's Come to This," a moving, inspired narrative about building a home, about coming to terms, about finding your place in the world.

It's an impulse equal parts generosity and selfishness, storytelling. The generosity of gift-giving, the selfishness of ego need and attention. But at the heart of the matter, and common to all these writers—each history as distinct as the next (academia to ranching, logging to environmentalism)—is a love for the place and its people. A devotion to the same land that has inspired the stories. In the eternal push and pull of favor and obligation, of debt and payment, we are pleased to offer this collection, a small weight added to the scales, one side or the other.

Author Biographies

Rick Bass is the author of eighteen books of fiction and nonfiction, including an anthology, *The Roadless Yaak*, and a fiction collection, *The Hermit's Story*. He is a board member of the Montana Wilderness Association, Yaak Valley Forest Council, Cabinet Resource Group, and Round River Conservation Studies. He lives in northwest Montana's Yaak Valley, where, despite there being nearly a million acres of some of the wildest country in the Lower Forty-eight, there is still not a single acre of designated wilderness.

Ralph Beer and his wife, Maggie, live in western Colorado where Ralph tinkers with old English motorcycles, while Maggie does most of the real work. Ralph is still typing away on his memoir in progress: *All Wrong All the Time.*

Jon Billman is the author of the short-story collection *When We Were Wolves,* and a forthcoming novel, *Embalming Will Rogers*. His stories have appeared in such magazines as *Outside, Esquire,* and *The Paris Review*. He lives in Kemmerer, Wyoming, with his wife Hilary, and son, Sam.

Kevin Canty is the author of two collections of short stories (*Honeymoon* and *A Stranger in This World*) and two novels (*Nine Below Zero* and *Into the Great Wide Open*). His short stories have appeared in *The New Yorker, Esquire, Tin House, GQ, Glimmer Train, Story,* the *New England Review,* and elsewhere; essays and articles in *Vogue, Details,* the *New York Times* and the *Oxford American,* among many others. His work has been translated into French, Dutch, Spanish, German, and Polish. Mr. Canty has won a Pacific Northwest Book Award, and three of his books have been named as "Notable Books" by the *New York Times Book Review*. A recent essay was included in the *Best American Travel Writing* 2002. He lives in Missoula, where he holds down Earl Ganz's old job in the MFA program at the University of Montana.

MARY CLEARMAN BLEW grew up on a central Montana ranch that her great-grandfather homesteaded in 1882. She has published numerous books of short fiction, essays, and memoir, and has edited several others, including the prizewinning *When Montana and I Were Young*, by Margaret Bell. She lives in Moscow, Idaho, where she teaches in the creative writing program.

CLAIRE DAVIS's first novel, *Winter Range*, from Picador USA, won the 2000 MPBA and PNBA awards for fiction. Her short stories have been published in numerous literary publications, including *Best American Short Stories* and the Pushcart Prize Anthology series. Her second novel, *Snake*, will be released from St. Martins Press in 2004, and a collection of short stories, *Labors of the Heart*, will be released from St. Martins Press in 2005. She lives in Lewiston, Idaho, where she teaches creative writing at Lewis-Clark State College.

RICK DEMARINIS is the author of eight published novels and five books of short fiction, with the sixth, *Apocalypse Then*, due out soon from Seven Stories Press. His fiction has appeared in *Esquire*, *The Atlantic*, *Harpers*, *GQ*, *Paris Review*, and twice in *Best American Short Stories*. He has taught at the University of Montana, San Diego State, Arizona State, and the University of Texas at El Paso.

JEANNE DIXON was born on Two Medicine Creek in north central Montana. She comes from a long line of Montana ranchers, lawmen, and ne'er-do-wells. Her paternal grandfather was the first district judge elected to the bench when the territory became a state, presiding over the Big Hole country during the bad old days of the vigilantes. Her dad was a fur trapper, bounty hunter, and sheep rancher on the east slope, later moving the family to the Flathead

Valley to farm. She loves to tell stories about life in rural Montana; "Blue Waltz with Coyotes" is one of these.

DEBRA MAGPIE EARLING is a member of the Confederated Salish and Kootenai Tribes of Montana. She is Flathead Indian. Her novel *Perma Red* received the American Book Award, the Spur Award, and the WILLA award, among others. She currently teaches at the University of Montana. "Real Indians" was first published in *Prairie Schooner* in the summer issue of 2003.

RICHARD FORD is the first writer to have received both the PEN/ Faulkner Award and the Pulitzer Prize for a single work with his novel *Independence Day*. He has also received a Guggenheim Fellowship, an American Academy of Arts and Letters Award for Literature, and the 1994 REA Award, which is given annually to a writer who has made a significant contribution to the short story as an art form. "Great Falls" first appeared in his short story collection *Rock Springs* in 1987. Each year he spends time at his cabin in Chinook, Montana.

PETE FROMM'S newest novel, *As Cool As I Am*, was published in the Fall of 2003. A three-time winner of the Pacific Northwest Booksellers Literary Award for his novel *How All This Started*, story collection *Dry Rain*, and memoir *Indian Creek Chronicles,* he has also published four other story collections, as well as more than a hundred stories in magazines. He lives with his family in Great Falls, Montana.

ALLEN MORRIS JONES has been writing professionally for almost twenty years, having published his first short story at the age of fourteen. He became editor of the prestigious *Big Sky Journal* at the age of twenty-five and during his five-year tenure, published most of the significant writers in the Northwest. In this same period, the magazine was nominated for four consecutive Maggie Awards for excellence in regional publishing. His first book, *A Quiet Place of Violence: Hunting and Ethics in the Missouri River Breaks*, was published in 1997. His second, a novel called *Last Year's River*, was released by Houghton Mifflin in 2001,

Mariner Paperback in 2002. His incidental essays and short stories have appeared in magazines as varied as *Men's Journal* and *Town and Country*; *Sports Afield* and *Gray's Sporting Journal*. He has just completed his second novel, tentatively titled *Landlocked*. He has also served as editor and co-publisher of Bangtail Press, a small book house specializing in limited-edition, fine-press releases of various regional titles. Among other books, he has published and/or co-edited *Where We Live: The Best of Big Sky Journal* (re-released by St. Martin's Press as *The Big Sky Reader*); *Flylines: The Best of Big Sky Journal Fishing*; and a collection of short stories by Jack Curtis, *Dawn Waters*.

WILLIAM KITTREDGE is a retired Regents Professor in Creative Writing at the University of Montana. His most recent books are *The Nature of Generosity, Southwestern Homelands,* and *The Best Stories of William Kittredge.*

DAVID LONG lives in Tacoma, Washington. His most recent novel was *The Daughters of Simon Lamoreaux*. He's currently working on a new novel called *Purgatorio*.

THOMAS MCGUANE was born in Wyandotte, Michigan, in 1939. He was educated at Michigan State University, B.A. 1962, Yale, M.F.A. 1965, and Stanford, where he was the Wallace Stegner Fellow in creative writing. He is the author of nine novels, including *The Cadence of Grass*, a book of short stories, a book on fishing, *The Longest Silence*, and a book on horses, *Some Horses*. He has also written several motion pictures, including *Rancho Deluxe, The Missouri Breaks,* and *Tom Horn*. McGuane was a finalist for the National Book Award, received the Rosenthal Award from the American Academy, the Montana Governor's Award, and the Northwest Booksellers' Award. His work has been collected in, among other places, *Best American Short Stories, Best American Essays,* and *Best American Sports Essays*. Thomas McGuane has lived on various Montana ranches since 1968, raising cattle and horses. He has competed in steer roping and cutting horse events since that time. He and his wife, the former Laurie

Buffett, are the parents of four children who were educated from rural schools to Montana State University; and four grandchildren, all of whom live in Montana. He and his wife live near McLeod, Montana.

NEIL MCMAHON was born in Chicago in 1949 and moved to Montana in 1971. He spent most of the next thirty years working as a carpenter to support his writing habit. His most recent novel is a thriller, *To the Bone* (HarperCollins, 2003). He's married and lives in Missoula, Montana.

MAILE MELOY is the author of the story collection *Half in Love* (Scribner, 2002) and the novel *Liars and Saints* (Scribner, 2003). Her stories have been published in *The New Yorker, Best New American Voices,* and *The Paris Review.* She was born and raised in Helena, Montana.

CHRIS OFFUTT is the author of *Out of the Woods, Kentucky Straight, The Same River Twice, No Heroes,* and *The Good Brother.* All have been translated into several languages. His work is widely anthologized and has received many honors, including a Guggenheim Fellowship, a Lannan Award, an NEA, and a Whiting Award. He currently lives in Iowa City, where he is a visiting professor at the Iowa Writers' Workshop.

MELANIE RAE THON is the author of the novels *Sweet Hearts, Iona Moon,* and *Meteors in August,* and the story collections *Girls in the Grass* and *First, Body.* Originally from Montana, she now divides her time between the Pacific Northwest and Salt Lake City, where she teaches at the University of Utah.

ANNICK SMITH is a writer and filmmaker who lives in Montana's Blackfoot River Valley. She was co-editor with William Kittredge of the Montana anthology *The Last Best Place.* She has published two volumes of essays, *Homestead* (Milkweed Editions) and *In This We Are Native* (Lyons Press), as well as a study of the tallgrass prairies of Oklahoma, *Big Bluestem* (Council Oak Books) for The Nature Conservancy. Her film credits include being executive producer of *Heartland* and a co-producer of *A River Runs Through It*.

KIM ZUPAN grew up on the east side of the Rockies in Stockett and Great Falls, Montana. Before and after earning degrees in English and creative writing at the University of Montana, he worked for several ranches in the Judith Basin. He received his M.F.A. in Fiction in 1984. He spent a decade as a professional bareback rider with the Professional Rodeo Cowboys Association. He has been a guest lecturer for the University of Montana, a substitute teacher in Great Falls and Germany, a fisherman for several summers in Alaska, and an instructor for Hellgate Writers in Missoula. His stories have appeared in such journals as *Epoch*, *Big Sky Journal*, and *The Montana Writers' Daybook*. His work is anthologized in *Where We Live* (Spring Creek Publishing, 1997), *Hunting's Best Short Stories* (Chicago Review Press, 2000), and *The New Montana Story* (Riverhead Publishing, 2003). Kim's first novel, *Why Do the Heathen Rage?*, is set in the Stockett, Sand Coulee, and Centerville areas of Montana. He lives in Missoula and spends his time as a writer, finish carpenter, husband, and dad.